And then there's YOU

TISA MATTHEWS

This book is dedicated to me.
After ten years of dreaming, I decided to write a book.
And then I DID.
I'm a fucking badass.

PROLOGUE

Me: *I'll never forgive myself for not throwing you bache-lorette party.* I text my best friend, as I wait for the rest of the plane to board.

Avery: *We could turn our current Australian plan into a girls' trip next summer. That would totally be forgiveness worthy. And maybe by then it can be a joint bachelorette.* She sends a row of wink emojis.

Me: *Yeah, we'll see about that. Let's focus on getting you married first! I can't believe your wedding is in two days!*

Avery: *I can't believe I get to see you in less than that! It's been way too long. Thank you for being here for this, Maci. It wouldn't be the same without you.*

Me: *I wouldn't miss it.*

After replying, I switch my phone to airplane mode and slip it into the pocket of my leggings.

My stomach twists. I wish I could claim flying nerves, but I know it's because I'm sick over being a bad friend. Yeah, I planned the end of my trip specifically around my best friend's wedding, but as much as this weekend should be all about her life-changing commitment, all I can think about is how it will be just as significant for me.

The decision I made before I boarded my flight will change everything.

That probably sounds dramatic. I know I'm only 22 and have plenty of time to make mistakes or take a different path if this one doesn't work out, but I don't want to go into this with one foot out the door. That being said, this choice will ultimately determine every aspect of my life forever. It'll impact what jobs I apply for, where I live and who I'm surrounded by. On top of that, it doesn't just affect *my* life.

22 or not, there's a lot of weight to that.

I've spent the past few months considering what is most important to me. Leaning into excitement and passion can be just as satisfying as a life that provides safety and comfort. I know I would love the story I'd create from either path and the version of myself I will become as a result. But I have to choose one or the other, and I have. Despite the emotions I feel about it, I'm confident I'm making the right decision.

CHAPTER ONE

1 year 8 months earlier

"Maci, you know you're going to have to *leave* our apartment on a regular basis to go to all these places, right?" Avery teases as we sit on the enclosed patio overlooking the swampy lake at my parents' timeshare. It's so cliché they got suckered into a timeshare in Florida, especially since unless you're at the beach, it's not as pretty as advertised.

I rest my chin in my palm and sigh. "I know, I'm the worst. I want to be better this year."

Anyone looking in on Avery and me would probably think we are sisters. We have the same long, brown hair falling over our shoulders and have been complimented more than once on our similarly bright smiles when we are excited. That's happened a lot over our nearly decade-long friendship.

My deep, brown eyes contrast with Avery's jade green ones, but both are now focused on a piece of torn notebook paper on a frosted glass table in front of us. We've been passing it back and forth, creating a list of countries we want to explore.

<u>Places We're Going Together:</u>
Costa Rica
Croatia
Thailand
Australia

Ever since we met in 6th grade, we've daydreamed about traveling the world. I'm not sure how it started, but in the nine years between when we met and now–two weeks before our last year of college–we've spent a lot of time talking about it. Neither of us has ever been out of the country, but each summer before the school year starts, my parents plan a trip somewhere in the U.S. Since I'm an only child, they let me bring a friend, and I choose Avery every time. We've been to eight different states now, a new one almost every year.

The summer after our high school graduation we worked hard filling out as many scholarship applications as possible–even ones we didn't think we'd be awarded. By the time we heard back from most of them, all four years were paid for at the University of Oregon–including enough to cover our small two-bedroom apartment near campus. It was more than we ever expected and gave us the ability to put any money we've earned straight in our travel fund.

We've always planned on adventuring the summer after we graduate, but now that it's approaching, I have a feeling it's not going to play out how we imagined it as kids. Avery's boyfriend, Miller, is a year older than us. He transferred to UO freshman year to be closer to Avery, and their unfolding love story leads me to believe she might be more settled down soon. I'm happy for her, even though I'll be sad if I have to travel alone. I've promised myself I'll still go no matter what.

I add "Spain" to the list after responding to my best friend's harsh but true remark about my reclusiveness. I've been using her spending so much time with Miller as an excuse to focus on school and keep to myself. It doesn't help that I get nervous introducing myself to people.

"Seriously, Mace. It's our last year before we have to live in the real world. You have to take advantage of it, so you don't regret it later."

I slouch in my seat. "I just don't know where to start."

"Okay, let's devise a plan." She leans forward, propping her elbows on the table. "What do you want more of this year?"

I twirl the pen between my fingers. "Maybe we can be better about weekly taco Tuesdays? I miss you."

"Done. What else?"

"Hmm." I rack my brain. "I think I want to do something that gets me out of the apartment every week, for something besides school or work."

"Like a club? Why don't you join the running club? I always see them around campus. Pretty sure they meet for pizza at Track Town a lot too. You love running, and you love pizza. It's perfect for you." She laughs.

I blink, surprised by how much I like her suggestion. "That's actually a really good idea. Okay, I'll look into that when we get back." Shifting in my seat, I debate saying what's been on my mind for a while now. "Also..."

"Out with it, Maci," Avery jokes when I hesitate for too long.

"I want a boyfriend."

Excitement is evident in her eyes and voice. "Why do you sound nervous? You could easily find a guy to date. You're a catch, Mace."

I manage a half-smile, appreciating the confidence boost. "It's just been a while, you know? I haven't been on a real date since high school. Did that even count?"

She relaxes into her seat, not concerned by my worry. "Try not to overthink it. Most people just want to get a feel for each other first too. It doesn't have to be anything serious. Taylor, Alexis and Kylie are always inviting us out, and I bet they could create so many opportunities for you to meet someone."

"Yeah, you're right. This doesn't really solve my real problem, though."

"Which is..."

"It feels like these are all just pieces to a puzzle, but I don't even know what the puzzle looks like. I still haven't figured out what I want to do with my life once this school year is over."

"I think all of this will help. An idea isn't magically going to come to you while you're sitting at home. Maybe being around new people and having different experiences will spark an idea."

"Okay. Yes. You're right." I sit up straighter, slapping my hands on the table with enthusiasm. "I feel good about this plan."

With a laugh, she stands. "Good, now that that's settled, let's go find your parents and go to the beach!"

CHAPTER TWO

The tunnel of trees that leads straight to the math building will likely make the walk to this particular class my favorite. The branches from either side intertwine where they meet over the only drivable road that runs through campus, with both a biking and walking lane built into it. It's officially fall as of a week ago, but the leaves are still green. It's beautiful and calming–one of my favorite parts of living in Oregon.

Holy shit, what is that smell? My mouth waters as I scan the sidewalk. I spot a food truck set up toward the end of the row of tables. This walk just got better. Why there's a mini street fair on campus, I have no idea, but I haven't had a funnel cake since I was probably 13, and I'm so here for it. Something tells me it'll bring me the comfort I'm looking for, and I have to have one.

There's nothing specifically stressing me out right now. It helps Avery and I came up with a game plan to make sure I make the most of my last year of college. Overall, I've just been consumed by anxiety because it's easier said than done. I know I'm in control, but as much as I love making plans and knowing what's happening, the follow-through doesn't always happen.

When I was younger, I had this plan to accomplish so much that would have put me ahead. Now, here I am, six weeks from my 21st birthday, and I don't even know how I'm celebrating that pivotal milestone. There's a lot I enjoy enough, but most days it seems like I'm just going through the motions. It kind of feels as if I'm checking items off a list to get me to this destination of graduating college and starting my life.

But the truth is, I have no idea what I will do once that happens.

Why isn't it as easy as I thought it would be back in high school? Avery and I planned to travel the world together, and I hoped it would all just come together. How naive of me. I don't have a job I love, I have never had a boy to love, and at this point, it doesn't feel like I have prospects for either. I'm not sure that second point would seem so important if I hadn't spent five years watching my best friend fall madly in love with her boyfriend, but it definitely feels like I'm running out of time.

I remind myself everything will be more likely to fall into place if I just stick to the plan. It's just overwhelming. And part of me holds onto hope I'll find a way to travel the world, fall in love with one of the cities I explore, maybe meet someone and then never leave. That would solve everything.

"Ummm, hello?" The irritated voice comes from a red-headed girl glaring at me from behind the funnel cake stand. My daydreaming has been getting out of hand. I order a funnel cake without any toppings besides powdered sugar, so I can eat it like a soft pretzel on my walk into class. After swiping my card in her machine, I take the flimsy paper plate from her. She's already yelling at the person behind me as I head off to statistics. I guess if anything can distract me from my life not making sense, it's something else that makes no sense.

I lick my fingers, but it's no use. This powdered sugar is too sticky, but there's no time to find a bathroom if I want a good seat. Tossing my plate in the trash, I try to brush the residual powder off my hands as I head up the stairs and open the heavy, green door that leads into the math building. As much as I love the walk to get here, statistics is the only class I'm not looking forward to this quarter. I tried to leave all my easy and fun classes for senior year but kept putting this one off because I'm worried about it being confusing. Math is one of those subjects I have to pay attention to without distractions or I won't understand it. I'm sure it will be much easier than I've made it out to be in my head. I tend to work myself up over nothing, more often than not.

Plus, Avery saved all her notes from last year for me. I need to remind her to get them next time she's home. The first two years after Miller transferred here from Oregon State, she was still around a lot. This past year, since Miller graduated, it hardly feels like I have a roommate anymore. After being apart for the year he was in college before us, he realized he couldn't stay away from her. The longer they are together, the more he seems to need her around. I don't blame him. She's been my best friend since I was 12 for a reason.

On the other hand, I can only imagine what it's like to want to be around someone all the time. In high school, I had a boyfriend. We did the whole "I love you" thing, but that hardly counts when you're 16, kissing someone for the first time and have no other experiences or people to compare them to.

I've been on a few dates–if you could call them that–since I've been in college. There was the guy I accidentally walked into at the gym when I wasn't looking where I was going. We kept walking around campus until we came across the school's lake and sat on the stone steps of the nearest building, talking until I left to catch dinner in the cafeteria before it closed. Very few things are worth my time more than food.

Freshman year, I met with a guy from my philosophy class. We went to his friend's apartment for a party. I still remember the buzz I felt from the Mike's Hard Lemonade. It was the first full drink I'd ever had. The only other time I had any alcohol was the night in high school when Avery and I took one sip of everything in her dad's liquor cabinet to see what it tasted like–needless to say, it kept me off alcohol for a while.

I've gathered that dating is synonymous with hanging out when you're in college. I didn't kiss either of those guys and never saw them again. We didn't have that "spark." I'm not convinced it even exists, but I'm choosing to hold out hope for it either way.

I walk down the hall, looking for the number 104, which I find outside the second door on the left. I pass through the propped open metal doors and bounce down the carpeted steps–it reminds me of airport carpeting–two at a time. Making my way to the second row from the front, I choose a seat barely off to the right. This is the plan I go with in every class, hoping I won't ever be called on, but I'll still be able to focus. It usually works.

The classroom is only a quarter full. I like getting there early on day one, so I don't have to choose who I sit next to, especially since even after three years here, I don't have that many friends.

Ugh, my stomach feels uneasy. Funnel cake for breakfast was a bad idea.

Or maybe I'm twisted up because it hit me all over again that I feel alone and without a plan.

I try to recall the list Avery and I made a few weeks back. We've made so many over the years, always wondering which country we would enjoy the most. She always thought it would be Australia, or maybe New Zealand, but my mind has always been set somewhere in South or Central America. I'd be happy going anywhere, though.

I read this quote by Graham Greene that said, "Once your passport has been stamped, your life will never be the same." I'm dying to experience that.

I should look into getting my passport soon. As much as I love Oregon, and the few other states I've been to, there's just something that feels so magical and life-changing about exploring abroad. I'm convinced traveling to a completely different reality gives you permission to be someone else once you get there. It's not that I don't like who I am, it just seems like the level of freedom to be who you want would be different somehow.

I'm startled from my thoughts when a blond-haired guy plops in the black folding stadium chair next to me. He seems distracted too. *Okay, stop staring, Maci.* I force myself to pull my eyes away from him as the teacher introduces himself. Before he even makes it through the syllabus, my eyes wander back to my right.

He's leaning forward on the hand furthest from me, which is propped up by his elbow on the desk, twirling his pen in his free hand. Why am I bothered by this? Or am I mesmerized by how intently his soft gray eyes are focused on his spinning pen? It slips from his hand, bouncing slightly off his desk, bringing him back to reality.

His eyes lock with mine when he reaches for his pen, but it feels as if he's looking through me. I uncomfortably shift my gaze toward the front of the class as he returns to his mindless twirling, appearing unaware of anything happening outside his head.

The rest of the class passes quickly, luckily without going over anything but a recap of what we should know from the prerequisite class. I'm reminded of how sticky my fingers still are as I slide my book into my bag. It distracts me long enough that by the time I stand to leave, there's no longer anyone in the seat next to me.

CHAPTER THREE

As I walk into Room 104 two days later, I find myself wanting to see the blond-haired guy again. I'm sure it's for no other reason than I like the comfort of consistency. I slide into my seat.

Avery left me her stats notes yesterday which is a huge relief. I must have barely missed her stopping by because they weren't there before I ran out for my first meeting with the running club, but they were on the counter when I got back. It'll help a lot if I can follow along with them. When I sit back up from pulling the pages from my bag, I startle slightly upon realizing he's sitting next to me again.

I wonder if he's there because he's a creature of habit, too. Surely, that must be the only reason. He seems a little less distracted today, and if we are going to be seat buddies, I should take advantage of the minute we have left before class starts to introduce myself. I promised myself I'd be better about that.

"Hi, I'm Maci," I say with much more personality than I intended.

He pauses for a moment like he isn't sure I was talking to him. "Troy," he replies, glancing over at me when he sees there's no one else around. He looks back down and pulls his notebook out, unlike Monday's class.

The next 100 minutes fly by, and as I'm packing my bag, I feel warm fingers graze over my arm. "Hey, sooo it seems like you're really prepared for this class."

I chuckle. "Don't be fooled. My best friend gave me her notes from last year. Math is not my strong suit, but I'm determined not to flunk a class my senior year."

"Yeah, same. At least we aren't on semesters like my cousin's college. Four months of this class sounds way worse than two and a half." He laughs lightly as he looks at me, then pauses, appearing lost in thought. Before I can respond he adds, "Still going to suck. Maybe we could be study partners?"

Seriously? A guy this hot actually wants to spend time with me? I know it's only for homework, but still. "Yes, please!" I reach back into my bag for my phone, but it slips through my fingers. I try to hide my nerves with a small laugh. Ugh, I'm so awkward and clumsy sometimes.

Hoping to escape the embarrassment I feel heating my face, I take a breath as I reach for my phone again and turn back toward him. When I do, he's holding his phone out for me with a new contact page open. I slide mine into my hoodie pocket before I take his and type my name and my number, going back to add "math class" in parentheses after my name. Taking it back from me, he glances at the screen and smirks. It's the first emotion I've seen since I met him.

"Hey, can I join you two later?" an unfamiliar voice interrupts us from behind. I didn't notice anyone else was still in the room. "Everything we learned today went right over my head."

I try to ignore the heavy, sinking feeling. I know nothing about the stranger next to me, but I like the idea of spending time alone with him. What's up with that?

Maybe he was just in the right place at the right time. I did kind of stumble across him in the middle of my quarter-life crisis, post stuffing my face with funnel cake and wishing I had a boyfriend who would have shared with me. And I mean, let's face it, Troy is hot. His perfectly styled blond hair against his light skin and soft gray eyes are apparently enough to qualify him as a candidate for that job. I snap myself out of my thoughts, hoping time hasn't betrayed me and made this interaction weird.

"Yeah, of course!" I say more enthusiastically than I feel, after I realize–quickly, thank goodness–I have no logical reason to say no. I exchange numbers with Carley after she ties back her red curls, and we make a plan to meet at 4 p.m. tomorrow in the main library to knock out our homework before the weekend. She bounces out of the room, leaving Troy and me alone.

My purple JanSport backpack sits on my lap, and I go to zip it. I sense Troy's lack of movement, still sitting in his seat next to me.

"Do you go to Sunriver often?" He points at the keychain attached to my bag.

"My best friend's boyfriend has a cabin there, so we go at least twice a year. It's one of my favorite places."

"That's cool, we've had a place there since I was a kid. You bring your boyfriend too?"

Smooth.

I ignore the butterflies in my stomach and laugh. "Yeah, I don't have one of those."

"Good to know." He winks at me, emitting such a confident aura–a complete 180 from the person he was on Monday when he seemed so in his head. "It must suck being the third wheel, though."

"I'm used to it." I shrug. "It would be nice to not be, but it's easy to be their third wheel."

"Well, I'll see you tomorrow, Maci." He stands, swings his backpack over his shoulder. and takes off up the steps and out the door.

Outside of math, I don't mind school. I'd go forever if it were free and if I could learn without the studying and the tests. I think I just enjoy engaging my mind; it's probably why I read so many thrillers when I'm not reading textbooks. I might not be outgoing enough to introduce myself to study groups, but I like being in the library, surrounded by other people wanting to focus too. It's how I know my way around the place so well. I've learned which study rooms are usually full and which are typically empty. I also know none of them have cell phone service, so I decide it's best to stay outside until my new friends arrive. Standing outside the giant brass and glass doors, at the top of the stone steps, I stare at the lawn art, trying to figure out what the hell it's supposed to be.

"You're not supposed to look confused until we attempt this homework," a voice interrupts my pondering.

I follow the voice to see Troy's face straight on for the first time. His gray eyes look a little bluer in the sunlight. His short, blond hair seems to sit there perfectly even though I can tell there isn't any gel holding it in place. He's wearing a gray school hoodie, the bright yellow "O" on the front contrasting his dark blue jeans that fit him well. They don't hang off him, showing his boxers like half of the guys here. I'll never understand why that's cool. His white Adidas are far cleaner than they should be living in a state that rains half the year. *Maci, stop taking inventory of his clothes before he catches you.*

I can't recall what he just said, so I laugh awkwardly and am thankful when Carley walks up the steps. We head inside, and I lead us to one of the study rooms connected to a section of the library that rarely gets seen. Relief washes over me when I take a seat at the round table, saving me the effort of figuring out how to sit next to Troy.

It's not that I haven't wanted a boyfriend since I got to college, I've just had other priorities. I have no idea why all of a sudden I'm drawn toward finding one, but it makes me hopeful someone paid enough attention to start a conversation.

We are getting through the homework fairly quickly. I should be happy, but I find myself wishing there was more. When we take a short break, I pretend to go to the bathroom down the hall. I know I won't have service, but I attempt to text Avery anyway. She asked for frequent updates. I told her it's only to study, we won't be alone, and he probably doesn't even remember my name. I know she just feels bad for spending so much time with Miller and wants me to find someone too.

It's causing me to get ahead of myself. I don't even know this kid's last name, but I feel like I need to know more than just that immediately. I shake the thought from my head, rolling my eyes as I walk back to the room. Troy and Carley immediately stop talking when I open the door. Maybe it's childish, but come on, that's classic "we were just talking about you" vibes. Nothing like that to make a girl self-conscious. We finish and go our separate ways, and I try to stop wondering what could have been said while I was gone.

I'm probably thinking crazy anyway. It's this quarter-life crisis I'm in. I feel like once I graduate, I cross over this line where I'm supposed to have my life together and know what I'm doing. I've heard my parents' story a hundred times. They met when they were in college at Oregon State and both knew they were meant to be after their first Education class they took together. They knew who they wanted to be with and what they wanted to do. They found jobs right away, and the rest is history. I love that for them, but I can't help but feel like I'm behind because of it.

CHAPTER FOUR

Even though I took the time to add loose curls to my usually straight brown hair and apply a little more makeup than the typical nothing I wear, I'm still early to class on Monday morning. I feel like a different person. Normally, I don't get out of bed until my alarm goes off five minutes before I leave. I throw on a hoodie, the one pair of jeans I own that I like and toss my hair in a messy bun with a scrunchie on my way out the door.

Of course, this is the day Troy is nowhere to be found, even by the time class starts at 9 a.m.

A few minutes into the lecture, Carley quietly walks down the steps, sliding into the seat next to me. When class lets out, she leans over and nudges me. "So... Troy was asking about you." She waggles her eyebrows.

My eyes dart to her. "Wait, what?"

"Yeah, when you went to the bathroom during our study sesh, he asked me if I thought it would be weird if he asked you to hang out, since he already has your number and all." The tone in her voice tells me she's curious to hear my reaction. I don't know her well yet, but I get the impression she's nosy and loves to be in on everyone's drama. Even if it only encourages her, I have to know more.

"Oh, what did you say?" I attempt to stay neutral and not give away that I'm freaking out inside.

"That there's no harm in asking!" she says with a shrug. A smirk reveals itself as she catches the smile I'm trying to hide slip across my face.

I waited all day hoping Troy would text me, hoping whatever kept him from class wasn't enough to keep him from wanting to hang out too. As I'm about to work up the courage to text him, my phone dings.

Troy: *Hey, I overslept and missed class. Any way I could get the notes from you?*

Me: *Sure! Just let me know when.*

Troy: *Maybe we could get coffee later and you can bring them?*

I pull my phone to my face to make sure I'm reading it correctly, especially since my hands are shaking. I steady them enough to reply.

Me: *Sounds great! I'm free around 2?*

Troy: *Works for me.*

I only have an hour break, so I head to the café Troy suggested as soon as my class lets out. I walk through the glass door, which is covered in a green and yellow poster listing the football schedule for the year, and see Troy at a table in the back. He's leaning forward on his elbows with a card in his hand.

"Hey," I greet him once I'm a few feet away.

He glances up. "Hey, Maci. Who is your favorite superhero?"

"What?" I scrunch my eyebrows together.

He holds up the card in his hand. "I found this stack of conversation starters on the table." He laughs. "So, who is your favorite?"

"Oh, Ant-Man, hands down."

"That feels... random." He looks at me with a quirked brow.

"No way. He's brilliant. He's hilarious. And so many game-changing moments wouldn't be possible without him. Who is your favorite?"

"Easy. The Joker."

"Does he even count as a superhero? Isn't he a villain? Does he even have powers?!" I roll my eyes.

"No less powers than Ant-Man! And he's arguably equally as intelligent. But I like him because he's the wild card. You never know what to expect, and that makes him awesome."

"Let's agree to disagree on this one. Or I'll cave and admit Heath Ledger plays one of the best superhero roles of all time."

"Deal. Okay..." He looks back at the card in his hand. "Apparently this card is themed. What is the worst superpower you could have?"

"Anything? Let me think, you go first," I say, searching my brain for the craziest thing I can think of.

"Hmmm. I think the worst superpower would be the ability to get turned on by only people you have no interest in."

I almost spit out the iced tea I ordered from the waitress. Of course he would say something like that, total man answer. "That would be terrible. Almost as terrible as being able to remember in detail every single bathroom you've ever been in."

"What?" He laughs. "That's the most random thing I've ever heard."

"It was the first thing that popped into my head." I shrug.

"You're weird. I like it."

The next 45 minutes fly by. We spend most of it going back and forth, answering nearly all the questions off the stack of cards. I haven't laughed this hard in a while. His answers are always random. He seems like the definition of fun–not what I would have expected based on day one. By the time I need to head to my next class, I haven't even taken out my notes. I pull them from my bag and give them to him.

"Thanks," he says. "You probably need these for the homework? I can give them back tomorrow. How do you feel about getting dinner after classes?"

Is he asking me on a date? Is that what's happening right now? I promised myself I'd be more open to opportunities this year, so now is as good a time as ever to take advantage. "A girl has to eat." I look at him, chewing on my lip. "My last class gets out at 4:50."

"Perfect. I'll pick you up on main street at 5."

CHAPTER FIVE

My stomach flips as I lean against the cool metal railing of the stairs outside the math building–conveniently next to where my last class of the day was. The steps leading down from the old brick building open up to the only drivable street that runs through campus, so it's the perfect place to meet Troy.

When was the last time I was this nervous? I can't remember. Sweat prickles across the back of my neck. I take my sweatshirt off and tie it around my waist, hoping to cool off by the time Troy arrives. Also crossing my fingers that jeans will be fine for the "adventure" claimed in a good morning text from him.

I move to sit on the second step from the bottom, keeping my eyes on the road. I have no idea what type of car Troy drives. I'm squinting to look through the windows of each car that goes by for blond hair when I catch a glimpse of a black and lime green motorcycle in my periphery. You don't see many bikes in Oregon, especially on campus. I've never been on one before. I wonder what it's like. My thoughts pause as the bike stops in front of me with the rider flipping the kickstand out with his foot.

I recognize the white Adidas immediately.

He pulls his helmet off. Confirmed, Troy.

I must have the widest eyes he's ever seen because he laughs as he reaches out with a plain black helmet. "Have you been on a motorcycle before?"

"Noooope," I say, rubbing my clammy hands against my jeans and internally thanking my morning self for not putting on the dress I considered.

"Guess I get to be your first," he winks, his blue-gray eyes glittering as he grins. He has the kind of confidence that sends a flutter through my stomach, rather than the conceited kind that makes me wish I was with any-one else.

I'm probably as terrified as he is amused. Are all the girls he dates this much of a baby? Or maybe they just think it's incredibly hot and that overrides their fear. I mean, he does look sexier than ever leaning against the black seat, still holding out his helmet for me.

I grab it from him. The buckle pinches my skin as I click it under my chin, but I pull the strap as tight as it can go until it's practically choking me. He swings his leg over the side and motions for me to do the same behind him. I assume this is like the movies and find little pegs for my feet to rest on before wrapping my arms around his waist. I guess we are skipping to the invading each other's personal space part of this date. Wait, *is* this a date? Or just dinner? I consider putting my sweater back on but my chest feels on fire as I lean against him. He yells back to me asking if I'm ready, then kicks up the stand and rolls back the handle once he feels me nod against his back.

We pull onto the street, my brown hair already whip-ping around the sides of my face. My heart races as fast as we drive, and I don't even care where we are going. I get the feeling spontaneity is Troy's thing. It's unlike me, but I'm already addicted to it. I know it seems contradictory considering it's my dream to travel to a bunch of countries I've never been to before, but even *that* I plan to make plans for. I like to know what's going to happen, but not knowing what Troy has planned for us doesn't leave me stressed like I thought it would. It thrills me, and I can see why people find spontaneity appealing.

Or maybe it's the magic of a lime green motorcycle and an extremely attractive man.

Before I have time to guess where we are going based on which streets we've turned down, we pull up at a little restaurant that looks like it's been shoved between two bigger ones.

If he didn't move first, I don't think I would have pulled away from him. Troy swings his leg over his bike, careful not to hit me. He takes in the sight of me and laughs. I can see in the reflection of his helmet that my typically straight brown hair is curly and crazy from the wind, and my face is flushed. He pulls his helmet off, takes mine from me and brushes a few wild hairs out of my face.

I hold my breath as his fingers graze my skin, releasing it only when he grabs my hand instead.

Unconsciously, I lean into his arm and the heat from us touching starts to warm my whole body. I hadn't realized it was so cold, but the shocking temperature change makes it evident. Looking up, I see the words "Off the Waffle" in green and blue neon letters pinned above the glass doors. We walk in, choosing a seat by the window, and a waitress tosses two menus on the table as she passes by.

Waffles with ice cream on top. That's what this entire place is, every flavor and combination you can imagine. There are both sweet and savory options such as bacon waffles with maple-flavored ice cream and baked cinnamon apples with vanilla bean. I'm always down for ice cream, but I've never had it for dinner. If decisions like this are what adulthood was actually about, I'd be signing up much quicker.

Usually, I'm that person who looks up the menu before they go places because I'm terrible at making decisions. I like to be prepared so no one has to wait on me. Between thinking I'm taking too long and my face heating from Troy's eyes on me as I read through the entire menu, my heart rate accelerates again after it's only recently calmed down from the ride over here.

I decide, and I'm about to ask Troy what he's going to have, but our waitress appears at our table again.

"Do you know what you'd like?"

Troy looks over at me with a small nod, letting me know to go first.

"I'll have the 'Hey Bob,'" I reply to her. It has caramelized pears, goat cheese, vanilla ice cream and honey drizzled on top. It's the "weirdest" one on the menu, but I almost always choose the most unique option and am willing to try anything. I feel a little self-conscious about my choice for absolutely no reason as I look up, waiting for Troy to order.

A smirk plays across his lips, lighting up his eyes. "Same," he tells her, taking my menu from me and handing them both to her before she walks away.

I turn to face him. "Well, I guess I realized I know nothing about you, considering I didn't expect you to show up on a motorcycle, and no one usually likes the weird options on the menu like I do."

The corner of his mouth turns up in a smile. "I forget it's something people don't automatically know. How was it?"

"Not as scary as I thought. I'm glad I wore pants to-day." I lean forward, resting my chin on my fist.

A curious expression washes over his face for a second before it clears. "Okay, so you know I own a motor-cycle now. What else do you want to know?"

Wow, that's a lot of pressure. I haven't been on an actual date with anyone besides my high school boyfriend, Grayson, and those feel different than this. Maybe I should have made note cards like Avery joked. I'm not sure what to ask, so I say the first thing that pops into my mind. "If you could travel anywhere, where would you go?"

"Hmmm." He looks toward the ceiling, pondering for a moment. "I don't know much about different places. I've only ever been to California. But I do think it would be cool to go to the airport one day and just buy a ticket for the next available flight."

"Wow, that's the definition of spontaneous. I'm not sure I could do it."

"Life is too short not to take a chance. I mean, some-times you can make a decision on purpose and not like where you end up, so why not chance all of it?"

I suppose that makes sense in a twisted way, but it sounds a little too stressful for me. I'm more of a reason and logic type of girl.

"Where would you go?"

"Anywhere and everywhere is on my list." I pause for a moment before I add, "As long as I know where I'm going before I go."

"You're no fun," he plays. "Okay, my turn, what are you most afraid of?"

I'm not sure if he's looking for an answer along the lines of spiders or heights, but I decide to say what first comes to mind. "Graduation. I have no idea what I want to do after I finish school."

"You're a psych major, right?" He leans back in his chair, and sips on his water, eyes fully focused on me.

"Yeah, I took a psych class in high school and loved it. There are so many different routes I can take with it. I've considered a few options, but nothing has been speaking to me. I guess I always thought I'd take a year off to travel before settling down, but I doubt that will happen."

He narrows his gaze. "What makes you think it won't happen?"

"It was something I planned to do with my best friend. But she jumped ahead to the settling down part, found the love of her life before the rest of us, ya know?"

"Yeah, I know how that goes..." The look in his eyes tells me he does know, although I'm not sure in what sense.

He goes quiet after that. When I think he's about to open his mouth and say something else, our food appears.

I get on his motorcycle again, this time with a lot more ease. Partially because it's no longer my first time on a motorcycle, but also because I feel comfortable around Troy. There's a warmth about him that makes me feel like I can talk about anything. He also has this fearlessness I want to explore. I don't ask him where we are going, although I hope it's not home. Considering he hasn't asked me where I live, I'm guessing the date isn't over.

We slow down when we approach what looks like the entrance to a hiking trail. A sign off to the side says "Skinner Butte." I'm surprised when he doesn't park the bike, but then realize the paved path continues up the side of the hill. This lookout point over the city has been on my list of places to check out, but I've never made time to come here.

Once he parks, we get off the bike and walk to the edge of the circular viewpoint that's lined with a black barred barrier. "Wow, it feels like you can see the whole city from here," I whisper.

The sun hasn't quite set, but I can see the glow coming from the houses below. I don't need light to feel him step closer. It always seems warmer when he's nearby, especially whenever he closes the distance between us. Within a few moments, the goosebumps covering my body under my sweatshirt start to fade. He's only a few inches away from my face, close enough I can smell his cologne. I can't place the notes, but it's a little sweet and a little spicy.

Even though no part of his body is touching mine, I get the feeling he might try to kiss me. Considering I don't know what's normal for dating these days, I'm slightly hesitant. I mean, I am in the middle of nowhere in the dark, with someone who is practically a stranger.

I kind of hope he leans in anyway.

His eyes flash to my mouth for a moment, but then he pulls back a little–as if he was too close to focus on me. He angles his body away from me slightly, shifting his gaze back at the city. "It's one of my favorite places here. I stumbled across it right after I got my bike." His eyes pull away from the view toward me as if he was referring to something different all along.

"It's beautiful," I say, forcing myself to study the trees rather than his face.

A few more minutes of comfortable silence pass. I can't tell if I'm disappointed he didn't kiss me–it's probably too soon for that–but I know I am not disappointed with this view. It's incredible out here, a blend of green, yellow and orange trees enclosing the town in front of us and the shadows of small mountains behind it all. I should come here more often. There's something about looking out into the world that puts into perspective how small you are in the grand scheme of things. It almost convinces you everything is going to work out fine, even if it's only temporary.

"Carley told me you were going to chicken out of asking me to hang out if she didn't talk you into it. Do you think you would have?" The words tumble out of me, breaking the silence before I can stop myself or know why I am saying them.

His eyes sparkle slightly in the orange glow of the sunset. "I guess we will never know."

"This is a date, right? I mean it feels date-ish. But just because she's not here, I'm not trying to misread this situation." Dear God, Maci, stop talking.

He laughs, wrapping his arm around me and squeezing my shoulder. Pressing his lips into my hair softly, he kisses the side of my head. "Definitely a date, but it's getting late. I should get home so I don't sleep through class again tomorrow. Ready to go?"

It's not that late, and I'd rather stay out here for hours than get enough sleep for school, but I nod instead.

We aren't very far from my apartment, so I nudge him from behind, directing him on the few turns he has to take to get me home. He pulls up in front of my first-floor apartment door and flips the kickstand out, without turning off his bike. I swing my leg over, pulling my helmet off for him. He removes his too, while reaching for mine. Pulling me into a hug, he whispers in my ear, "Thanks for the adventure, Maci."

"Thanks for not killing me on your motorcycle."

He pulls back, chuckling, and puts his helmet back on. I turn around when I get to my door in time to see him wave goodbye.

CHAPTER SIX

Thanks to my parents' neighbor, Sharon, the Dean of Admissions here, I got the perfect college job at a little café and convenience store on campus. It's easy enough, and I only work one day a week for spending money since I got scholarships to pay for school. Sometimes I pick up an extra shift so I can add to my travel fund. It's a nice break from my schoolwork or if I need to get out when Avery has been with Miller all week, and I don't feel like day drinking with the girls.

It's only weird because I don't like coffee–so I'm not even sure if what I make tastes any good. I usually have to hide my scrunched-up face as I make it and hand it to whatever zombie student has wandered in. No one has said anything negative, so I'm hoping they can't tell I don't even like the smell of what I'm making. Today though, I feel like I can't smell anything. I'm staring blankly as I ask the girl in front of me her name for the third time, like *I'm* the zombie.

It's been over a week, and I haven't heard from Troy at all. I texted him as soon as I got in bed after he dropped me off to let him know I had a great time on our date. At least I thought it was a date. I mean, he confirmed it was. He paid for dinner too. But the next morning, he never showed up to class, unless I didn't see him.

Carley questioned me about it this week, and I didn't know what to say. She was as confused as I was after hearing the rundown. He's missed three classes now. Did he drop it? Or is he just not showing up? I shake my head, trying to clear all the possible scenarios currently running through it, and some of the coffee in the drink I just made sloshes over the edge. I instinctively drop the cup when the hot liquid burns my skin, spilling all over the counter.

Dammit. This is why I have spent three years sticking to schoolwork at school.

CHAPTER SEVEN

If voluntarily attending school on a Saturday doesn't scream how much I need a distraction, I have no idea what else would.

At the start of the quarter, my Psychology of Crisis Intervention professor told us about this eight-hour weekend course we could take in place of the final if we were interested. I still don't know what direction I want to go when I graduate, but I do know I probably won't figure it out unless I explore all my options.

So, here I am, on a Saturday morning, waiting for my Psychology: Human Trafficking course to start. I didn't get to choose the topic, and it sounds dark, but it'll get me out of the final. Plus, I have been fascinated by anything connected to how the mind works ever since I took a psychology class in high school.

I'm probably also curious because sometimes I feel like it's impossible to figure out how some people's minds work.

I'm still sitting here, just staring at the front of the now-empty classroom. Even the professor left a few minutes ago. After the first time Avery and Miller had sex, she ran to me screaming about how her world had been rocked. She claimed she knew at that moment he was the one because of how it made her feel. This is the weirdest comparison, but I feel like my mind was rocked. Eight straight hours, minus a short lunch break, and I wasn't bored or distracted once. Every heartstring was pulled on, and more than once it took a lot of willpower and self pep talk to keep tears from falling.

This is my thing.

Okay, well, saying human trafficking is "my thing" is probably not the right choice of words. But I've been so worried about finding my purpose, that one thing I want to use as my vehicle for making a difference in life, and now I know what it is. Unfortunately, I still don't know how exactly I'm going to tackle this issue, but knowing I want to in some way is such a huge step for me.

In the class, we learned about how much of a problem trafficking is, even as close as Portland. That's less than two hours from here. Most commonly, a lot of these women and children are promised by these men that money will be sent to their families if they come to work for them. It turns into more of a kidnapping, and they are forced into sex labor. Sometimes it's years before they are rescued, and at that point they are behind in education, not to mention traumatized. My teacher mentioned a few organizations that help with the rescue and rehabilitation of these women. I make a note to research them later.

CHAPTER EIGHT

I've never been much for Halloween, but this is my last year in college and there are already so many experiences I have missed out on by always choosing sweats and a book. Even Avery is ditching Miller and their typical couple costume so we can go all out for our last college Halloween with our girl friends.

If we do include anyone else in our plans, it's only ever Alexis, Taylor and Kylie. We met them last year at a just for fun women only kickball tournament over Spring Break, and since then, we've gotten together for a few random fitness events on campus or house parties. They are our go-to girls when we are in the mood for an adventure.

We know life won't be the same once we graduate, even if we all stay around Eugene. It hasn't been said aloud, but I know we want our last year before we enter the real world to have as many high notes as possible. It's why we all agreed on a group costume. Alexis had the idea for us to go as the Spice Girls. After the rest of the girls jumped to be their favorite, I was assigned "Posh Spice.".

On my third thrift store of the day, I was about to give up and order a generic costume online. But the third time proved to be a charm–I found the perfect outfit. It's a dark gold strapless dress with a ridiculously high pair of gold platform shoes. I guess you can find anything you need these days if you search hard enough. Even though I'll probably freeze, considering it's going to be 47° out, a wave of giddiness washes over me.

"I hate you for this idea. Why didn't we go with something that had pants?" I whine at Taylor as I tug on the bottom of my dress. I was right. It's fucking freezing.

"I'm wearing pants." She sticks her tongue out at me as she shoves a red Solo cup in my hand with at least two shots worth of amber liquid swirling around the bottom. She's got on a pair of old school, loose-fitting Adidas sweats. They are royal blue with bright yellow stripes up the leg that match perfectly with her yellow sports bra. Her shoulder-length brown hair is pulled back into a ponytail. "But your dress is perfect. You look like a total babe. Here, take this shot, it will help you warm up!"

"Warm up or throw up?" I laugh before I gulp it down, making a face once the Fireball hits my tastebuds. *Gross.*

"Okay, let's go!" Kylie's voice gets louder as she comes into the kitchen from the bathroom. She's wearing a red wig over her usually short blonde hair, a British flag dress–that might actually be a shirt it's so short–and mid-calf red platform boots.

"Daaaamn," Taylor and I yell in unison when we get a good look at Kylie as Alexis and Avery come out of

Avery's bedroom in equally skimpy clothes. Alexis has her long, white-blonde hair pulled into high pigtails, a silky, light blue spaghetti strap dress that looks more like lingerie and white Go-Go boots.

Avery was made for the Scary Spice look. Her dark brown hair is twisted into two space buns on top of her head, tightly wrapped with gold ribbon, zigzag part and all. She's got on a cheetah print crop top, black spandex shorts and black combat boots. We all look perfect.

"Where are we going tonight? We should find a costume contest somewhere. We would totally win," I declare. If we look this good, we might as well make the most of it.

"Oooohhh, There's one at Rennie's! Let's go there!" Alexis squeals.

"I still have a week until my birthday," I remind her.

"Ehhh, it'll be fine. I think they are doing wristbands tonight, I'll yank mine off to give to you and go in twice!"

It's so crowded here. Is this what all the bars are like, or only because it's Halloween? I'd be worried about losing my friends, but there isn't any room for them to escape the area where we are standing by the bar. Despite the crowd and the chaos, I keep catching a glimpse of the same guy. It's probably because he's nearly naked.

His George of the Jungle costume consists of only a leopard print loincloth. A LOINCLOTH. I'm freezing in my dress. I can only imagine how cold he is, not that he seems to mind. If he had entered the crowd-judged costume contest, surely he would have won, considering there are more girls here. I haven't gotten a full frontal view of him, but even in the dark anyone would be able to tell how sexy he is. The dim lights cast shadows on his back, highlighting the muscles in it and his golden brown hair has that messy, sexy thing happening.

"Maci!" Avery breaks me from my thoughts as George starts to turn around. Before I have a chance to look, my best friend reaches her hand down to help pull me onto the bar with her, which requires all my focus, so I don't fall off it. We won the costume contest. It wasn't even a competition between everyone who entered.

Apparently winning requires a dance party on top of the bar. I know this contest was my idea, but I wasn't prepared to be in the spotlight like this. I stand anyway, making sure my legs stay closed as I reach down for a prize shot from the bartender. I probably don't need another shot, but everyone screaming "Wannabe" as it blares from speakers has me too hyped to turn it down.

This is exactly what I needed. I may not know what my life is going to look like once graduation hits, but I'm happy I'm here now, with my friends, making these memories. I tug on Kylie's arm, leaning my head on her shoulder. "I loooveee you. Thank you for forcing me to get out tonight," I yell at her over the music.

"You mean every night we go out?" Her hand pets my hair as she laughs. "I think you've had enough to drink, Maci."

"Okay, yeah, probably, but the night is young! We are still young! Donuts?!" I turn the other way, facing Avery. "Donuts?!"

"Yes!"

Before the song is even over, I've managed to help all my friends down from the bar. We decide to walk. It's a little less than a mile, and there's streetlamp-lined sidewalk the entire way there. In the daylight, you can see all the fir trees behind the lights, but right now there's only the stars above us. It's perfect, minus it being so cold I'm shivering more with every step. We can make it there before an Uber would get to us in this Halloween traffic, though, so no reason not to walk and make the best of it.

"Oooh, grab bag, please!" I squeal at the lady behind the pink and black striped counter at Voodoo Doughnut. After 1 a.m., they toss all the leftover donuts into bags and sell them for a couple of bucks each. It's perfect, especially when we are all too drunk to care what kind we get.

I wrap my arm around Avery as she practically holds me up, her go-to vanilla scent washing over me. "Thanks for being my best friend," I tell her, while simultaneously shoving a donut in my mouth.

"You're stuck with me forever you weirdo. Mixing your alcohol makes you so mushy." She laughs.

"I know, I knooooow. I just want you to know that I love Miller so much, even when he takes you away from me."

"I already told him the guest bedroom of our future house is basically yours." She stops walking and turns toward me. "You know you're going to find someone too, Mace." Her arms wrap around me again as I pull the bag of donuts out from between us to do the same.

"I hope so."

CHAPTER NINE

Today is November 9th. It's also my 21st birthday. I probably don't feel any different because all that's changed is I can legally get alcohol in public. It's never been an issue to get it while in college anyway. It wasn't hard to sneak into the bar on Halloween, and since Avery turned 21 a few months ago, we can make margaritas at home on taco night if we feel like it. The happy hours at the college bars are good deals, but I still doubt I will go often. Avery and I have a pact to save as much of our money as possible for the trip we want to take someday, even if it isn't as grand as we used to dream.

We do have plans tonight. I'm excited, even though going to a bar where I'd get carded isn't part of the plan.

Once I get home from my last class of the day, I get ready. I touch up the waves I made earlier in my long, brown hair and add mascara and lip gloss. It won't stay on long, but surely we will take pictures for the memories.

I pick out my favorite swimsuit–black bottoms and a black top with neon pink straps. I jump into my jeans, put on a pink tank top, and grab my black North Face jacket since it's freezing outside. It is the beginning of November in the Pacific Northwest after all. Luckily, there isn't rain in the forecast tonight, but it wouldn't matter anyway.

"Avery! Are you ready?" I call around the corner as she walks out of her room at the same moment, nearly crashing into me.

"Ready!" She chuckles, tying her hair back in a low ponytail. She's in black leggings and a matching long sleeve shirt with her cheetah print bikini strings poking out the top. As we slide on our flip flops, our front door swings open. Alexis, Kylie and Taylor come bouncing in carrying five bottles of wine between them. Luckily, I'm not worried about us drinking too much because we can walk nearly everywhere in this town. Class might suck tomorrow, but I only turn 21 once.

I spin them all around to head right back out the door before they talk me into shots and we never get where we are going. The red and yellow of the setting sun streaks the sky as we find our way to the cross walk around the corner from our apartment. Three more corners down, we giggle our way into Track Town Pizza. This is easily my favorite pizza place in town, mostly because of the vibe. It's cozy, the tables are light cherry wood, and the cushions in the seats alternate green and yellow. Old photos of past track stars and both running and football memorabilia hang on the wood panel covered walls between each booth. This entire town has so much school spirit, and I love it. The five of us squish into one of the booths, each of us hiding a bottle of wine inside our jackets.

We practically inhale our BBQ chicken pizza once the server drops it off, anxious for our next stop. Tonight's events might feel lame for a birthday, especially a 21st, but we can go to a bar any time. It's almost completely dark when we walk outside. Despite it being only a two block trek, Avery pulls out her phone to play music.

Taylor Swift's "22" blasts as we skip dance our way to the wooden shack. We've already reserved a room, so Alexis checks us in and gets the key. As I walk by the stand, I catch a glimpse of messy, sandy blond hair out of the corner of my eye. He might be cute, but I can't really tell because it's dark. My attention falls back to my friends ahead who are already yanking off their sweaters. Avery is almost down to only her swimsuit already, hopping out of her leggings as she takes off.

This place is cool. It kind of looks as if you were to take a hallway of hotel rooms, rip the roof off, and place the whole thing in the middle of an oasis. There are rows of doors on either side of us, made of the same wood used for saunas–but instead of hot rocks and benches behind the doors, there are hot tubs.

Alexis slips the key into the first door on the right. The ceilingless room is small. There's a hot tub, ready to go, with the cover already pushed back and steam coming off the water. There are a couple of plants in each corner, a chair for us to set our belongings on, and that's about all the space there is. We make a pile of our clothes on the chair, and Taylor starts pouring wine into the paper cups she swiped from the pizza place earlier.

With taco Tuesdays being the only time I regularly drink, I'm fairly drunk by the time 9:30 hits–three Dixie Cups of wine and a half hour into our hot tub party. I haven't known Alexis, Taylor and Kylie that long, but I really like them. It's been nice having them around. I don't want to be one of those girls who studies her entire time at college and doesn't make any real memories, although that seems to be what I've done for the last three years. These girls thrive in social situations, and they've proven a few times now that I'll always have something fun to do if I want to go with them.

We've been in the warm bubbles for nearly an hour, and our time is ending. It's late enough now that the stars above us stand out brightly, and it's so peaceful I could stay here all night. Mostly we've been joking around, the girls sharing about what parties were epic last weekend, and who hooked up with who. I haven't tried talking to any guys since my date with Troy a few weeks ago. I cringe, pondering for the hundredth time what the heck happened there. I should put myself out there more, but I'm hesitant, especially with the last time being an epic disappointment.

"You know what sounds good right now?!" Avery exclaims out of nowhere.

"What?" I laugh, questioning my best friend.

"Ummm, the cookies 'n cream ice cream cake that is waiting in our fridge for you." She smiles, knowing it's my favorite flavor.

"Why are we still here?!" I immediately stand and step out of the tub, my friends following closely behind.

Realizing we forgot towels, we all try to shake ourselves dry a bit, but are drunk enough we mostly just laugh, knowing it's pointless. I zip my jacket and toss the cups in the small trash can next to the door. My hair is now pulled back into a low messy bun, with the kind of frizz that only comes from hair that has dried after chlorine steam has been soaking into it.

We walk through the small oasis entryway of the place, surrounded by twinkle lights I must not have noticed when we came in. Stopping by the stand to pay on our way out, once again I notice the sandy blond haired man. Now that I'm on an active search for a boyfriend, I'm surprised he hasn't crossed my mind in the last hour. His eyes are as brown as mine, maybe even darker. They look almost black. His skin is barely tanned, like it's trying to drag out the summer sun as long as it can.

He's sitting on a spinning bar stool in a navy Carhartt jacket and dark dusty blue swishy looking pants that I swear are the kind that zip off at the knee. I had no idea they made those anymore or that anyone over the age of nine wore them. Despite the pants, I feel my cheeks heat slightly because I have never been more attracted to someone in my entire life. I've never considered myself having a "type," but if I do, this man in front of me is exactly it.

I'm frozen, paralyzed as I can't take my eyes off him. Alexis is distracted by something Taylor is saying as she hands over the room key and starts to walk away. I somehow will my feet to move in her direction and beg my eyes to follow, but an urge washes over me, and I turn back around. A rare boldness bursts out of me.

"Do you have a girlfriend?" I blurt at this guy, who is intently reading the pages of a book held open by his fingers.

Reggae music plays softly from somewhere behind him, although I'm surprised I've noticed because it feels like someone I don't know, someone braver and more impulsive than me, has possessed my body.

Silence.

If I wasn't already soaking wet, I would probably notice I'm sweating. I'm sure it's only been a few seconds, but it feels like so much longer waiting for him to respond.

He finally looks at me, and our eyes lock. "No," he says, hesitant and curious. Closing his book and setting it on the small desk in front of him, his eyes captivate mine as he returns my question. "Do you have a boyfriend?"

"No. Do you want to go out sometime?" The words tumble out of my mouth before I can stop them.

"Yes," he says, giving me a slight smile, with a hint of dimples. Pulling out a pad of sticky notes, he pushes them toward me. As he takes the cap off the pen and hands it to me, my stomach flips. I've never had butterflies like this before. That must be what this is? I feel like I'm going to throw up.

His hand grazes mine as I take the pen from him, and I'm not sure if it was static, but I swear some sort of electrical current speeds through my finger and explodes into my entire body.

I scribble my full name–not sure why I felt it was necessary–and number across the bright blue sticky. Hopefully he can't tell my writing came from shaking hands.

"Dean." He introduces himself as he reaches for the notepad and pulls it closer to him, an unreadable expression on his face, but questions in his eyes.

"Okay, bye," I mumble as I take off like a third grade girl on the playground after someone jokes about her having a crush on a kid in class. This feeling makes me uneasy. I'm not usually like this. Despite my parents and Avery swearing by it, I've never been convinced love–or "this will be love"–at first sight exists. It makes no sense to me. I've never felt that magnetic pull to someone like it's claimed in the movies, but whatever that was a second ago... I don't know how else to describe it besides chemistry. It had to be.

Avery, who is waiting for me with our friends on the other side of the parking lot, is wide-eyed as I approach.

"Ummm, hi, who are you, and what have you done with my best friend?!" she shrieks.

"What just happened?! I think I blacked out!" My voice is far too loud for how close I'm standing to her. My entire body is shaking, and my heart is racing.

"He was cute!" Kylie exclaims. "What was that all about?!"

I can tell my face is red by the way my skin burns, and if I hadn't asked a boy out for the first time in my life, I would have thought it was from our hour of hot tubbing outside in the middle of winter. I tell them, hardly believing the story myself, even though it just happened.

"Do you think he's going to text you?!" Kylie chimes in again.

I shrug my shoulders because I've reached the point of being so cold it's hard to talk. I'm soaking wet, and my lips are practically numb. We are already about halfway home and thank goodness it isn't much further. I hope he texts me.

At that moment, a small buzz comes from the pocket of my jacket.

Dean: *Hey, Maci Jackson.*

That was fast.

As much as I hoped for it, I didn't expect him to text me. He probably lied about not having a girlfriend. It was dark. Did he even get a good enough look at me to see if I was worth a date? We are in college, he probably only wants sex. I can't remember the last time I had sex. It's my senior year of college, and all I know is the last time was senior year of high school. I feel hands on my shoulders and snap back to reality as Avery shakes me, laughing.

"Helloooooooo. Earth to Maci. Are you going to answer him?"

I feel like such a loser. Maybe I'm in my head because I'm drunk, but I also know I have a lot less experience with guys than my friends. I mean, my only serious boyfriend was Grayson in high school, and that doesn't count as an adult relationship.

"Hey," I reply back, adding a heart-eye emoji at the end, but replacing it with a smile instead before I hit send.

Dean: *I'm going to see my friend's band play tomorrow night. We could get dinner first?*

I must be reading this wrong. It's not that I don't think I'm pretty. I'm fairly confident about myself physically, and I've never been self-deprecating about my looks. Avery gets hit on whenever we go out, so it boosts my confidence when we get mistaken for sisters. We both have an athletic build, even though we don't workout consistently anymore. All four years of high school, I was on the swim team and Avery played volleyball, and we always went for runs together on the weekend. We also have nearly the same color hair, but overall all my features are much softer than hers, and I'd have to spend way more time outside to get my skin as golden. She's much more outgoing, though, and before Miller, more willing to put herself out there. I always wondered if that was the main difference between us when it came to dating, and this seems like my answer.

I'm still holding out my phone, to get confirmation that I have a real date proposal in front of me, when Avery rips the device from my hand, replying for me.

Me: *Sounds great!*

I'm definitely still drunk, and I feel like I might pass out. I'm not quite sure if it's because of the wine or the high I seem to be on right now.

Twenty minutes later, I'm in my pajamas, sitting cross-legged on my living room floor eating cake with my friends. When I blew out my giant 2 and 1 numbered candles, I wished for the perfect date tomorrow. I try to be a little vague with my wishes because being open leaves the possibility for something even greater to happen than I could imagine. I know I'm potentially getting my hopes up a little too high, but you never know.

It's after midnight by the time I'm crawling under my fluffy purple comforter. As I plug my phone in, it dings with a "see you tomorrow" response from Dean. I set my phone on the nightstand without replying. I roll over to try and sleep, but between all the panicking and daydreaming, I don't drift off until after 3 a.m.

CHAPTER TEN

"Ready or Not," by Britt Nicole, blares through my eardrums, and my head pounds as I reach for my phone. 7:30 shines dimly on the screen over a picture of my friends and me on Halloween. I hit the snooze button before I close my eyes again. Avery must have changed my alarm tone to her favorite hype song before we went to bed last night. She's convinced that's the secret to a successful day.

I wipe the sleep from my eyes and stumble into the shower, mentally searching through my closet to choose an outfit for tonight. I think I've decided, but I'm glad the girls volunteered to come over after class to help me get ready. I feel like I'm in high school, but after whatever happened with Troy, I don't want to mess anything else up, especially with Dean.

What am I even thinking? I know nothing about this dude. I saw him for maybe two minutes, in the dark, while I was drunk. I could be imagining how cute he is. But could I be imagining the electricity? I recall the tingling I felt as it traveled up my fingers and through my arm. I shiver at the thought despite the shower being hot enough to nearly burn my skin.

By the time I get home, it feels like I've been gone for a week. All morning I was stressed wanting to know the details for tonight, but I didn't want to come off annoying, so I refrained from texting Dean. Sometime during psychology he texted me. I saw a notification as I packed my bag.

Dean: *I'll pick you up at 7. What's your address?"*

"Okay," I replied, along with my address. I didn't want to sound too excited in case all he really wants is sex. I don't think I'm that type of person, even if that's what college is about for a lot of people.

I realized too late that I gave a stranger my home address. I'll make sure the girls stay until he gets there.

Tuesdays are my long day at school, so I only have an hour to get ready. Luckily, even hungover, I was composed enough this morning to pick my outfit and lay it out on my bed.

Black jeans, black leather jacket and a flowy teal tank top with gray heeled boots. It's an outfit Avery picked out for me after I made my resolution to get out more at the beginning of the school year, but I haven't had anywhere to wear it until now. It's not really my style, but it feels right for a night out of dinner and music.

Certain the confidence in my outfit should reflect the confidence I had that made this date happen, I jump into my jeans and slide my tank top carefully over my freshly curled hair. I reach for my eyeliner to do my makeup as the front door slams into the stopper on the wall behind it.

"We're here!" Alexis sings. The girls head straight toward me, which is a direct line from the front door, catcalling to me as they make their way past the living room to the bathroom. Taylor takes the eyeliner from my hand, signaling me to sit on the toilet so she can do my makeup for me. Thank goodness.

As the time ticks down, my nerves get higher. Are first dates always such a big production? I guess it's something I'm going to have to get used to. Unless this was my last first date ever. Wouldn't that be nice? Albeit probably a little hopeful.

7 p.m. on the dot.

Dean: *I'm here. Just come out when you're ready, no rush.*

Me: *Be right out.*

I grab my pink shimmer lip gloss and shove it in my small black crossbody purse along with the apartment keys and head for the door. Avery slaps my ass as the rest of them holler after me to "have a good time" and "use protection." I roll my eyes as I walk out of our first-floor apartment and scan the row of parking spaces in front of our building for Dean.

I hope I recognize him. It occurs to me once again that I don't know what the person picking me up drives. Within a second, I spot his slightly ruffled, sandy blond hair. He's leaning against an old white truck, his feet crossed at his ankles and his hands shoved into his front pockets. Wow, he's taller than I expected–he's got at least six inches on my five foot six.

I can tell from four parking spaces down that his jeans hug him perfectly. A gray shirt under a dusty red and blue flannel covers his broad shoulders. The sleeves are rolled up barely below his elbows, highlighting his muscular forearms. I practically have to stop myself from drooling. His entire look might not seem like the sexiest thing to a lot of people, but at this moment, I realize it's *my* thing.

He follows me with his dark eyes, and when he catches my heated gaze, he flashes me a dimpled smile. He's definitely as cute as I thought, and despite the way my body heats, I'm a lot more at ease. By the time I make it to his truck, he's walked around to the passenger door, holding it open for me as I slide onto the leather seat.

"Good thing I'm not a serial killer since you gave a stranger your address," he jokes. Oddly enough it's more reassuring than unnerving.

I smile. "Yeah, good thing."

CHAPTER ELEVEN

We pull up to a freshly painted sky blue house, and he parks alongside the street. I'm confused at first, but then realize it's an older house that has been converted into a restaurant.

Before I unbuckle my seatbelt, the door opens and Dean's hand reaches out for mine. The second I lift mine to grab it, tingles of electricity shoot through my fingers. *Must be static again.* Maybe I should use dryer sheets with my laundry. Climbing down from his truck, I keep an eye on my feet, knowing if I don't, I'll probably trip over the curb wearing these heels.

He drops my hand when we reach the front door so he can open it. Once I'm through, he gently guides me with his hand on my lower back, leading me up a flight of stairs directly in front of us. It feels like he's been here before. I wonder how many times and with whom.

When we get to the top of the stairs, the host greets us, asks for Dean's name and seats us at a two-person table in the corner. Dean pulls my chair out for me, and I sit, taking in my surroundings.

The room is dark, lit only by small, soft yellow lights. The vibe is more romantic than I expected for a first date. Part of me feels weird about that, but my heart thumps more quickly in my chest anyway. I'm trying not to get my hopes too high again, especially after I had such a good time with Troy and then he disappeared on me–but Dean is not Troy. Like Avery reminded me, it's only fair to give him a chance because "you never know when your Miller will come along."

The restaurant turns out to be like the Melting Pot, except with a small, intimate, family-run feel. We order a cheese pot, a meat and broth one and of course chocolate, which our waitress assures us she'll space out properly. I turned down a cocktail when she offered and ordered water instead. Even though I was excited to get carded for the first time, I was already nervous and figure I'll have a drink at the bar. Better to stay focused for now.

"So..." I break the silence that washes over us when the waitress walks away. I look up and his eyes are already on mine, all his attention on me. "Have you worked at the hot tub place for a while?" I feel dumb because I can't for the life of me remember what it's called.

"Yeah, since I was old enough to work. A family friend owns it. It's just the two of us running the place."

"Oh wow, so you've lived here most of your life? Do you like it?"

"Yup, in the same house until I started college. I'm pretty sure my parents will live there forever. What about you? Did you grow up around here?" He leans back in his seat, and his comfort eases my remaining nerves.

"In Albany. My parents are hardcore Oregon State fans. Imagine their reactions when I decided to come here instead." I laugh, recalling the memory of sitting on our couch, with Avery there for support, as I broke the news to them.

We both pause to thank the waitress as she drops off our first course of assorted bread and vegetables with a cheese pot. I reach for a fondue fork as Dean picks up our conversation.

"I would have loved to have been a fly on the wall for that conversation." He chuckles. "I bet it makes game day fun." He reaches for his own fork, stabbing a piece of bread with it.

"It does. It's all in good fun, though. Especially since both schools are within an hour drive of home, it doesn't really make a difference."

"Do you see your parents often?"

"Mostly on holidays. They were always around before I left for college and through my third year, but now they are taking full advantage of their empty nest, gallivanting around the world with every chance they get."

"Ahhh, traveling is the way to go." His brown eyes light up at the mention of travel, but he changes the subject. "So you know what I do so I can afford to take out all the girls who ask me out while I'm working." He tacks a smirk onto the end of his statement. "Have you been working while you're here?"

My hands fly to cover my face in embarrassment. My skin heats under them, but I pull them away before I speak. "Does that happen a lot?"

"Nahh, it was a first for me. Can't say I didn't like it though." Holy shit whatever little laugh to himself he did behind his smile was the most adorable thing I've ever heard. It came out more like a half cough, half laugh, like he was trying to hide it, or hide what he was thinking, but couldn't.

My new goal is to get him to do that again.

Before I get more lost in my thoughts, I answer his question. "I work one or two days a week at a café near the student union. Total dream, I know. But I got enough scholarships to pay for school and housing so it's mostly to add to my travel fund. It works for now. Do you think you'll stay here forever, like your parents?"

"Scholarships? I like a smart woman." He adds a wink that makes me want to roll my eyes, but I bite the corner of my lip instead. "For me, Oregon is home. It has everything I love–camping, hiking, mostly outdoor hobbies. I think even if I went somewhere else, I'd come back here in the end."

The rest of dinner flies by, and our conversation flows better as we keep talking. He told me a little about his friends we are meeting with after dinner. When we were dipping marshmallows into the chocolate pot, he told me a story about when they went camping, and his friend Marcus' marshmallow caught on fire. He started flinging his stick really hard to put it out–because blowing on it would have been too easy. It flew right into the tent, burning a hole through the fabric.

Apparently, they were too drunk by the time they went to bed to remember the hole, and the next morning they all woke up covered in welts from all the mosquito bites. It wasn't that funny of a story, but the way Dean became so animated, waving his hands through the air, dramatically imitating Marcus and his flaming dessert made me nearly choke on my water. After a few more similar stories, I got the impression they have all been friends for a long time, since before college at least. When I asked, he said that he met Marcus in kindergarten, and Aden only a few years after that. They seem for him how Avery is to me, and I can't wait to meet them.

After dinner, Dean leads me down the stairs. When I turn toward his car, he gently reaches for my wrist and tugs me down the sidewalk instead. We only walk a few blocks until we stop in front of the entrance to a bar that doesn't have a name on the outside. It's dark and grungy looking, but that's the vibe in almost every bar around here–at least from what I can tell walking by them, considering I turned 21 yesterday.

After showing our IDs to the bouncer, we walk in, Dean's hand pressing into my lower back, softly pushing me forward. A bar lines the entire left side, and we walk toward the back of a room that is much longer than it is wide, until we get to a high top table with a couple of guys standing around it. Dean does a cute hand grab and bro hug with his buddies that makes me swoon a little. I think the type of friendships people have say a lot about them. He asks me what I want to drink and heads off to the bar, leaving me standing there with two dudes. Greeaaat, his reunion with his friends distracted him, and he forgot to introduce me.

Welp, now is the time to try and make a good impression I suppose.

"Heeeyyy. I'm Maci," I say, trying to sound as cool and confident as possible. If Dean is acting so casual about this hang out with his friends, I want to come off that way too.

The guy closest to me has dark brown hair tied back in a bun. His gray jeans and black V-neck T-shirt hug him perfectly. He introduces himself as Marcus, and I can't help but smile at the thought of his fiery marshmallow flying away from him. He reaches around to side hug me, and it's surprisingly not awkward at all. I'm immediately relaxed in his presence. The other guy reaches his hand across the table, introducing himself as Aden. His dark hair is short, the facial hair he's trying to grow is a little patchy, and he's got on a band T-shirt of someone I've never heard of. He smiles at me and even though these two guys give me a totally different vibe look wise than Dean, the level of ease I feel around them is comparable, especially after hearing a few good stories about them. Dean walks over with my whiskey sour, smiles at me, and rests his hand on my lower back, not realizing he never introduced me to his friends.

It's a lot less chaotic than I expected–nothing like the bar on Halloween. Even though it's already 10 p.m., no one seems too drunk, everyone chatting amongst themselves while they wait for the music to start. The screech of a microphone being turned on fills the room and halts all conversation as everyone looks to the stage in unison.

"YEEEAAAAH!" Aden yells from behind me with a fist pump. I know Dean said his friend was playing tonight, but I'm not sure which one he is, or if it's all three of the guys on the small stage in the front corner of the bar. They start playing, and I'm immediately drawn in. It seems a little reggae and a little indie. It's not what I usually listen to, but I love live music.

And the company.

I look over as Dean laughs at something Marcus said, his messy, blond hair swishing across to the other side of his forehead and his dimples coming out strong. He pulls a toothpick to the corner of his mouth and starts chewing on the end of it. He's still grinning, currently giving his attention to his friends, but his hand is still on my back where he scratches his fingers every once in a while, letting me know he hasn't forgotten I'm there. It sends chills up my spine every time he does. I'm already addicted to the way it feels when he touches me and find myself waiting for his hand to come back whenever he pulls away.

I try not to stare, but it's so hard not to. This man is truly the most gorgeous creature I have ever laid eyes on–despite the fact that he still comes off a little mysterious, and I can't tell whether his "super chill" attitude around bringing me here with his friends is a good thing or something that doesn't phase him because he's done it a million times.

I'm trying to simply enjoy the moment and not think too much about it, but I'm falling for this guy already. It's so different than anything I've ever felt before, even with Grayson after nearly two years. It feels like there's an electrical current pulling us together, like there are sparks flying, and I can't quite tell if something will explode or if fireworks are going off. Am I crazy or does he feel it too?

The band continues playing for two hours. When they start packing their equipment, the boys head toward them, and I follow behind. After congratulating them on a good show, to my surprise, Dean turns and pulls me in front of him, introducing me as *just* Maci. I'm not sure what else I expected him to say but it feels like a letdown for no valid reason.

After a few more minutes of chatting, we walk outside. Was it this cold when we were out here before? It's getting foggy out, and the streets are nearly empty from all the bargoers who have caught an Uber back to campus. We say goodbye to Marcus and Aden, and with his hand falling back to me like it's magnetized, Dean leads me back to his truck. It's the only car left parked on this street that's almost completely dark.

I'm not worried about him driving–we each only had two drinks. But I also don't want to leave yet. I didn't learn as much about him at dinner as I wanted to, and once we got to the bar it didn't feel like we were spending time together, even though he included me in the conversation with his friends as much as possible. When we were talking, our conversation flowed well. I never felt like I had to find something to fill empty space. It was refreshing. It wasn't particularly anything of substance though–more like a bunch of random memories that were triggered from something the other person said.

I know I can't learn everything in one night, and there's no reason to rush it, but I find myself wanting more. I also find myself unsure what will happen once I get back home, wondering if he will want to see me again and if I'll get the chance to keep discovering what makes Dean "Dean."

Staying here might keep me in suspense, but at least I can pretend the outcome is good if I don't know what it is.

CHAPTER TWELVE

Dean unlocks the passenger door for me, opens it and starts to walk toward the driver's side. I'm not sure if he notices I haven't made a move to get into the truck or if maybe he's drawn back to me too. Either way, he takes the few steps until he's back in front of me, staring into my eyes that immediately fix on his. Before I can say anything, his hand slides along my cheek, moving into my hair and gripping the back of my neck. I watch his eyes flash to my lips, then they are back on my eyes as if asking for permission.

But then he moves so close everything goes out of focus. My heart races. He hovers with the smallest distance between our lips before he closes it, pressing his mouth into mine, while simultaneously twisting my body so it's pinned against his truck.

His kiss starts out as pure lust, pressing into me with a sudden, uncontrollable urgency, my lips parting for him as if they had no choice. His tongue swipes over my bottom lip before he deepens our kiss. As soon as he does, the tension I didn't realize I was holding in my entire body melts away. I reach to his waist, pulling him toward me while helping me stay steady. His kiss that felt so desperate in the first few seconds suddenly calms as if he's more in control. A flash of worry crosses my mind that he lost interest as quickly as he seemed to gain it, but he doesn't make any sign to pull back from me. His urgency faded, but the intensity is still there. As his tongue moves in sync with mine, my thoughts start to fog. Even though I'm not, I feel intoxicated as he pulls my head closer to his face, as if it's not enough.

I need to come up for a breath, but I don't want to break our kiss. I'm not sure I physically could even if I wanted to. This is by far the most heated kiss I've ever experienced, and I don't want it to end. As if he's reading my mind, he pulls back slowly, presses his forehead to mine for a split second, and whispers, "I just needed to do that." He gives me one more soft kiss and turns away to get in his truck. I climb into my seat, holding onto the doorframe to steady myself. My hands shake as I buckle my seatbelt and take a deep breath, hoping to calm my racing mind.

Before he starts his truck, I catch him running his thumb over his bottom lip. He glances my way, a look in his eyes that says he's replaying that kiss over in his head like I am.

The drive back to my apartment is quiet besides the wind whistling through the cracked windows. It's so cold that even with my jacket on, I'm shivering. He must notice because when we stop at a light, he rolls up the windows and reaches into his back seat, pulling a maroon hoodie forward. "Sorry, my heater is broken. You can wear this." He holds it out for me, nudging it a little closer when he sees a hesitant look on my face.

"Thank you." I slide it over my head, my body and heart warming immediately. It's nearly one in the morning and completely dark out other than a few streetlights by the time he pulls into the parking spot in front of my apartment. He puts his truck in park but doesn't turn it off before getting out. We meet in front of his truck and walk to my door, where I hesitate, digging for my key and holding it in the lock.

"I want to come in," his voice pierces through the silence of the night. "But I'm not going to," he finishes his statement with certainty. Then he leans in to kiss me–a kiss in which I don't think I participate in because I'm standing there shocked and processing what he said. Then he spins on his heel and heads back to his car. When he reaches it, he turns back around. "I had a good time tonight. See you around, Maci."

Without giving me a chance to reply, he hops into his truck and drives off. I stare until he disappears before walking inside and closing the door. Leaning against it, I try to sort through what happened. I'm shocked by how the ending to this night played out so differently than the few scenarios I had worked out in my head. Did my birthday wish for a perfect date really come true? I'll definitely be wishing on candles every birthday from now on. I sink to the floor and lean against the door as I pull my hands into the sleeves of Dean's hoodie.

Oh, oops, I forgot to give his sweatshirt back. It smells so good. It reminds me of when you're camping, first wake and unzip your tent–like wood and fresh air maybe. I wonder if he let me keep it on purpose. That "see you around" comment he added in there is the only thing throwing me off, but I won't try to figure that out right now because the second his lips touched mine, I felt something for the first time.

It was like when you have two magnets facing away from each other, pulling to be together, but they get stuck at a certain distance. Then you turn them around and they fall perfectly together, creating a force that becomes harder to separate.

Whatever magic that was, all I can think about is how I need it again.

CHAPTER THIRTEEN

Lying down on my small, two-seater blue couch, I swing my sock-covered feet over the back–my favorite reading position. I finally finished my homework, so I'm starting *The Silent Patient,* a novel that's been sitting on my nightstand for a few weeks now. I open to the first page but can't seem to make it to the second because my thoughts keep drifting to Dean.

It's been two nights since our date, and I haven't seen him since. I wonder what he's doing tonight. Based on how often he said he works, I assume he's there, but I'm trying not to come off needy by bugging him. Even though we did go on a date, and his date etiquette was perfect, a gut feeling tells me he's not the boyfriend type. As much information as he was willing to give me, I also felt like there was a lot he was holding back. He appears a little enigmatic, and I can't figure out if it's in a secretive way, or if it's just how he is.

Since it's only been two days without hearing from him, I'm trying not to be crazy, but all I've thought about since our date is wanting to see him again. That and replaying our kiss over and over. His sweatshirt immediately became my new loungewear. It smells like him, mostly woodsy with a little bit of bonfire, and I love it. I noticed when I took it off the other night it was from his high school. At least that's my guess because his last name, which I'm now assuming is Porter, is printed across the back. It might be weird that I'm wearing it, but no one is here to see me cuddled in the oversized sleeves, so it doesn't matter.

I start over at the top of the page for the fifth time. One line in, my phone vibrates against my side where it rests on the couch.

Dean: *What are you up to?*

My heart leaps, and I answer. *Reading, you?*

Dean: *I'm coming over for a sleepover.*

Well, that's presumptuous on so many levels. Thank goodness Avery is at Miller's tonight.

My fingers feel paralyzed, hovering over the keyboard trying to figure out what to say. Play it cool, Maci. Get it together. I delete the emoji I have after the *ok* before pressing send and get up to brush my teeth.

I unlock the front door, take off his hoodie and hang it over the edge of the couch so he doesn't know it's my new favorite. I find my place back on the couch, which is directly to the left of the entryway. Picking my book back up, I face away from the entrance to my apartment so I don't stare at the door.

Fifteen minutes later a knock startles me. "Come in," I call.

I wasn't sure my voice was loud enough until my door slowly opens. I attempt to stay focused on my page because I know if I let myself be excited that he's here, I might freak out. I don't know what it is about this guy, but this strong pull I feel toward him is hard to deny. It's not only when he's near me, but even through the phone. I have this urge to kiss him, to leap at him and to run my fingers all over his body, to want to know everything about him. *Stay cool, Maci.* I sense him coming toward me, but I keep my eyes on the page of my book.

He kneels on the floor next to me as he pulls the book from my hands and places it on the table behind us. Then he presses his lips softly against mine, like he comes home to me every day and does this. It's weird and wonderful.

As soon as he leans back, I bite my lip, trying to calm the surge of energy that seemed to transfer from him to me as we kissed.

"You made me lose my place in my book," I tease.

"It's okay, I've already read it. I'll tell you what happens." He says it matter-of-factly.

Wait, he's read this book? I noticed him reading the day we met, but not the book he had. It would be cool if we are both into psychological thrillers.

Sitting and turning to fully look at him, I can tell he just got off work. He's wearing those stupid pants I recall from the night we met. They are, in fact, swishy material, and you can tell they zip off at the knees in case you want to make them shorts. Somehow though, he looks attractive in them, and I have the urge to rip them off.

Clearly I've zoned out because I catch his hand waving in front of me. "Maci! I guess I'll give myself the grand tour then!" He laughs and stands to look around. His laugh is so quiet as if he's only laughing to himself, and my stomach flutters.

I snap out of it when I realize he's about to see my room. He peeks his head into the kitchen, off to the right when you first walk in, directly opposite where I am in the living room. I open my book back up quickly to find where I was and slide in my bookmark. Leaping off the couch, I follow after him. He opened the door to the right of the bathroom before I could get to him, but he must have somehow known it was Avery's room because he closed it right away. Now he's standing in front of my doorway on the left, pausing to take a look around before walking to my bed, which is pushed against the back wall. I don't have much else in here besides my dresser, a bookshelf and a ton of pictures, mostly of Avery and me. Dean picks up the frame I just got a few days ago that holds a picture of my friends and me on Halloween.

He sets it down and my heart races, hoping I have a little more time to prepare for this "sleep"over because I'm not sure I'm quite ready. I'm torn from the freak out happening in my head when he starts piling the pillows in his arms and pulling my purple comforter off my bed. He flashes me a grin as he walks right past me back to the living room.

I consider asking what he's doing, but I'm more curious to watch it play out. Reading my mind, he looks over his shoulder and says, "I told you we were having a sleepover." I watch as he releases everything in his arms and pushes the coffee table across the carpet until it's out of the way. Then he lays the dark purple blanket that had been folded at the end of my bed on the floor. He tosses the rest of my bedding on top as if it were actually a bed and then pats it. Sensing my confusion, he adds, "What? Did I not mention it's a *middle school* sleepover? No funny business, just movies on the floor."

I continue to stare.

"Come on, what did you think I meant? Get your mind out of the gutter, Jackson." He uses my last name through a dimpled grin then takes his shoes off and sits, rubbing the spot next to him for me to do the same.

"What do you want to watch?" he asks, as if this whole night is totally normal.

Relief washes over me, but then I question it, not sure if that's how I feel. Either way, this is the most cheesy and adorable thing anyone has ever done with me, and my excitement starts to outweigh my nerves.

I grab the remote and join him on the floor, flipping through the "recently added" section of Netflix. I push play on the first option–*Starsky and Hutch*–because I'm far too curious what this mysterious guy has playing through his head to search for something. Plus, I like this movie. He scoots down, and crosses both hands, resting them on the pillow behind his head. I lie down, staying a few inches from him, ignoring my body begging me to move closer.

Once the opening credits start playing, he turns on his side so he's looking straight at me. I hesitate before slowly twisting my body to meet his, moving an inch closer in the process. He reaches his hand out and runs his fingers through my hair, locking them behind my head and pulling me to his face. The instant our lips meet, a shiver runs through my body, covering every inch of me in goosebumps. His kiss is so soft and perfect, and yet all I want to do is crash into his mouth harder, as if it will bring me closer to him.

I lean up on my arm, and it forces him more on his back. My free hand finds its way to his hip and grabs onto it forcefully as he presses his lips harder into me, his tongue dancing with mine. My assertiveness surprises me, as I run my fingers along the edge of his pants, and slightly under his shirt. I trail my fingers up his side, and then back down again, before pulling myself closer to him.

I sense his hesitation right before he pulls back, breaking our connection. "Maci! Let's keep it PG. I told you, sleepover! Did you do this when you were in middle school?" he jokes.

"Probably for the best because I don't have any condoms." Why did I say that? I'm so awkward. He stares at me like he's just as shocked the words came from my mouth. "But I am on birth control. I don't do this often anymore. Sex, I mean. Ugh, why am I telling you all this?" I bury my face into his chest, and his laugh vibrates through our bodies.

"Are you finished?"

"Yes," I nod into his chest before he pushes on my shoulders lightly until I'm looking at him.

"Maci, relax. I'm here because I want to spend time with you."

He rolls onto his back again, but this time he puts his arm around me, pulling me into his chest, before making some comment about Owen Wilson. Apparently, we are watching this movie and having a sleepover. If I hadn't seen this movie before, I would have no idea what is going on as I lie here wondering what is happening in my living room. Does he not want to have sex with me? I mean, he also didn't come in the other night when he dropped me off. Does he not feel this intense pull toward me that I do toward him? Mine is so strong, he has to feel something, right? I remember the way he lingered during our first kiss the other night.

Is he really just here to spend time with me?

I know it must still be the middle of the night when I wake because there's no light coming through the crack in the curtains. I'm uncomfortable from lying on the floor, knowing the only reason I fell asleep was because I was curled into Dean with my head on his chest. I shake him gently until he stirs.

"Come on, let's go to bed," I whisper.

"Shhhh," he mumbles and tries to pull me into him. "This has to be our bed tonight."

I'm not sure what he means by that, but he's half asleep and might not be sure himself. I stand, grabbing a couple of pillows and his wrist, tugging on him until he reluctantly stumbles up and follows me to my room. I set the pillows down and let him fall into bed while I go to flick the light off. He mumbles something about a sleepover, but I can't understand him. I pull my pajama bottoms off before I climb in because I'm so uncomfortable sleeping in them. I don't usually sleep in anything except my underwear, but taking my shirt off might be a little weird.

I lie down next to him, leaving a little space between us. Just because we fell asleep cuddling, doesn't mean he likes to sleep that way. As soon as I go to pull the sheet over me, Dean reaches for my waist. The second his fingers land on the edge of my panties, he rubs them against the lace. He must realize I took my pajamas off because his eyes shoot open. There's a combination of lust and anger in his eyes, but by the way it startles me, it seems like more of the latter.

"I said this was a PG sleepover," he growls before rolling onto his back, staring at the ceiling, much more awake than he was a minute ago. "You're making that very difficult," he adds when I don't say anything. I can't tell if he's actually mad or not.

I'm still half asleep, but I'm not stupid. I know he's talking about the fact that I took my pajamas off. I'm not sure if I did it for any other reason than comfort, and maybe I still shouldn't have, but I don't think I was subconsciously expecting anything. I close my eyes and whisper for him to go back to sleep. He stills and assuming he listened, I take a breath.

I know I've started to drift off because it feels like I'm dreaming. His fingers slowly smooth over my skin, tracing the line where it meets the lace. He makes his way closer to my center, then pulls back, his hand resting on my hip. He grips slightly harder, tugging me to him until there's only an inch or two between us. He leans his head toward mine and whispers in my ear, "How do you feel about PG13?"

My heart races, but I'm so drawn to him, there's no way my answer could be anything different. Instead of using words, I lean in and kiss him hard on the mouth, pulling our bodies together, closing the gap between us. He breathes out like he was holding his breath waiting for me to respond. He kisses me again, his tongue parting my lips with urgency. It's like he was being tortured and is making the most of his freedom before it's taken away again. It's ironic because he is the one who put a limit on what happens tonight. I'm still a little confused by that.

We haven't had a conversation about what we are doing, we've been on one date. Having sex already would feel quick, but he seems like he's putting in enough effort for it to not only be about that. Considering this is only the second day spending time with him, I'm nervous to bring it up so soon and scare him away, but maybe he would tell me if I was brave enough to ask for clarity.

I snap back to the present, wanting to ignore this anxious feeling I've constantly had since Troy disappeared. I lean more into our kiss, wrapping my arm around him, digging my fingers into his back with the same intensity I feel about wanting him to be closer than he is right now. I feel him growing hard through the scarce amount of fabric that separates us, and knowing that he's turned on makes me want him, without question. A thought flashes across my mind how weird that is because I've never been a boy crazy kind of girl or the type to jump into bed with anyone. I've also never felt this level of connection with someone or had this pull toward anyone I just met before. I wonder if it's because of him or because I've never really put myself in this type of situation.

A slight hesitation snaps me out of my thoughts. I pull back and open my eyes, and he does the same. It only lasts a split second before he kisses me again. This time, his urgency seems to have faded. Instead, he runs his fingers through my hair, behind my ear, and whispers, "Goodnight," with a smirk and a wink before rolling over and pulling the sheet to his shoulder. Did he just wink at me? *This guy.* I don't know whether to smile like a giddy teenager or roll my eyes until they get stuck back there.

CHAPTER FOURTEEN

I'm not entirely sure why, but when I wake, I'm surprised Dean is still in my bed. He's already awake, lying on his back, staring at the ceiling. "Finally, you're awake!" He grins. "Let's go get breakfast!"

I rub my eyes, thinking about what's in my fridge right now. Absolutely nothing. "Brail's?" I ask, rolling on my side to face him, careful not to open my mouth too much because who knows what my breath smells like.

"I'm in."

Joy, the owner of Brail's, greets us when we walk in. She doesn't know who I am, but Avery and I have been here a few times, and her name matches her personality so well it's impossible to forget. "Would you like a table or the bar top?" She directs the question toward both of us, a genuine smile on her face.

Dean looks at me, allowing me to choose. "Bar please!" I respond to Joy, before turning back to Dean. "I like the spinning stools."

He doesn't say anything, but his eyes give away the amusement the rest of his face tries to hide. His hand grazes my lower back, guiding me in front of him to follow Joy to our seats. She walks us to the gray laminate bar, and we both slide onto a red leather stool. Immediately I twist my body, so my seat spins until I'm facing Dean, a smile on my face.

"You're not hard to please, are you?" he asks, his grin matching mine.

"Nope!" I shrug. "Did you expect something else from the girl who spent her 21st birthday in a hot tub with her friends?"

His hands fall to each of my knees, and the contact sends a spark through me. He quirks a brow. "The night we met was your birthday?"

"Yup!" I twist my chair until I'm facing forward and pick up the menu in front of me.

I feel him staring as I try to read the menu.

Turning to face him again, I'm drawn straight to his muscled forearms, resting on the counter, as he holds his own menu. He's got his dark gray long sleeve shirt pushed up to his elbows, and I'm immediately distracted. This isn't a body part I've ever been attracted to before, but I can't look away. He looks strong. I wonder if he works out. He must. Either way, it's hot–kind of the way my face is getting as my memory flashes to our first kiss when he gracefully pushed me against his truck and pulled my lips closer to his.

"What?" he chuckles, breaking my trance.

I clear my throat and shake my head slightly. "Nothing."

"So, you didn't even get carded on your birthday?"

"Nope. First time was when I went to the bar with you. I didn't even get to order my first legal drink out," I joke.

"Oh, sorry. Next time I'll make sure to not to buy you a drink." He smirks, and my stomach flutters hearing him talk about the next time. "So, how'd you get all the wine you snuck into the hot tub?"

Something between a laugh and a sigh comes out. I guess we weren't as sneaky as we thought. "All my friends are already 21. My best friend, Avery, has been since the beginning of summer."

"Which one was she?"

"Long, dark brown hair. The bombshell of our group, she's hard to miss." There's no jealousy in my words–it's just the truth that my best friend is gorgeous.

"Hmm. I didn't notice." His gaze meets mine for a moment, and my stomach flips. I'm not the best at accepting compliments–if that's what that was. I hope that is what it was. "Have you been friends for a while? Didn't you say you grew up in Albany?"

"Yeah, since we were 12. We both grew up there. She's practically my sister, and my parents treat her that way too. It's great."

"Old friends are the best," he says, picking up the menu but making no motion to read it.

"Yeah, they are. Avery is the only one I'm close with from before college, but she's more than enough for me. I bet you have a lot of friends around since you grew up here?"

"People who are raised here tend to stay, so it helps. You know Marcus and Aden. Practically everyone I attended high school with is still around too. Also had all the same neighbors forever."

"What happens if you want to escape someone?" I laugh. I'm not someone who runs into people they know every time they go to the grocery store, so I can only imagine what that must be like.

"Short of running away, I'm not sure." His tone is playful, but his eyes tell a different story I wish I could ask about.

"I like to run!" I'm trying to be funny, but it's also true.

"Is that so?" It looks like I've piqued his curiosity.

"Yeah, I joined the running club at school this year. I kept putting it off without the accountability."

"Makes all the difference."

"I guess not, considering I was supposed to go this morning."

"I'd say I'm sorry, but I'm not." He shrugs and glances at the menu.

I shove playfully on his shoulder. "Hey!"

"Okay, fine, a little. You could have gone."

I've been enjoying the running club, and everyone is nice enough, but I haven't bonded with anyone in particular yet. "I'd rather be here."

His gaze meets mine as Joy's bubbly self graces us with her presence again.

CHAPTER FIFTEEN

Thank goodness this statistics class is easier than I thought it would be. Sometimes Carley and I get together to study, but mostly for the company. I've been able to get through the class on my own. I'm working on my stats homework right now, in between my Monday classes, sitting at one of the outdoor picnic tables in the middle of campus. It's as chilly as you'd expect for the middle of November, but I can't help but want to be outside when the sun is out. Based on how quiet it is around me, it appears I'm the only one who feels that way.

Our campus is covered in open fields, grass the perfect shade of green. Every walkway is lined with trees, and each building is surrounded by them. The leaves have been transforming into beautiful shades of orange and yellow over the past few weeks. They are finally starting to fall to the ground, taking over the paths to class, regardless of how many times the groundskeeper tries to clear them.

It's absolutely beautiful and not worth missing, even if it means suffering in the cold. I also just love the smell of it here, like fresh air and trees. It reminds me of Dean and the way he smells if you added a campfire to it.

Although I'm not sure yet if that part of his sweatshirt smell came from him or an actual fire.

I haven't heard from Dean since he took me to breakfast on Friday morning after our sleepover. I texted him on Saturday to say hi, but he never responded. I'm proud of myself for not texting again as much as I wanted to. Popping my AirPods in my ears, I push play on one of my Spotify playlists and try to push away the insecurity not hearing from him makes me feel by focusing on the math problem in front of me.

The sway in my body to my music freezes when hands land on my shoulders. *What the.* I tip my head until I see him.

Dean.

He squeezes his hands a little tighter before taking a seat next to me, straddling the bench of the green metal table. He's so close that one knee rests against my back, the other touches my thigh, and his hands press into the small space between his legs. I turn to face him, pulling out my earbuds.

"Umm, hey."

"What's up, Jackson!" He picks up one of my earbuds and puts it in his ear. The song I was listening to just ended, so I'm not sure what's playing, but he eyes me like he's trying to read me through my music choice. Either that or he's waiting for an answer to his question.

"Killing time before my next class. You?"

"Yeah, same."

"What's your major, anyway?" I ask before he can change the subject. I don't know enough about him.

"Sociology. What about you?" His woodsy scent heightens that outdoor smell I was already enjoying as he reaches in front of me, picking up the edge of my textbook like he's trying to guess my major before I tell him. As he does, his other hand rubs across the small of my back.

I start to say "psychology" but realize I'd rather know what type of job he wants. As I open my mouth to speak, I'm cut off by a good looking guy with chocolate brown hair and way too much swagger walking up to us.

"Hey, Dean. Hey." The stranger directs the second one at me with a small head nod.

I give a small wave as Dean replies, "Hey, man."

"Party at your place tonight still?"

"Yup, I'll see you there." I can tell Dean is trying to end the conversation, and the stranger takes the hint, waving at both of us before turning and walking away.

Before I have a chance to question him, Dean stands. "Well, I'm off to do college things. I'll text you later?"

"Mhmm," I mumble, but he's already gone. What party was that guy talking about? Why am I not invited? I know I sound needy, but don't guys know they can't do this to women? We read into literally everything. I'm tempted to invite myself like he invited himself to my apartment, but I don't know where he lives.

When he's near me, I swear he's drawn to me the way I am to him. Any time I've been within reaching distance of him, he finds a way to touch me, like he did a moment ago. I lost track of how many times his hand found my back on our first date, and even though he refused sex the other night, his hands were on me almost the entire time we were together.

But as soon as we aren't in the same room anymore, it's almost like I don't exist, or at the very least like a wall disconnects us temporarily. Maybe he's not big on texting, but he hasn't even tried to make plans with me again, and it's frustrating–especially because I thought both times we hung out went really well.

I pick up my earbud to see which song was playing for Dean. The outro of Taylor Acorn's "Are We" whispers into my ear. *Do I play it cool like you're just another guy I accidentally ran into, oh. Is it all in my head? Or are we just friends?*

At least someone understands me.

I wish I better understood his intentions. Let's be real, though, until he stops touching my back the way he does, and it stops lighting me up from the inside out, there's not a chance of me walking away. Regardless of how much I could potentially be misreading the situation.

I try to focus on my assignment. Who knew math would end up being less complicated than the men I'm meeting this year.

Finally finishing my homework, I slam the book shut, shoving it away from me on the coffee table. My brain cannot handle statistics after 10 p.m. Ready to relax, I reach for the TV remote, but my phone vibrates before I can push the power button.

Dean: *Hey.*

Me: *Hi.* Isn't he at his party right now?

Dean: *Whatcha doing?* Maybe he does want to invite me.

Me: *Just finished my homework. You?* I ask him, even though I know.

Dean: *Just chillin.*

Me: *Yeah, partying on a Monday is how I relax too.* I add the laughing emoji.

Dean: *Need to take advantage of every opportunity while I still can.* Or maybe he doesn't want me there, since he clearly ignored that. Why is he texting me then?

Me: *Totally get it, I made a pact with myself to do that too.*

Dean: *Oh yeah? What opportunities are you looking for?*

Me: *Normal ones. I mostly want to get out more, make the most of senior year. Maybe go to a frat party.*

Dean: *Frat parties are overrated. Do you party? I didn't peg you as the type.* Maybe that's why he didn't invite me.

Me: *What type did you peg me as?* This could be my chance to see what he thinks of me.

Dean: *I'm not sure yet. But not the party on a Monday type, definitely not the frat party type. You didn't even go out on your 21st birthday, Maci.*

Me: *Well, maybe I am the party type but don't know it.* I add the shrug emoji. How would I know if I've never really tried?

Dean: *Why are you trying to get out more?*

Me: *I don't know. I guess I don't take initiative often or leap at opportunities in front of me, but I don't want to miss out on things that might only happen in college, ya know? I don't want to regret it later.*

Dean: *It sure felt like you were taking initiative the other night.* He double texts me with a wink emoji.

Me: *Yeah, look how well that turned out.*

Dean: *What do you mean? I had fun.*

Me: *Oooohh, it's fun to turn down a half-naked girl in bed?* I'm hopeful the emoji with the tongue sticking out shows him I'm not actually mad.

Dean: *Whoaaaa. Don't act like that's something I wanted to do.*

Me: *Then why did you do it?*

Dean: *It's never the best idea to make decisions when you're half asleep.*

I think back to this morning when I woke an hour before my alarm and in my hazy state easily convinced myself to reset it for a later time. I guess it's a logical thought, but it doesn't mean I didn't want what my actions showed.

Me: *Okay, that's fair.*

Me: *But I'd still be down. Even not half asleep. Just so you know.*

Dean: *Good to know.* He adds a wink emoji.

He changes the subject, and we continue chatting about random things. My eyes are burning by one in the morning, not wanting to stop talking. Though, it doesn't slip away from me how weird it is he spent his whole party talking to me through a phone when he could have just invited me instead.

CHAPTER SIXTEEN

My last class for the week just ended, and I've never been more thankful that I managed a schedule with no classes on Fridays. It's been exactly a week since the night Dean came over. We've been texting on and off, but nothing as much as Monday night. I want to see him, but I'm being petty about not getting invited to his party. I thought I'd made it clear I'm interested in seeing him, but he hasn't attempted to make plans with me.

I searched for him on social media. Based on the pictures, the parties don't look exclusive by any means. Of course a million thoughts have run through my head. Maybe he doesn't want to hang out again. But why would he bother coming over to interrupt my studying? Why would he spend his entire party talking to me? What I do know is that if I don't get out tonight, I'll go crazy at home sitting by myself snuggled in his hoodie.

I text Avery asking if she and Miller want to grab drinks at Jameson's. Dean mentioned Jameson's is his go-to bar when he does go out, so the chances of potentially running into him are higher than if I went anywhere else. But they also have the best Happy Hour on Thursdays, and Dean is probably at work anyway. Avery replies back almost immediately they'll come as long as I agree to play a game of pool with Miller. She is over being the only one who gets stuck playing with him.

Sold.

Putting my phone down, I walk to my closet. Usually when I'm the third wheel with my best friend, I stick with my go-to jeans and a sweatshirt because, who is there to impress? But now that I'm actively trying to find a boyfriend, and on the off chance I could run into Dean, I want to at least look better than I feel on the inside. All the clothes that have been in the back of my closet waiting for the day I was confident enough to wear them sure have been making more appearances lately. Avery always says "If you want to feel good, you need to look good" and very strongly believes in the whole fake it until you make it concept. She's convinced an outfit can change your energy, and your energy is the most important factor in getting what you want. I pick out dark jeans with a silky navy tank top, toss them on my bed and grab my black booties from the rack by the door.

It's the first time I've been inside Jameson's, even though I've passed by it more than once. I can see why Dean likes this bar. It's ugly, but in a fun way. It's got a retro vibe, like it was pulled out of *That '70s Show*. When you walk in, brown leather booths line the wall that connects to the front door. A long, worn, wooden bar lines the back wall, and off to the right it opens into a room with four orange felt-lined pool tables. The lights hanging above the tables are all encased by dusty red covers, and a soft orange light glows from the ceiling above the bar. Unlike every other bar I've been in, this one has carpet floors, an ugly green and brown design printed into it.

There isn't any art on the wall in the main bar area, but square canvases line the wall in the billiards room, alternating between circular and lined patterns all in shades of burnt orange and brown. It seems older in here, in both the look and the clientele, and I'm hopeful we'll avoid the rowdy college crowd.

I head to the bar and order one well whiskey sour and two tequila orange juices. I know Miller will make fun of me for my old man's drink of choice, but as long as he gets tequila and a pool partner, he knows better than to mock me too much. I head over and claim one of the pool tables in the side room before it gets too crowded. Avery and Miller walk in as I finish racking the balls. Avery smiles, running to hug me, whispering in my ear, "Take my man from me! I love him, but I can't play another game of pool anytime soon without sacrificing my sanity or relationship!"

I laugh and hand Miller a cue. I love that being a third wheel is never awkward with them, and I get along well with Miller. He's attractive, from an objective perspective of course. He's tall, with dark brown eyes and hair that's typically styled into some sort of professional fauxhawk, and most of the time he wears squared black framed glasses. It looks like he came straight from work. He's got on slacks with a plain V-neck T-shirt he was probably wearing under his dress shirt earlier. I'm still not sure what he does exactly, but I do know that he is exceptionally smart and works in a fancy office downtown. He also treats my best friend like she's the greatest gift in the Universe, and me the same by association, so brownie points all around. As much as I'm comfortable being around only the two of them, part of me still wishes I could add a fourth person to our night out plans. At least every once in a while. I have this vision of double dating being so much fun.

I let Miller break because I am an absolute terrible shot and can't scatter the balls to save my life. He doesn't mind that I'm not great; he's just happy to play.

We take a few turns each, and I still haven't hit a ball. Miller has already knocked in most of the stripes, and Avery ran off somewhere, bored watching us. Miller moves behind me to adjust my hands on my cue and help guide my shot. I try again and finally get one. Go me! I do a little happy dance as Miller steps away to avoid getting smacked in the face with my cue and to let me hit the next one without his help. As I'm lining up my next shot, a hand slides across my lower back. A shiver runs through me, so I already know who is behind me without looking.

"Hi, Maci," Dean whispers, his voice confirming what I already know. I take a breath and ignore him, focusing on the ball in front of me. I glance at Miller for a moment, noticing the questions in his eyes as they shift to the space behind me. I realize he has no idea who Dean is and probably thinks some random guy is way too close to me. I roll my eyes, hoping it reassures him everything is fine. Miller nods in both acknowledgment and for me to hit the ball. The second Dean pulls his hand back, I take my shot, and to my surprise, the green six ball makes it into the pocket.

"Yes!" Miller pumps his fist into the air like he's shocked but excited I made another one. When I look to flash Dean a small smile and acknowledge him, his eyes have narrowed and are focused on Miller instead. As I make my way around the table to the cue ball, his gaze shifts to follow me, but he walks toward Miller. It distracts me as I take a third shot, and I miss.

"Hey, I'm Dean," he growls at Miller as he reaches out his hand assertively. I'm a little annoyed, but I also have to refrain from laughing at how he's suddenly territorial.

"Miller." He smirks but doesn't extend a hand or anything cordial. Instead, he leaves Dean standing there as he takes his shot. He plays until the rest of his balls are in the pockets, leaving five of mine still on the table. Dean stands there with as much confidence as I feel uncomfortable, although I note his fist is clenched at his side. Miller starts to set up another game, completely ignoring him. This guy will keep going until someone cuts him off, but I also know he's doing it for his own amusement right now too.

Luckily for me, Avery chooses this moment to reappear. She walks up to Miller, greeting him with a kiss on the cheek. Then she glances to the side, her eyes raking up and down the very attractive stranger standing only a few feet from her. I watch Dean's fist relax as he puts two and two together. I know I mentioned Miller's name the other day, but he must not have made the connection until now.

"I have to go to the bathroom," Avery declares, looking over at me and implying I need to follow her. I break my eyes away from the gray jeans and blue flannel in front of me. It's such a typical Oregon man look, but on this specific man, it looks so much better.

"Yeah, sure." I pull my attention toward her. It takes all my self-control to not look back and give him the attention his body language begs for right now, but

I have enough self-respect to require him to use his words to tell me what he wants. I think.

"Umm, is that Dean?" Avery whispers a little too loudly as she drags me to the bathroom in the back of the room.

"Sure is," I say, rolling my eyes.

"What's up? Why aren't you more excited, especially after how much fun you said you had with him last week!" She's not trying to whisper anymore.

"Shhh." I cover her mouth, noting the three other girls standing in front of the bathroom mirror. I know there's nothing all that personal about what she's saying, but the college bar scene is small, and you never know. Especially when I don't know. Plus, out of the corner of my eyes, I see the blonde in a lacy red tank top muttering what feels like gossip, leaning into her friends as she unscrews the wand of her lip gloss.

She shrugs, with her hands on her hips, waiting for an answer.

"That's exactly why I'm not excited. I thought last week was perfect. He stayed over and didn't try to sleep with me, but not in an uninterested kind of way. Then the next morning we went to breakfast, he paid, and then he dropped me off back home. The only other time I've seen him was when we crossed paths at school, and he was talking to a buddy of his about a party he didn't invite me to. Oh, and then he texted me all throughout said party but *still* hasn't made plans with me. Then all of a sudden, he *just happens* to be in the same bar but doesn't come over to me until he sees me playing pool with Miller? I mean, I could tell he got the wrong idea, but it doesn't seem like it's any of his business if he isn't making an effort to spend time with me in the first place."

Avery rolls her eyes at me this time. "Have you tried asking him to hang out first, Mace?"

My deadpan expression confirms I haven't.

"Look, I appreciate your level of self-respect right now, but I was at the bar talking to Taylor while you were playing. I noticed a guy staring at you but didn't re-alize it was him at first. He couldn't take his eyes off you. When Miller was showing you what to do–since you're worse than me–his eyes glossed over with jealousy. I could tell even through these dingy red lights. The guy clearly has feelings for you."

"Yeah, maybe." I try to believe what I'm saying as I open the door to leave the bathroom. I need another drink.

I walk back toward the bar and attempt to get the bartender's attention. I'm leaning against the counter, waiting for her to notice me, but as soon as she starts my way, Dean slides in next to me and catches her attention first. "Hey, Jess, two whiskey sours please," he says with a wink, although I'm not sure at which of us it's directed.

He turns to me, pulling his toothpick back to his teeth, chewing on the end as he smiles at me. "Hey," he says in a deep, possibly drunk but definitely sexy voice.

"Heeeey," I draw out the word with hesitation.

He leans close enough for me to hear his whisper, his hand squeezing my hip. "You look good tonight, Maci." God, he smells good, like the fir trees in my parents' backyard. His hand catches under the silk at the edge of my tank top and his fingers slowly slide under, pulling my shirt up slightly as his thumb brushes across my bare skin. The sensual contact causes an involuntary gasp to escape my lips. He smirks like he's aware of the effect he has on me. He's about to say something else but right then a petite blonde with her boobs spilling over the top of her lacy red tank top squeezes into the small space behind Dean, pulling his attention away.

"Hey, Dean." I recognize her from the bathroom.

"What's up, Julia?" He sounds annoyed, not that she seems to notice.

Jess comes back with his drinks, and before Julia can reply, Dean cuts in. "Well, have a good night." He slides one of the drinks over to me and turns away from her, leading me away with his hand on the small of my back.

We head to a booth by the pool tables, where Miller and Avery are leaning into each other, focused on Avery's phone that rests on the table as she scrolls. Apparently, he couldn't talk her into playing a game.

My friends glance up as I slide in first, and Dean follows. "Hey, man." He nods at Miller before directing his gaze to Avery. As far as I can tell, he's not embarrassed about his incorrect assumption from a few minutes ago. He seems comfortable even.

"I'm Avery. The..." I kick her under the table, knowing that if I don't, she'll go into an entire "don't hurt my girl" speech. That's the last thing I need to add to this situation.

"Oh yeah, hi. I think you were at my work on Maci's birthday?"

"Yup, that's me!"

"You two do know most people who come to my work are there to hook up, right?" Dean chuckles.

"What you're saying is you basically run a brothel?" Avery scrunches her face and laughs.

"Your words." His eyes dance with amusement. "The amount of chlorine we put in the water kills the germs. It's fine," he adds with a smirk.

"Well, we definitely weren't there for sex," I shrug.

"Yet," Dean mumbles so softly, I'm not sure I heard him correctly until my eyes lock with Avery's wide ones.

Right as Miller is about to say something, Dean's phone rings.

He glances at it, before looking at me. "Hey, I'm sorry, I need to take this." He stands and walks away. Once again he exits a conversation leaving me with questions. Both the door and the rest of the bar are behind me, so I'm not sure which way he walks, but hopefully he comes back soon. That pull I feel toward him came back as soon as he touched me earlier. Not to mention, I'm willing to admit I'm enjoying the attention from him, especially after not seeing him for a week and definitely after he turned his back on another girl to walk away with me.

CHAPTER SEVENTEEN

Twenty minutes go by and Dean hasn't come back. I'm irritated, and I'm ready to leave. Heading outside with Avery and Miller, I decide to only focus on the fact that I'm starving. I scan the four corners of the cross streets that most of the downtown bars are on until I spot my favorite little food cart. It's called Dump City Dumplings, and they have the best dumplings I've ever tasted. I mean, I'll make a new assessment if I ever make it to Asia, but for now, these are it for me.

Every week they have new flavors, and if you have a punch card, every tenth one is free. We started going before we were old enough to get into the bars. It's a tradition Avery and I created our first quarter in college. After both of us finish our last final, we get a box filled with dumplings then go eat down by the river next to campus. Maybe it's partially the sentiment, but they are undeniably good. They are also the perfect distraction right now.

I don't know what I expected when I was secretly hoping we would run into Dean, but I can tell you, it wasn't this. It's weird he won't make plans but acts like he wants to see me when we are apart or when he happens to be around me. It's been a yo-yo of butterflies in my stomach, and confusion in my brain. Now that both are mixed with whiskey, the only solution is dumplings.

I order 6 four cheese pizza dumplings to split with Avery and Miller, and we take a seat on the curb, inhaling them before we can decide what to do next. Avery pulls out her phone and scrolls through pictures of a house she and Miller like. They aren't ready to buy yet, but they have fun looking, and she shares a couple of new links with me every day. That also means I need to figure out what I'm going to do with my life once I graduate. Anxiousness overwhelms me when I let thoughts invade my head.

"I'm tired, I'll call an Uber. You two ready to go?" I stand.

"Yes!" Avery smiles as they stand together, and she leans into Miller. I can't wait to have what they have. It's sweet and wonderful. I sigh, and Avery catches it.

"What's up, babe..." she trails off and her eyes narrow.

I turn to follow her gaze to Dean standing behind me, confident and flawless, with one hand still holding the toothpick he's been chewing on, and the other stuffed into the front pocket of his jeans. "Hey, Maci. Do you want to get out of here?"

Every reason I would have had ten seconds ago to turn him down floats from my head as I stare back. I'm about to use Avery as an excuse until she speaks first.

"Yeah, she does. We are heading out anyway. Nice to meet you, Dean." She pushes me toward him.

I turn to give her a look before turning back to Dean, trying again to find some reason why this is a bad idea. A smirk flashes across his face as he catches the glare I've directed at my best friend. He gets serious as he reaches for my arm, holding me in place before we go anywhere. "Sorry I had to take that call. I didn't plan to dip out, but I'm all yours for the rest of the night. Or I can give you a ride home if you don't want to come over?"

"We can go to your house." I appreciate him giving me an out, even if it was more out of courtesy than anything. I'm eager to spend time with him and see where he lives.

His hand guides me down the street. I look back at him for a second, and he gives me an unreadable look before slightly nodding his head and pointing his eyes to his truck, which just came into view.

I hop into the passenger seat, sending a quick "I'm nervous" text to Avery before he slides into the driver's side. It's not that I'm not happy to be spending time with Dean. It's just that twice now we've had such a good time together, and then I leave wondering if I've slid over into an alternate reality where, based on his apparent inability to make future plans, he might not feel the same.

Since Taylor, Alexis and Kylie haven't been in any serious relationships since I've known them, Avery has been the only person my age to give me an insider's look into an adult relationship. Maybe she and Miller are an anomaly, but I love seeing how the two of them interact, how well they communicate and how much they love each other. I'm around them enough to have experienced arguments and watched them work through them. I've felt how much Miller cares from all the times he's taken over my role as comforting best friend anytime Avery has been upset. The guy also moved back here simply because he couldn't stand to be away from her for a day, let alone a whole week.

Knowing a relationship like that is possible makes me not want to settle for anything less.

Yet, here I am, in a truck with a guy who can very clearly spark a fire inside me, but I have no idea if he could or would ever put a literal fire out for me. He hasn't given me a real reason to push him away, and something keeps telling me to push toward him until I figure out if he's going to give me one.

Ugh. Get it together, Maci. It's been like two weeks since we met. Just because your best friends and parents experienced "love at first sight," doesn't mean that's normal. What is it about this guy that steals all my patience?

CHAPTER EIGHTEEN

After about ten minutes of driving, we pull into his long gravel driveway. I follow him to the front door that opens without him using a key. Down the hallway there's a glow from a TV off to the right, and it occurs to me he might have a roommate. I'm relieved when I see the back of Marcus' head.

"Hey, man," Dean says, reaching to shake his shoulder.

"Hey. When you ditched me, I thought you'd be out later." Marcus' eyes stay glued to the TV, but there's humor in his voice as he raises one hand off his video game controller to give a slight wave.

"Hiii," I chime in, catching a glimpse of a smile on Dean's face in my periphery.

Pressing pause on the controller, Marcus turns around. "Oh hey, Maci. I didn't know you were here!" He says it like he's genuinely happy to see me, but I don't miss the surprised look he throws Dean's way.

"Yeah, well, I'll end up anywhere someone asks me to go when I have dumplings in my system." I laugh, wondering if that came out more creepy than I intended. I know Dean spent the night last week, and I practically told him I was down to have sex, but now that I'm in his space and we might actually do it, I'm so nervous I can hardly process my thoughts enough to form sentences.

"Dump City? I love that place! You know they are trying to open an actual restaurant?"

I'm about to answer, but my attention redirects to Dean whining at me from around the corner, "Maciiii!"

"As long as they keep their punch card, I fully support that. Have a good night, Marcus." Somehow I know I won't see him again tonight. He pushes play on his game as he says goodnight, and I take off in the direction of the voice I'm pretty sure could lure me anywhere.

I walk through the kitchen, pushing on the slightly opened door on the other side of it. "Nice room," I muse, my eyes wandering around his space. There's hardly anything in here. There's nothing on the walls and only a mattress on the floor, made lazily with a few pillows and a gray blanket thrown on top. It looks exactly like the room I'd expect from a college guy who moved out of a dorm room. "I don't even need to make up a PG sleepover bed on the floor since that's where you sleep already."

His brown eyes flicker with amusement as he takes a step closer, close enough to touch me, although he doesn't. "Damn, I knew I should have sprung for the bed frame."

"I don't think a bed frame is a requirement to graduate from PG." *Holy shit.* I can't believe I said that. If he was trying to figure out what I hoped was going to happen between us tonight, I cleared it up for him.

He takes another step, closing the distance between us until his breath is on my cheek. "Is that where you see this night going?" he asks.

"Well, yeah, now I do. Don't you?" I mean it, but my teeth bite into my lower lip, and my eyes fall to the floor.

"Now? Talk to me, Maci." He brings his finger to my chin, gently pulling my gaze back to his.

I take a breath to ease my nerves. "I'm thrown off because I didn't expect to see you tonight. But now that we're here... it's definitely something I've been thinking about."

"Yeah, I know it feels out of the blue today, but this isn't a random hookup for me. I've been thinking about this too–about you."

My stomach flutters at words I'd never heard before and didn't expect to come from him. His voice is rough when he speaks again. "If something happens right now between us, I want that. But only if you do." His fingers touch my wrist, and the electricity that immediately flows through my body renders me speechless.

I look up until my eyes meet his and realize he's looking for confirmation. I nod. "I do." As soon as the words leave my mouth, his other hand makes contact with my other wrist and both of his hands slowly sweep up my arms, leaving chills in their wake. By the time his hands reach my neck, mine find his hips, and I lean into him. His hands are soft as they grip the side of my face, and his thumbs run along the edges of my cheeks.

His steps forward force me backward, until we are against the edge of the bed. His hands fall away from me, the point of contact replaced by his shirt as it brushes over my skin when he pulls it over his head. My heart races as I glance behind me before lowering until I'm sitting on the mattress. He follows me, kneeling so he's straddling me. His hand finds its place near my spine as he slowly lowers me down, his mouth connecting to mine at the same moment his body presses mine into the mattress.

Shifting his weight back to his knees, he slowly runs his hands up my sides, pulling my shirt along with them and tugging to encourage me to lift my arms, his eyes locked on mine the entire time. I follow his lead, letting my shirt slide off easily and fall to the floor beside us. He leans back slightly to get a better look, and self-doubt rushes through me until a smile spreads across his face, and I watch his eyes darken.

His hands fall to the side of each of my breasts as his mouth finds my neck. Massaging lightly, one of his thumbs snags over the edge of my bra and pulls it back. He's a little rough as his hand rubs over me, my nipples getting hard as he pinches one between his fingers. This feels like an out-of-body experience. I mean, Grayson and I had sex almost our entire senior year, but that's the only experience I've had. I wouldn't say it was bad because I always enjoyed it.

But this... we haven't done anything yet, and every-where our skin touches, it's as if there's electricity shooting through me. It would make sense for me to be more nervous than I am because it's been so long, but for some reason, I'm not. All the nerves I felt on the way over here have disappeared.

His hands trail down my body, his mouth following closely behind. When he reaches the button on my jeans, he undoes it with a quick twist of his fingers. I feel the zipper being tugged down slowly, and when it catches at the end, he looks at me watching him, as if asking for permission again. I give him a look that I hope says "Do whatever the hell you want" and apparently he translates it well because he tugs my jeans down my legs, pulling them inside out as they come off.

His hands graze over the outside of my thighs, the pressure increasing as they make their way to the back of my legs. He leans down, pressing his lips right above my knee, and continuing a trail of kisses up my inner thigh until he can't go any higher.

A sensation I haven't felt in a while rushes through me, but at a level I've never experienced before. I'm not sure I've ever wanted to be with someone as much as I do at this moment. His fingers slip under the lace, one of them looping around the top edge as he slips the delicate material down my body.

Running his hands up my body as he goes, he climbs on top of me. His look of want escalates to pure lust, and any softness around what was happening is replaced by intensity in the air around us. His eyes catch in my gaze. I try to read them as I reach between us, undoing the button on his jeans, but it's no use. I can't see past the desire in his eyes. At the same time, my gut tells me it's more than that, it's the reason I didn't stop him when I realized where this was headed.

His eyes drift from mine as he reaches into his back pocket. There's a crinkle of what I assume is a condom wrapper, which is confirmed when he tosses the purple foil on the bed next to me before kicking off his jeans. His eyes close as he takes my breast in his hand and sucks my nipple into his mouth. I suck in a breath, the sensation from that alone turning me on more than I've ever been. On instinct, I reach down, taking him in my hand, and a small moan escapes his mouth, vibrating against me. He's already hard but gets all the way there as I slide my hand up and down his length. I'm already getting wet–him being turned on turns me on more than I thought it would.

He leans up on his forearm, his hand gripping the side of my face as his mouth meets mine with urgency. Without wasting any more time, he rolls the condom on before he slowly pushes inside of me. My head falls back from losing my breath for a moment. His fingers lace into my hair behind my head and pull my mouth back to his. "God, you feel good." He groans against my lips.

His next kiss is forceful, like he has no control over what he's doing and can't get enough, and it spurs on my arousal. I imagine what his abs look like, contracting above me as I run my fingers up his side, the muscles in his forearms flexing next to my face as he holds himself up. His sandy blond hair is long enough to barely brush my forehead as he hovers over me, his dark brown eyes nearly black from desire. Watching him want me, even if it's only in this moment, is enough to pull me to the edge.

He's pushing in and pulling out of me so slowly, it's almost torturous. My hips press up so he goes deeper, wanting more. He smiles in our kiss, like he knows he's tormenting me. "Not yet," he whispers in my ear, but he doesn't pull away. The air around me is hot, and hearing his breathing pick up makes me want him more.

As if reading my mind and not being able to hold back any longer himself, he pushes my knee toward my head, pinning it beside me with his arm as he thrusts into me, deeper now. We moan in sync, and pressure starts to build inside me at a much quicker pace than it was before. I'm on the edge of tipping over. The muscles in my stomach tighten as he pushes into me, over and over. With every pull back, I crave the feeling of all of him inside me for the split second he's not. I'm tightening around him as his breath hitches, and we both ride our orgasms out together.

He collapses onto me. I feel his breath in my hair as he reaches to run his fingers through it, letting his hand rest beside me once they work their way through. After a minute of stillness passes, he pulls out of me, rolling onto his back. Not wanting to lose contact, I roll into him, so my head falls onto his chest. He hesitates for long enough that I wonder if I shouldn't have done that. Maybe this *is* supposed to be just sex.

Right as I decided to move, he wraps his arm around me and pulls me into him. The sweat from his body is wet against my face, but I lean into it, my arm reaching around his waist. I'm trapped in a euphoric state, barely registering the kiss he presses to the top of my head before sitting and pulling me with him.

He bends down to grab his briefs off the floor as I stand there, a little uncomfortable.

"Umm, do you mind if I rinse off quickly?" You would think after being that intimate with someone, I wouldn't be nervous to ask a simple question, but I feel awkward.

"Yeah, of course," he doesn't hesitate as he looks up and points toward his bathroom. It's in his room, thank goodness.

I tie my hair up so I don't have to sleep with it wet. I'm assuming I'm going to be staying here, but this is the first time we've had sex, the first time I've even been to his house, and I have no idea how comfortable he is having someone in his space. Not to mention, we aren't dating, are we?

I step into the shower, pulling the curtain closed behind me. I close my eyes and let the scalding hot water fall onto my face. What the hell am I doing? Sleeping with someone I hardly know doesn't feel like me at all. There's something about Dean I can't say no to though. *I don't want to say no to him.*

When he runs his hands through his hair, he's so damn sexy. The way his dimples show when he smiles as he chews on the end of a toothpick, it makes my stomach flip. There is this pull toward him. I've felt it since the moment I saw him on my birthday–this need to kiss him even though he was a complete stranger. Whatever just happened on his bed, there's no way he can't be on the same page as me. Right? I mean, that was easily the best sex I've ever had. I know it's been a long time for me, but I would have remembered if it felt that good. It has to be because of the intense chemistry between us. Unless it wasn't as good for him? Or maybe he's amazing in bed because he's had a lot more recent experience than me. Either way, I wish his hands were all over me again. The moment I think it, something touches my side.

I pull my face out of the water, spinning around so fast, I almost slip. *There's that freaking smile.* My hand falls to my chest, and I shift my feet to balance myself. "You scared the shit out of me." I manage to let out a small laugh in the process of trying to catch my breath.

"You alright?" He laughs, more to himself than at me.

"Mhm," I manage to get out. He just saw me naked a few minutes ago, but I'm suddenly self-conscious in the well-lit bathroom. I start to move my arms to cover myself.

"Good." He bites the side of his bottom lip, filling the space between us before my arms have the chance. His hands slide around either side of my back, pulling me to him before he steps me backward, through the stream of water and against the wall. Out of instinct, my hands go to my face, brushing the water out of my eyes and clearing them to see the guy standing in front of me. I press my hands lightly against his chest as I look at him and only have a second to let insecurity seep in again before his mouth presses into mine.

Every thought that doesn't belong in this moment fades away. His hands don't wander, but his fingers dig into that place on my lower back he seems to love, pulling us as close together as we could possibly be unless he was inside me again.

His tongue sweeps inside my mouth, deepening our kiss as water flows around us. He doesn't pull back for at least ten minutes. When he does, I finally open my eyes to see him standing there, water dripping off the ends of his hair and beading all over his body. What Dean does to me is something unlike I've ever experienced. When he's around, it seems like he can sense what I want without me telling him. I am seriously about to be on my knees begging for round two if we do not get out of the shower right now. Who am I? Is this who I am? Or who I am with him?

I pull open the curtain, step out to grab the two towels sitting on the counter and reach back to hand one to Dean. I immediately wrap mine around myself, feeling unsure now that we are no longer in a heated moment. He brings his towel to his face to dry it before rubbing it over his hair. Seriously, Maci, get a grip.

"I wasn't sure if you had anything going on early tomorrow morning, but if not, you can stay here, and I can take you home in the morning."

"Okay, thank you. That works." I wander out of the bathroom in search of my underwear. Once I pull them on, I find my shirt on the other side of the bed. I usually sleep naked, and even though the shirt I wore tonight is not the kind you sleep in, it feels weird to not wear anything. I didn't notice he was standing behind me, but he must have seen my hesitation because he tosses me a folded black T-shirt. When I unfold it, I notice it's a shirt for his friends' band we saw on our first date. I decide then to steal it. Maybe collecting his clothes will keep him close.

After sliding the shirt over my head, I look at my phone before setting it on the floor. It's already 3 a. m. My mind is wide awake turning over my thoughts about everything that happened tonight, but exhaustion overpowers it. I can hardly keep my eyes open as I crawl onto my side of the bed.

CHAPTER NINETEEN

When I wake, the room is dark. I flip my phone over on the floor, clicking the side button to light it up and check the time. It's a little before seven and Dean is still sleeping. I have no idea why I'm awake–possibly because I'm in desperate need of a glass of water. I roll off the bed quietly, in hopes I don't wake him, then slide my bra under Dean's shirt in case I run into Marcus. The six inches of height Dean has on me makes his shirt long enough I'm comfortable leaving the room without putting my jeans on. I doubt he's up anyway.

As soon as I walk into the kitchen, I immediately regret that decision and feel self-conscious when I see Marcus sitting at the kitchen table. He looks up from his phone, his surprise evident. It would be more awkward to change now, so I decide to go with it. "Oh, hey, Marcus. I was looking for a glass of water." I tug on the edge of Dean's shirt, as if it'll make it longer. Thank God I put my bra on at least.

He sets down his phone, walks over to a cabinet and pulls out a glass for me. As he hands it to me, he smirks. "Hey, Maci, didn't know you were still here."

"Umm, yeah." I turn on the sink and fill my cup. Uneasiness washes over me with the expression on his face. "Is that okay? Sorry about my lack of pants. I didn't think you'd be awake already."

He laughs. "I'm not surprised about the lack of pants so much as I'm surprised to see you here at all."

"Oh, why? I was here last night." I shift back and forth on my feet, waiting for him to clarify.

"Oh, I know. That was weird too." He can see my confusion. "There usually aren't girls staying over." He pauses for a beat. "It's good though. I mean, the dude won't shut up about you." It comes out more playful than annoyed.

"Oh, really?" I wouldn't be able to hide my surprise if I tried, but I take a sip of my water in an attempt.

"Didn't expect him to act on it. It's just weird..."

Right before he finishes his thought, Dean walks into the kitchen. He's shirtless, only wearing forest green basketball shorts, and his blond hair is sticking in every direction. He's sexy, especially with the way his eyes rake over my body in his shirt. My cheeks heat as he stares like he can't decide if he wants to keep admiring the way it fits or rip it off me.

The moment he's close enough, he wraps his arm around my waist, on a mission and confident about what he wants, even in his half-awake state. I can't help but smile at his gentle possessiveness, but I'm still a little confused about whatever Marcus was saying. He tries to hide his smile, but I catch it as my feet slightly skid across the floor as he pulls me into him, the water in my glass nearly splashing over the edge. I take an-other small sip before reaching behind us and setting my glass on the counter. Once he has my full attention, he kisses my hair before whispering, "Good morning."

"Morning," I say under my breath, and he squeezes me a little tighter.

"Morning." He looks up, directing this one toward Marcus. "What's weird?"

"You, dude." He shakes his head at Dean before turning to walk out of the kitchen.

Dean runs his hand through his hair, like he knows Marcus is calling him out on some secret I haven't been told.

As soon as Marcus is out of the kitchen, Dean shakes his head like he's shaking away a thought. Then he turns to me, his arms draping over my shoulders. "Hi," he whispers as if we aren't alone.

"Hi." I match the volume in his voice.

"Sooo, last night..." He doesn't finish his thought–waiting for my reaction first.

It occurs to me he could regret what we did. Feelings can get distorted when it's late. He's said before that you can't trust tired decisions. I can hear the insecurity in my voice when I say, "It's okay if it was a one-time thing."

His brows pinch together. "I mean, I was thinking one time wasn't enough. But is that what you want?"

My teeth rake over my bottom lip.

"What is it?" His eyes meet mine, and his fingertips brush against my skin as he sweeps a strand of hair away from my face, leaving his hand to rest at my neck.

I shake my head softly. "I don't want it to be a one time thing. I just didn't want to misread the situation."

"You didn't misread anything."

"Okay, I don't want you to think I expected anything since we haven't talked about it."

He pulls me into him before he brings his mouth to my ear. "Well, we could talk about how I want it to happen again... or we could go do it again, you know, to confirm we are on the same page about how great it was."

I can't help but smile and start to nod against him, but something catches my eye, distracting me. I pull away from Dean to walk to the counter, running my fingers over the cover of the book. It has a picture of a beautiful mountain surrounded by jungle. It's titled *Guide to Central America*. "Is this yours?" I pick it up and turn back toward him.

He nods and eyes me for a second before he speaks. "I'm going on a trip with my family in a few weeks."

New energy flows through my body at the mention of travel. My eyes must light up because the edge of his mouth tugs into a smile as he watches me. "That's so cool. My parents are in Croatia right now. Where are you going? I really want to go to Costa Rica. It's at the very top of my list." I'm rambling and remind myself to take a breath. When I look up and let my brown eyes meet his, I notice the smile is gone from them. That's weird. What could I have said?

"We are going to Honduras." His eyes flicker across mine like he's debating whether or not to tell me whatever else is on the tip of his tongue.

He's pausing too long in his indecision. I thought maybe we were about to bond over travel, but it makes me uncomfortable enough to want to change the subject. What's safe? "Sooooo." The book in my hand reminds me of when he first came to my apartment. I set it back down on the counter. "What other books do you like? Did you actually read *The Silent Patient*?"

Reaching out, he runs his hand down my arm until his fingers link with mine. He slowly starts stepping out of the kitchen and toward his bedroom, laughing to himself as he responds. "I did. I'm actually kind of a nerd." He says it like it's an embarrassing thing to share, but I love it. "I like psychological thrillers, but I tend to read anything that specifically focuses on the human mind, or how people interact and connect."

Okay, is it weird I'm turned on by the fact that he loves to read? Liking it in the first place would have been attractive, but the fact he loves books that will teach him something is even hotter. I refrain from sharing those thoughts. "Oh yeah, you're a sociology major. I don't think it's nerdy. I'm the same." He gives me a half-smile as he continues walking us slowly down the hallway.

Sometimes he's open—other times he seems uncomfortable talking about himself. I don't want to push it all at once, so I attempt to lighten the mood. "How do you feel about conducting your own research on how two specific people can connect?" I try to be clever, but I'm awkward.

He humors me. "For the sake of research, it would be a shame if we didn't at least test out a few theories." A smile lights his face before he reaches his arms around my back, pulling me into him as he pushes his way through his bedroom door.

CHAPTER TWENTY

Thursday night with Dean has been playing through my head on repeat. I wish I was counting down the minutes until I was going to see him again, but he hasn't asked to make plans, and we've hardly talked since he dropped me off yesterday morning. I'm considering seeing what the girls are doing tonight as a distraction, but I don't want to go to a party. As I open my phone to our group chat, it buzzes in my hand.

Avery: *Miller's buddy has tickets for the student seats to the game this afternoon. He can't go anymore and offered them to us. Do you want to come? What are your plans?*

Me: *That is my plan now! I'll meet you at the stadium at like 3:30?*

Avery: *Yes! Do you want to invite Dean? Miller suggested it. Thought we could at least try to get to know him this time.*

Me: *Haha I doubt he'll want to double date considering I'm pretty sure he doesn't think we are dating, but I'll ask him.*

I wish I wasn't unsure of myself when I'm not around Dean. When he's with me, he gives me his full attention, and that gives me more confidence. Maybe I feel like the time we spend together is only ever on his terms. I just don't get it. How much he acts like he enjoys being around me doesn't align with how much time we spend together. But the worst that can happen is he says no, so I might as well try to make plans.

Me: *Hey.*

Way to be bold, Maci. I roll my eyes and set down my phone, half expecting him to ignore my vague, purposeless text, but it buzzes almost immediately.

Dean: *What's up, Jackson.*

Me: *Nothing much, just getting ready for the game.*

Dean: *The football game?*

Me: *Yeah, are you surprised?*

Dean: *Just didn't know you liked football.*

Me: *I don't go to a lot of games. But Avery and I try to go a few times a year. College experience and all. We wanted to catch one more before the season is over.*

Dean: *Ahhh, got it. Your pact with yourself to do all the things this year.*

Me: *Do you want to go with us?*

Me: *Avery and Miller*

Dean: *Sure*

Me: *Really?*

That was easy. Maybe I need to take more initiative like Avery said, and like I promised myself I would.

Dean: *Yes. lol Really.*

Me: *Okay, meet you out front at 3:30?*

Dean: *Sounds good. I'll see you soon.*

I change into my favorite pair of jeans and tug on a long sleeve shirt and my green school hoodie, hoping I'll be warm enough. On my way out the door, I pull up my text thread with Avery to let her know I'm on my way and opt to walk the half mile to the stadium in case I decide to drink. Plus, parking is a nightmare on game day.

The moment I spot Avery and wave at her, I also see Dean. I'm not sure why I'm surprised he's on time. He showed up exactly when he said he would for our first date. He's wearing black joggers and a green school hoodie, the yellow "O" slightly faded on the front. His sandy blond hair messy in that sexy "I just woke up like this" way, paired with his dark eyes is enough to keep my gaze locked on him. He's looking down at his phone, so he hasn't seen me yet, but when Avery follows my gaze to him too, he must feel it because he looks up. He flashes a smile and meets me where Avery and Miller are standing, waiting for us. As soon as he's close enough, his hand reaches out, settling on my lower back as he leans in and kisses my hair.

"Hi," he says, casually, to both me and my friends.

"Hey, man, good to see you." Miller reaches out to shake his hand, and Dean pulls his away from the small of my back just long enough to return the gesture. Then the four of us head toward the stadium entrance. Once we get inside, the guys head to the beer line after asking what we want, and we take off to find empty seats in the student section.

I was not prepared for how cold the metal bleacher would feel through my jeans when we sit. I berate myself mentally for not dressing warmer as Avery texts Miller to let him know where we are sitting. We should have brought a blanket.

My best friend's voice pulls me out of my head. "Okay, seriously, he's bonding voluntarily with Miller, and he seems affectionate. I thought you said you weren't sure if he's really into you? Looks like he is to me." She shrugs.

"I know... I just don't want to get my hopes up. I remember when you and Miller started dating, you couldn't stay away from each other. I'm not saying the guy has to be obsessed with me, I just don't want to want to be around him all the time if he doesn't want the same."

"First of all, you can't compare relationships, Mace. Everyone is different. And you can't assume he's not thinking about you or doesn't want to see you because he doesn't make plans all the time. Maybe he's busy. Try enjoying this and see what happens."

"Yeah, you're right. I don't know why it makes me self-conscious. I don't know why I can't ignore the feeling that something seems off. I guess we will see. Can we talk about today's jerseys? They are sexy!" They're different for almost every game. Most of today's uniform is black, with silver wings on the jersey shoulders and neon yellow names and numbers printed between them.

Before Avery can respond, the guys appear at the end of the row. Miller shimmies past me and Avery to get to the seat on the other side of her as Dean sits next to me. "Hi," he greets me again and hands me a beer. "What's sexy?"

"Thank you." I take it from him. "The jerseys. Did you know that the co-founder of Nike is an alum, and he's made it his mission to make sure the team always looks good? He thinks it'll attract the best players and enhance the perception of the team." I don't know much about football, but I know this fun fact, and I'm excited to share.

He's been smiling at me since I started talking, a slight glimmer in his eyes. "I did know that, but I love that you know it." As soon as his words leave him, he leans in to kiss me. It's quick and soft, but it's the first time he's done it in public. I shouldn't be greedy, but I can't help it. As soon as he pulls away, I lean back in and kiss him again. He flashes a smile, and his eyes meet mine before he turns his attention to his beer and the field.

"Soooooo, do you come to a lot of games?" I question Dean as I take a sip of my beer. Before he can answer, a voice comes from behind us.

"Hey, Dean."

"Oh, hey, Coop." Dean turns around to greet his friend.

"Surprised to see you here and not in your usual seats." His friend leans forward. His short, light brown hair noticeably contrasts his bright blue eyes as he tugs on the strings of a maroon hoodie that looks similar to the one I still have of Dean's.

"Yeah. Sophie wanted to bring her boyfriend today." He shrugs.

"Boyfriend?!" Cooper whisper-shouts. His jaw clenches. He closes his eyes and takes a deep breath through his nose. When he opens his eyes again, the anger has cleared from them. His next words come out unaffected by emotion. "I'm Cooper by the way," he says, directing his attention to me and reaching out his hand as if he's completely flipped a switch.

I'm a little confused by his reaction, but I reach out my hand to shake his. Before I can say my name, Dean cuts in. "Oh yeah, sorry. This is my... Maci." He hesitates before saying my name like his instinct was to introduce me as his girlfriend but he realized his mistake. I catch his quick sideways glance of panic before he adds, "Cooper's parents live next door to mine."

Was he about to call me his girlfriend? I nearly stop breathing from how quickly my pulse picked up. What else did he just say? I focus on Cooper, my hand frozen in his. I pull back and wing my response. "It's nice to meet you." He seems nice, and I love that every person I meet who knows Dean allows me to know him a little more.

"Yeah, you too. I think I'm going to head out though. Let me know when your next party is."

"Will do," Dean agrees as I wave goodbye.

Cooper reaches to fist bump Dean before abandoning his seat and taking off upstream through the crowd of students looking for seats.

Dean settles himself facing forward again. His hand falls to my thighs, wiggling his fingers between them, and gently tugging so I'll move closer. When I do, he doesn't pull his hand away. The heat radiating off them warms me, and it's impossible not to lean into him more.

"I hope Cooper is okay."

"Me too." He sounds concerned as his thumb rubs against my thigh.

"Well, I guess that answers my question about you coming to games," I joke, hoping to lighten the mood.

"Yeah, we have season tickets, somewhere over there." He subtly tips his hand holding his beer toward the 50 yard line on the opposite side of us. "My parents have been dragging my sister and me here for as long as I can remember."

"Are you close with your sister?"

He nods as he takes a sip of his beer. "Yeah, she's cool. She's three years younger than me, a freshman this year, so kind of a weird age gap growing up since we didn't spend a lot of time at the same school. Now that she's older, it's better. We hang out sometimes." He offers this information freely, like he hasn't been mostly vague this entire time when talking about himself.

"That's nice you have her at least. Avery is the closest thing I have to a sister." I look over toward my best friend, but she's so into whatever Miller is saying she doesn't notice. Dean's thumb rubs against my thigh, and it brings my attention back to him. "So it's safe to say you like football then? Because if so, I'm going to need you to explain a few things."

He does that little to himself laugh I love so much. "I used to play. All through high school."

I didn't expect that. "Oh, wow, really?"

"Yup, I got a scholarship to play here freshman year, but I turned it down. It was more of my parents' dream than mine."

"Were they mad?"

"Nah, they are great. They'll support anything I want to do." He pauses for a moment to take another sip of his beer. Looking into his clear plastic cup, he adds, "Even if it's crazy," under his breath in a way that makes me believe I wasn't supposed to hear it.

"Sooo... what's *your* dream?" I'm going to take advantage of all the personal information he's willing to give me right now.

He glances sideways at me like he knows what I'm doing. "That is a great question, Maci." He doesn't add anything else, just goes quiet. As if the Universe has his back, the game starts, and the stadium roars to life.

CHAPTER TWENTY-ONE

After the game, Dean offered to walk me home since it was getting dark and Avery said she was going to Miller's. I was freezing during the game. It was my fault for not dressing appropriately, but I blamed Dean for buying me cold beer. He responded by pulling my face into his and warming my lips with his own, kissing me like no one else was around. Then he promised me hot food as soon as the game ended. He's definitely making it easy to fall for him the more time we spend together.

My stomach is growling, and my fingers are freezing, even stuffed inside the middle pocket of my sweatshirt. I'm not sure whether food or warmth is a more pressing matter right now. After we get out of the stadium, Dean looks over to see me shivering and without hesitation he slips his hand into my pocket, lacing our fingers together. Holding my hand is not something he's done, and the rush that flows through me is more than just from his body heat.

"Food first? Or do you need me to warm you up first?" He waggles his eyebrows at me.

His excitement to get me in bed is tempting, and I'm about to choose the second option when I look up and notice we are passing Track Town Pizza–the place I went to with my friends on my birthday. He must see my eyes widen with excitement. "Food it is, then." He laughs, reaching for the door handle, but he hesitates before opening it. He leans in to whisper in my ear, "I'll warm you up after."

I can't help but smile and glance up at him, our eyes locking before he pulls me inside by our intertwined fingers.

The rush of hot air from the restaurant burns against my nose as I look at the menu hanging above the order counter at the entrance. "You pick. Whatever you want," he says, squeezing my hand before he lets it go.

"*Anything* I want?" I want pineapple and jalapeño. It's what I've been craving all week, but no one ever wants to eat that with me. He nods, a "give me your best shot" look on his face.

"Pineapple and jalapeño?" I ask, still hesitant.

Without more than a smile, he steps up to the counter and orders for us.

I wondered if he was only being nice, but he eats half our pizza like he loves pineapple and spice on pizza.

When we get back to my apartment, Dean follows me inside as I unlock my door. Fine by me, especially since he alluded to what's next. I had such a good time at the game. I usually watch without really knowing what's happening. Dean patiently explained answers to every question I had, his hand lazily rubbing my lower back or locked between my thighs almost the entire time. I know I still haven't known him very long, but I already want this to be more than it is. When we are together, it's great and then earlier I swear he almost slipped and called me his girlfriend. I know he stopped himself, but I felt crazy for thinking I was already falling for him. Maybe I'm not. I want to bring it up, but I'm not sure how to approach it.

Closing the door behind me, I veer to the right, into the kitchen to grab a water. "Do you want anything?" I turn my head back to look at him.

"Yeah, I want to stay over. If you're cool with it."

"I meant something to drink." I can't help but smile. "But that works too." I reach into the fridge, and by the time I close the door and turn back around, Dean is in front of me. His hand wraps around my lower back as he pulls me into him while pushing me against the fridge simultaneously. His lips land on mine, soft and sweet, and the kiss is shorter than I expected. He pulls back, tugging my water bottle from my hand and taking a sip before handing it back. "Good because I want to do a lot more of that."

When he's blatantly sharing his attraction to me, I'm at a loss for words. I've never had someone act this into me physically before. It doesn't make me uncomfort- able–I love it, at least with Dean. I just don't know how to respond, so I change the subject.

"I like meeting your friends. Cooper seems nice."

"Yeah, he is. He's a year younger than us. We played football together, and he's always lived next door, but he and Sophie are better friends."

I feel like being nosy. "Maybe I'm off base, but he seemed upset when you mentioned her."

He nods. "Yeah, I noticed that too. He's always had a crush on her. They had a thing in high school. I thought it was short lived, but maybe he's not over it."

"Well, I hope he's okay. Have you met Sophie's boyfriend?"

"No, it's pretty new I think." He moves his hand to my shoulder and starts twirling my hair around his finger, his interest in our conversation fading.

I take a drink of my water before working up to the real question I want to ask before we head to bed. "I wonder how it went with your parents meeting him."

He shrugs, his free hand sliding under my sweatshirt against my skin. "I'm sure it went well. They are super chill," he mumbles into my neck before kissing me.

"So, they've liked all your girlfriends?"

He pulls back to stare at me. That probably wasn't the most subtle way to mention his slip earlier. I'm so awkward. It feels like he's studying my face for the answer I want to hear. "I wouldn't know," is what he lands on.

Well, that didn't go as planned, not that I had a solid plan. Clearly. Way to ruin the moment, Maci.

Before I can maneuver out of this conversation, he adds, "I haven't had anyone important enough to bring home. Yet."

"Oh, okay." I feel defeated before he adds "yet," but I'm still unsure.

"Maci."

"Yes?" I break eye contact, looking to the strings of my hoodie as I tug on them.

His hand leaves my hip and reaches to tip my chin until my gaze meets his. "Do you want to ask about whatever it is you actually want to know?" The way he locks his eyes onto mine and runs his fingers through my hair fills me with more hope than maybe I should have.

"I don't want to sound crazy." My eyes shift across his face as I try to read his reaction.

"If I thought you were crazy, I wouldn't be here." There isn't any judgment or amusement in his voice.

"It kind of felt like you almost introduced me as your girlfriend earlier." The words come out slowly, but then

I panic and quickly add, "But that's crazy because we hardly know each other, right? I must have misheard, I'm sorry. Just forget I said anything. I don't know what I'm talking about."

"Are you finished?" He looks amused now.

"Yes," I whisper.

"You're not crazy." His smirk drops and he hesitates before adding, "But I don't want to mislead you. I'm not sure why I almost said that. I can't put a label on this right now."

"Okaaay?" I draw out mostly in hesitation, partially in confusion. I'm not sure what to say next.

He evades elaborating on the girlfriend thing. "But there isn't anyone else I'm spending my extra time with." He says it like he knows I need reassurance. "It's just you."

"Okay." I repeat my previous response but smile this time, satisfied with his level of commitment for now, and choosing to push any other thoughts to the back of my mind. I didn't expect him to want to be my boyfriend yet anyway.

He leans in to kiss me on the forehead. When he pulls back, he slides his hand into mine but waits for my lead on what happens next. Exhilaration runs through me when I imagine him in my bed. Keeping my eyes on him, I slide out from between him and my fridge and tug him toward my room.

CHAPTER TWENTY-TWO

Dean is traveling in Central America for the next week with his family, which obviously makes me jealous. But stronger than my pull to the world right now, is my pull to him. It's devastatingly painful and very annoying. This version of myself is overwhelming. There's no room left in my brain with how much it's flooded with thoughts of Dean.

We hung out twice between the football game and when he left. I've been taking initiative and asking him to hang out first like Avery suggested. I think I was just in my head about it, especially considering the way he keeps saying yes and can't keep his hands off me when we are together. I contemplated asking what prompted him to clarify he didn't want a label, but my intuition told me not to, and not just because it's only been a few weeks.

I can sense something holds him back, but he's definitely been more open the past few times we've hung out. I'm glad I don't have to worry about him seeing anyone else, and it sounds like he's busy. The other day he told me he was taking an extra class this quarter because he wants to do more than the minimum requirements for foreign language. It makes sense. We are required to take two years to graduate but it's not enough to be fluent. If you're going to go that far, you might as well make it worth it. I'd consider it if my ability to retain a second language was a skill I had at all. Even if you're good at it, I know how much work it is, so it makes sense why Dean has seemed busy and distracted.

He left the night before last, and they don't have service where they are going, so I'm impatiently waiting to hear about his trip. It doesn't help that it's Thanksgiving weekend. Usually, I'd go to my parents, but they extended the trip they are currently on in Europe. I'd be sad, but I get to talk to them every few days about their adventures. I'm happy for them because after both teaching for thirty years, they've been able to take a few off to travel. I hope I'm like my parents someday. I do miss them, but at least Miller's parents invited me over for their Thanksgiving dinner yesterday, and they are like family too.

My phone vibrates, snapping me back to reality.

Kylie: *Put on your skinny jeans and take the tag off that sexy red tank top hanging in your closet. We are going out. I'll be there in 15 minutes.*

I don't know why I assumed she drove home this weekend.

Twenty minutes later, I'm ripping my black leather jacket off the hook as Kylie pulls me through the door by my other hand. Her short blonde hair flips over her shoulder as she stops in her tracks to face me. Her light green eyes sparkle with mischief before she speaks. "Maci. Are you excited?"

"Umm, yes? Where are we going?" I just assumed it was a party.

"Let's just say it's going to be a bucket list kind of night," she says with a wink. She's the dramatic and sassy one of our group. Turning back around, she continues tugging me down the sidewalk, as if I'm not walking fast enough. She goes on about how much fun we are going to have, her energy hyping me up. After all, her mention of a bucket list must mean she's taking me to a frat party, and I've been joking all year about going to one.

When we walk through the front door, I look around, and it's everything I expected and nothing like I thought all at the same time. The entire living room is painted black, except there's also neon paint that looks like it was flung all over the walls. It's glowing from the black lights that line the edges of the ceiling. Off to the left is a wooden bar with a few bottles of liquor lined up next to a stack of red Solo cups. In the middle of the room is what I'm guessing is the main attraction. There's a large circle of people around it. Holy shit, is that an ice sculpture? It's a giant mountain made of ice, with a shot luge running through the middle of it. I didn't know things like this existed, let alone in a fraternity house in Oregon. It's like I walked into a movie scene.

My eyes continue to wander around the room. Wait, maybe I walked into a practical joke instead.

I stare a second too long, and when Troy looks up, our eyes lock across the room. A few different emotions flash through his eyes, but I can't decipher them when it's so dark. Surprise and an apology, maybe.

My brain floods with chaotic information, so I just make a decision on what to do. This time I grab Kylie by the hand and yank her toward the ice luge. Someone, I assume a fraternity brother, is standing there with a bottle of Smirnoff. He tips the bottle back upright, after having dumped far more than a shot onto the ice and watching it slide into a pretty blonde's mouth. I get his attention by stepping closer. "Can I have a shot?" I definitely don't need it, considering Kylie and I each had a bottle of wine we had poured into water bottles before our walk over here. Everyone in the room is already slightly out of focus, and I can hardly concentrate on what I'm doing. But with the new uneasiness of seeing Troy, added to the anxiety I was already feeling about missing Dean so soon, it seems like a good decision at this moment.

He smiles and points to the end of the luge, where I squat slightly before tipping my head back and positioning my mouth directly under the opening. Before I have time to mentally prepare myself, cold alcohol splashes onto my tongue. It keeps coming–way more than a shot–and I try to swallow it before it overflows out of my mouth. It's a wasted effort because I choke anyway–but I'm too frazzled to be embarrassed. No one seems to be paying attention to me. I step back as Kylie slides into my place to get a shot of her own.

The second I move backward and out of the way, a warm hand lands softly on my shoulder. I know who it is before I turn around to look at him. When I do, Troy's gray eyes meet mine. I wasn't imagining the surprise in them, but I wasn't mistaken about the apology either. How could this dude think an apology is acceptable this late? I'm about to ask him, although I know it will come out as more of a demand. But at that moment my two shots of vodka seem to be mixing with the wine I had earlier, and my stomach flips.

I spin away, out of his grip and take off down the hall, opening the first door I come across. Thank the Universe it's a laundry room with a trash can.

I close the door behind me, instantly yanking out and leaning over the white plastic bin that was in between the washer and dryer. Ugh, it tastes worse coming up than it burned going down, and my stomach aches with the heave. Surprisingly, it's short lived, and I feel better physically–lighter. But my head continues to spin, filled with thoughts that shouldn't mix at all–like that wine and vodka–in an otherwise empty stomach.

The door creaks. *Please be Kylie or someone random.* I already know it's not because I can sense caution in the way it's opening. Of course I'm not that lucky. By the time he slips in through the door and closes it behind him, I'm sitting on the floor with my back against the wall, my arms draped across my knees, my eyes closed. I hope this is all over soon.

He sits down next to me. We aren't touching, but the warmth radiating off him lets me know he's close. "Maci," he whispers. "Are you okay?"

Even though the room is spinning, I open my eyes and turn my head slightly in his direction. He looks good. A plain baby blue shirt hangs perfectly on him and brings out the blue in his usually gray eyes. He's wearing dark jeans and his white Adidas, with his legs kicked out in front of him. His hair is perfectly in place, and I have a flash to the guy pouring the Smirnoff a few minutes ago. Wait, is Troy in this fraternity? I guess I don't know much about him at all considering I haven't talked to him in months, after misreading what I thought was the perfect date.

I stare back at him with the best glare I can muster, though it's probably outweighed by the tears burning my eyes. Through the spinning and the blur of the room, I get one moment of clarity. It almost feels like I'm not drunk anymore, and I take advantage of it. "I'm fine, but I don't want to hear it, Troy. Get out, please," I tell him, not breaking our eye contact so he knows I'm serious.

He hesitates a moment, and I can tell he's considering his options. "Maci, let me explain, please. We can go outside, get some fresh air."

"No." I'm firm because I don't think I can handle a serious conversation right now, and at this moment I don't care what his excuse is. "Please leave, I know you know how." Okay, that was a little harsh, Maci. "I'm sorry," I add under my breath. I reach out, my hand falling to his thigh. "I'm just really drunk, Troy. I don't want to have this conversation in case I don't remember."

"Okay, maybe later."

He looks away from me as he stands, then locks our eyes again as he backs away toward the door, not breaking contact until he's out in the hallway with the door between us.

I wish my head would stop spinning–it's not helping me steady my thoughts. I get the impression he was being genuine, and maybe I should have listened now. I don't really know why I'm upset. It's not like I ever developed real feelings for Troy. Maybe I'm anxious about the rate at which I'm developing them for Dean, and frustrated that Troy is willing to communicate when I'm convinced there's something Dean is keeping from me. Maybe that's just an insecurity caused by Troy, though. Hmm. That's actually a reasonable thought. Wow, what an epiphany. Hopefully I remember it in the morning.

I stay on the floor a few more minutes before willing myself to stand and steady myself. On my way out the door, I spot Kylie in the corner of the room chatting with one of the fraternity brothers. I decide to leave without interrupting her. I'll text her when I get home and let her know I made it. On the way out the front door, I can't help laughing to myself, remembering when Dean told me frat parties were overrated.

CHAPTER TWENTY-THREE

Dean was supposed to come home yesterday. I'm not sure what time, so it could have been late. It's not that I expect him to let me know he got back or make plans to see me, but part of me does hope he missed me even a fraction of the amount that I missed him. I check my phone for notifications, and there's still nothing. Needing a distraction, I pack my books and drive to the library.

The sensible thing to do would be to go inside the library, where cell phone service does not exist and I could actually get some work done. Instead, I sit on the wooden bench outside, telling myself it's because it's an unusually nice day in Oregon for the beginning of December. As I pull my books out of my bag, I admit to myself that it's really because I'll have cell service out here.

I'm distracted reading about psychotropics in my Psychology of Drugs book when my phone vibrates against the bench next to me. I'm sure it's Avery asking me to grab margarita mix for taco Thursday tonight. Picking up my phone, I sigh, knowing I won't see the name I'm hoping for flashing across my screen.

To my surprise, I do.

Dean: *Whatcha doing?*

Me: *At the library, you?*

I'm trying not to give away how much I've been going crazy over getting any text at all from him.

Dean: *On my way, I'll be there in 10.*

I love how he seems to show up whenever he wants to see me. I want to be better about saying and doing what I want. I stay cross-legged on the bench, my knee bouncing while I pass the time by staring at my book. I've read the same line over and over but haven't retained any of it.

The scrape of his truck tires against the gravel of the library parking lot brings my attention to Dean, smiling through the open window at me. He's wearing the purple sweatshirt I noticed he wears on days he wants to be comfortable, and his skin glows from the type of tan you only get on vacation.

"You hungry?" he asks, as I zip my backpack, slide my flats on and start toward him.

I sink into his passenger seat cautiously, nervous about making the first move to kiss him. He doesn't lean to kiss me, but he reaches to put the truck in drive and then rests his hand on my thigh. Instantly, I feel that spark as he touches me and look over at him. I'm not going to overthink anything. He said we are exclusive after all.

"How was your trip?" I ask, my eyes on him as he stops at a red light.

"Great. Part of me already wants to go back." Keeping it vague as usual.

"Umm no. I need more than that. Tell me everything about Central America." I grin. I'm jealous he went but excited to hear about it.

His eyes roam my face for a moment as if he's contemplating telling me but then shares all about the place they stayed and their excursions. I soak it all in as the hot air blowing from his vents hits my face. He finally got his heater fixed. He's also got the windows rolled halfway down, letting fresh air swirl around us. I thought I was the only one who did that.

We pull into a dirt parking lot of a Mexican restaurant I've never been to before. We head for a round, light blue wire table, and as we sit, two waters and a basket of chips and salsa appear in front of us. I go to pick up the menu to look it over, but I pause, noticing Dean hasn't glanced at his. He's staring right into my eyes when I look up.

The table is small enough that he's easily able to reach over and brush a strand of wind-blown hair out of my face. Tucking it behind my ear he says softly, "I lied to you the day we met."

"Wait, what?" It comes out as confusion, but my heart races in anticipation of hearing something I don't want to know. What could he have lied about? We hardly talked that day.

"Well, not really lied. I told you I didn't have a girl-friend. Which wasn't all the way true. She wasn't my girlfriend, I don't do girlfriends. But I had been seeing someone casually. Julia. I haven't seen her since we met, though. Well, not like that, I mean."

"Wait, Julia?" The name sounds familiar. "That girl we saw at the bar?"

"Yeah, I had only met her a few weeks earlier. I told her after the first time you and I hung out that I didn't want to see her anymore, but I guess she didn't think I was serious."

I don't know how to respond or what to think. I'm not quite sure why this is unsettling. If anything, it should be reassuring. I was unjustifiably worried about him keeping things from me, and he's being honest, so I want to be thankful for that. The timing just seems weird. Why would he out of the blue tell me he specifically stopped seeing this Julia girl?

"Okaaay." I say, a little hesitant and at a loss for other words. It's only been about a month, and I had talked myself into being okay with the pace we are going. But this announcement throws me off. I did promise myself like a half hour ago I'd take more initiative in what I wanted out of this. "Can I ask you something?"

"Yeah, what's up?" He asks in a way that tells me he thinks I'm changing the subject.

"What are we doing here, Dean?"

"What do you mean?" His brows scrunch. "I thought you like Mexican food."

"I do... I mean what are *we* doing?"

"Oh."

I try to keep my voice calm because showing my frustration with not being able to understand his thought process isn't going to help. "You said you didn't want a label or anything, and that's fine, but it's confusing when you bring up something like telling me you're not sleeping with someone I didn't know you were sleeping with, for seemingly no reason at all. Especially since last week you told me you don't want to spend time with anyone else. I'm a little confused about what's going on in your head."

He seems a little panicked when he responds, like he didn't expect me to call him out, but also like he doesn't want to upset me. "I don't know, Maci. I'm not sure why I felt the urge to tell you that. It was something I was thinking about, and I didn't want to keep it from you. I'm not good at this, but I'm doing the best I can right now. I like spending time with you. Like I said, only you.

Can we please leave it at that for now?" His eyes beg me to let it go.

I get the feeling he's not intending to be confusing. "Yeah, we can." It comes out with a sigh, but I swap it for a half-smile before adding, "For the record, I like when you tell me things, so thank you."

His eyes don't wander from mine, but he doesn't add to the conversation.

CHAPTER TWENTY-FOUR

The front door swings open as I click the burner off from warming the tortillas. It didn't occur to me I'd be having the same meal twice in one day, but a girl can never have too many tacos. Avery sets the bottle of tequila on the counter then leans into my hug. "Soooooo, you had lunch with Dean today? Tell me all about it." She laughs in anticipation of a better explanation than the one I texted her earlier.

"Yeah, apparently to tell me about some girl he dumped after he met me? That's all I know. The guy is confusing as hell, but he's also the most captivating human I have ever met."

She pulls away from our side hug to look at me. "Your eyes look dreamy and mushy." She laughs again. "Look, I get it, Mace. I mean, when I met Miller, I couldn't stay away. It's something I could never quite explain. Miller was also clear from the beginning he felt the same and wanted to be with me, though. Did Dean give you any details about this Julia girl? What was his point in bringing it up?"

"Your guess is as good as mine, and apparently he didn't know either." I shrug, wanting to forget it.

"Well, it sounds like he's trying to communicate and be relationship-y to me. He's just a little awkward at it." She laughs.

"Yeah, that's probably it. Sooooo, you said you had something to tell me!"

"Do you want to see my engagement ring?!" she shrieks so loudly that I nearly drop the plate of tacos I'm holding.

"Ummm, what! This is the only thing we should be talking about tonight! Where is it?!"

"Oh, well, he didn't propose." She shrugs. "I just happened to see some tabs open on his computer when I went to print off a paper earlier. I have no idea which one will be mine, but I love them all." She pulls out her phone, opening an image with a glare streaked across it from taking a picture of a screen. "I had no idea what I wanted, and I didn't picture anything like these at all, but I love them so much." She sighs dreamily as she scrolls through the three other pictures. Each ring shares a big oval diamond in the center but have different bands. They are simple, but in an elegant–and expensive–way. Knowing Avery, Miller can't go wrong with any of these choices.

"I think you just love Miller so much." My comment isn't meant to take away from how gorgeous these rings are, but I also know the guy could propose with a twenty-five-cent ring from a toy vending machine and she would be as happy. She deserves something like one of these, though. "When do you think it'll happen?"

"I'm not sure. I told Mack he better call me the second he talks to Miller. He'll probably go to him to ask or tell or whatever guys do these days, you know, since it's mostly been just us," she refers to her brother.

"Do you think Mack will warn you?" I take a bite of my taco.

"Probably not. He's a little shit." She shrugs before shoving half of her taco in her mouth.

My laugh causes me to choke on my food a little. "He's your big brother, it's his right. Plus, I read somewhere that only 44% of men ask for permission to marry anymore. I don't know if that's true, but if Miller is a good enough guy to do it, let him have his moment, and don't ruin it or his surprise."

"You know what the best surprise would have been?"

"What?" I ask as I pour us each a shot of tequila and splash a little margarita mix on top.

"If I had let my brother date you in high school. Then we might be planning a double wedding right now! That would be fun!"

"Are you drunk already?" I've learned to take everything Avery says when she's drunk with a grain of salt.

"Not that drunk." She laughs.

"Well drink this then." I hand her a shot glass, and we clink them together before shooting them back.

CHAPTER TWENTY-FIVE

Jameson's is practically dead when we get there. It's the middle of December, and it's also the middle of finals week, so not a lot of people are out celebrating, but Dean and I both took our last tests today. This last week has been fun. He's been staying at my apartment almost every night, coming over when he gets off work. I have dinner ready for him, and then he makes us both study for an hour before we do anything else. I love how seriously he takes school, and we've each taken one of the classes the other is currently in since some Psychology and Sociology classes overlap, so we shared our old quizzes. Grades won't be in for a few more days, but I'm confident in both of us enough to be out here celebrating.

After at least an hour of talking about nonsense, a few drinks and a lot of playing footsie under the table like we aren't old enough to be in a bar, Dean and I abandon our booth next to the pool table room to go to the restroom.

I stare at my reflection in the mirror. I look really good. Yeah, I have on a cute, long sleeve forest green dress that hits barely above my knees and makes my waist look great, but I also look happy. I've been enjoying soaking up all the extra time with Dean this past week. Smiling at myself, I tuck my straight brown hair behind my ear and pop the cherry from my whiskey sour in my mouth before heading into the stall. I choose the big one so I can pull down the changing table for my purse and drink. Especially in gross bathrooms. Wait, why is there a changing table in a bar? Weird.

I'm buzzed enough to not care about bringing my drink in here with me but also conscious enough to realize how ridiculous it is that I'm floating in here like a lovesick teenager who doesn't want to be away from her boyfriend for more than two minutes.

We still haven't put a label on our relationship, but ever since I asked him what we were doing, he's acting like this is just as real and serious to him as it is to me. I wake to a text from him almost every day he doesn't wake up in my bed. It's typically about something random, but still. Plus, he kisses me whenever he finds me on campus now, which seems to happen daily. I sigh happily at my own thoughts. Setting my purse and drink on the changing table, as usual, I turn around to lock the stall.

Before it clicks, resistance comes from behind the door, and it slowly swings open. Standing there with a goofy smirk on his face is that sandy blond-haired man with his brown eyes slightly glazed over. He hastily pushes me backward so he has enough room to follow me into the stall, closing and latching it behind him.

My mind buzzes, trying to put together what is happening. Before I can figure it out, Dean's body presses into mine, until my back is against the wall dividing the two stalls. His hand reaches for mine, pinning it above my head. Instantly that electricity shoots through my body, blurring my vision this time. I can't think clearly enough to know if I should stop whatever is about to happen, or just go with it. Before I have a chance to make up my mind, Dean lets go of my hand, pressing his fingers into my skin as he drags them slowly down my arm, continuing down the side of my body. When he gets to the skirt of my dress, he grabs a fistful of it, bunching it at my waist. He pauses, like he's contemplating ripping it off me.

Then he locks eyes with mine before he slides his other hand under the fabric, over the top of the black lace panties I carefully chose this morning, not expecting this is how he would see them. His palm puts slight pressure on the front of me, and his middle finger catches on the edge of the lace before pulling it to the side. He traces the edge of my opening before his finger enters me, sending a surge of energy through my body and eliciting a moan. He pumps in and out, slowly at first as his lips meet mine to silence me.

His mouth trails away from mine, kissing my neck, sending a shock through me with each one. I'm so distracted by the way he's sucking at my skin, that I'm not reminded of what else is happening until he presses a second finger inside of me. I suck in, losing my breath for a moment. He smiles against my skin and slowly starts to pull out of me. I whimper when our contact breaks, and he laughs quietly, twisting my dress more in his hand to give him better access. I go to help him pull my panties off and he swats my hand away, tracing the outside edge of them down to where I'm already soaking wet. He slides his fingers back in. They pump in and out a few times, coming out for only a moment. I'm surprised by his hardness that slides in place of his fingers with ease from how turned on I am. I don't know how or when he got his pants undone, but I can't focus on that with the insane rush that's pulsing through my entire body.

My toes curl into my booties as he thrusts inside of me, pressing me into the unstable stall divider behind me. His finger, which hasn't drifted far, finds its way to my clit and moves quickly, faster than his thrusting–vibrating almost. I try to hold off as long as I can, but the electricity surging through me is too much. Overwhelm consumes me as I tighten around him, paralyzed by the energy running through my veins. Grabbing the back of his neck roughly, I pull his face to mine, kissing him hard enough to make my lips tingle along with the rest of my body.

The second he pulls out, the door of the bathroom flies open, slamming against the wall behind it and shocking me back to reality.

"Dean! Maci! You two in here?" a familiar voice comes from a few feet away. I recognize it as the bouncer, Jace, who we've made friends with since we started coming here every few nights.

"Yeah, man, we're in here." Dean laughs, but I can see his face turning as red as mine feels. He runs his hand through his hair then leans his neck back into it as it rests behind his head.

I'm assuming Jace is waiting for us because I haven't heard the door shut or his steps walking away. We adjust our clothes, and I throw my hair in a ponytail quickly. Shoot, I still need to pee.

"Come on, guys, don't make me have to do this. You know I need to kick you out."

"Yeah, we know," Dean replies through the door.

I shove his shoulder lightly. "I have to pee. I'll be right out."

"Okay." His eyes wander over my face for a moment, and he smiles before he brings his hand to my neck and kisses me on the forehead, easing my nerves. Then he slides through the stall door, pulling it closed behind him, and encourages Jace out of the bathroom.

Once I'm finished, I reach for the handle, now close enough I can hear them. "You know I love you guys, but you can't come back."

I slip out the door to see the two of them standing there, Jace with his arms folded across his chest, not looking too happy. I feel bad we put him in this position. He and Dean have been friends for a long time, but he still has to do his job. I lean into Dean's back, trying to hide my embarrassment. He chuckles as he pulls me from behind him and leads me to the entrance of the bar, following Jace.

"Come oooon man. I've been coming here forever, and I bring all my friends every week," Dean says in a slightly begging, but a little bit "this is bullshit and you know it" tone.

"I know, I know, okay, stay away for the next month. When you come back, no more of that." He flails his hands around in the direction of the bathroom, with a laugh and an eye roll.

"Thanks, Jace! See ya in a month!" He laughs again, his hand on my back, guiding me through the door.

As soon as we are outside, I cover my face with my hands in total embarrassment. I do not know what came over me. I mean, I do know. I'd do anything Dean asked me to, but I'm not sure why it's Dean that makes me feel this way.

He grabs my hand and drags me a block down the sidewalk, then pulls me into the alley between Jameson's and the next bar over. Before I can say anything else, he pushes me against the brick wall, his lips finding mine in the shadows. I melt into his kiss because I can't help myself. Bringing my arms around his neck, he pushes both his tongue and his body into me more. His lips unstick themselves from mine as he kisses gently up my cheek until he reaches my ear. "Worth it," he whispers, then grabs my hand and pulls me back out onto the sidewalk.

CHAPTER TWENTY-SIX

I'm finishing a shift at the café when my phone vibrates in my pocket. I pull it out and smile.

Dean: *"Hey, you. End of the quarter party tonight, my house, bring your friends."*

Ooh yay! Finally an invitation to one of his parties.

Me: *"Only the single ones?"* I joke, knowing every time we are at the bar he tries to push Marcus and Aden toward girls.

Dean: *"You know it."* He adds a wink emoji.

I group text Kylie, Taylor and Alexis and let them know we have plans tonight. I don't include Avery because she and Miller took off to his parents' cabin for winter break vacation right after she finished her last final yesterday.

Thirty minutes later, shortly after I get home from work, someone bangs on my front door. Taylor yells through it. "The car is running, let's gooooooo!"

I run to my room, unzipping my work jeans as I go and pull my favorite long sleeve maroon dress off the hanger. I know it's December and freezing outside, but this dress cinches perfectly at my waist and makes my boobs look great. Plus, I'm betting Dean will have a bonfire out back since there will probably be way too many people to be inside. I'm sure I'll be fine. I grab a school sweatshirt on my way out in case I need it and hear Alexis honking her horn as I lock the door.

It's clear they are ready to party because before I can buckle my seatbelt, Taylor wiggles a flask in my face. "No thanks." I laugh.

I've seen pictures on social media of the parties Dean throws. It's why I'm making assumptions about the bonfire. I've still never been invited to one, so I'm curious why now. I'll take what I can get, though. I wonder if this is a sign he wants to make us official.

The bonfire flames are so high I can see them from where we've parked on the street. Since Dean always comes to my apartment, I've only been to his house the one other time. I don't know my way around yet, but it's easy enough to follow the light. Heading around the back of his house, Taylor and Kylie are already giggling as they pass the flask back and forth between them. As soon as we get to the edge of the yard where the fire blazes, I spot Aden and Marcus, along with a bunch of other people I've never met.

Marcus comes over right away, pulling me into a side hug, his sandalwood aftershave making me linger an extra second. He's easily my favorite friend of Dean's that I've met. He's about to offer me his own drink when another red Solo cup appears in front of me, attached to Dean's hand.

"Hi," he says, waiting for me to take the drink from him, not offering any affection along with it.

"Thanks." I sigh, gazing into the fire. He's been so good lately about giving me attention, I wonder if something is wrong. It's only been a minute though, so I shouldn't jump to conclusions.

Dean starts talking to Marcus about something, but even though I'm standing between the two of them, I've already zoned out.

Besides the moment when we first got here, I haven't seen Dean. He wandered off a few minutes after he brought me a whiskey. My cup is empty now as I spin in a slow circle, my eyes searching for his sandy blond hair and his flannel that doesn't match his cargo shorts at all. I finally spot him standing under the porch light with a blonde girl I've never seen before. She's cute. How the hell is she not freezing in that skimpy skirt and tank top she's wearing? She's practically flashing him.

"That's Cassie," Marcus' voice breaks through my thoughts. "We've known her forever, and she is Dean's ex-whatever you want to call her, from last year. Be careful around her. She acts sweet and like she's your friend but swoops in the second she sees him near you. She's been trying to get his attention again for months."

"Oh, okay, thanks for the heads up." I feel like Marcus has been on my side since I started seeing Dean, whatever that means in our situation. It's nice having someone in my corner.

"Not that you have anything to worry about, though. Not about him wanting another girl anyway."

I want to question if there's more meaning to that second statement, but Taylor stumbles up to me. "Maaciiiii, let's get out of here, I'm hungryyyy," she wails. I put my hands on her shoulders to steady her as she falls slightly into me. I don't want to leave, but I'm also not having much fun either. Not to mention it seems like Alexis started drinking and someone has to make sure my friends get home safely. I give Marcus a hug and wave goodbye to Aden as I round up my friends and get them into Alexis' car. I'm not in the mood to stop and wait for a pizza, so I order one to be delivered to their apartment before we leave.

As we pull up to the complex, a text pops up on my phone.

Dean: *Where are you? I miss you.*

My stomach drops seeing the words he's never said to me. I go to grab it, but somehow I'm not as quick as Alexis, who rips it off the phone mount. "Awwwwww how sweet is thiiiiis," she says in her high pitched drunk voice, showing the screen to our friends in the back seat. She's shaking it far too much and they are way too drunk to read it.

I roll my eyes, but no one sees.

"Be back soon, babe," Alexis sends back with a kissy face emoji before I'm able to process what she's doing and grab my phone back.

"Ugh, whyyyyyy, Alexis?!" I practically scream at her.

"'Most beautiful man I've ever laid my eyes on.' You said that, remember? Don't act like you don't want to go back. Take my car and get out of here. There's not enough pizza coming for you anyway." She winks dramatically.

I'm more worried about the girlfriend-y word she attached to the end of the text than admitting I want to go back in the first place. Before I can figure out what to do, my phone buzzes again. I hesitate, nervous to see his reply.

Dean: *Hurry, please.*

I panic for a second thinking something is wrong, but then I note the "please" and figure it must not be anything truly urgent or important. Come to think of it, nothing ever seems urgent or important to him. I actually think it's something I like about him. It's helping me feel less in a rush and less like I need everything to be planned right this second.

The girls get out of the car, but not before they shoot me a few wiggling eyebrows, make a few kissing noises and tell me to have fun. Eye roll again. I wait to make sure they get inside their apartment before I pull out of the complex.

I make the ten minute drive back to Dean's, questioning myself the entire way. He told me to come in the first place but didn't hang around at all. Now all of a sudden he misses me? I'm confused, but I want to see him more than anything. How could I not when I walk down the hill of his backyard and he turns around, a smile instantly lighting his face when he sees me? Seriously, the most beautiful man I've ever laid my eyes on. He doesn't walk to meet me, but as soon as I get within reach, he pulls me into a tight hug. The earthy smell of his body wash fills the air around me, and I breathe into his chest until he lets me go.

"Where were you!" he exclaims, but then immediately turns to respond to something Aden said. I choose to ignore his question and sit on the log that has been turned into a makeshift bench in front of the fire. A minute later Dean realizes I've sat down and grabs my hand, pulling me to my feet. "Let's go inside," he says with a glimmer in his eyes.

Ooook. So *that* is why he wanted me to come back.

A ton of people are still partying in his backyard, but even though everyone is drunk, it's pretty quiet. Quite a few people are chilling by the fire or sitting in the camping chairs on the back porch. "Let's get a drink instead."

Without saying anything, he just smiles and leads the way to the porch. He man hugs his buddy when we make it up the hill. I don't get a drink because I didn't actually want one. Whenever I'm around Dean, my mind is intoxicated enough. I've been confident about how each night will end with us for a while now, but we are in a new situation and with how hot and cold he is tonight, I don't want to count on anything. I want to make sure I'm good to drive if I want to leave.

He introduces me to his friend, who is also a psychology major apparently. We start talking about the professor for the Psychology of Drugs class we've both taken because wow, did that lady seem like she was the one on drugs. His friend, whose name I've already forgotten, is telling me a story when I see Cassie, the girl Marcus pointed out earlier, approaching from the corner of my eye. Ugh, what is that bitch still doing here? I've already decided I don't like her even though we have never met. The last thing I want is competition for Dean's attention. She takes advantage of the fact that he's standing there, half listening to us, but not engaged in the conversation.

"Heeey, Dean," she says in a flirty voice.

"Cassie," he replies in a flat tone. "Have you met Maci?" His fingers brush against my arm to get my attention.

"No." She glares for a split second before she plasters a fake smile on her face and reaches out to shake my hand. Rolling her eyes, she turns into Dean's friend, leaning far into him like she's trying to make a point, which is evident by the way she looks back to see if Dean is watching.

That quiet laugh escapes his lips right before he winks at me then pulls me into another hug. He whispers into my ear, "I'd choose you over her any day, babe." It wasn't lost on me that he used the word "babe" for the first time, though not loud enough for anyone else to hear it–like he was sensing and trying to ease my insecurity.

The back porch lighting is dim, but I can see Cassie glaring. He puts his hand on the small of my back–the place it tends to gravitate–and starts talking to no one in particular. "Well, we are headed in for the night, friends. Someone put the fire out when you leave!"

I don't like what he's implying to everyone by us going inside together, but the look on Cassie's face is worth my uncomfortableness thanks to his public declaration.

When we get inside, he closes the door behind us, heading straight ahead to the kitchen sink to grab himself a glass of water. He stays quiet as he takes a sip then sets his cup on the counter. I pick it up to take a drink too, keeping my eyes locked on him the whole time, searching for answers. I am seriously conflicted. Sometimes he has me questioning if he's hiding something or being weird. But then other times it feels like that might all be in my head. More often than not when he's with me he acts like he doesn't care about anyone else in the room and isn't afraid if they see that. I sigh and look away from him as I set the water down. He walks around to the side of the counter that I'm on–his hand finding my back again–and leads me to his room.

We sit on his bed, silence filling the space between us for a second. I have no idea what the hell to say to him right now.

"Where did you run off to earlier?" He seems genuinely curious.

"I was taking my friends home. They were convinced they needed pizza at that very moment."

"Oh, so you're not drunk?"

"No. I wasn't sure when I would be driving home, so I didn't want to risk it. Why?"

"What do you mean? I invited you over. I don't want you to leave. I never want you to leave." There's confusion in his eyes, like he doesn't realize his actions contradict his words tonight.

"Were you drinking?" I question because I can't really tell with him. He's usually chill all the time. Although maybe it's that I don't know him well enough to see the difference.

"Nah, wasn't feeling it tonight," he says with a nonchalant shrug as he leans in, his body pushing me backward until I'm flat against the mattress and he's hovering over me. "I prefer something else as my drug of choice." He leans down and kisses my collarbone softly, continuing up my neck, until he reaches my mouth. All of a sudden he pulls back, bringing his eyes to mine. "You know, you're the only girl I've ever not used a condom with." He says it quietly, but matter-of-factly, as if it was a sentence people say all the time. His lips crash back into mine, this time with much more intensity and urgency. I'm trying my best to not totally freeze and to participate in what's happening, but what? I pull back to say the last part aloud, along with a nervous laugh. "What?" Surely he can see the confusion in my scrunched-up face.

"Yeah..." His voice gets softer, like he realizes it was a weird thing to say but knows he can't backtrack now. "When we were at Jameson's... I didn't plan on that happening. I usually think before I act. I've never followed through on something I was unprepared for like that, but I didn't care about anything but being closer to you."

He's talking as if this is a big deal for him. As weird of a confession as it was, it felt genuine, and if it's true–I don't know why it wouldn't be–he *must* be feeling a similar connection to the one I do. He runs his hand up my arm before it catches around the back of my neck. It shoots a tingle through my entire body. There's no way he doesn't feel something like this when he touches me. I mean, it's nearly impossible to help myself around him. I swear I'm under some spell that's created a current constantly pulling me toward him.

"I really like you, Dean." The truth tumbles out of me quietly as I search his eyes. I can hear the nerves in my own voice at my confession.

"I know. Me too." He hesitates, like he wants to say something else. Instead, he leans back down to kiss me. Once I give into it, there's never any talking myself out of it.

Avery: *Hey, do you have a date with Dean this weekend?*

Me: *We don't really make plans in advance. Why, what's up?*

Avery: *I was thinking we'd ditch boys and go on our own date! Sweet Cheeks Winery is having a girls only night! It can be our Christmas date a week early since Miller and I are going back to the cabin with his parents in a few days. You in?*

Me: *YES!*

"Have fun ladies!" Miller yells out the window as we climb out of his car in front of the winery. Avery reminded me this was a date and made me turn back around to put on my black fit n flare dress and tights when they stopped by to pick me up earlier. Especially the last few years, her focus has been mainly on Miller, and I can't fault her for that. If Dean wanted to spend as much time with me as Miller does with Avery, I can't say I wouldn't be the same. That being said, when it's just the two of us, she's all in, and I love that about her.

We find a table inside by the full-wall window that overlooks the vineyard after ordering a full bottle of Rosy Cheeks at the bar–it's the best wine they have, hands down.

"Sooooo," Avery starts. "What's up with Dean these days? Taylor said she didn't see him at all at his house last week?"

"I think he was just busy since it was his party. When I went back, he wouldn't let me out of his sight. There was some other girl there. It was like he was trying to make her… I'm not sure. Mad?" I take a sip of my wine and look away, knowing my best friend will be a little judgy about this. I'm not sure why I brought up that part.

Her eyes narrow. "Like… trying to make her jealous or trying to show her he's taken?"

"From what Marcus said, I think more to get her off his back. But he sure wasn't shy about ditching his party for me." I lean forward onto my fist and sigh happily recalling the end of that night.

"I just want you to be happy and be in a relationship you deserve. If he's giving you what you need, then I'm happy."

"I really like him, Avery. Like I've never felt like this about someone. I know that sounds crazy because it hasn't been very long, and especially since I still don't know everything about him, but our chemistry is un-real. I can't imagine that's easy to find, and that has to count for something."

"It does, and it's a good starting place for sure. Checks off a box on your senior year plan too!"

"Right! I mean he is basically my boyfriend, just with-out the title. Taco Tuesdays ended up being more like taco Thursdays, but whatever, still counts. And I have gone to run club every week, sometimes twice. I'd say

I'm doing well for only being a quarter into the school year!"

"Feels good, huh?" She grins.

"Yeah, it really does."

CHAPTER TWENTY-EIGHT

The only time we go to Dean's is when he hosts parties. Apparently, since Marcus and Dean moved in, it's been the go-to place for all their friends because they are the only ones with a house and a yard instead of an apartment. I like the parties and his friends because they are chill–nothing like the insanity of Troy's fraternity's party.

The fire is already blazing by the time I get there. I'm dressed much more appropriately tonight than the first party here, but I still put in effort. I can't help but want to look good for Dean. I've got on dark blue jeans that make my ass look great, and I curled my hair and put on more makeup than just mascara. I was going to wear a cute sweater, but at the last minute opted for Dean's maroon hoodie he let me borrow on our first date. He never asked for it back, and I never offered it. It's a little big on me, but this color looks good against my hair, and it's comfortable. I'm hoping I can get it to smell like him again.

I walk down the hill to where Dean is throwing a few more logs on the fire to make it bigger. Marcus and Aden are the only other ones here so far. I passed them stocking the coolers on the patio on my walk over to the fire. When Dean catches sight of me, he pauses mid log throw.

"Hi! Anything I can help with?" I look at his hand holding the wood.

He drops it into the flames, his heated eyes ripping his clothes off me. Without saying anything, he walks up to me, picks me up and tosses me over his shoulder before heading up the hill. I can't help but giggle the entire way to the patio, slapping my hands playfully on his back, half-ass begging him to put me down. As he opens the sliding back patio door, Marcus looks up from the cooler, a smirk on his face.

Forty minutes later, with my fallen curls tied into a ponytail, I slip back outside. Dean had to run to the convenience store around the corner to get ice, so I decide to get a drink while I wait. At least twenty people arrived while we were inside. I head to the cooler and pick out a lemonade Truly. I crack the top and turn to walk toward the fire. As I lift the can to take a sip, hearing my name causes me to freeze mid-drink.

"Maci?"

I spin on my heels to face the patio again. "Troy? ... Hey. What are you doing here?"

"I'm here to party?" he says, like it's obvious, but adds, "I played football in high school with one of the guys who lives here."

Wait, he and Dean are *friends*? That's weird. "Ooh, okay, that's cool."

"Yeah, what about you? You're the last person I expected to see tonight."

"Don't worry, I won't be repeating the mistakes I made last time." I genuinely laugh at myself, thinking back to how drunk I was at his fraternity's party. I have been much smarter about my alcohol since then.

"Sooooo, you'll let me talk to you this time?" Ironically, his joking tone is what halts my laughter.

"Umm, I mean if you want. But I'm sure whatever we were going to talk about then doesn't matter anymore." I say it gently–I'm not trying to be rude. I truly don't care why he ghosted me anymore. If he hadn't, I probably wouldn't have met Dean, and as much as I wanted to see where things went with Troy at the time, the way I felt around him is nothing compared to the way my body lights up in response to Dean.

"I guess not, but I did want to explain myself. I figured I at least owe you that."

"It's okay, Troy. Really. Water under the bridge or however that expression goes." My skin itches, begging me to leave the conversation. It's not that I'm upset by Troy being here–I've moved on from it. I'm searching my brain for a transition to another topic when a hand lands right on my ass. I turn my head back to see Dean as he speaks.

"Troy." He says it firmly, in a "back off" tone, but still reaches his free hand out to fist bump his friend.

"Hey, Dean." His eyes flash back to me, landing first on Dean's sweatshirt covering me, then to where Dean's lips meet my hair as he kisses the side of my head. "Ahhh." Realization flashes across his face, and he smiles like he's genuinely happy about this new information. "I'll see you guys around. Talk to ya later, Maci."

As soon as he is out of earshot, Dean turns to me like he's waiting for an explanation of my interaction with Troy.

"Are you okay?" I ask, trying not to laugh at the way his eyebrows are furrowed together. I don't know why this entire situation is funny to me.

"You two had a thing, didn't you?" He's upset, like he caught me in a lie.

I wrap my arms around his waist and pull myself into him. He's hesitant at first but then lets me. "I wouldn't call it that. We went out once, and he ghosted me. Apparently, my type is guys who can't commit." I shrug and laugh to myself. I'm not mad, I just think I'm funny.

He isn't amused. "That's not funny. So, if he hadn't done that, you'd probably be with *him* right now."

I stand on my toes to kiss him. His eyes don't even close. "Dean." I switch my tone to match his seriousness though I don't know why this created an argument. "You know how I feel about you."

"I have an idea," he mumbles.

"I don't want to be with anyone else. You know I want to be with you. What's gotten into you?" I'm still on a high from the way Dean ravished me in his bedroom a half hour ago. How could I think about anyone but him? His jealousy is absurd, to the point it's comical. "You're acting all commitment-y. If it makes you feel better, you could just decide to let me be your girlfriend right now." I grin at him, not expecting him to take the bait or necessarily caring if he does. I'm surprised when he stares back at me like he's actually considering it, but he doesn't respond. "Or we can go back inside, and I can return your favor from earlier if you need a little help relaxing." I attempt a wink at him.

Finally, his face cracks with a smile. "Later." He pulls me into him and leads me toward the fire.

CHAPTER TWENTY-NINE

Me: *What are you and Miller up to tonight?*

Avery: *Hanging out with his parents at the cabin. We might as well be married already. Haha What about you? Plans with Dean?*

Me: *I wish, but no. He has to work tonight.*

Avery: *He's still at the hot tub place, right? Isn't he the only one there when he works? You should go hang out with him.*

Me: *I guess I could ask.*

Avery: *Just show up!!*

Me: *It's not crazy?*

Avery: *He shows up last minute whenever he wants to see you all the time. It's only fair you're allowed to do the same. Do it! It's New Year's Eve, Maci. What better way to start the year than showing him you want to spend it with him?*

Me: *Yeah, you're right. I knew you were my best friend for a reason.*

By the time I pull into the small gravel parking lot of Dean's work in my dusty red Corolla, there's only an hour until midnight. I start to think of reasons why showing up unannounced is a bad idea, but remember what Avery said. Dean and I have been hanging out for two months now, and if we are going to act like we are together most of the time, spending almost every night together, and him acting with the possessiveness and insecurity he did around Troy, then I have every right to make choices based on that.

It's reasonable to want to revisit the idea of putting a label on our relationship at this point. It's time to figure out what's holding him back from taking that small extra leap and giving us a real chance and a label.

I get out of my car and lock it, looking over toward the check-in counter. I can see Dean from here, but I doubt he can see me, even if he turned around. His "office" is a freestanding five by five room. There's a door on the side nearest to me and a giant open window on the wall next to it with a counter directly below it. It's made of the same type of wood as the hot tub rooms–cedar, I think. He's sitting on his swivel stool, in his usual navy Carhartt jacket and blue swishy pants, facing away from the opening. It looks like he's on the phone. I wonder if his phone voice is different from his regular one. Sometimes my customer service voice comes out when I work at the café, and it drives me crazy.

I'm not trying to eavesdrop, but as I get closer, it's easy to make out some of what he says. He sounds like his normal self, but I can hear annoyance in his voice. "I know I need to. I'm going to tell her soon." He twists slightly back and forth. One of his feet is propped against the back wall creating the motion. My stomach drops. Who is "her?" I'm not trying to assume it's me, but it's hard not to jump to conclusions. I wonder who is on the other end of the call. Sounds like someone he's willing to be vulnerable with.

Whoever is on the other line must pass the conversation back to him. "Mom, I will, I promise. She's just going to be upset." Another pause. "It doesn't matter how I feel about it." His irritation is evident as his foot kicks off the wall hard enough this time to spin him around. I'm still a few feet back from the building, but I'm in his line of sight now. He grips the counter to stop his spin. "I have to go, Mom, I'll talk to you later." He sets his phone down.

"Maci, hi." The way he's looking at me, I know he's trying to determine how much of his conversation I heard. "Sorry, I didn't see you there."

"It's okay, I just got here. Is everything okay?" I try to hide my anxiousness as I take a step closer, and he opens the door to let me into the little office.

"Yeah, it's fine." He pushes the door shut behind me after I walk through.

"Is it okay that I'm here?" I was confident by the time I got here, but now it seems like I've invaded his space.

"More than okay."

"Are you sure? Sorry I didn't text you first. I just wanted to see you and wasn't sure if you'd check your phone at work." I'm still about a foot away from him.

"Come here." He reaches out for me and pulls my body into him, both his arms wrapped around my neck and crossing over themselves. When he holds me like this, my head lands perfectly at the top of his chest. My arms wrap around his waist out of instinct. "You could show up anywhere, and I'd be more than okay with it," he mumbles into my hair.

I try to pull back from our hug, but he doesn't let me. Instead, he tightens his hold, like he's worried I'm going to leave him.

I stay close to him this time but loosen my arms from around his back, letting my hands slide forward to his hips. "Dean?"

He relaxes his hold on me enough that I can see his face now, his dark brown eyes shifting over my face, his blond hair pushed to one side, and his face a little red from how cold it is. "Yeah?" His tone comes off... sad? Defeated?

I chicken out of what I actually want to ask him and say the first thing that comes to mind. "I've never kissed anyone on New Year's Eve before. I thought maybe you could help me with that."

His smile is half-hearted. "I *can* help you with that." His arms loosen all the way from their hold around my neck, and he runs his hands down my arms. The way his entire body language exudes vulnerability for the first time in my presence gives me a moment of courage.

"Ummm... also..." I pause. My heart beats so loudly in my chest I can hardly hear my own thoughts. I've told Dean I like him before, and I've asked for clarification, but I've never been *that* clear on how I feel about him. I can't expect it from him if I'm not willing to give it too. And I'm pretty confident we are on the same page.

He gently guides me back toward the stool. I push my feet off the floor, helping myself up to sit on the seat. He takes a step forward, positioning himself between my legs. My knees fall on either side of his thighs, as he holds me in place with his hands on my hips. He waits patiently for me to finish my thought.

"I want to tell you..." I bite into my lip before continuing. "I've never felt this way about anyone before, like I need you. It kind of makes me want to throw up." Nerves swirl in my stomach, threatening to expel themselves at any second. "Can we talk about us being officially in a relationship or what's holding you back? Did you go through a bad breakup or something?" It all comes out of me in one breath that I breathe back in as soon as I'm finished. I can feel the tension and worry in my face as my lips pinch together in silence. I stare at him, waiting for his response.

A soft sigh leaves him before any words. His eyes close for a moment, and when he opens them, the words come too. "No, this isn't about anyone else. I've never been as serious about anyone as I am about you. But–"

"Hey, I'm here to check in." A man's voice comes from behind me, and Dean's attention shifts toward him.

Dean shakes his head as if to bring himself back to a world that consists of more than only us. "Hey, man. Yeah. 11:00?"

"Yeah."

By the time Dean finishes checking in the guy and his girlfriend, there are a few other people waiting as well. I slide the stool to the back of the office so I'm out of his way while he's working. All the possible options about whatever he was going to say flash through my head. *I have to calm them.* I pick up the book he's been reading,

Eat Smarter, and smile. I love that he reads books most people wouldn't read even if they were assigned them in school. I open it and start reading.

The next almost hour flies by and with check-in times every 15 minutes leading to midnight, Dean is constantly helping someone get set up with their room. When I checked earlier, my weather app said it would get to 35° tonight. I'm cold, even through my puffy black jacket. A 103° hot tub, looking at the stars? It sounds like a nice way to spend the evening. Although it kind of ruins it when I remember Dean telling us most people come here to hook up. I suppose after our sexcapade in the bar bathroom stall, I shouldn't judge.

I check my phone at 11:58, as the only customers I can currently see are walking away from us, toward their room. As I look over to Dean, the guy who interrupted us earlier comes back into view. "Hey, I wanted to check to see if there was any way we could stay an extra half hour longer?"

"Oh yeah, of course. It's not a problem." Dean doesn't seem bothered by the late request.

"Thanks, man. I thought my girl might want to go home after we got engaged, but turns out she wants to stay here. The stars are something else tonight, huh?"

"Yeah, it's nice out here. Congrats, man. Take as long as you want." I can't see Dean's face from where I'm sitting, but I can hear the genuineness in his voice. Right then he looks at his watch. "It's almost midnight though, you should get back to your girl. Especially since I'm going to need a minute to kiss mine." He doesn't wait for the guy to respond before he turns toward me.

I don't have time to smile in the two seconds it takes him to make the three steps that close the distance between us. As he does, both of his hands slide through my hair. His fingers are warm against my cold ears and hot air from his breath heats my face for a second before his mouth lands on mine. His intensity causes the entire stool to slide back until it hits the wall. A gasp slips from me, but he swallows it, as he deepens our kiss. It's hot and needy, almost desperate, and I can't get enough. As I pull him back between my knees, I feel him hard, against me. He groans into our kiss at the gained connection between us.

We are a tangle of tongues, our hands running all over each other's fully clothed bodies for a half hour straight. We don't stop until we finally notice the line of customers ready to check out. By then I'd temporarily forgotten our conversation remained unfinished.

CHAPTER THIRTY

I'm dreading this entire week. It's the first week of the new quarter and nothing is going on besides going over the syllabus, but I still show up so I don't miss anything. I grab the metal door handle, but when I tug on it, a hand stops mine. Before I can look, I'm being pulled away. My heart races, and from the tingle shooting through my wrist and up my arm, I know it's Dean before I confirm it.

I always know.

He pushes through the exit door that leads to the stairwell, pulling me through and waiting for it to slam behind us. As soon as he hears the click, my back is against the wall, his fingers thread into my hair, and his mouth crashes into mine as if it's an emergency only cured by my kiss. My arms finally relax, falling to his waist and pulling him into me. I'm addicted to the times he acts as if he *has* to be close to me.

His kissing slows, as if he got what he needs to survive and now only needs to make sure his life support doesn't go anywhere. After what must be at least ten minutes, he pulls back enough for us to lock eyes for a moment. I'm about to question how he knew which class I had, but his eyes flick to the door as he says, "Let's go back to my place."

Ugh, why does he have to look the way he does when he wants something like that? He's wearing dark khakis that fit him very well and a nice maroon and burnt orange flannel with the sleeves rolled above his sexy forearms. His hair has that messy, sexy thing going on, his smile looks like he's up to something, and he just looks like Oregon. I love everything about it. I'm so distracted by taking him in that I forget he asked me a question. "Maci, you coming?" He pulls me back to reality with his words and a single kiss.

"Umm, I have class."

"Nooo, play hooky with me," he whines, only a few inches from my face. This side of him is a little more playful than usual. He tugs on my wrist again.

"Fine, fine." I wonder what's different about today. I want to find out, so I let him lead me out of the building and toward his truck.

Holy shit. Every time we do that, I swear it gets better, and I have no idea how. Something felt different about this time. The way he took his time with me, I swear he was making sure no part of my body was left untouched, unappreciated. It felt less lusty than normal and more... I'd say like lovemaking, but that's a little far-fetched. More savory, maybe? It could be my hopefulness, but it did feel as if... he had a little more feeling invested in it than normal. Either way, my mind is mush. I shake my head to try and clear it. We never finished our conversation on New Year's Eve because

I wasn't sure how to bring it up again. He's been busy every day since then, so this is the first time I've seen him.

Getting up to go to the bathroom, I glance back to a satisfied looking Dean on his bed, hands folded behind his head, abs begging for my hands to run over them again. Maybe things *are* about to change between us. Finally. I wonder if I could get away with bringing up the shift I'm feeling, if he'd be more open this time, especially without anyone else around to cause a distraction. My gut tells me something has changed.

When I come back, he stretches one arm out, waving me back to him. That's weird. We aren't really the cuddling type. Even though he's pretty affectionate, especially lately, we haven't cuddled after sex at all since the few seconds after our first time.

I slip my underwear on, then grab his T-shirt off the floor and slide it over my head before crawling back onto his bed and sitting cross-legged facing him. "Hiiiii." I say it with a bright smile. I can't help the way he's making me feel today.

I watch his eyes scan my face. "You look happy." He gives me a half-smile, but then it fades.

"Yeah, why wouldn't I be?" I pause. "I mean, we are pretty good at that." I laugh, my hand falling to his thigh, but the way he glances at where our skin touches makes me uneasy all of a sudden. I can't put my finger on it, but something is off.

Grabbing a handful of my shirt, he tugs until my mouth is on his. He doesn't deepen our kiss but moves his hand from its hold on my shirt so he can slide his fingers into my hair.

He breaks our kiss, and when I pull back slightly, he looks at me like he's studying my face. After a few moments, he maneuvers slightly to reposition me so I'm lying next to him rather than on top. When I'm where he wants, he pulls me into him until my head rests in the place it fits perfectly on his chest. After a moment of lying there, I wrap my arm around his waist, and he squeezes me closer to him. I can feel his heart beating hard with my ear pressed into him. Something is definitely off because he rarely seems nervous. His name is coming out of my mouth at the same time he starts talking.

"So... there's something I need to tell you."

I swear my heart rate jumps by at least 50 beats as I try to sit again so I can look at him. The arm he has wrapped around me keeps me pinned to his chest, as if he can't say what he needs to if I'm looking at him. Panic rushes through me in the seconds he's letting pass by without continuing his thought. I search for possibilities in my mind, but it's filled with nothing but fear.

He scratches my back softly and releases a deep breath. "I'm moving." He pauses before he adds, "To Costa Rica."

My stomach immediately knots. I must have heard him wrong. Did he say moving? "Wait, what?"

"I'm graduating early, I'm actually already finished. Now feels like the right time."

My mind goes blank. "Well, that's... cool." Cool? Maci, what the hell is wrong with you? Why did I say that? What is happening? This isn't cool.

His thought matches mine. "Cool?" He does that little laugh he does before letting out a sigh.

"That was a dumb thing to say. I don't know what to say. I'm confused." This time when I move to sit and face him, he lets me.

"I know. No one really knows. I've been wanting to tell you but..."

"...But you didn't want me to stop having sex with you? Or what, Dean?" I don't recognize my voice with the anger that's laced through it. I couldn't stop myself.

"You know this isn't about that," he whispers.

"I know, I'm sorry. I didn't mean that," I say much softer. My eyes fall to my hands folded in my lap. All of a sudden overwhelmed with emotion, I'm fighting back tears harder than I ever have.

When he sits too, I'm reminded about the intimate moment we shared a few minutes ago and how little clothes we have on. This feels weird. I feel naked and vulnerable but not just physically. He moves one of his hands to rest on mine, his thumb rubbing slowly back and forth across my skin. "This is harder than I thought it would be." It's a whisper, under his breath, as if he was talking to himself.

Pain shoots through my gut as his secret runs through my brain again and an ache consumes my entire body. "Hard for who, Dean?" My eyes flash to his, which are focused intently on me. "On New Year's Eve I basically told you I lov..." My voice breaks on the words I can't say and his thumb freezes against my hand. I watch his whole body tense. His reaction makes me angry, so I take a breath in an unsuccessful attempt to calm myself. "And you were going to say what? *That you want to leave me?*"

His lips part slightly, and he starts to say something. Immediately, he closes his mouth. I search his eyes for a hint of what he's thinking. I could swear they are screaming out against this moment, like his soul doesn't want this to be happening any more than I do, but I must be mistaken. I must be projecting what I wish he was feeling because there's no way he loves me too. If he did, he wouldn't be doing this.

I pull away from him, my face falling into my hands in defeat. I can't look at him, at what's happening.

When his voice finally breaks through my thoughts and the silence, it's soft. "What I was going to say doesn't matter because it doesn't change anything." He gently tugs my hands away from my face, then cups my cheek, nudging my gaze back to him again before he continues. "I don't want to leave you, or us, but this is something I have to do, and I'm not sure when I'll be coming back."

"There's an us?" My voice cracks again, and I know he can see the tears in my eyes as I glance up. We've basically been in a relationship without the title, but this feels like a breakup for a commitment he never officially made. That stands out more to me than the news that he's moving or whatever else he's refusing to tell me.

"I'm sorry. I know this screws up what we have," he whispers without directly answering my question.

His words are a weight, crushing my chest and making it hard to focus on anything else. "When?" It's the only other thing I can seem to say aloud.

"I leave on Friday."

"That's in three days." I'm surprised I can figure out the math right now.

"Yeah, which is why I wanted to let you know..."

I cut him off, my voice strangled. "Let me know? I don't understand why you're leaving." I swipe angrily under my eyes to catch a couple of tears before they fall.

"I don't think you will. No one else seems to." Through my blurred vision, I see the conflict in his eyes, like he wants to try and explain but he's had a similar conversation with someone else, and he doesn't want to risk it going badly again.

I'm torn too, between needing an explanation and wanting to lean into him before he's not here anymore. The way he's acting feels final, like even if I tried, there would be no changing his mind. He's also never elaborated on anything before, so I doubt he'd start now. Without saying anything else, I lie back down but face away from him. He lies down too, the heat of his chest against my back warming me, though I can't stop shaking. I scoot back into him. He wraps his arm around my waist, pulling me to him, as close as he can. Tears sting my eyes as I attempt to process what he told me. I'm cursing them to not fall, but they disobey me.

"Maci," he whispers.

I shake my head against him.

Quiet sobs come out of me and don't stop. His forehead presses into the back of my head and he tightens his grip around me with each cry that escapes aloud. The way he's holding me contradicts everything else that is happening. My heart is breaking for me, but an unexplainable gut feeling makes it shatter for him. I don't understand how it can feel like this is so hard for him when it's his choice, but I'm overwhelmed by my thoughts and whatever emotions are radiating off him. I'm confused about what's happening, and the longer we lie here, the harder I cry, until I'm exhausted enough to fall asleep.

We leave his house for what is probably the last time, after what was the best sex I've ever had–until he sprung his big news on me right after. The car is completely quiet. We don't speak, and there's no music on the radio–nothing to drown the overwhelming static from my thoughts. Trying to make sense of how yesterday was about to end perfectly, then actually finished with me realizing it would be the last time that could ever happen, seems impossible.

He shifts his truck into park in front of my apartment. With the engine still running, he looks over at me. My hand is already on the door handle because as much as I don't want this moment to be over, I need to be as far away from it as possible right now. I hold his gaze until I feel the tears coming back. I wish he'd kiss me. Or say something. Mostly, I wish he'd tell me this is a joke. But I know he's not going to, so I can't stay here any longer.

I close the door softly behind me and walk up the path. Right before I reach the door, I swear I hear my name, but when I turn around, Dean isn't there anymore.

In three days he won't even be in the country anymore. He's getting on a plane and moving to Costa Rica. He's not just going on vacation. He's packing and leaving without any intention of coming back for the foreseeable future. Like the idiot I am, I didn't ask a single question. I didn't say much besides "That's cool!" because what the hell do you say to the guy you're crazy about picking up his life and taking it to another country? Also, I didn't know he was graduating two quarters early. What's his rush? I've been "not dating" dating this guy for months now. How did I not know this?

Maybe the same way I didn't know he was moving to another country until a few days before he was leaving. He didn't want to tell me.

This is why he never officially committed to a relationship. Last night was the first time the thought of it ever came from him since his almost accidental slip up, and now that I'm thinking about it, we don't even know each other's middle names. I'm crazy to think this was anything real. But damn, I'd say we were at least together enough for a little bit more warning than that. I mean how many other girls does he have no condom sex with? He told me none. *That* seemed like a necessary thing for him to note, but this didn't?

Walking through the front door expecting to be alone, I'm surprised to find my best friend sitting on the couch, phone in her hand. The second she looks up and sees me, tears pour from my eyes. By the time Avery realizes what is happening and makes her way to me, I'm already on the floor, my back against the door, choking on sobs that shake my entire body. She wraps her arms around me tightly, waiting for me to speak.

Somehow, I manage a few sentences. When she pulls back, confusion covers her face, not because she couldn't understand me through my tears, but because she just doesn't understand.

Welcome to the club.

CHAPTER THIRTY-ONE

I can't be mad. Traveling the world is something I have been dreaming about for as long as I can remember.

Jealousy? I feel like that's justified.

But how can I be mad at Dean for following a wanderlust as strong as mine–arguably stronger since he is acting on it–and I'm over here just making lists. I'm assuming that's why he's going. I can't believe I didn't demand more information. I was upset, shocked. Either way, did he have to just up and leave? What kept him from telling me? Could he have waited and taken me with him? Could we have tried long distance? Would that have been crazy to ask?

His last text to me–the only one since he dropped me off–said: *I'm glad I met you, Maci. I'll be happy if we run into each other again down the line. Also, I'm going to be living in and visiting some pretty amazing places, and I would love for you to visit.*

I never responded because *what the fuck*. It felt like there was both a level of finality and an open invitation. One last time, I was left confused and exhausted from attempting to decipher his thoughts. I've been trying my best to ignore it because it's only been a week since he left, and I'm losing my mind. I want to be done.

It's also been a week since I've gone anywhere or done anything. I only showed up to my classes to avoid sitting at home, trapped in my head. Thank goodness it's only the first week because I'm too busy attending my own pity party to spend time studying.

I'm going out tonight. I need to. I don't want to be around anyone, but I'm self-aware enough to know I shouldn't be alone with my thoughts.

I drag a brush through my tangled brown hair and swipe on mascara, for my own sake. I change out of my sweats and into jeans for the first time this week. When I walk into Jameson's, a friendly face greets me at the door. "Hey, Maci, has it been a month already?" Jace jokes.

"Oh shit, I think so. I don't know, I'm sorry," I mumble apologetically.

He catches onto my lack of usual friendliness, and his voice softens. "You know I don't care. I mean, hell, I can't even blame Dean."

I cringe at hearing his name. "Yeah, I know. Thanks, Jace. I just need a drink."

"Well, you're in the right place. I'm sure Jess has a spot at the bar for you."

I find a seat at the end of the bar, in the dark corner closest to the bathroom, where the low lighting match-es my mood. Jess comes over almost immediately when she sees me. "Hey, girl!" She sets a whiskey sour in front of me. "Missed seeing your face around here, maybe you could stay out of trouble... or out of the bathroom for a little while," she jokes. Great, will this be a thing from now on? I don't know why I thought going out would help me escape Dean. Then again, coming to this particular bar probably wasn't appropriate for that goal. I just want to feel connected to him, even though I can't be.

This is pathetic.

"Don't worry, the trouble isn't coming back." I mean it in more than one way.

"Oh no, what's up?" She glances at the rest of the bar. "Actually, I need to work, we are slammed. I'm sorry, we'll chat later?"

Before I have a chance to respond, a voice comes from behind me. "Don't worry, Jess. I'll take it from here."

Marcus sits on the empty black leather bar stool to my left, and I turn toward him. His dark brown hair is pulled back into a messy bun, and he's grown a thick beard since the last time I saw him a month ago. He looks good this way and better than I look right now. When his dark brown eyes meet mine, I only see pity in them. "Hey, Marcus." I lean into the bar, my head barely being held up by my hand.

"You look like hell." He laughs.

I stare back at him, unamused.

"Come on, Maci. Cheer up. You deserve more than to let a guy take you down like this."

"This all could have been avoided if he didn't lie to me," I spit at him, but he doesn't seem offended by my tone.

"I wouldn't call it a lie. It just took him a while to tell you. He kind of kept it from everyone." He shrugs before reaching for the bourbon Jess set in front of him.

The way he lumps me in with "everyone" makes me hate myself for thinking I meant something different to Dean. I shift to self-preservation mode, on a mission to prove how shady he was, like it'll keep my heart from crumbling more.

At least a dozen memories shuffle quickly through my head, trying to find an example of a lie. My thoughts stop on our moment in the kitchen, the morning after the first time we had sex. Wait. I repeat myself aloud. "Wait. The first time I stayed at your house, he knew then, didn't he? I mentioned Costa Rica when I saw that book on the counter, and he got all weird."

"I don't think he had decided anything at that point." He's not necessarily defending Dean. It seems like he's trying to help me control my thoughts. He doesn't have to be here, and it's nice of him, but it's hard to reign in my frustration.

"Okay, but what the fuck? He could have at least mentioned it. I should have seen this coming. I'm such an idiot," I mumble into my red straw before taking another sip of my drink.

"I know it might not seem like it, but telling you was really hard for him. He wasn't trying to intentionally hurt you. Dean is a good guy, and he knows this is his loss."

I want to believe him. "I wish that made this easier."

"It sucks, but if you truly care about him, you should support him doing what's best for him, even if it means leaving. Just like he did what he thought was best for you by breaking things off before he left."

I hadn't thought of it that way. Even if I still don't understand why he left, he genuinely seemed torn up telling me he was leaving. I could sense how off his energy was that entire day from when he pulled me out of school to when he took me back home the next day. But the way Marcus talks about Dean's feelings... it's lacing my thoughts with false hope I can't afford when being together isn't a possibility anymore. It doesn't matter if he felt the same because he's gone. If I don't believe that, I'm not sure I'll ever get past this.

After another drink, both the conversation and I lighten up, and Marcus and I end up going dancing at the bar next door. I'm having so much fun, for a moment I think I'll be okay. I stop dancing mid-song, reaching my hand out for Marcus' muscled bicep. He turns toward me.

"Thank you for this."

He pulls me in for a hug, bringing me close enough to smell a trace of sandalwood and sweat. "I'm here if you need anything." He pulls back and digs his phone out of his front pocket, opening it to a new contact page before handing it to me. "Dean asked me to look out for you, but just because he isn't here, it doesn't mean we can't still be friends too."

He keeps making statements that contradict my new beliefs of how Dean feels about me. I don't know what to think about it. But I've liked Marcus since we met, and it can't hurt to have another friend. I take his phone from him and enter my number. I text myself and wait for the vibration in the back pocket of my jeans before handing his phone back.

CHAPTER THIRTY-TWO

I need to knock off this pity party. At least I'm not drowning in my thoughts anymore–rather walking through the water and refusing to choose dry land. I don't do anything but go to school and pick up shifts at work. I haven't been out with the girls since... long enough ago they stopped asking me. I quit showing up for the running club. The last time I went anywhere was Jameson's that first week in January. It's March now. It's clearly driving Avery insane because she comes home even less. For sure it's driving me insane. I'm annoyed with myself. I have got to get out of this funk.

I pull up my best friend's name from the favorites section of my phone and send her a text. *Taco Thursday?*

See you at 5! Flashes across my screen before I even set my phone down.

One of my favorite parts of my friendship with Avery is we get over everything quickly, regardless of who pissed off the other, or what happened. I know she's not mad, but I also know I haven't exactly been a pleasure to be around.

The second our apartment door swings open, I practically leap at her, wrapping my arms around her neck. "Hi, best friend! I love you. I'm sorry I'm a psycho over a boy. I'm done with that now."

She giggles and pulls away to show me the bottle of Patrón she brought with her.

"Just what the tacos need!" I exclaim.

We are two shots in before the tacos are ready, reminiscing about the time we drank a shot of every type of liquor in her dad's alcohol cabinet in high school. We play the voicemail we left for ourselves that night so we could recall our experience the next day, to make sure it's still there, and to take pride in how far we've come since then.

"Sometimes it doesn't feel like I've come that far since high school." My laughter is replaced by a sigh.

"I've been thinking about your dilemma, and I have a possible solution," she says as she pours us another shot in the green and gold glasses my parents sent us from Ireland for my birthday. We took at least two more during our flashback. I've lost count of what number this is.

"Oh yeah, what's that?" I roll my eyes.

"You should hit up Mack."

"Mack, your brother Mack?" She must be joking.

"That's the one!" she says as I stare at her, trying to discern if she's serious or just drunk.

"I mean, you're my best friend, and he's my brother. I brought it up jokingly a few months ago, but the more I thought about it, the more it made sense. I know you both better than anyone else does and think you'd be great together. A dating app can't even be that certain!" The level of volume in her voice has increased with her level of drunkenness.

Avery and I have been best friends since the 6th grade. Her brother is two years older than us, but even though our high school years overlapped, and he's close with Avery, I never spent much time with him. He was either out with his friends when I was over or playing in his band. I think the last time I saw him was at our high school graduation. I remember him being there and joining Avery and me at dinner with my parents since their parents never showed.

We must follow each other on Instagram because I see pictures of him here and there. I know he lives in California. I know he has the same dark brown hair Avery does, and the same piercing green eyes–because that's not something you forget. Outside of that, however, I don't know much.

"I'm serious!" she practically screams at me, seeing I'm still unsure of her intention. "He asks about you all the time."

"Really?" I narrow my gaze. "I mean, I am your best friend, so it makes sense."

"No, no!" She waves away my thought. "He asked me last week if you were still seeing that guy from high school. You know, he's coming here next weekend for a visit."

"You know I'm all for wanting to leave the state I'm in, but I don't think it would be fair to anyone, let alone

Mack, to jump into something new when I'm not completely over the old thing."

"It's been two months, Mace. You haven't heard from Dean once. He's not coming back, and you can't wait around forever to see if he does. I'm not saying you have to marry Mack, although that would make us sisters sooooooo."

"I can accept we aren't supposed to be together, or at the very least, we got screwed by poor timing. It's that I worry if I had no idea this was coming, how can I trust myself not to get into the same mess again?"

"You live and you learn, Maci. Maybe you will get hurt again or make another mistake. You're going to keep learning until you're ready for whatever the right thing is. But that right thing won't come along if you don't give it the chance and you don't keep trying. You might be surprised what you come across on your path if you just keep walking."

Her drunk honesty stings a bit. I know she's right, but I don't want to deal with it right now. I change the subject to Miller, knowing it's a topic that will distract her. She goes on about how they are hoping to find a house by the end of the school year and how she hopes he proposes soon because it's killing her not knowing which ring he picked.

We've talked about this before, so I know it's coming, but it still makes me sad to think about losing my best friend. I know she won't be far, but it won't be the same. My sadness clears when we shift to wedding planning. Even if it's not set in stone yet, it's inevitable, so it doesn't hurt to brainstorm.

We eventually stop drinking when we realize we've made it halfway through the bottle. Thank goodness tomorrow is Friday, and I don't have anything to do until work at night. I pull out a spare toothbrush and my face wash–knowing Avery has moved practically everything she owns over to Millers'–before I head to bed.

CHAPTER THIRTY-THREE

The sun streaming through my window burns my eyes, and my head pounds. I need water. Knowing Avery is already gone, I don't bother dressing before heading into the kitchen. After chugging an entire glass, I set it on the counter and pick up my phone. 11:17. I really slept in. I turn down the brightness on my screen before checking the two text notifications. The top one is from Avery: *Love you best friend! See you next Thursday to finish that bottle!* I cannot handle drinking that much. Even three months ago when Dean was still here and we were going out all the time, I only ever had one or two drinks, so I never built a tolerance. I rub my temples as if it will help my headache then refill my water. I take a sip as I look at my other text.

It's from a 541 number, but not one saved in my phone.

Hey stranger. I heard you and my sister have learned how to manage alcohol better these days. There's a wink emoji sent in the following text.

I freeze with my water glass in my hand then set it down, like holding my phone with two hands will help me focus. Obviously, it's Mack. What did Avery say to him? Did she talk to him last night when we were drunk and joking about us dating? Or this morning when she was sober?

Me: *Hey, we did the best we could with no one around to teach us the way.*

I lean my hip against the counter, waiting for the three dots to turn into words.

Mack: *I may have known how to control my alcohol back then, but I don't think I would have been able to control myself around my sister's best friend while drinking it.* He leaves off any emojis he could have added for context. Is he serious or joking?

There is no way he looked my way back then. Did he? I mean, I hardly ever saw him, and I can't recall a specific conversation we had before this one.

I still haven't decided on an appropriate response when another text comes through.

Mack: *I thought you knew I had a crush on you. Didn't mean to spring that on ya, Mace.*

Avery is the only other person who uses that nickname for me. I would have thought it would be weird coming from anyone else, but my stomach flutters when I read the word.

Me: *I thought you were kidding.* I throw in a laugh emoji to make it clear I'm not upset about this revelation. At least, I don't think I am.

Mack: *Oh yeah, Avery had to talk me down so many times. She always made me leave the room when you were at our house. She mainly didn't want me stealing any of her time with you. Didn't keep me from being curious, though.*

Me: *You know I had a boyfriend like all through high school, right?* I laugh to myself about the oddness of this conversation.

Mack: *Oh, I know. But you don't have one now, do you?*

What is happening? It's weird having this conversation out of the blue. That and the fact Mack is so forward–which is not something I'm used to.

Me: *Nooope. You'd think I'd have time to find one with how often Avery is with Miller, though. Speaking of, if anyone knows, it's you. When will I get to start wedding planning?*

Mack: *Wow, Maci, at least let me take you on a date first.*

Me: *You know what I meant!* Eye roll.

Me: *A date couldn't hurt, though.*

I feel a little guilty sending that text, knowing very well there is a part of me that isn't over Dean yet, maybe ever. I would never want Mack to feel like I was using him to help me with that, but also, it's Mack. Even if I don't have the same relationship with him as I do with Avery, he has still been in my life for over a decade, and that sounds like a safe place to start.

Mack: *Don't sound so excited. Lol Sunday then? I get in Friday night but promised Avery I'd hang out with her Saturday before her "best friend steals me away forever."*

Me: *Wow, she's not putting pressure on this at all. I mean, I love you by association and all, but I haven't seen you in years.* I hit send before I realized the I love you part was weird.

Mack: *Are you surprised? That's my sister for you. Look, no pressure coming from me. How about we ignore Avery this weekend and any plan or ideas she throws our way? Whatever happens, happens.*

Me: *Okay, okay, deal. I'll see you this weekend, Mack.*

CHAPTER THIRTY-FOUR

The door swings open, and Avery hops up from the couch. She leaps at her brother, completely ignoring Miller, who has barely had a chance to make it into the entryway. Mack's deep laugh is muffled against his sister as he steadies himself so he doesn't fall over. When she steps back to let him walk into the room, he looks exactly how I remember, just a little older. His hair is a darker brown than Avery's, but he has the same jade green eyes. I know he played soccer in high school, and I vaguely remember him coming home from the gym with his friends on occasion or from a run on the weekends. I always considered him attractive and fit, as much as you would consider your best friend's older brother while you were in a relationship.

He still has a varsity team preppy vibe, but now, something about his body seems different. More mature maybe. He's a little edgier with his backward hat and a hint of scruff on his face. His blue jeans hug his ass perfectly, and I can see the definition of the muscles he has now under his plain black T-shirt. When he looks over to me, he smiles enough to light up his eyes, and my face burns.

He walks to the couch, waiting for me to greet him. When I stand, my anxiety spikes with each of his steps, but the second he pulls me to him, a wave of calm rushes over me. It's similar to the feeling I get around Avery, like I'm safe and have nothing to worry about. This is another level, though–like I'm melting into his arms.

"Hi, Maci." He says it like I've been away far too long and have finally arrived home.

He smells like cinnamon, but a little sweeter, and I lean into my urge to breathe him in. "Hi," I whisper on my exhale.

I snap back to reality when I notice Avery's matchmaker eyes staring at us as she wiggles her eyebrows enthusiastically. Pulling away, I sit back on the couch. Mack slides down next to me, close enough our thighs touch, as Avery walks over with a potholder and a tray of pizza rolls she just pulled out of the oven. Miller stops her before she reaches the living room and demands a kiss. After appeasing him, she sets our dinner on the coffee table in front of the couch.

"Thanks for picking up Mack from the airport," Avery says to her boyfriend.

"Anything for you, babe. And Maci." He shoots me a wink before sitting on the floor on the opposite side of the coffee table.

Oh great, he's in on the scheming too. I should have known they would be conspiring together on this like they do everything else. I roll my eyes. Mack chuckles but changes the subject. "This is such a warm welcome," he jokes as Avery runs back to the kitchen for plates and hot sauce. "I guess this is you returning the favor after all those years of me making the two of you after school snacks, huh?"

"Yeah, except I'm a broke college student, so I skimped on the veggies you always forced us to eat."

Avery sticks her tongue out at her brother as she joins Miller, sitting cross-legged on the floor.

An image appears in my mind of Avery and me sitting at her kitchen table after school doing homework, like we did at least a few nights a week. Her dad was usually at the bar, or at least that's where we assumed he was. I don't remember Mack being there whenever I've recalled this memory in the past, but he clearly materializes into the picture as I think of it now. He always made us something to eat when we got home. It was usually simple like pizza rolls or spaghetti, but now that I'm thinking about it, there were also always vegetables. That's such a strange thing for a teenage boy with no parental guidance to be conscious of. It's weird enough I feel the need to mention it. "Wait, what fifteen year old always remembers the vegetables?"

Avery pauses, a pizza roll halfway to her mouth, now curious too.

Mack stares at me like he can't remember the answer. "I thought you knew."

"Knew what?" Avery asks, a look on her face equally contemplative as mine.

His glance bounces between the two of us, before settling his eyes on me. "Your mom. At the beginning of the week she'd bring over a box of precut veggies and freezer meals. She'd tell me it was because she didn't want you eating all our food, but I knew..." he trails off as I sit there with my mouth open. I guess at thirteen we didn't even question it even though it's clear now what my mom was really making sure happened. Something I love about Avery is that she has never been ashamed of her parents or used them as an excuse for how anything in her life has turned out. She's proud of herself for how much she's grown despite them. By the way he delivered this new information, I can't tell if Mack feels the same.

A surge of love for my mom overwhelms me, but I also feel a rush of emotion thinking about Mack and how hard it must have been for him to take care of not only his sister but also me. I'm not sure what to say in response to this revelation. Thankfully, Mack speaks again with a change of subject. "So, how's house hunting going, Sis?"

"Oh yeah, about that..." she trails off. "Miller and I are looking at a few tomorrow. There are a few we love, and now that we have our loan pre-approval, I don't want to risk losing the perfect one. Don't hate me, but, rain check?"

"I fly all the way here from another state to visit you, and then you ditch me. I see how it is," he jokes.

"Oh shush. Maci told me she doesn't have plans tomorrow, I'm sure you two can find something to do instead." She shoves her last pizza roll into her mouth. "Also, I'm getting kind of tired. I think we'll head out and stay at Miller's tonight. You can sleep in my bed, Mack. Only if you need to." She sends an obnoxious and exaggerated wink our way.

Subtle.

"Avery!" I catch a slightly hurt look on Mack's face as I say her name with evident frustration. It's just a lot all at once. I know Avery is trying to help get rid of the currently super lame and depressing version of me. Plus, we are at the age where instead of being annoying, it would be a dream to have your best friend and brother fall madly in love. I just don't want her to get her hopes up. Before I jump into anything, I want to make sure I'm confident in what's going on and how

I feel, and I don't know him well enough to make any kind of judgment yet.

Ignoring me, she hugs her brother and grabs her purse off the counter. "I love you both!" She reaches for Miller's hand, ready to leave. She walks out, but I follow them both before the door swings closed.

"Avery," I plead. "I can't believe you're not staying tonight. You know how awkward I am. He's going to wish he hadn't come before the night is over. It's like you're leaving me alone with a stranger!"

"Okay, first, take a breath," she laughs. "This is Mack we are talking about. You have known him since you were like 12. It's going to be fine. He's such a good guy, Mace. As much as it would be magical to have my best friend date my brother, you know I wouldn't be pushing this if I didn't think you would be good together. If it doesn't work, it doesn't work, but I think it's worth a try."

"Okay." A mix of defeat and nerves washes over me.

"It'll be fine, Maci," Miller chimes in, giving me a reas-suring shoulder squeeze.

"Okay, now go back in there and have such a good time you feel weird telling me about it!" She smacks my butt as I turn around to walk back inside.

I close the door behind me and engage the deadbolt. "Well, that was…"

"Predictable?" A smile lights Mack's face as I return to my spot next to him.

"Yeah, that." I know I look nervous as I pick at the chipped, dark purple polish on my nails. His hands reach over and cover mine, calming them.

"Maci, take a breath. I'm not here to murder you. I know you probably thought you had more time before you were stuck with me alone, but it's kind of your fault if you didn't expect this move from Avery." He chuckles.

There's something about the way he talks to me. He takes everything seriously but also makes it lighter. I'm much calmer just being this close to him. "Let's turn on a movie and hang out, exactly what we would be doing if my sister hadn't ditched us."

He flips on the TV, putting the remote down before he even attempts to scan the channels for something to watch. Be normal, Maci. You can do this.

I turn toward him and pull my knee up, so it rests against his thigh. "So, tell me all about California." I imagine my eyes go starry because I can't help but instantly daydream about any place that's not here. It's not that I don't love Oregon–I do. There's just so much more of the world out there, and how will I know if there's a place I love more if I don't explore it?

"Hmmm, what do you want to know? The weather is perfect all the time. There are as many taco stands as there are Dutch Bros Coffee here. Where I live is only forty minutes from the beach. You would love it."

"You hardly know anything about me, so how would you know that?" I tease, knowing I would, in fact, probably love California.

"What's not to love about sunshine and tacos?" He smirks. "Tell me, what *do* you love, Maci Jackson?"

"I don't think I know." He looks at me with an arched brow, so I clarify. "I mean I know what things I love. Day trips to the beach with Avery. Live music, anywhere. Those pizza rolls were freaking good. Oooh, I took an interesting psychology class a few months ago that I loved." I'm rambling now. "I want to say I love to travel, but I haven't really been anywhere. I mean in the U.S. I have, but I want to try international travel. I guess I don't feel like I can know what I truly love or want if I haven't experienced enough. Does that make sense? Is that weird?"

He looks at me like he's studying my face. "Nah, it's not weird at all. I get it. I kind of felt the same before I moved to Cali. I had my band here and the guys I played soccer with, but nothing that really got me excited. Even though my band moved with me, it's different. We have a real stage to play on, we get to go on tour every once in a while, it's a different experience." He shrugs. "Plus, home should be somewhere where there are as many tacos as there are in California."

I twist my body slightly so I can lean into him and rest my head on his shoulder. It's a bold move for me, but if I'm going to make an effort, I want to commit and feel out my chemistry with him. It's comfortable, like I've known him forever, but I'm trapped in this weird place of knowing I technically have and haven't all at the same time. "I think I'd like California."

"You should come visit sometime." He doesn't seem bothered by our new level of contact. "I keep inviting Avery. Maybe you can talk her into coming down sometime before the wedding."

I shoot up. "Umm, are you holding out on me Mack Michael Torres?!"

"That's not my middle name." He laughs as he wraps his arm around me, pulling me back closer to him.

"Don't change the subject. Do you know something I don't?"

"Nope." He pops the P. "I wouldn't tell you anyway." He rubs his thumb along my shoulder. I can feel him smiling through the way his body shifts.

"What if I was your girlfriend? Then would you tell me?"

Panic rushes through me at the same moment he pulls back enough that my head falls off his shoulder. "Wait, let me backtrack. That came out wrong," I blurt before he can say anything. "I mean–"

Amusement splashes across his face before he cuts me off. "Are you always this nervous, or do I just bring out the best in you?" He says it more jokingly than judgmentally, trying to ease my nerves. Something about the way he talks is soothing.

"Well, I'm always awkward, but I mostly blame you for the nerves." I held back my thoughts so often with Dean, worried I'd scare him away more from the commitment he was never willing to make. I don't want to do that again.

Mack's face goes serious. "Are you nervous because of the situation or because of me?"

"Ummm." I take a moment to think about my response. "Both? I rushed into things in my last... not relationship. I fell fast and let my emotion cloud my ability to read the situation. It shouldn't have been such a shock when he left."

"Try not to beat yourself up too much. We are always a little blind when it comes to the people we care about most. I think one of the reasons my dad started drinking so much was because he felt guilty for not seeing a sign my mom was going to leave. It's easy to feel like it's your fault, but all you can do is be upfront and learn where to draw the line if others aren't willing to do the same."

"I tried not to worry about making it an official commitment because the rest of it was there. I should have been more concerned about the reason we never took that step. Maybe if I had realized that was an important line, I could have saved myself from the inevitable heartbreak." I sigh, feeling that pain creep back in.

He nods. "Is that important to you? A title?"

I turn toward him, sitting crisscrossed. My heart races, but this level of transparency is what I want. "I tried to convince myself it wasn't, but I guess I want to feel like if I'm all in, the other person is too? Now I'm nervous because I don't want to get hurt again. I'm afraid I won't be able to navigate a relationship any better this time." *Dang it. I did it again.* "Wait, sorry. I'm not trying to make it sound like you and I are going to be a thing."

He tries to hold back a smile, but it slips through for a second. I instantly worry what I've told him was dumb. "I understand. Well, for the record, here's where I'm at: I was in a serious relationship before I moved to California. I was with her for a few years, and we lived together. In the interest of full transparency, it was my fault it didn't work out. I realized I had a lot of shit to work through because of my parents' relationship, or lack thereof. It took a while, but it's finally all sorted, I think. I can't say I'm perfect, but I can say that when I do decide to try again, I'll be ready to commit."

The way he offers so much information freely is encouraging. "Thank you for telling me all that. So, this girl..."

"Not in the picture. Even if the timing had been right, we weren't right for each other." He rests his hand gently on my knee. "I'm not naive enough to think you and I could be right together when we don't even know each other as adults. But so it's clear, I'm interested in taking the time to find out."

"A few days ago I would have been against the idea, but being with you right now, I'm a lot more comfortable than I expected. I think it's worth trying to see if there's anything here." I laugh quietly and add, "If not for our sake, at least to get Avery off our backs."

He smiles and pulls me in until I'm leaning against him again. "I think so too."

CHAPTER THIRTY-FIVE

I'm lying on the couch, with a blanket folded over me when I wake to the smell of coffee. Gross. The best part about Avery always being at Miller's is the morning coffee smell left with her. Wait, I thought Avery left last night?

Oh. Shit. *Mack.*

Did I tell him last night I would try this? Am I really ready to date? Dean still partially occupies my mind. I don't want to hurt anyone if it could be prevented, especially Mack. According to Avery, he's had a crush on me since high school. This isn't something I should rush into knowing he already feels stronger about me than I do about him.

"Morning." His voice comes from the kitchen, a little scratchy from using it for the first time today.

I sit, an involuntary smile appearing on my face. "Morning."

"I made coffee. I wasn't sure how you liked it, so I tried to make it the way Avery likes it."

"Ummm, I actually hate coffee," I say, dramatically covering my face with my hands, peeking through my fingers to check his reaction.

"Oh, thank God, so do I. I have no idea if this would even taste good to someone who liked it." He laughs as he dumps the entire cup into the sink. He's making such an effort already. As long as I'm honest with him, I at least owe it to myself to try. Bad timing isn't a good enough reason not to explore this, and it's not like Dean is coming back to sweep me off my feet. "So, we have the whole day to ourselves! If you are free or don't feel the need to run away from me yet." He breaks me from my thoughts, looking at me and waiting for an answer.

"I was planning on going to the Saturday Market. Can you still handle the cold, or are you too 'California' now?"

He smirks. "You might need to hold my hand to keep me warm."

I grin, shaking my head as I stand from the couch to change.

Despite not getting a lot of sleep last night, I'm not tired. Poor Mack, I've been dragging him up and down every aisle of the market. On Saturdays, the city blocks off a few streets downtown, covering them in at least seven or eight rows of folding tables and pop up tents. He's patient as I stop by every booth. He stands just behind me with his hands in his pockets, and I feel his eyes on me the entire time. There's nothing I want to buy, but I love experiencing how excited all the shop owners are about their crafts. It's cool they've found something that makes them so happy they are willing to stand in the freezing cold to share it with the world. I hope I find something I love enough to freeze for someday.

After I've thoroughly checked out every single table, I send Mack to find us somewhere to sit while I head back to the food stands. He tried to come with me so he could pay, but I insisted on putting together the perfect brunch for us. I don't know what he prefers yet, so I play it a little safe. I land on two different types of crépes, a matcha fruit smoothie, a freshly squeezed lemonade and a plate of french fries because that's always a safe bet.

"Wow, this is quite the assortment," he declares, helping me with the three plates and two cups I carried across the Market.

I shrug. "Sometimes you have to go with your gut, even if it makes no sense, ya know?"

"I do know." His expression says he's referring to something else entirely. "So, what did you get us?"

Either I got lucky with my choices, or Mack really isn't a picky eater because all our food is gone within a few minutes. As he's throwing away our plates, a band starts setting up on the lawn stage. "Ooohhh, can we please stay? I looovee live music." It's already easy to be myself around him. I'm not sure if it's because I assume he knows what I'm like, since his sister is my best friend, or because I'm genuinely comfortable around him.

"Of course. You know I play live music... like for my job... all the time, right?" His eyes flicker with amusement.

"Oh yeaaah, well, it's easy to forget when I've never heard you play before."

"You knooooooow," he drags out dramatically. "I'm playing at a local bar in a couple of weeks. By local I mean to me, obviously. You could come if you wanted."

I search his face for confirmation he's being serious. It's one thing for him to come here, where his sister lives, and spend time with me, but it's another for me to go someplace I've never been.

I go with my gut. Not listening to it didn't work out for me before, so maybe it's time I do. "Alright."

His eyes go wide. "Wait, really?"

I nod as he pulls me into a hug and kisses the top of my head.

The band is good, but I keep finding my thoughts wandering between what it'll be like to see Mack play and slightly freaking out about how I agreed to go to California in a couple of weeks. I'm broken out of my trance when Mack's phone dings with a text. A moment later he stands, reaching out his hand for mine. "Let's go! We have somewhere to be!"

"We do?"

"No questions, Mace, just trust me."

We pull into the driveway of a house I've never seen, in a part of town I haven't been through. It's nice. There are a lot of gated communities and beautiful trees that arch over the roads. *Where are we?* A rope swing hangs from the oak tree in the front yard. The surrounding grass is mostly brown but sprinkled with green now that it's almost April and the sun has been making an appearance. The one-story house is freshly painted light blue with white trim. We get out of the car, and I follow Mack to the door, which he opens without knocking.

I stand frozen in the doorway, trying to put together what is happening. The house is completely empty, but I didn't see a "For Sale" sign in the yard, at least not that I can remember. Sensing my hesitation, Mack turns around and smiles, grabbing my hand and tugging me into the entryway. "Maci, come on."

I follow him down a hallway until it opens into a kitchen on the right. When my eyes scan to the left, I panic. Avery is standing there, collapsed into Miller's arms as he holds her. It sounds like she's crying. She looks up at my gasp.

"Maci," her voice cracks. She pulls away from Miller and runs toward me. She flings her arms around my neck. I sigh in relief when I realize her tears aren't sad. "It was perfect. I didn't want to jinx it in case something happened, but we found this house last week, and we fell in love with it. Our offer got accepted today. We came back to walk through it again." She's talking fast and crying so much I can hardly understand her. "He said, 'Avery, the only thing that would be more perfect than this house is if you would be my wife.' And look!" she shrieks, pulling away from me so she can shove her hand in my face.

After fully examining the most beautiful ring I've ever seen, I glance up to see that Mack has made his way to Miller. He's looking at his sister with the biggest grin on his face, and I can see how genuinely happy he is for her. Earlier today he told me how grateful he is that Avery is part of such a healthy relationship. Since their dad is an alcoholic and their mom left the year before I met Avery, they haven't had the best role models for relationships. From what Avery has told me, her parents used to fight so much, it was a relief when her mom ran away. As much as my heart breaks for them, and I can't wrap my head around how parents could abandon their kids–especially kids like Avery and Mack, it makes me melt a little on the inside watching how proud Mack is of Avery for choosing a different path. I'm thankful they have each other.

Avery pulls her hand away from me to run back toward the boys. She slaps Mack on the shoulder. "You knew about this, didn't you! I can't believe you didn't tell me!"

Mack laughs as Avery leans into Miller, holding her hand out in front of her face to examine her ring again.

CHAPTER THIRTY-SIX

After a celebratory dinner with Taylor, Alexis, Kylie and a few of Miller's friends from high school, we agreed to meet everyone at the bar. We arrive first, at Jameson's. The location was Mack's suggestion. Apparently, this is one of his favorite bars too. He walks in first, and I'm surprised when Jace greets him by name. "Hey, Mack! Haven't seen you in a while. How ya been?"

"Hey, Jace. I'm great. Just visiting from Cali for the weekend. This is Maci." He steps forward, giving me room to stand next to him.

"Maci! Haven't seen you in a while either."

At the same moment Mack looks to me to get confirmation I already know the bouncer, I watch Jace's eyes flash between Mack and me, confused, as if he forgot Dean was gone.

"Oh, I didn't know you two knew each other! Small world," Mack exclaims, unbothered.

"Yeah, I've come here before," I respond to neither of them in particular.

"Yes, you have." Jace winks at me, and thankfully Mack doesn't catch it.

Eye roll.

"I'm going to the bathroom, get us drinks?"

"Deal." He smiles and makes a beeline to Jess, who is behind the bar.

I leave the bathroom and head straight to the bar. It's busy, so I doubt Mack has gotten our drinks. I spot him right away, but he's not alone. The guy next to him stands there in his go-to gray jeans and black V-neck. *Oh shit.* That can't be good.

Marcus must sense someone standing behind him because he turns toward me as I approach. "Maci, hi!" He immediately leans into a side hug. He's got his hair pulled back like the last time I saw him, and I can smell his sandalwood scented beard balm with his face so close to mine.

"Do you know everyone here?" Mack laughs.

"Do you know Marcus, too?" I question, pulling out of the hug.

"Oh yeah, we go way back to two minutes ago. How do you two know each other?" He's more curious than threatened.

I glance at Marcus for a moment before deciding which truth to go with. "He's Dean's friend." I look over at Mack to gauge his reaction, which is total confusion, seeing as I've never said Dean's name, and he hasn't put it together.

Marcus cuts in. "Hey, we are friends too."

"Thanks, Marcus. Well, this is Mack, in case you didn't get that far." I don't introduce him as my best friend's brother like I would have in the past. Part of me doesn't want to see him that way anymore.

"Nice to meet you, Mack." He reaches to shake his hand. Mack does the same, and I wonder if realization has hit him that Dean must be the guy who wrecked me.

"Yeah, you too."

"You look much happier than the last time I saw you, Maci. I'm really glad. I'll see you around?"

I nod, leaning into another hug before he walks off with his bourbon.

By the time the bars closed last night, we were all far too drunk off love and tequila shots to organize the sleeping situation and a bunch of Ubers going to different places. The four of us ended up going back to mine and Avery's apartment since it's closer than Miller's. The second we walked in the door, Avery and Miller stumbled into her room, with their lips and eyes locked on each other the entire way.

"Gross," Mack had commented with a laugh. He slept on the couch, even though I offered to let him share my bed so he could be more comfortable. He did come into my room after I brushed my teeth and was climbing under the sheets. He pulled my purple comforter over my shoulders and whispered something about having a great day with me, kissing me softly on the forehead before heading out to the couch. It was sweet. I had a great day with him too.

The sun shining through my window woke me. Not long after, Avery came into my room, flopping herself onto my bed hard enough I wouldn't be able to go back to sleep if I tried. Now we whisper random comments to each other as we lie under my blankets, scrolling social media, waiting for the guys to wake. I'm half listening to whatever she's rambling about, and half paying attention to my Instagram feed as I scroll aimlessly. My thumb freezes on the screen when I see a picture of Dean holding a surfboard on the beach, and my heart instantly does that weird thing that happens when you take a big drop on a roller coaster.

I haven't thought about him much this weekend, so it was more of a gut punch than I expected. As I'm clicking on his name to unfollow him for my own sanity, Avery notices the crack in my composure.

"What's up?"

"I'm freaking out a little. Tell me everything that's wrong with your brother because he seems too great." I'm dead serious, but she laughs.

"I told you he's great, but you didn't believe me. That shouldn't be a problem, Mace."

"I know. I'm just worried, I guess. I don't want to hurt him because I'm still hurting from Dean. And I'm worried because there's no way dating my best friend's brother could be as magical as it sounds. It's normal and comfortable to be around Mack. It's too good to be true–it has to be."

She grabs my shoulders, shaking me far too violently for how much I drank last night. "Take a breath. Mack is a good guy, and he's not Dean. It's not fair for you to place the same worries on him when he hasn't done anything to deserve it... yet." She laughs, trying to lighten the mood before she continues. "You deserve something good, but you're only going to get it if you give everything a chance to work out, okay?"

"Okay, okay." Right then, there's a knock before Miller's face appears in the doorway.

The four of us are squished onto the couch, there's a soccer game on TV, and Miller ordered us a pizza. Mack's flight leaves tonight, so we don't have a lot of time left together.

I walk to the kitchen to get plates and napkins so we are ready when the pizza arrives. When I return to the couch, Avery and Miller are in their own little world chatting about the wedding and the house. Mack looks up from his phone when I sit next to him again. "Soooo, were you serious about wanting to come out in a few weeks?"

"If you are."

"Your birthday is November 9th, right?"

How does he know that? "Yes."

"Okay good..." he clicks on his phone screen before looking back at me. "Because I booked you a flight."

"You didn't have to do that. I could have gotten it." I bite into my lip, holding back a smile.

"It's not a big deal, I'm the one who invited you. Plus, I owe you for buying me lunch yesterday." He shoots me a wink.

I grin at him and lean into his shoulder as he wraps his arm around me. I definitely want to give this a chance.

I pull up in front of the passenger drop-off area and walk around to where Mack steps out of my car. Before I can say anything, he pulls me into a hug, his sweet cinnamon scent warm and comforting. "See, that wasn't so bad, was it, Mace?" he whispers in my ear.

"Hmmm?"

"Whatever scenario you had worked up in your head from all the pressure Avery put on this weekend." He pulls back slightly with a grin on his face.

I bite the edge of my lip, breaking our eye contact. So many possible responses run through my head before I decide on, "I suppose it could have been worse."

He squeezes me tight again before turning to walk away. "See you in two weeks!"

I wait until he's through the automatic glass doors before getting back into my car. It hadn't occurred to me until that moment that we haven't kissed. I mean, I want to–I really want to–but it doesn't feel the way it did when I was around Troy or Dean. I haven't doubted his interest in exploring this at all, and I don't feel like there's a rush. Patience is foreign to me, but I'm excited to see what happens next with us. It's easy to be around him, and I'm comfortable with how things have progressed these past two days. Like Avery said, I just need to relax, enjoy it and let it play out how it's supposed to happen.

CHAPTER THIRTY-SEVEN

Me: *Still on for tonight?*
 Mack: *Duh, did you decide what we are watching?*
 Me: *I was thinking Pitch Perfect? It's my favorite movie! And they just added it on Netflix.*
 Mack: *Sounds great, babe. See you tonight.*
 He's never called me that before. It feels normal but makes my stomach flutter anyway.

My laptop is on my coffee table with the movie paused on the opening scene, ready to press play. I know it sounds lame to call this a date, but it feels like it. Plus, it's the closest thing we can do right now. We've been texting all week, but I haven't seen his face since he left a week ago. I'm not sure why that makes me anxious. My finger is hovering over Mack's contact when his incoming Facetime call pops up. My heart races as I hit accept.

"Hey, babe." I can see his smile reach his emerald eyes when the videos load. His phone is propped against something in front of him, and he's sitting on a couch, adjusting his black backward hat as he greets me.

"Hiiiiiiii. I miss you! Is that weird? I've only seen you once. I'm weird. Ignore me. How was your day?" I word vomit at him.

He laughs. "Maci, we've known each other for like half our lives. It's not weird."

"I mean, not reaaaally. No offense, but you were always just Avery's older brother I never saw." I cover my face with my hand that isn't holding my phone and peek at him through my fingers.

"Ouch. Well, I'll have you know I always saw you."

I stay hidden behind my hand, my face heating against my fingers. Mack is sweet. He's easy to talk to and be around. He communicates so well. He says what he's thinking, and he's sexy as hell. Just thinking about his backward hat and his zip-up hoodie has me wishing I was in California already. The biggest difference between him and Avery is that I have an overwhelming urge to kiss Mack. I'm not exactly sure when the shift occurred, but I've caught myself being distracted on more than one occasion, wondering what he tastes like or what it feels like to have his hands running through my hair.

"I wish I was there." I mean to think it, but it comes out of my mouth as I pull my hands away.

He smiles, his small dimples coming through. "You ready for our date, or what? Push play riiiight NOW!"

CHAPTER THIRTY-EIGHT

The second I exit the boarding bridge and enter the Los Angeles airport, I dial Avery's number. "Just breathe," she laughs before I speak. "It's just Mack. You haven't shut up about this trip since he invited you. You're fine!" It's like she has best friend ESP.

"Yeah, you're right," I mumble into my phone.

Also knowing I need to be kept off the ledge for a few more minutes, Avery starts her classic reassuring best friend pep talk. I'm walking toward arrivals and the path there is a cement tunnel, so right before she finishes the words "BE SAFE," the call drops, and I'm on my own. My panic instantly returns.

Leaving the tunnel that opens into baggage claim, I see him right away. He stands there with a smile on his face and flowers in his hands, and all of a sudden, I'm calm. This is exactly where I'm supposed to be. I've been questioning it every day the past two weeks, wondering how I could go from not being over Dean, to being consumed by thoughts about the next time I'd see Mack. But seeing him right now, I'm confident he's not a distraction or a rebound. I'm genuinely pulled toward him.

The moment I'm close enough, he wraps me in a hug, nearly crushing the flowers between us, and I'm reminded how good he smells–like when you walk by a Cinnabon and can't resist. Combined with the roses, I'm intoxicated, and I'm pretty sure it's a feeling that won't leave me the entire weekend. I want him to kiss me right there in the middle of the airport because I'm struggling to wait any longer, to know what it's like, but somehow, I know he won't. Instead, he takes my backpack from me, swings it over his shoulder and then grabs my hand.

I follow him through the short term parking lot until we get to his freshly washed black Jeep. It's the perfect combination of Oregon and California, and with the guitar in the backseat it screams "Mack." He tosses my bag in the back with his guitar before opening my door for me.

The entire drive to his apartment we don't talk much. He's got one hand on the steering wheel and one holding mine in my lap. He looks great in his plain black T-shirt and backward hat. He keeps looking over at me and smiling. The air between us is filled with anticipation and nerves. With anyone else, I think I'd be uncomfortable, but the silence works for us.

We pull into the parking garage and walk the two flights up the dimly lit cement stairway to his floor. When we enter the hallway, his apartment is immediately to the right. He unlocks his door, holding it open for me to slide through. As soon as it closes behind us, he sets my backpack and flowers on the floor and turns back to me. He grabs my face with both hands, leaning in until our foreheads connect. His lips touch mine, softly at first as he runs his fingers from the side of my face into my hair.

Then he kisses me again, my lips parting and our tongues melding together in a smooth movement that feels more like we do this every day, rather than something we've never done. I could see it in his eyes a second ago, and feel it right now he already wishes we could do this all the time.

He breaks our kiss but lets our foreheads touch again. His eyes flick open and they are the most intense green I have ever seen. I don't think I could look away even if I wanted to.

"I wanted to wait, but I couldn't. I'm sorry." He looks guilty.

"I'm not." I kiss him softly, smiling against his lips. He tastes the same way he smells, like cinnamon sugar, and I decide right then it's my new favorite flavor. My memory of when Avery told me about her first kiss with Miller flashes into my mind. She said she just knew the second their lips met he was the one she was going to marry. She couldn't describe it any other way besides she had a feeling at that moment. Even after they were together for years, I still thought it was crazy and illogical she could know something like that, like a kiss was a switch that flipped. I loved Dean–maybe part of me still does or always will–but this kiss with Mack tells me I'm going to love him too, and I somehow know it'll be different this time.

He's reluctant when he pulls back. "I wish we could stay right here, especially now that I know how you taste, but I need to get ready for my show. After that though, I'm all yours for the rest of the weekend."

The venue is grungy on the outside. It has an old mar-quee letter board above the door that's rusted enough it probably wouldn't pass an inspection. Inside, it's a to-tally different story. It smells like lemon cleaner instead of the musk I expected. Not far from the entrance is a sleek, black square bar that traps the bartenders and the alcohol safely inside. The wooden stage that ex-pands across the back of the room looks newly remod-eled and bright white lights still flood the space since it's an hour before the show starts. The place is pretty much empty, so I plan on sitting at the bar until then. Mack walks me over to one of the black leather-covered stools as a pretty blonde pops her head up from under the bartop.

"Oh, perfect. This is Lexy. She'll keep you company." He shifts his attention to her. "Lex, take care of my girl for me?"

"Careful what you ask for, Mack," she responds in a flirty tone.

He laughs into the kiss he places on the top of my head and then disappears somewhere behind the stage.

"I'm Maci. He left out that part." I roll my eyes. "Why do guys always seem to mess up introductions?"

"Let this one slide. I already know who you are." She winks. "But also because boys are idiots. Whatcha drinking?"

"Whiskey sour?"

"That is, like, the most old man drink you could possibly order. Let me make you a drink." Her eyes are so blue and light up with her smile.

"Okay, as long as I don't get too drunk before the show. I want to be able to tell Mack I loved it without wondering if I'm lying or not." I laugh.

"Is this the first time you've seen them play? How long have you two been together?" she asks while pouring a chaotic amount of ingredients into a shaker.

I have a feeling she already knows but answer anyway. "Ummm, I'm not sure we are officially together. I mean, I've known him since I was in middle school, but we just started hanging out. My best friend kind of set us up."

"Ahhh, classic tale. Well, Mack is a sweet guy. L.A. isn't always kind to newcomers, but he's lucky he found me, and I'll take him any day over any locals." Her words don't have a hint of threat in them, giving me the impression there's no romantic history between them. "Mostly it's just the two of us sticking together."

She pushes a very blue drink across the counter. I take one sip through the straw and nearly choke on how strong it is. "What is this?" I scrunch up my face. It tastes like it has five different types of alcohol in it. I might as well just take shots.

"A chill pill." She laughs. She's sassy, and I can see why Mack is friends with her. I know I'm going to love her already. "Seriously, why do you look so nervous?"

I lean forward, resting my chin on my fists, hovering over my drink. "It's nerve wracking, being in a city I don't know... with someone I don't really know." I wonder how much Mack has told her about me.

"If it makes you feel any better, I've lived here my whole life and still don't understand this city." The spark in her eyes disappears for a moment before she perks back up. "As far as Mack goes, that's what this weekend is for, right? To get to know each other better?"

"Yeah, you're right. I know we have time, but I also want to know everything at once. You know?"

"Not really." She shrugs. "I don't date. Mommy issues." She squats down to pull freshly washed glasses from the dishwasher.

"Oh. Well, it's a roller coaster for sure." I want to know more about her, but that's a conversation for a different time.

"But what I do know is until a few weeks ago, he never mentioned anyone special, let alone brought them around. I've never seen him serious about getting to know someone until now. So, I wouldn't worry."

Once people start filtering in, Lexy gets busy making more drinks.

It's crazy we are living completely different lives in different places. I know I'm getting ahead of myself, but if I keep coming back to visit Mack, it'll be nice to know someone else in L.A.

I finally hear the slight screech of a microphone and look up from my drink. "Hey everybody, thanks for coming out tonight. I'm Mack, and this is Where We Are." He turns to look at his band as the room goes dark and the lights shine bright on the stage. It's a fairly small venue, so I can see Mack perfectly. He's wearing the same jeans and a T-shirt I saw him in an hour ago, but now he's holding a guitar. Instead of his backward hat, his dark brown hair is free and messed up in a sexy way. In a very sexy way. I can't stop staring. Seeing him looking like that–on a stage–gives me feelings I never expected to have.

He plays a few chords, and that's when I hear his singing voice for the first time. "Holy shit." My mouth falls open.

Lexy must have been standing right behind me when I said it. "Get it together, Maci. You look like all the other lovesick twenty-something year olds in this place." She laughs, handing me another drink.

I shake my head to snap me out of my trance. "Thank goodness I don't have to lie about him being good. But you could have given a girl some warning."

"What? That your boyfriend sounds like an angel?"

I haven't heard the term boyfriend in association with me in so long, but I like the way it sounded. "I mean, I was going to say like the American version of Jamie Miller, this singer who was on *The Voice UK*. But yeah, same thing, because I'm equally as obsessed. How am I supposed to not jump him on stage?" Wow Maci, calm down.

"Chill out tiger, you still have a 90 minute set to get through." She's still laughing as her blonde ponytail swings over her shoulder, turning around to help the obnoxious guy throwing straw wrappers to get her attention.

The rest of the night flies by. I stop after my second drink because I have limited time this weekend to figure out if whatever Mack and I have going on is more than just comfort, attraction and really good kissing.

That kiss earlier, it was something else, and I can't help but let my mind wander to it. It was different from kissing Dean. With him, it was like electricity was running through me. But this, I don't know how to describe it other than it just felt right.

I know there's technically no rush, but living a plane ride away makes me feel like we need to decide when I leave here if this is worth pursuing or not. There I go again. Avery isn't even here, and I'm putting pressure on this myself.

"Another one?" Lexy yells over the music.

I shake my head at her.

Half the crowd pays their tabs, while the other half filters out of the venue. I'm sitting antsy on the bar stool, watching Mack put his guitar away. When he looks up and catches my gaze, he jumps off the stage and heads my way.

Falling into the space between my legs, his hands immediately go to my hips. "So, what did you think?"

"She thinks you're an angel," Lexy yells from the other side of the bar.

"Hey, those were her words, not mine." I throw my hands up in surrender. "But seriously, I feel like I don't even know you, Mack Andrew Torres!"

"Well, for starters, my middle name is Ryden." He's amused. It occurs to me I now know this tidbit about Mack I never learned about Dean.

"Is it really, though?" I scrunch up my nose before leaning in for a kiss. "You're amazing. You know how I feel about live music, but that was..."

He grins, taking the compliment well, before kissing me again when he realizes I'm not going to finish my sentence. It's like we broke the seal when he kissed me in his apartment, and there's no going back now. I want more of all of it. "I want to know all the things about you right now."

"We've got plenty of time, babe." He leans over the bar to where Lexy digs for something in the fridge.

"Sorry, Lex, I'd stay and help you close, but..."

"Yeah, yeah get out of here." She waves us away. "See you soon, Maci!"

By the time we get back to Mack's apartment, it's nearly two in the morning. Between traveling, the excitement of seeing him, and the two very strong drinks Lexy made for me, I'm tired, but I want to make the most of my time here.

I chug a glass of water, hoping it will help wake me up while Mack showers. I pull out my phone and see a check-in text from Avery. She's probably asleep by now, so I'll text her back in the morning.

Mack comes out of his room in plaid pajama bottoms, the band of his briefs peeking out at the top and his dark hair is sticking up everywhere from being towel dried. I sit from where I was lying on the couch to get a better view of his abs. *Damn*. He walks over and sits next to me, and I turn to sit crisscross facing him.

"I'm so glad you're here." His hands fall to my knees.

"Me too." My clammy hands are folded in my lap, like I'm an awkward teenager who doesn't know what to do around the guy she has a crush on.

"So, how was Lexy? She's cool. I thought you two might get along."

"Yeah, I like her a lot. I didn't get to talk with her much because you have some crazy fans."

"That's L.A. for you. It's a wild card on any given night around here."

"Sure is good for people watching. A lot of people who might have wanted to jump you even more than I did." I laugh. "Is that why you haven't brought any girls around before?" The words tumble out of me before my 2 a.m. brain can focus enough to filter my thoughts.

"Maybe I shouldn't have left you alone with Lexy." He chuckles, rubbing his hands up my thighs. "What did she say?"

"Nothing really. Just that she's never seen you bring a girl around before. It's confusing to me because the more I learn about you, the more I like you."

That makes him smile, and he answers the question I didn't ask. "Things weren't great when I first moved here, and I had the wrong priorities. I mostly play music and do my own thing now."

I stop myself before pressing for details about what it was like when he first got to California. "But you hang out with Lexy a lot?"

"Yeah, usually after my shows. We go to the beach once or twice a week too. I'm glad I have her here." He pauses for a second. "Just as a friend." He looks at me like he's concerned I might be worried. I wasn't, but I'm happy he cares about easing any of my possible fears.

When I smile back and shake my head as confirmation I hadn't thought anything contrary, he continues. "I didn't decide until recently I was ready for a relationship again and haven't found anyone worth bringing around until you. Even that was unexpected. At first, I thought Avery was joking when she called me last month wanting a favor."

"A favor?" My eyebrows scrunch together.

He laughs. "Yeah, she asked if I could sweep her best friend off her feet when I came to visit. I brushed her off until she convinced me she was serious. She told me you had been kind of depressing to be around lately and thought I could be the cure. I thought she was being a little dramatic, and I wouldn't have considered it if it was anyone else. Then I felt a little guilty like maybe we were tricking you. But you've always been there in the back of my mind. I honestly didn't know you were single. I couldn't imagine why you would be. Once she insisted, I knew I had to at least see you when I was in Oregon for her engagement."

"I don't want you to think you're a rebound," I trail off into a whisper, embarrassed, but wanting to be upfront with him.

"You don't have to talk about it if you'd rather not."

"It's okay. You know, you being so forward has been refreshing. Despite communication not always being my strong suit, I have never been with someone I've felt I could be completely open and myself with in the first place. I don't want to attempt a relationship that makes me feel unsure about who I should be. Not that we are in a relationship yet," I add, looking to gauge his reaction. His face doesn't give away anything except he's listening. "Maybe my idea of what a relationship should be is skewed because the one I'm most familiar with is Avery and Miller. They seem to love each other so well, you know?" I can see in his new smile he's thankful for the love his sister found. It's one of the things I've already decided I love most about him.

"We could be, ya know, in a relationship."

I stare. I can't help but love the way he's willing to commit, without hesitation. I'm also at a loss for words.

When I don't say anything else he adds, "You know, I've listened to so many love songs. Hell, I've written so many, but sometimes when I hear about serendip-itous moments or having a feeling something is right, it seems like it's a made-up thing to write a catchy song. But being around you, Maci, it feels like some weird full-circle moment that's exactly where we are supposed to be. I'm not afraid of giving this a shot or of giving you the girlfriend title while we do. If you want it, it's yours." He says it with a half-smile, and I can tell he's hesitant about being this forward.

I study the vulnerability in his eyes, wondering how I will ever be able to come up with words that compare to someone who writes love songs for a living. I stick with a simple "yes" and lean in to kiss him before he waits on me to add anything else.

His hands immediately leave my legs and find their way to the sides of my face, pushing his fingers through my hair and pulling me closer. I slide forward, unfolding my legs to wrap around him. Our kiss deepens, and I'm already consumed by him. I run my fingers up the back of his neck, into his still damp hair, but suddenly, he pulls back.

He studies what I'm sure looks like fear in my eyes before he says, "I don't think we should have sex yet."

I breathe out both relief and confusion. "Okaaaay." It's not that I was planning on it, either way. I'm going with the flow and letting whatever I want to happen, happen, and not stress about it too much.

He wraps his arms around my waist, keeping me close to him. "Look, I don't know what exactly happened in your last relationship, and I don't need to know. But I do know I want you to be sure about this, about us. Plus, if I mess this up, my sister might actually kill me. So, everything is on your terms, and when you're ready, okay?"

I nod and lean in to kiss him again. It's different from the intensity between us a few hours earlier when we kissed for the first time. It's almost lazily, like we are in no rush or at risk of ever having to stop. I love it.

CHAPTER THIRTY-NINE

We kissed last night until I physically could not stay awake any longer. Around four in the morning, we crawled into bed. This time, I easily talked him into not staying on the couch. I was out before he could give me another kiss goodnight.

Mack lightly shakes my shoulder until I open my eyes. I rub them until he comes into view clearly. "What time is it?" I ask groggily, still half asleep.

"It's only nine, babe, don't be mad. I only have one full day to show you around, and I want to make the most of it!" He sounds like he has a lot more energy than anyone possibly could after only four hours of sleep and no caffeine. I smile as I sit.

"Where are we going?"

"You'll see!"

I slide a blue sundress over my body and slip the straps into place. Walking out to the kitchen, I find Mack filling two water bottles. He freezes in the middle of screwing the cap on to look me up and down.

"What?" I ask, knowing very well, based on the heat in his eyes, what he is thinking. Once I got out of bed this morning and it hit me where I was, I thought about how out of character this entire situation is. I feel like a different Maci than I was when I woke up yesterday. It's not a bad thing. If anything, I feel more like myself, or more like the me I want to be. I put on this dress that was another "back of my closet for a more confident day" outfit. As I slipped into it, no doubt crossed my mind. I don't know what it is about Mack, but being around him makes me more sure of myself, more in control.

He sets the water bottle on the counter and takes three steps that land him in front of me. His hands reach for my waist and pull me closer as his eyes meet mine. "You look beautiful." He pauses for a moment. "God, Maci, I've thought about being with you for so long. It was easier to be patient when I thought it would never happen." He shares his thoughts so freely, and I love that about him.

"Hey, I thought we were taking things slow?" I joke, my smile uncontrollable.

His thumbs rub against my hips. "We are. I just want you to know how I feel about you. Does it freak you out if I say stuff like that?"

"Umm, I don't think anyone has ever felt that way about me, so I'm not used to it, but it doesn't freak me out."

"Okay good. Promise you'll tell me if it does?"

I nod, stepping more into his embrace. "I promise."

"Now." He grins. "Let's get to making you love California so you come back and see me again."

"I already want to come back, and I haven't even left," I whisper before I press my lips against his. I smile into our kiss, partly because of his confessions, but also a little amused by the flash of a memory of my first day of senior year when I was feeling everything opposite of what I am right now. A path for my future might finally be forming. I know in reality, it's been the entire past school year that has changed everything, but in this moment, it feels like it was just the day I chose to give Mack a chance that did.

Our first stop is the café down the street from Mack's apartment. He leaves the car running while he goes in and comes out with two fruit smoothies and a bag of bagels. "I think the thing I love most about you is you hate coffee too." A moment of surprise flashes across his eyes when I say it, and I make a mental note to think about my words before I say them. That's the second time I've done that. I didn't mean love like love, but hi, my name is Maci, and sometimes when I'm sleep deprived and falling for a boy too quickly, the things I say don't quite come out the same way I mean them. *I'm falling for him.* That's the first time I've admitted it to myself.

"Helloooooo, Maciiii." He waves a cream cheese covered everything bagel in front of my face, and I snap out of my trance.

"Hi, yes, bagel, thank you!" I lean over to kiss him, hoping to wash away my feeling of awkwardness in myself.

He smiles. "Alright, to the beach we go!"

The Santa Monica Pier surprisingly looks exactly like I imagined it would. We spent the morning walking along the boardwalk. He's been telling me about all the places he's been since he moved to California and everywhere he's been on tour, which is 12 different states so far. He moved here on a whim a few weeks after he graduated college when one of the guys in his band used a connection to get them a residency spot at the bar we went to last night. After about a year of playing there every week, they started traveling the West Coast to play at other venues. They still aren't very well known, even now, because making it in the music industry is a challenge, especially in California.

The four of them lived together when they first got here to save on rent. Now, with traveling and playing at bigger venues, they make enough to pay for their own places. Mack seems satisfied with the amount he makes since he gets to do something he loves. I love his priorities. I've never been big on money being the most important thing as long as I can do what I love. My problem is I still don't know what I love.

I do know, however, I love food. "Can we get something to eat?" I chime in when there's a break in the conversation.

"Anything you want, babe. How do you feel about poké? There's a great place right here." He points down a walkway leading off the boardwalk.

"I'm from the Pacific Northwest. If I didn't like seafood, it would practically be a crime."

He smiles, picking up my hand and pulling me in a different direction than we were walking. Every time I realize we have something else in common, it's like another piece of my doubt chips away.

We take our bowls and walk to the end of the pier, sitting when we find an empty bench. "You know what's crazy?" I say as he takes his first bite of tuna and looks at me, curious. "We spent two years in the same high school, and I hardly remember seeing you at all." Amusement flickers in his eyes. "What?"

"Mace, you know we had a class together, right?" I must look as confused as I feel. "Psych. I needed one more elective class senior year."

"Wait, seriously? How do I not remember this?" Genuinely wondering how I could have gone an entire semester without noticing. It's not like we weren't friendly. I saw him at least a few days a week after school. Then again, those memories came back only recently.

"You sat at the front of the class and actually paid attention. I remember one day thinking how into the lesson you were when everyone else was passing notes or drawing in their notebooks. I was always in the back writing lyrics, but every time I looked up, I'd notice how focused you were. I'm not surprised it ended up being your major."

I hate that he remembers more than I do, and I don't like feeling like maybe we could have had more time together if I hadn't been so blind. I push the thought away, knowing it can't change anything. "Yeah, if only I knew what I wanted to do with it. I'm a little jealous of you. You've always known what you wanted to do, and then you did it. I'm proud of you too, for the record."

I can see his cheeks get a little pink, which is a first. "Thanks, Mace, but don't worry. You'll figure it out. Is anything particularly interesting to you?"

"Not really. I took this weekend class last quarter about human trafficking, and I think about it all the time. Not in, like, a morbid way. The professor told us about these organizations, like this one in Costa Rica, where they rehabilitate girls who have been trafficked. They are usually behind on their education and struggle to work through their trauma, so they need a lot of one-on-one help so they can confidently reintegrate into society. Sometimes I think it would be fun... Well, maybe that's not the right word... to do something like that for a while. I want to do something that matters, you know? That makes an impact in someone's life. Like you do with your music."

"I would love it if my music had that power."

"I guarantee it does, Mack. I've heard 90 minutes of your lyrics, and I can tell you words like that matter to people, make them feel like they aren't alone. That can make all the difference sometimes."

"Thanks," he says sheepishly and makes eye contact with me. "Music was there for me when my parents weren't. I'd love to help other people have that if they need it. You can make any impact you want, too, Mace. It'll happen, I know it."

I smile as I spoon the last bite of my lunch into my mouth with my chopsticks. It's weird to think we lived our lives right next to each other as near strangers. Now here we are, living a thousand miles apart and trying to exist together. Being together now almost feels like enough to make up for all those years we weren't.

CHAPTER FORTY

An intense blend of orange and pink lights the sky through the window, making the whole kitchen glow as we enter Mack's apartment. He walks to the fridge to grab water, and I can't help but watch him. Leaning my elbows on the counter, I rest my chin on my fists. He turns around and catches me staring. "I had the best day with you." My voice sounds dreamier than I intended it to be.

"It's not over yet. Is there anything specific you want to do?"

I walk around the edge of the counter, pulling the water bottle from his hand to set it on the counter behind me. Since we've been in public all day, we've hardly had any physical contact, and now that we are back in his place, alone, I don't want to stay away any longer. He seems to be on the same wavelength because he takes a step closer as I do the same, closing the distance between us. His hands fall to my waist and mine press against his chest. The moment his lips touch mine, that newly familiar calm rushes through me. It's like any anxiety or stress built up in my body disappears. His tongue parts my lips and slides between them. Our mouths sync right away, as if we've been doing this for years. My hand reaches to tug on the hair at his neck fervently, pulling him closer. The new movement causes him to flinch.

"Maci." He looks at me with pleading eyes. I know he's telling me I need to be the one to slow down because I can feel his want for me radiating off him. My eyes scan him for the answer he's waiting for from me. I take a dramatic stomp back, a whimper escaping my lips.

He chuckles, and pulls me into a side hug and starts walking us over to the couch. "I know it feels like we don't have time since you're leaving tomorrow, but we have time. I promise you, we have time." God, he's so sweet, enough to overpower the throb between my legs–for now at least.

I scroll through Netflix while Mack orders us a pizza from the authentic Italian place down the street. It's different here than Oregon. It's more chaotic, but you also have everything you could ever want, practically at your fingertips.

After we eat, we make it to a second movie, with me leaned into him and his arm wrapped around me. Every once in a while, he kisses the top of my head and squeezes me to him a little tighter. I'm not sure how I can be so comfortable and content, while also wanting so much more.

I'm woken by him rubbing his thumb over my shoulder as the credits roll on the TV. My body has slipped down so my head is on his lap. When I sleepily gaze up at him, he's looking at me. "Ready for bed, babe?"

"Mhmm." I sit, and he reaches for my hands, pulling me up with him. Leaning into him, I link my arm through his, my eyes mostly closed as he leads us into the bathroom and gets our toothbrushes ready. I steady myself on my own enough to lazily brush my teeth, staring at him in the mirror as I do. It's such a strange feeling, to be so at ease with someone. The few times I was at Dean's, I would use my finger and toothpaste, too afraid to show up with a toothbrush or ask for one. I've never felt this comfortable with anyone before. It's different, in the best way possible.

It's dark in here other than the stream of light from the city coming through at the edge of the curtains. I turn so I'm facing Mack instead and am surprised to find his eyes are open and looking back at me. I'm not asleep, but I'm not quite awake either, and everything feels like a dream. "You're awake?" My voice comes out raspy.

"Can't sleep," he whispers, reaching to tuck the piece of fallen hair behind my ear. That feeling is as good as I was hoping it would be. Instead of pulling his hand back, he leaves it there, twisting his fingers into my hair. His touch makes me want to drift back off to sleep, but I don't close my eyes. We stay like that, staring at each other until my eyes have adjusted to the dark.

I'm not sure which of us make a move first, but all of a sudden, his mouth is on mine and my patience to stay in the previous moment forever turns into a surge of urgency flowing through me. His hips slowly scooch across the bed, bringing him closer. He's close enough I can feel him, hard, against me. His hand slowly slides down my neck, my arm, stopping at my hip, gripping it with more pressure than there was a moment ago. There's a shift as his want overpowers his hesitancy.

My hand finds his side under the sheet and explores a little further, lightly tracing his abs. Overcome by the urge to let them wander further, I run my fingers along the edge of his briefs, that lie slightly above his pajama pants. His hand moves from my hip and his fingers softly trail along my forearm until they reach mine. He squeezes my hand slightly, stopping my fingers in their track. "Maci?" His eyes lock onto mine.

"Mack." I say it more as a statement than a question as I lean forward until my lips barely graze his. I already know what he's going to say.

"It's hard to keep my hands off you."

"Then don't," I whisper.

He squints a bit, trying to read me through the darkness. "Are you sure?"

"I know you're right next to me, but it's not enough." That's all the confirmation he needs.

His hand releases mine, and he lets it slowly slip to the edge of the lace between us. Dipping his fingers underneath it, he tugs it down, and it rolls into itself as it slides down my legs. His hand moves slowly up my legs, light as a feather. When he gets to the edge of where my hips meet my leg, his finger traces a path to my center before sliding over my entrance, gently pulsing, teasing me. My legs naturally fall apart to give him better access, and I surprise myself with my lack of hesitancy. Taking it as another sign of permission, the pressure of his fingers intensifies, and I suck in a sharp breath as he slips one inside.

Mack's lips press into mine, and I can sense by the way he's kissing me he's not getting enough of what he needs. I reach to release him from his briefs, but he nudges my arm away with his. I hesitate for a second, worried something is wrong, but he shakes his head slowly into our kiss. He smiles as he pulls back enough to whisper, "I need more of you first." His mouth meets my skin, right at the edge of my face before he starts trailing kisses down my neck. His finger slides out of me, and his hand lands on my hip, gently pushing me onto my back. Propped up on one arm, his other hand slides under my tank top, stopping when they reach the bottom of my breasts. I help him by gripping the edge of my shirt and pulling it over my head. As soon as I do, he places a kiss where his hand was and works his way down my body with his mouth. His fingers dig into my thighs, spreading my legs as he moves in between them.

Without even taking a moment to tease, his tongue makes a long, slow drag over me, the wetness of his tongue adding to the wetness that's already there. He repeats the motion, using enough pressure to drive me crazy but not enough to push me over the edge. Damn, that's hot. My patience has disappeared, and I need more. My hand grips his hair, and my hips lift into him. I'm not usually comfortable asking for more in moments like this, but in this dream-like state, it's way past being in my control. His tongue flickers inside of me and my stomach muscles contract, my entire lower body involuntary spasming, without warning. Holding my legs in place, his tongue continues to roll against me, putting pressure in the perfect place. My orgasm rips through me, leaving a tingling sensation in its wake.

Holy shit. That was way more intimate and intense than sex has ever been. I catch my breath as Mack's kisses work their way up my body until his head rests on my chest. I'm still shaking from that experience and too turned on for it to be over. My hand reaches down to reveal how ready he is. I scoot down on the bed slightly, so our faces align. Gripping my fingers around him, I move it up and down slowly until he is completely hard, loving the feel of him in my hand and the way he groans in response. "I'm ready," I whisper. "For you," I add in case it wasn't clear.

His eyes study mine, full of both question and need. Deciding I'm right, he closes the distance between our lips, his hand caressing the side of my face. Breaking our contact, he turns and reaches behind him into the drawer of his nightstand. I don't even hear the tear of the foil before he's turned back toward me.

Hyper sensitive to every sensation, the calluses on his fingers from playing guitar seem rougher than normal as they run over my hip. He locks his eyes with mine again.

"I'm positive," I reassure him, knowing that's what he needs. Adjusting myself to hover over him, I guide him into me slowly, taking him in an inch at a time. His eyes close, and his head tips back as he bites into his lip. Witnessing him so turned on is everything I need to feel confident about this decision. He regains control after his moment of initial ecstasy and looks up before pulling me into him and flipping us both over in one swift movement.

Leaning into one arm, the other hand threading through my hair, he pushes into me again. God, he feels good. I feel so connected to him, like everything that's ever happened brought me to this moment for a reason. No part of me wants to be anywhere else. We find the perfect rhythm with our bodies, and he continues pushing deeper into me until we are as connected as we can possibly be. Another orgasm builds, and I can tell he's getting close too by the way he rocks into me, less controlled than before. He hits exactly the right spot, and I tighten, pulsing around him as a second wave of pleasure shoots through me. That sets him off, like it's all he was waiting for, and he rides us through our orgasms until we are capable of coming back to reality.

"That was..." he trails off.

"Perfect," I find the right word for him.

"Better than anytime I ever imagined it."

My arm covers my eyes in embarrassment thinking about all the years he was thinking about me while he barely crossed my mind. *How did he never cross my mind?* "I'm dumb for wasting all the years we could have been doing that." It comes out more like a whine.

He plants a few kisses along my arm covering my face. "Just think about all the years we can do it now," he mumbles into my skin. "I might be able to sleep now."

I lift my arm enough I can see him, an uncontrollable giddiness washing over me. My next words come out quiet and shy. "But what if I don't want to?"

The grin that comes over his face is the only thing I need to light my fire again.

As I step onto the curb, tears sting my eyes, and I will them not to fall. Mack shuts my door and turns to me, sliding his hand into my hair and pulling me into him. "I don't know when I'm going to see you again." My tears betray me by silently escaping. He pulls back and swipes his thumbs over my cheeks to brush them away, then tilts my face until my eyes meet his. "I'm sorry I'm emotional about this. I don't know what's gotten into me."

"Nothing to be sorry about, babe. I already miss you." He kisses my forehead. "I know it's hard because I have so many shows coming up, and you're about to graduate, but we will figure it out."

"Okay," I mumble as he kisses me softly. I grab my backpack off the ground and swing it over my shoulder, walking toward the airport entrance. A hand tugs on my wrist, forcing me to spin around and right back into Mack's arms. He pulls me into him, this time kissing me with much more intensity than before. I forget where I am until he pulls back and my surroundings come back into focus.

"Okay, now get out of here." He gives me a half-smile.

CHAPTER FORTY-ONE

I can't remember the last time Avery and I adventured together besides our date at the winery. I don't mind Miller being around, but it's nice to have time with just my best friend, and I'm excited for this weekend. Miller is away for his brother's bachelor party, so Avery asked if I wanted to take a trip to California as one final girls' trip before she moves into her new house. Mack is out of town for a show, but he will be back around 2 a.m. Saturday morning. This way, I get the best of both worlds seeing him after six weeks apart and spending quality time with Avery. Mack is letting us crash at his place, so he left a key for us with his neighbor.

As soon as we drop our bags inside the front door, we turn right back around to get in the Uber and head to dinner. Lexy recommended a place called Saddle Ranch on Hollywood Boulevard.

The restaurant isn't far from Mack's. It looks like a horse ranch and a bar were mashed together. Every-thing is made from wood, there's a mechanical bull in the corner and the lights are dimmed low. As we sit at our table, a waitress walks by with a stack of cotton candy that's literally the size of half of me. Lexy was on point when she referred to this place as more an experience than a meal. It takes me the entire time we eat the best truffle mac and cheese we've ever had to convince Avery to ride the mechanical bull.

When she mounts the worn, brown leather, it's worth every second. She is surprisingly good and lasts six seconds. We didn't realize agreeing to ride also counted as entry to a contest, but her performance was long enough for her to advance to the next level of the competition. She makes it through two more rounds before she's kicked out of the bracket, and by then I have more than enough footage to send to Miller. "Okay, let's get out of here before I throw up mac and cheese!" she declares as we sign our tab and head out front to meet our Uber.

Our driver drops us off at the entrance to the Santa Monica Pier. It's crowded since it's Friday, the Pier lit with carnival lights, games and a Ferris wheel at the end. As much as we claimed to be down for adventure, we are ready for a mellow rest of the night since we have plans with Mack all day tomorrow. We peek our heads inside a few bars, searching for one where we like the atmosphere.

A couple of blocks from the pier there's one that just feels right. It reminds us of the bars we go to in Oregon, more laid back instead of crammed with preppy rich kids like so many of the places here. I order us two glasses of wine, while Avery finds us a seat at the bar top at the window. Even though it's getting dark, you can still see the ocean, and it's perfect.

Avery has been going on about Miller for the last hour and showing me pictures of the furniture they want to buy for their new house. I can't believe we are getting to the age where we do things like get married or buy houses–not like that's happening for me anytime soon, but still.

Around 10 p.m., we finish our last sips of wine and walk toward the boardwalk entrance to call an Uber. For some reason it's not busy anymore, unless everyone is out on the pier. The bar wasn't very crowded, and there's hardly anyone close to us now.

All of a sudden, a hand is on my arm, yanking me backward. Avery pulls me into a dark alley that runs in between the bar we left and the one next to it.

My face scrunches as I glance from her to where she grips my arm. "What are you doing?"

"I need to talk to you about something," she whispers.

"Okay..."

"You love Mack, right?" Her voice is barely audible.

I stare back at her, wondering why she's bringing this up in an alley, at this very moment. It's weird, and something doesn't seem right.

"Okay, so," she acts like I've said yes, even though I haven't responded. "I want you to think about how you love Mack... now, think about it backward."

Wait, what? I say it both in my head and aloud to her.

"Just think about it okay." She starts to walk back in the direction we were headed.

I begin to follow her, but before I can move, she spins around, and her hand forces me against the wall by my throat. My heart races as I gasp for air. "Avery." Her name comes out in a broken and struggling whisper. She looks straight through me like she's in a trance. Her hand grips tighter around my throat. It's not a strong enough hold that I can't breathe or get away if I violently force her off me, but it's enough that I feel trapped between her and the wall. "Avery," I choke out again.

It's only been a few seconds, but it feels like I'm in an alternate reality where time has slowed and everything around us moves accordingly. Her gaze is still on me—or through me. It's like she knows what she's doing while simultaneously not realizing at all. In my periphery, I see a car slow as it drives by us. There's a guy poking his head out the window, and for a moment I assume he's checking on us, but then I realize he's taking a picture. I'm scared and confused, someone is taking a picture of this moment, and I can't wrap my head around what's happening. The only thing I can think to do is call for help, but my voice hasn't gotten me very far. I slowly reach into my pocket and slide out my phone. I glance down at it quickly, pulling up the emergency contacts, where I've already saved Mack, and hit the call button. I don't bring it to my ear, I just don't know what else to do. Mack is probably still a few hours away, so I don't know how he could help anyway.

The street is quiet and empty now, so when Mack answers, I hear his voice coming through the phone even though it's by my waist. It's what snaps Avery out of her trance. She pulls her hand back, but her eyes stare ahead as if they can't focus on anything. I twist to the side so I'm no longer between her and the wall then stare at her, frozen.

She walks toward the parking lot, slowly, like she's not in any rush, and like all the intensity that was there a moment ago has been flushed from her. She doesn't look back to see if I'm following her. It's like she doesn't remember I'm there. She can't possibly be drunk. We only had one glass of wine. Thoughts are spinning through my brain, trying to make sense of what is happening. I finally hear Mack's voice yelling through my phone. He sounds panicked. I look down at my phone and see his name with a heart next to it lit up on the front of the screen, but I can't bring myself to say anything or move it closer to my face. I take off in a run after Avery, and when we both reach the parking lot around the same time, I notice an empty cab.

I pound on the passenger side window and watch for the driver to motion for me to get in. I hold up my finger, and he nods. I take the few extra steps to where Avery is still walking slowly, as if she's in a dream. I wrap my hand around her wrist, gently, trying not to startle or trigger her. She looks at me with that same vacant expression, then slowly to where our hands connect. "Come on, Avery. Let's go home," I say, and realize for the first time I'm crying. I'm surprised when she lets me lead her to the cab. She gets in first, and I slide in but stay on my side of the back seat.

It's a thirty-minute drive back to Mack's apartment. I just have to get us both there safely. *Mack.* I glance down at my phone that's still in my hand, but this time I don't see his name on the screen. I can't call him right now. I know he's freaking out, but I can't form words aloud, let alone put together a sentence. I just need to get us home. Then we will figure this all out and everything will be okay.

We make it a few minutes from the apartment, slowing as we come to a light on the back road a few streets away. Suddenly, Avery's door flies open with the cab in motion, and she tumbles out of it.

What the fuck.

I freeze. What is happening? Is she okay? Why did she do that? What is going on? Luckily there aren't any cars on this road since it's so late. She gets to her feet and starts running, but it's so dark I can't see which direction she goes. In the same instant I turn my head to try and follow her with my gaze, the cab driver slams on his brakes. "What the hell?" he screams. "Are you staying in or getting out?"

"Getting out," my voice shakes as I frantically pull cash from my purse and all but throw it at him.

Slamming the door behind me, I take off in the direction Avery ran. Though I lost sight of her, I run four blocks, frantically searching each side street I pass. With no luck, I stop, my hands falling to my knees, my breathing ragged. I'm outside, but I need air; I feel like I'm suffocating. I don't know what to do. I take in my surroundings, recognizing them. I'm in the parking lot of the café where we got bagels. It's only two blocks back to Mack's. Hopefully she found her way there.

When I get to the apartment, I pound on the door. Avery has the key, so if she's made it here, she should be inside.

No answer.

I slam my fist against the wood again.

Nothing.

I take off down the stairs I just ran up, opening the stairwell door to cool night air. I need to keep searching, but I can't make my feet move. Even if I could, I don't know where to start. I collapse onto the curb instead.

I brush my hands over my face, wiping the tears blurring my vision, but it makes me cry more. Within a minute, I'm sobbing so hard my body is convulsing, my arms wrapped around my head resting on my knees.

It feels like hours have passed, but my phone is dead, so I have no idea how long it's actually been. I've finally stopped crying. The only light is the glow of the street lamps. I'm probably not safe out here by myself, but I'm not sure I'd feel safe anywhere right now.

Footsteps approach, and it crosses my mind that I should be apprehensive, realizing I'm no longer alone on a street in Hollywood. But I don't have the energy. I hear a sigh that sounds like a mix of relief and panic, and it takes everything I have to lift my head for the first time in however long I've been sitting on this curb. I start to stand, but Mack is quicker, sitting and pulling me to him. Sobs break out of me the moment my face hits his chest.

A few minutes go by, and I pull back. "Avery, I don't know where she is." I'm not sure he can even under-stand me.

"Shhhh." He runs his hand over my hair, trying to calm me. "She's in my bed. What happened, Maci?" He speaks softly, but I can sense his confusion.

"But is she okay? I need to know," I whisper, a pang of guilt flooding through me.

"I think so. I mean I don't know. She's breathing, she acknowledged me when I woke her to ask where you were, but couldn't fully come to enough to talk to me. She's just drunk... right?" The newfound worry in his tone is evident now. "Are you okay? What happened, Maci?" he asks again.

"I don't know. I'm confused." My tears slow but con-tinue to silently slip out as I rehash the events of the night. When the story brings me to the present mo-ment, I reiterate how sorry I am and how guilty I feel for stopping my search. "I don't want her to wake up alone. Someone should be with her, but I don't think it should be me," I admit. I don't tell him how much I need him to stay with me.

"It's okay, baby, it's going to be okay. We will figure this out." He's reassuring, pulling me back into him, his thumb rubbing across my shoulder. Chills shoot up my arm, and I realize for the first time how chilly the night has become.

He pulls out his phone and sends off a text to someone, then sits with me a few more minutes before he stands, pulling me with him. Right as I find my feet under me, his phone dings, and he looks at it. "How do you feel about going to Lexy's?"

I look at him, my eyes welling with tears. There's no way he can't see I don't want to leave him.

"I know. I don't want to let you out of my sight, but we also don't know what's going to happen when Avery wakes. We don't know what happened in the first place, so this might be easier for now." He guides me toward his Jeep parked in the alley next to his building.

I nod as he opens the passenger door, and I crawl onto the warm seat.

We stand in front of Lexy's apartment door for at least five minutes, Mack holding me, rubbing his fingers across my back. I'm out of tears and out of energy. He reaches behind me and knocks softly on the door. It opens almost immediately, and Lexy–still in her bartending uniform, jean shorts and a black tank top–steps back, making room for me to enter.

I don't want to talk about it, and I'm thankful Lexy doesn't push. She makes up her couch for me and gets me a glass of water and a set of pajamas. I change, curl myself under the gray fur blanket, and try to calm myself. I stare at the ceiling, simultaneously tired and wide awake. The thought hits me like a smack to the face. *I know what happened.* Why didn't I realize sooner?

Grabbing my phone off the coffee table, I text Mack.

Me: *I think she was roofied. I read about it in my psych of drugs class. For most people, it puts them in a foggy and dream-like trance. But for some people, it makes them aggressive. That has to be it. I don't know why I didn't see it before. I'm sorry.*

Mack: *It's not your fault, Mace. I'm going to wake her and take her to the hospital. I'll keep you posted. You feel okay, right? Like are you sure this didn't happen to you too?*

Me: *I'm not okay but in a different way.* I wish I could be as calm about this as he seems right now.

I startle awake when Mack crouches next to the couch and runs his thumb across my cheek. "Hey, baby," he whispers.

Squinting to avoid the sunlight seeping into the room, I scan his face. "What time is it?"

"A little after one."

One in the afternoon? Why did I sleep so late? Wait, where am I? I open my eyes more to take in my surroundings, and it all comes flooding back. "Avery..." I start to say.

"She's okay. You were right. And they were glad I brought her in. They said this has been happening a lot recently. There are guys going around dropping pills in as many drinks as possible, then waiting to see who leaves alone."

My eyes widen. "What?" It's not that I don't understand what he's telling me, it's that I don't understand how someone could do that. "Where is she? I need to tell her how sorry I am that I left her. I'm sorry I left her. I was just so scared. I didn't know what to do." My voice breaks as a few tears escape.

Still kneeling on the ground next to me, he pulls me to him. The growing panic inside me slowly starts to dissipate as his hand rubs up and down my back. "She's okay, Mace. Physically too. Just a few scratches from when she jumped out of the car. I wanted her to stay with me, but she begged me to take her to the airport so she could get back to Miller. He's going to call me as soon as he picks her up."

I let out my breath before taking a deep one.

It's okay. Everything will be okay. But it's not. I'm angry at whoever did this to my best friend. I'm upset I didn't notice what was happening sooner. The guilt for not staying with her no matter what consumes me. I'm tired, confused and sad. I'm afraid of what this will do to our friendship.

We spend the rest of the day lying together in bed watching movies. Mack picks out a new comedy every time one ends. I fall in and out of sleep because I'm so emotionally exhausted. Mack lets me, and he's always right next to me every time I wake. He orders us a pizza at some point, but I can't eat more than a few bites. I hate that I'm wasting our limited time together, but I can't seem to find the energy to do anything.

I don't want to leave him tomorrow. I've lost my sense of security, and I'm anxious about going home alone and not having him next to me. Every time I think about Avery, all I see in my mind is her hand pinned against my throat. Then, the shame of giving up my search for her sets in. I don't know how to handle it. I think I'm too busy wishing it wasn't something I even have to deal with for me to actually work through it.

I'm not sure if he's that in tune with me already, or if it's a coincidence, but every time I feel a rush of overwhelm, Mack pulls me closer to him, and it calms me to my core, even if it's temporary. I just have to make it through the next month. I graduate in three weeks, so I'll be busy. Then his band starts a West Coast tour, and he'll be in Portland only two weeks after that.

When I get back to our apartment, I'm not surprised Avery isn't there. Despite what happened, I wouldn't have expected her to be, but I was still holding out hope. I haven't talked to her at all, and even though it's only been two days, it feels like longer. I call her, and she answers on the second ring.

Avery: Hello?

She sounds exhausted.

Me: Hey, I just got home. How are you?

Avery: Tired mostly. The doctor told me the side effects might last a few days. Miller has been taking care of me. It's almost annoying how he won't leave my side.

She manages a weak laugh.

Me: Let's be real, he's always like that. I'm so sorry I couldn't find you, Avery. I was scared and lost, but that's not an excuse.

Avery: I know, I don't blame you. I hardly remember it–I don't even know how I got back to Mack's–but I think I would have done the same thing. It's not your fault. It's whoever did this to me, to us.

Me: I love you. You're my person. I don't want you to worry you can't count on me.

Avery: I know, Mace. Let's not let him win. It's over now, and it can't have control over us unless we let it.

Me: You're right. Well, I'll let you get some rest. Just wanted to let you know I made it back, and I love you.

Avery: I love you too.

CHAPTER FORTY-TWO

I've texted with Avery here and there, but time has gotten away from us, and it's the first day in three weeks I will see her in person. I'm not sure what to expect. Everything seems fine between us, but today is graduation, and it's nothing like we planned. We were going to get ready together and wear the new sundresses we bought. We were supposed to come home from our trip and decorate our caps. But the plan shifted. I texted Avery asking if she wanted to meet before the ceremony so we could walk in together and if she and Miller still wanted to go to dinner with my parents after. We agreed to meet outside the stadium.

I spot her in the sea of green graduation gowns before she sees me. I take a step toward her but wait until she notices me before closing the distance. When she's right in front of me, we simultaneously fall into each other's arms. A sense of relief washes over me, the same calm feeling I get with Mack, that I've always felt with Avery. The breath I let out feels like one that's been trapped inside me since the last time I saw her when she was running away from our cab.

Without pulling back, I whisper, "I've missed you." Tears roll down my cheek and into the soft brown curls of her hair.

Her hug tightens. "I missed you too." She pulls back and reaches to swipe her thumbs under my eyes. "Now, are you ready to do this, or what!?"

"As ready as I'm going to be. Let's do it." We head in to find our seats.

"There's my two favorite girls." His voice cuts through the chaos of the stadium.

There's no possible way Avery could have turned to see him faster than I flung myself into his arms. "You're here," I breathe into his neck as he grounds himself from my tackle.

He chuckles. "You thought I was going to miss this? I'm so proud of both of you."

I reluctantly release him so Avery can hug her brother. It gives me a second to rake my eyes over him. He's dressed for the occasion in nice black jeans and a black button up with the sleeves rolled past his forearms. He skipped his backward hat-rare for him-but his deep brown hair is perfectly tousled. Although it would look better with my fingers running through it. He shoves his hands into the pockets of his jeans as he shoots me a perfect grin. It's been so long since I've seen him-too long.

I move to get back in his arms, but before I'm happily in his embrace, my parents excitedly rush between us. My dad wraps me in a hug and my mom squeezes Avery before they switch. When they step back, my mom says through teary eyes, "I'm so proud of you girls." They've always treated Avery like their own daughter, especially once they realized her parents didn't. She turns to Mack, flashing him a knowing smile. "Mack, it's so good to see you again. I assume you will be joining us for dinner?"

While we were waiting for our food, my parents surprised me with a $5,000 travel fund as a graduation gift. Their wanderlust is one of my favorite qualities about them, something that was passed down to me. Knowing they support me taking time to figure out what I want to do with my life and encouraging me to explore the world has been a gift in itself. This money is more than I ever expected, and I'm so thankful for them. I'm not sure what my plan is or how I will use it, but I can decide later. I do know this money nearly doubles what I have already saved and whatever adventure I use it for will be epic.

After dinner, my parents head home, and Avery and Miller go downtown. Mack and I sit inside my car, deciding what to do for the rest of the night. My thoughts wander to Avery and how relieved I am after seeing her today. I'm pulled back to reality when Mack's hand reaches over the center console and lands on my thigh, sending a wave of comfort through me with the contact. As if he was reading my mind, he says, "It was nice seeing you and Avery together. How was it?"

"It was really good. I'm still angry about the situation. I'm not quite sure how to let go of what happened. But Avery and I are okay. We have to be. She's my person."

"Hey!" he jokes.

"You're my person now too." I lean in to kiss him.

"It's strange. It feels like yesterday I was driving you two to pick out homecoming dresses. I was jealous you were with someone else, and you hardly knew I existed." He laughs. "Now look at us." He squeezes my thigh.

He's unlocking all these memories of our past–*like he was holding onto them until I was ready.*

His browns knit together. "What?"

"It's just... you've been there for me, even when I didn't realize it. Thank you for being here and for being you. Everything's better because of it."

His hand slides to the nape of my neck, tugging me gently toward him. "I don't want to miss anything important in your life," he says before stealing another kiss. "Now, let's go celebrate."

I know my friends will end up at their self-made graduation party–an escape room and karaoke night we had planned with Taylor, Alexis, Kylie and their boyfriends weeks ago. Even though I would have been the odd one out, I was excited. Now that Mack is here, there isn't anywhere I'd rather be than alone with him. Celebrating for us means going back to my apartment to spend this unexpected time together, and luckily, they all understand.

As soon as we walk through my front door, I veer to the left, landing on the couch to immediately strip off my wedges. Mack sits next to me, pushing up the sleeves of his black button up before pulling my feet onto his lap. He gently massages his thumbs into my cramping feet, his forearms flexing as he does. Damn, my boyfriend is sexy.

I lie back, my head resting on the armrest of the couch. A quiet moan of relief leaves me as his hands release the tension in my feet, and he raises his gaze to meet mine. "Thanks again for coming, Mack. It means a lot to me. To Avery too."

"There's no way I was going to miss it. This is a big deal, Mace." He pauses, shifting my legs off his lap, so he can reach into a pocket of his black jeans. He pulls out a small white box and holds it out for me. "I got something for you."

I sit and reach for it, my heart racing. I haven't gotten a gift from a guy since high school. I gently lift the square lid. Under it lies a shiny, silver charm bracelet. "Wow, this is beautiful, Mack."

He smiles. As I reach for it, his hand stops mine. "Wait, can I show you what they all mean?" I nod and he reaches for the jewelry. I set the box on the coffee table, and when I turn back to him, he's holding the bracelet between us. The links are small, with different charms dangling from every few. He adjusts it in his hand, singling out one of the charms. He's excited to show me, and it's adorable.

"Okay, so... I know lately you've been worried about figuring out where you're supposed to go in life. I wanted you to have something that reminds you every day you're going to see the world and make a difference in it. I want you to know how much I believe in you."

Tears well in my eyes, and the thought that I might love him flashes through my mind. He continues. "I've watched Avery and you make lists for years, of all the places you want to go. That's what some of these are." He holds the palm tree charm in front of me. "This one is for Costa Rica. I know that's on the top of your list." I love that he remembers. He scoots his fingers along the chain until he's pinching the edge of the next charm between his thumb and pointer finger. "This elephant one is for Thailand... The four leaf clover is for Ireland, and good luck of course." He holds up the cutest silver kangaroo charm. "Obviously this one is for Australia. Just throwing the idea out there, you could take me with you when you go there." He doesn't give me time to respond to any of his comments. He's talking quickly like he wants to show me all of them at the same time. After another minute of explaining charms, there are only two left I haven't seen up close. The first is a small plain charm cut to the shape of Oregon State. "This one is obvious. Oregon will always be your first adventure, ya know?" I nod in agreement. As he rubs the last charm between his fingers, his enthusiasm disappears and is replaced by nerves.

"What's the last one?" I'm even more curious now as I study the hesitation in his emerald eyes.

He releases the charm from his fingers, and he lets the bracelet fall into his palm, holding it out toward me. My eyes follow. The way it lands, I can see it's a simple heart covered in tiny diamonds.

"I know you are working on a plan for where to go from here. I was thinking maybe you could try to figure it out in California. I want... I hope you'll consider letting me be your next adventure. Now that you've graduated, and your lease is about to be over, will you move in with me?"

His eyes lock onto mine again, vulnerability shining in them. It must have taken him a lot to suggest this. He's lived with a girl before, but that didn't work out, and it would still be a big adjustment for him too. My thoughts race. I've never lived with anyone besides my parents or Avery–which is completely different from a boyfriend.

Before I have a chance to pull myself out of my head, he adds to his thoughts as if he needs to justify them. "I know we haven't been together that long yet or even spent that many days together. I know it would be a lot more of an adjustment for you, I know this is a lot to ask, but I feel really good about our relationship. If you're not ready–"

I cut him off by wrapping my hands around his outstretched palm, still holding my new bracelet. "Part of me is nervous and a little scared, but all of me wants to say yes. So yes. I want to live with you, Mack."

He breathes out a sigh of relief and smiles. "I can't fucking wait."

"Okay, well, I can't wait for you to put my perfect new bracelet on me." I shove my hand in his face and wiggle it around.

He laughs and undoes the clasp before linking it around my wrist.

As soon as it's on, I fall back onto the couch again. My feet are on Mack's lap, my head is on the arm of the couch, and my wrist is above me, my bracelet dangling in front of my eyes so I can examine it up close.

I'm examining the charms when Mack's calloused hands rub slowly up the outside of either calf. He grips my left ankle, gently moving it behind him as he turns toward me, now in between my legs. His hands run up my legs, pausing at the bottom of my thighs and applying slight pressure. I shift my gaze away from my bracelet to see what he's up to. "Don't mind me, I'm just working on part two of your present." He smirks before he dips his head, kissing the inside of my knee softly. My breath hitches in anticipation.

His hands move torturously slow along the outside of my thighs, gently pushing the hem of my blue flowered sundress with them. Light kisses graze my inner thigh and stop only for the brief moment it takes him to hook his fingers around the edge of my navy lace thong and slide it off. When his hands connect with my skin again, it's along the backside of my legs. They wrap around the outside of my thighs, simultaneously pulling my legs apart and guiding them over his shoulders. He slides to the floor, his knees finding their place, without letting go of me. Then in one smooth motion he tugs on me lightly, pulling my back flat against the couch, and bringing me to him. It gives him perfect access as his mouth lands on me.

His tongue drags soft and slow across me, and my entire body aches to have more of him. A whimper escapes, and he spreads my legs further apart, burying his face between my thighs and groaning into me. He teases, alternating between long slow drags and a few short licks that dip only slightly into me. He knows exactly what he's doing–keeping me riding the edge. It's pure ecstasy and torture.

When I can't handle the building pressure inside me any longer, I search for release by linking my legs behind his head, pulling him even closer. He laughs at my need for him and it vibrates through me, bringing me to the tipping point. I weave my fingers into his dark hair, the charms from my bracelet mixing into the strands as I tug on them. His tongue dives deeper, hot and firm against me. Every muscle in my body tightens, and I'm gasping for air as I ride the contracting waves of pleasure. He leaves his tongue pressed against me until I beg him to stop and squirm away.

As soon as I come down, he lifts himself on the couch, hovering over me, an arm on each side of my face. He plants a soft kiss on my lips before whispering, "I really like doing that."

"I really like you." The words come out without any hesitancy. "I feel good about my decision. And not just because it means more of that." I smile, and he returns the gesture.

"Good," his says before pressing his lips to mine.

CHAPTER FORTY-THREE

The morning after graduation, I wake to Mack sitting on the edge of my bed, his forearm muscles flexing in the sunlight streaming through the window as he laces his black Nikes. *What a beautiful way to wake up.* He's so sexy, even from the side and first thing in the morning. He's already got his black hat on, backward, with strands of his dark brown hair sticking out from under it. His jaw is more defined than the younger version of himself, lined with stubble that wasn't there when we were kids. The muscles in his arm flex under his plain black T-shirt as he finishes tying his shoes. I get a good twenty seconds of staring in before he realizes I'm awake.

"Hey, babe." He turns so he faces me more and smiles. "Go back to sleep, I'm going for a run."

"Noooooo, don't leave me. Can I come with you?" I whine. I did well meeting with the running club every week for the first few months of school, but I haven't been once since the new year started. I need to get back to it. Plus, I don't want to be away from him.

"You want to? Let's go!"

"It's been a while, so you might have to wait for me. I don't want to ruin your run."

"I'll always wait for you. Come on!" He reaches for my hand and pulls me up.

Five minutes later I'm in black leggings, a hot pink sports bra, and lacing my matching Asics. "Okay, I'm ready."

Mack looks up from his phone, his now heady eyes roaming over my entire body. "You need to get out that door before we don't leave at all." There's a seductive rasp to his voice.

My cheeks flush as I hide my smile. I walk out the door, waiting for Mack to come through before locking it behind us. Following his request, I take off in a jog, directing him to the right, toward a running trail behind our apartment complex. One of the things I love about Oregon is how outdoor activity friendly it is. There are biking and running trails everywhere. Avery and I chose this apartment specifically because it's next to one of our favorite greenways that runs along a river and leads you straight to campus if you go far enough.

"Why are you smiling?" Mack's voice breaks through my thoughts about the time Avery and I first ran this trail and got so lost our three mile run turned into eight.

"I'm thinking about how many times I've done this with Avery. It's not that I didn't think about you being crazy enough to run for fun too–I know you played soccer–I just never imagined we'd be doing it together."

He glances back and slows his speed to fall into line with me. "I've thought about a lot of things we've been doing together."

"Really? Like what?" I ask, a little out of breath.

"I don't know. Everything. Going out on Saturday nights, staying in for lazy Sunday mornings. I want it all with you." His voice is sweet and genuine, not affected at all from the first mile.

"Every weekend we spend together makes me wish we could have that all the time. I love being able to do whatever you're doing. Like this. Soon, we will get to."

"I love this too. When things calm down with the band, we will have even more freedom. We could do whatever we want."

"Wait, what do you mean calm down?" I shift my body so I'm nearly running sideways, trying to discern what he means from his body language or face somehow.

"I don't know. I mean, I've loved playing, especially this last year, but it's not something I plan on doing forever. I've realized there are other priorities in my life now."

"Do you mean me?" My stomach flutters at the thought even though I shouldn't assume. "I don't want to be the reason you don't live out your dream."

"It's not like that. I love music and my band. I just don't see us getting big enough to justify it being my whole life. I've realized as I get older, I want more than that.

"What do you want?"

"Eventually, I'd like to come back here. When I'm ready to settle down, buy a house, start a family and all that, ya know? I want to be closer to Avery for that too. I don't want to miss out on being there for her, since our parents aren't around. And I'd like you to be there for all of it too. If that's something you want."

Wow, this got serious. My heart rate picks up, even though our running pace hasn't. I loved hearing his vision. It's more real than just an invitation to pick up my life for him right now. He's actually thought about what our future could look like.

"Does that freak you out?" I must have gotten lost in my head for a little too long. "I'm sorry, I'm trying to be honest. I know our relationship is moving fast and you just agreed to move in with me, and that's a big enough step in itself..."

I stop running and reach out to run my fingers along his wrist to get his attention. He stops and turns toward me. Worry is evident in his eyes, and I can't help but to want to calm it. "Can you find us a house next door to Avery and Miller?" My smile is big enough he must know I'm serious.

"Wait, really?" He still seems unsure.

I step so close I can feel the heat of our run radiating off him. I lace my fingers through his before looking at him. "Honestly, I hadn't thought that far into the future. Deciding to move to California last night was the most direction I've taken in my life in a while. But hearing you lay out that vision... Just because I don't necessarily know what career is in my future, doesn't mean I don't know who I want to be in it. I'm enjoying this so much. *Us.* I love where we are headed, now and in the future that exists in your head." As I talk, I watch light replace the worry in his eyes.

He unlinks one of his hands from mine. Bringing his free hand to my chin, he grazes his fingers along my jaw, tilting my face to his. His other hand moves to grip my hip, pulling me to his body as his lips press into mine. He doesn't try to make out with me, just stills for a moment against me as we stand in the middle of the paved path, enclosed by trees.

His lips pull away from mine, but his hands don't. Our gaze stays locked, so I see the smirk in his eyes before it crosses his face. He steps away from me and takes off running.

I take off after him.

CHAPTER FORTY-FOUR

Pulling up in my dusty red Corolla, I see the tour bus already parked in its place behind the bar. I check my makeup in my visor mirror one last time before stepping out onto the pavement. It's cold tonight, but I know I'll be hot once I'm inside surrounded by a few hundred people, so I'm wearing black jeans and a plain gray T-shirt. I text Mack to let him know I'm here and not even a minute passes before the side service door opens, my perfect boyfriend sticking his head out with a grin on his face, waving me over. As soon as I reach him, he wraps his arms around me–like he didn't see me two weekends ago–surrounding me in his cinnamon scent. He pulls back only to kiss me, letting his lips stay pressed into mine for a moment before he turns to go back inside.

I follow him in and see they are almost finished setting up. One barback wipes the counter while another dumps ice into the well. This venue is way bigger than the one he usually plays in California. There's a side of the stage sectioned off by a curtain. He has a stool set up for me by his extra guitar and some mic stands, so I can watch the show more comfortably. I'm excited to see him play again now that I know what to expect and have listened to every song enough times to have them memorized.

His show was perfect. I love seeing him in his element because he looks so happy when he's playing music. But after they finish packing their equipment, he finds me with a smile on his face that I love more. He's got a box of equipment in his hands and motions for me to come with, so I follow him to the underneath storage of the bus, where he slides in the last box.

Grabbing my hand, he leads me onto the bus and walks me to the back. There's a community space lined with black leather couches with a small coffee table in the middle. We sit on the side of the couch and Mack's arm instantly reaches around my shoulder as he kisses the side of my head. As he watches his buddies, he plays with my hair, twisting it around his fingers to tug on it–and tugging on my heart in the process. I wish I never had to be away from him. I can't wait to be in California together. His touch, even just his presence, is enough to comfort and ground me every single time.

My attention pulls away from him as the drummer dumps a white powder from a small baggie onto the table. I know it's cocaine, despite never having seen it before. I watch it being scraped into a thin line with a credit card. As I look at Mack with wide eyes, the drummer also looks in our direction. "Mack?" He nods in the direction of the table, with a smirk on his face.

"Come on man, you know I don't do that shit anymore." There's a flash of hesitation in his sideways glance to me, and I watch regret set in when he realizes he didn't think fast enough to leave out that word.

We've never had this conversation before, and it's very clear he was never planning on it.

My heart pounds wildly, the beat loud in my ears. Before I can say anything, he stands, links my fingers with his and pulls me toward the bunks that line the hallway of the bus. He slides the curtain on one of the bottom bunks open to reveal his "room." It's smaller than I imagined, a strip light along the back edge, and his backpack full of clothes jammed in the corner. I have no idea how the heck both of us will fit in there, which was my plan until two minutes ago. Despite my reservations he can surely feel, he pats his bed, nodding at me to get in. I slide in, lying on my side with my back to the wall because there is no other option if we expect both of us to fit.

He slips in next to me, after taking his Converse off and stuffing them in the space above his backpack. Wrapping his arm around my waist, he pulls us closer but stays far enough back that he can look at me. His hand moves to the lock of hair that's fallen into my face and gently tucks it behind my ear–vulnerability in his eyes. He knows my mood shifted and why I'm bothered. Since the first day he came to my apartment, it seems like he's been able to gauge me so well. I look toward the ceiling two feet from my face. His hand still resting on my cheek, he pulls my gaze back to him.

Music blasts from the back of the bus so he has to talk at normal volume for me to hear him. This conversation seems like it should be done in a whisper, so it feels more intense. Discomfort tingles against my skin, but he doesn't break eye contact with me. "Listen, babe, I was a different person my first year on the road. Everything was new and exciting, and I cared too much about fitting in with the guys." It starts off sounding like excuses, but then his voice softens, and his eyes shift away for a moment, like he's embarrassed. "I know how dumb that sounds looking back, but I can't change it, and I wouldn't. It may have taken forever for us to find our way to each other, but I know every choice I made is what led me back to you. I know you hate this, but please know that's not me anymore. The person I've been with you these past few months, that's who I am, and it's who I want to be."

I suck in a deep breath to calm myself before I start talking. My voice cracks anyway. "How bad was it?" I hold my breath waiting for his response.

He sighs. "Bad. I was high all the time. I wasn't sleeping. The guys get away with slipping up on stage, but I started fucking up lyrics–not so easy to cover up. I had one really bad show that thankfully helped snap me out of it."

I absorb what he's said. "Even after a whole quarter learning about it, I've never had an opinion about this before–maybe because it's not something I've had to deal with personally. But I'm already feeling insecure about what I'm doing with my life and feeling out of control. Then everything happened with Avery and it was such a scary situation, with someone I could always count on to be safe in my life. With one decision, it felt like that security was taken from me. That wasn't even her fault. We lost control of a situation without doing anything wrong. But knowing you could potentially *choose* to do something unsafe, it worries me. And not telling me about it, when you're usually so open with me, is upsetting, especially if I'm going to move all the way to California for you. You can't keep important things from me."

He sighs, hurt filling his eyes. "I never want to make you feel unsafe. All I want to do is protect you. It's *why* I'm so happy you are moving in with me. I know what it's like to live with someone you can't count on, and I don't want you to feel that way."

"That means a lot to me. You are my safe place, Mack, and I'm sure I'll feel even more strongly about that when we live together. I know you can give me everything you never got at home. I don't doubt that. I never want to compare you to your dad because you aren't him. But I saw the impact his choices had on you and Avery. Now that I know you're surrounded by this all the time, and it's an urge you've given into before... it's not that I don't trust you. It just scares me that one choice could potentially change everything. I don't know what I would do if drugs took you away from me."

He takes a moment to study my face, and the look on his makes me feel like he's torn between saying two different things. "I don't want to think about us not being together." He pauses. "I know I should wait for a time when you're not upset or we aren't crammed into this excuse of a bedroom, but I have to tell you." He pauses again, like he's trying to clear the nerves from his voice. When he talks again, it comes out perfectly clear. "I love you, Maci. I knew it was inevitable the moment I walked into your apartment three months ago. I could feel it. You don't have to say it back if you're not ready. I just want you to know how serious I am about you and us. I don't want you to have any doubts, especially when I'm on the road and we aren't together. I'm sorry I didn't tell you about this before. I wanted to leave it in the past and focus on our future together."

A tear that's been sitting in the corner of my eye finally falls. I was afraid when I saw those lines sitting on the table, but my love is stronger. Despite the fact we've only been together a few months, I do love Mack. I know it, without any doubt, because it's like nothing I've ever felt before. I love how safe I feel when I'm around him. I love how reassured I am not only by his words and his touch but simply by his presence. In my world that has felt chaotic in the past year, he's been the thing that helps me feel grounded, despite this new information.

"I love you too, Mack," I whisper right as he reaches to wipe the tear off my cheek. He pauses with his hand still on my face, and his eyes go wide-right before he closes them and closes the distance between our lips.

I cannot get close enough to him fast enough. I reach down and unbutton his jeans then tug at the zipper. I pull on his jeans, but get stuck, considering I can hardly move in this six by three foot shoebox. He helps me, kicking them off right before he reaches for the button on my jeans to do the same. The next few minutes are a frazzled, tangled mess of an attempt to get our clothes off. It would be funny if I wasn't overcome by the weight of realizing this is the first time I've ever been in love with someone who has told me they feel the same. Yeah, I'm frantic trying to get closer to this man right now, but my soul is calm, despite my racing heart trying to convince me otherwise. It's like the feelings of my need for him and knowing I have all of him now have finally melded together.

I roll on top of him, careful not to hit my head on the top of the bunk. Reaching between us I feel how hard he already is. My heart pounds, loving how much he wants me, in every way. The ache between my legs begs for relief as I take the condom from him, rolling it on before guiding him into me. I intended to let him fill me slowly to savor every second of this, but an urgent need for him wins out.

One hand framing his face and the other pressing into the bunk wall, I steady myself, sliding down onto him faster than he expected. A groan escapes his lips, and his eyes roll back. His calloused hand grips my hip, and I continue to ride him. He sweeps the hair out of my face with his other hand gently, but the next sensation is anything but as he tugs my face to his with a firm grip on my hair. Sliding his hand down until he's palming my breast, he rolls my nipple between his fingers, a flutter shooting through me. I grind into him until he's so deep inside, I feel him everywhere. It's almost painful and uncomfortable but still not enough.

I rock into him, pulling back slowly, before taking him in again, each time still feeling like we aren't close enough. I want every inch of my skin touching his, for my body to consume him the way my heart already has. Both my hands grip the sheets now, twisting them as my stomach contracts, pressure starting to build. There's no stopping it. I shove my face into the pillow behind Mack's head to muffle my moans as my orgasm consumes me. Waves of heat flow through my body as I feel his release pulsing inside of me. It's so much more than a physical sensation. This feeling of wholeness floods every part of me. I didn't realize how much I want this–how much I want Mack.

Our breathing steadies, and I pull back, settling my chin on his hot chest so I can look at him. He pushes the sweat soaked hair from my face, his green eyes dark and full of fire as his teeth tug on the corner of his lip. I watch him, trying to memorize the way he looks. He laughs lightly, and it vibrates through us. Confusion washes over me.

"I... planned on that being more lovemaking than... me frantically trying to have you faster than possible." I smile as he leans up to kiss my forehead. "I love you."

"I love you too."

CHAPTER FORTY-FIVE

I left my books for last. I'm the worst at letting go, but I know I won't need them now that I've graduated, and I don't need to drag them all the way to California. Some of these textbooks are ridiculously heavy and big anyway, so I decide to box them up and drop them off at my parents' house before I leave. After a month being in the states around graduation, they are back to gallivanting around the world but support this move 100%. When I shared my concerns, my mom reassured me. She said, "Sweetie, you only have one life. There's no way to know if the choices we make are right. We can only know what makes us happy. If you think this will make you happy, then you should go. And not that it should be a deciding factor, but you know how much we love Mack." My mom is the best.

I pick up my statistics book to toss it in my box but notice the corner of a piece of paper sticking out of the top, between two of the pages. That's strange. I don't usually keep notes in my books. I pull it out.

It takes me a moment to realize who it's from. My mouth drops open as I start to read.

Hey, Maci, In case you've forgotten about me already, I was the one who took you on your first motorcycle ride, we ate waffles, and had the most incredible night before

I ghosted you. I was just thinking about you. I've been thinking about you a lot lately. Wanted to say I didn't forget about you. When we met, I was heartbroken. I've been single this entire time, and I'm doing much better now. If it hadn't been for that, I would have loved to date you. The truth is, the night we spent together is what I needed to get my confidence back and feel like I was deserving of someone, and I wanted that someone to be you. But I didn't realize it until I thought it would be too late to call. I still regret not kissing you that night and giving us a chance. Anyway, I'm not sure if you'll still be around by the time you read this, but if you are, give me a call. -Troy

I reread it three times before folding it back up. It doesn't matter now. I'm moving to California to be with Mack, and I love him. It's just crazy to think about what could have happened if I'd found this letter sooner. How long has it been here? It had to be from before I ran into him at Dean's. *How did it get here?*

I toss the letter in my box of random knickknacks I'm bringing. I'm not sure why I don't throw it away, but it doesn't feel right. I spent weeks trying to figure out answers to questions I had about Troy, and now I finally have them. I got to a point where I didn't wonder at all anymore, and now I'm living this different life where I don't and can't know what would have been possible, but finding this piece of an old puzzle is still nice.

I'm distracted when I find another piece of paper loose between two books. It's an old list Avery and I made, covered in doodles of palm trees and airplanes and places we want to visit. The travel fund from my parents is still in my account, but I've yet to come up with a plan. Rather, my international travel dreams have been put on pause for my move to California. I am okay with it for now.

I twist my charm bracelet from Mack through my fingers. I might be unsure of exactly who I am, or what direction I want my life to go, but I'm certain about him. I repeat my mom's words to myself. Follow what makes you happy. Mack is currently at the top of that list. I have plenty of time to figure out what's on the rest.

CHAPTER FORTY-SIX

I knock on the door, and it opens immediately. Before I'm fully in the entryway, Mack has me scooped up in his arms. Taking a step back, he spins me around before setting me down. I tighten my arms around his neck. "Hi, baby," I whisper in his ear like I didn't just get off the phone with him.

He offered to fly to Oregon and drive with me, but I didn't think it made sense. The drive was my last opportunity to be alone, and I thought it would be a good segway into the next phase of my life. But then I ended up talking to Mack for about half of the 13-hour drive since I got tired driving so far.

"I can't believe you're finally here!" he says, voicing my thoughts. "I'll help you get your clothes." He's already pulling away from me and heading to the door.

My hand stops him by tugging on his wrist. "I haven't seen you in like five weeks, Mack. I don't care about my stuff." It takes him a second to register what I'm saying before he kicks the front door shut and picks me up again, with that signature grin of his on his face.

None of my things made it in the apartment last night. I let Avery keep all our furniture from the apartment because she has a whole house to fill now, and we don't need anything else in Mack's place–our place now. It only takes a little over an hour to get everything carried up and put away in the space Mack emptied out of his closet. This will to be strange since I've only ever lived with Avery, and the past year it felt like I didn't even do that. Avery is so excited about this move. She's sad I'm leaving her, but she's also getting very ahead of herself planning our future as sisters. She and the girls took me out a few nights before I left as a sendoff party. They promise they will come visit me.

I'm happy I'll have Lexy here, and she's excited too. Mack said I'm her only girl friend, so it'll be great for both of us. I've promised myself I won't take her friendship for granted by spending all my time with Mack. I'm beyond thrilled we get to be together all the time now, but I'm also a little worried. Some of what I learned in my Psychology of Relationships class really stuck with me–like it'll be better if both of us have something to do outside of each other. Mack already has music, and until I figure out my thing, I know having Lexy around will help. This is such a big step for me. I'm not only moving in with a guy for the first time, but I'm also in a new and unfamiliar place, and I don't want to be one of those girls who doesn't have anything to live for besides her boyfriend.

I finish hanging my last shirt as arms wrap around me from behind. I lean back into his shoulder, and it feels so comfortable, like my being here is the right choice. "Are you hungry, babe?" he questions. "I was thinking we could walk over to the café and get lunch."

Mack orders us two bagel sandwiches and fruit smoothies from the café counter, and we find a table while we wait. I keep finding myself here, but I've never been inside. It's modern, mostly stained brown wood and white with sage green accents scattered artistically throughout. The vibe is very California, and I love it. I know Mack comes here regularly, and I won't mind. I think being a regular somewhere will give me more of that small town feel I know I'll miss about Oregon.

As I finish scanning the room, a beautiful and petite brunette stops in front of our table with our order. "Oh, hey, Mack!" she exclaims.

"Hey, Abby. This is my girlfriend, Maci. She just moved here." He grins and squeezes my hand across the table. It's the first time he has ever introduced me as his girlfriend, and my stomach swarms with butterflies.

"About time. Maybe I won't have to hear you going on about her every morning now," she jokes. "Any chance she needs a job? We need someone to start right away." They both look at me.

"Actually...That would be great!" I don't have any idea what direction I want my life to go right now outside of Mack. It'll take me a while to learn new running routes around here, if I even feel comfortable going on my own. It's not that I couldn't read all day or hang out with Lexy, but having something to show up for might be nice. I want to contribute financially, too, though Mack has claimed we would be fine without it. I'm not sure if that's completely true and he just likes to take care of me, though. Either way I like this idea, and maybe I can work it out so some of my shifts overlap while he's gone.

"The real question is, is your opinion on coffee the one thing you and Mack fight about?" Abby laughs, curious.

"Nope, I'm a weirdo too. But I've been told I make a cup better than my opinion of it!"

"Perfect, you're hired! I'll see you in the morning around 8?"

I nod, squealing with excitement. It's not that working at a coffee shop is my dream, but everything feels like it's falling into place, or at the very least, heading in the right direction.

CHAPTER FORTY-SEVEN

My first day of work went well, and Abby already put me on the schedule for next week. Luckily whoever quit was willing to finish out this week so I get to spend my first few days here with Mack before he goes out of town this weekend.

"Ready, babe?" he calls from the entryway. I pull on my Asics before meeting him at the door. When I look up, I stop mid-step. He's wearing black basketball shorts, a green Oregon hoodie that matches his eyes, his backward hat, and his guitar is strapped around his back. It's nothing fancy, but holy shit, he's sexy. I can't believe I'm here and that he's mine. Seriously, why did it take me so long to *see* him?

He catches me staring. "What's wrong? Do I not match or something?" He looks down at himself, concerned.

"Ummm, are you sure we have to go? I'm thinking what would be a better idea... is if we stayed here. But more specifically, in our bed, without your clothes on, clothes that look very good by the way. Totally match." I start tugging on his wrist.

He smiles, but I can see his hesitation as he considers my offer. "Babe, no! We have plans. I have a surprise! Let's go!"

"Fiiiineee," I drag out the word dramatically, and he plants a soft kiss on my lips before I follow him out the door.

"I'm still confused why you brought your guitar on our hike. That thing is your baby, what if a bear eats it?"

"First, you are my baby, and second, there are no bears out here." He scans the woods. "I'm pretty sure."

I can tell Mack worries I'll miss Oregon too much because he keeps comparing California to back home. He planned this hike today for the same reason. It's a little cold with the breeze closer to the water, but after a half hour of walking uphill, I'm warm enough to tie my sweatshirt around my waist. "Are we almost there?!" I ask, tugging on the knot and jogging a few steps to catch up.

He glances over his shoulder with a wide grin. "Yup!"

When I look up, I'm surprised by the view. I've only seen the city parts of California, but this is incredible. We are on a cliff overlooking the ocean. It's a little scary, but also breathtaking. When I scan my surroundings for Mack, I find him back a few feet with his hands shoved awkwardly in his pockets.

"What's wrong? Are you afraid of heights? Come here. I'll hold your hand!"

An uneasy laugh escapes him. "No. Okay well, yeah I am, but that's not why I'm nervous." He pauses. "I wrote a new song. I wanted to play it for you."

"Oooh, that's exciting! Am I'm the first to hear it? I feel so special! Why are you nervous? You sing songs you've written literally as your job."

"I've written songs about my experiences... but I've never written one for someone, let alone played it for them."

He wrote a song for me? About me? This is the sweetest thing someone has ever done, and I haven't even heard it. "Mack, your song could suck and I would still love it. But I know it won't. Play me my song!" I shriek at him, excited as I sit on the rock next to me to wait.

He hesitates, glancing at me before looking back down to make sure he's about to play the right chord.

We'd known each other forever,
but that day something changed,
though you didn't see me
the way I saw you,
I knew even then I was gonna fall.

Loving you is easy. It's like breathing,
it's second nature. Maybe there's a God
out there who brought you back to me.

I walked into your house,
after all those years.
You hadn't changed at all.
I knew now again,
I couldn't help but fall.

Now that we are together,
I'm never gonna let you go.
You make me want to be
a better man,

I'll live all of my days for you.

Loving you is easy.
It's like breathing,
it's second nature.
There has to be a God out there
who brought you back to me.

Loving you is easy...
it's the best high I've ever had.
Loving you is easy...

After the first line, the nerves left his voice like I knew they would. His confidence is one of my favorite things about him. As soon as he finishes, he hardly has time to swing his guitar to his back before I leap into his arms. "I can't believe you wrote me a song! I love it so much. I love you so much. I'm so excited for this chapter of our lives!"

"You have no idea." He squeezes me a little tighter.

Lying in our bed that night, I roll onto Mack's chest as he reaches his arm out, calling me to him. "I'm so in love with you," he murmurs into my hair before kissing the top of my head.

I smile against his bare chest before leaning up on my elbow. "Oh, well, isn't that a coincidence because I'm so in love with you." His green eyes light up. My heart swells in my chest with how happy I am to be here with him. An urge comes over me to put it into words. "You know what I was thinking about today on our hike back?"

"Tell me." He positions the hand not wrapped around me behind his head, like he's getting comfortable waiting for me to share a story.

"I was thinking about how crazy it is I moved here, without a plan really. I'm usually big on plans. But for some reason it doesn't feel crazy. It feels right."

He smiles. "You might not have known this was a plan, but it was always my plan."

I shove at his chest playfully. "Hey, it's not fair. You had more time to think about it."

"Not my fault you couldn't tell I wanted you long before you were mine." His grin widens.

"You're right. It's Avery's fault for keeping you away from me."

He chuckles. "I blame her for everything."

"But you should thank her too." I brush my hand over his chest. "She practically forced you on me."

"That's true. I guess that wins out, huh?"

"At least we don't have to waste any more time now. I was also thinking about what you said after graduation. About someday moving home. Do you still want that? Even though I just moved here."

"Absolutely." There's no doubt in his voice. "I love California. I love it even more now that you're here. But I don't see us here forever. I see it more as a chapter of our story, ya know?"

"That's what I was thinking too. I'm excited for this phase and to live in our own Hollywood world. But I'm also excited to settle down and live in the house you promised me right next to my best friend."

"So she can babysit for us whenever I want to have my way with you?" he jokes, pulling me on top of him.

I fold my arms on his chest and rest my chin on them. "This really doesn't freak you out thinking this far into the future, does it?"

"Why would it? You're it for me, Mace. I'm not going to change my mind about that."

"Thank you for giving me the chance to realize I feel the same about you." I lean in to kiss him, thankful every night can be like this.

CHAPTER FORTY-EIGHT

People and their coffee are *a lot* here. Oregon is much more laid back and simple. College kids only care about whatever will keep them awake through class. California is all about who can have the most fancy, complicated order and come up with a cool name for it. I find myself rolling my eyes constantly, but the tips make it worth it. Not to mention, I still haven't figured out how to translate and pursue my desire to help trafficking victims since I took that class. It's always in the back of my mind, but I'm okay with my relationship being the priority right now, and this job helps me get by.

It's helpful I've been able to pick up extra shifts lately because Mack has been out of town a lot. The first week I was here was perfect, but this past month alone, I've only seen him for five or six days. I'm not sure what I expected, or maybe I didn't fully think about it. I knew he was getting booked at more venues before I decided to move. Even with him being gone, I see him more than I did before, so I shouldn't complain. But whenever I call him lately, he's been too busy to talk, and I feel more alone than I thought I would.

CHAPTER FORTY-NINE

Mack (7:37 p.m.): *Hey, baby. Sorry I missed your call again. We've been so busy.*
    Me (7:38 p.m.): *It's okay, how's it going?*

    Me (12:03 a.m.): *I miss you.*

    Me (2:17 a.m.): *Going to bed, I know you're probably tired, so maybe you're already asleep. Just wanted to say I love you.*

CHAPTER FIFTY

I'm sitting on the couch scrolling through Netflix when the front door swings open and Mack comes through, his hands full with his guitar and travel bag. He drops everything in the entryway, making his way to me. A kiss presses to the top of my head. "Hi, baby."

I tip my head back to see him, reaching my arms out for him.

"Nope, get up! We are going out!"

"But you've been out for a week," I state the obvious and note how tired he looks.

"I know, which is why I'm taking this opportunity to start my week with you off right."

I smile so wide my cheeks hurt. "What are we going to do?"

"I was thinking mini golf. Then we can go to that new sushi place you've been wanting to try."

"Yes, please!" I shout, hopping off the couch to change out of my pajamas.

We played three rounds of mini golf before Mack finally had enough of me beating him. Hole in ones are one of my secret talents. Mini golf for me is like how pool is for Miller. I always want to play, and no one ever wants to go with me. It's not lost on me Mack will play even when he knows I'll win.

As we get in the car to head to sushi, Mack's phone rings. I instantly get a knot in the pit of my stomach, a bad feeling washing over me.

He answers and puts the phone to his ear. "Hey." Silence. "Okay," Mack responds to the voice I can't hear. "Yeah, I'll get on it, and call the guys... Yeah, I'll see you tomorrow."

Looking at me, he chews at the corner of his lip and sets his phone down hesitantly. I hold his stare without saying anything, waiting for an explanation for something I have a feeling I'm not going to like.

"I'm sorry, babe. That was our manager. I guess one of the bands on a tour up the East Coast had some emergency, and we've been asked to fill-in at the last minute..."

I already know the answer but ask the question anyway. "And you're going?" I manage to keep some of the frustration out of my voice, but it cracks and betrays me at the end.

"I know this sucks. I don't want to leave you. To be honest, I never thought this would happen for my band. You know this isn't the end game for me, but this is a huge opportunity for us to do a couple of shows in new places, to get more ears on our music. The guys are going to be psyched." He sighs. "This *is* their dream. I don't want to let them down." He keeps explaining as if it'll lessen the blow. "I know this is bad timing because I just got home. You know I'm doing this for us too though, right? This is the best way I can contribute to building our life right now. I want us to have more than an apartment off some street in Hollywood and be able to work toward our dream of going back home someday. This can help with that."

Do I know that? He's so genuine every time he speaks, and I know he truly believes he's doing this as much for us as he is for himself and the band. But right now, there hasn't been a whole lot of us. "I know," I whisper, looking down at my fingers twisted together in my lap. "It's just that I've hardly seen you, and you just got back." I hear the selfishness in my words as I say them.

He reaches over lightly caressing the side of my face, putting enough pressure to encourage me to look toward him. "Hey, I love you, Maci. This isn't going to be forever. It's just for now, it's just a chapter, remember?"

"How do you know that? You guys are so good. People are noticing, like they should. You're only going to be more in demand from now on. I know it's selfish of me to say this, but I'm struggling with sharing you."

"I'll be home in a week. It's only five shows. When I get back, we will reevaluate and devise a plan. We will figure this out, okay?"

I nod, and he leans in to kiss the side of my face before driving us to the sushi restaurant.

CHAPTER FIFTY-ONE

I haven't seen Mack in almost three weeks. The tour on the East Coast is going so well, they canceled the smaller shows that were scheduled on the West Coast for last week. The band that dropped out had to miss more shows than expected, so this is a big opportunity for Where We Are. I'm not trying to sound unsupportive; I'm so proud of him.

I'm just so lonely.

I'm worried if I talk to anyone else about this, they will lecture me about how I was crazy for following him to California or how much of a mistake it was to make this big of a commitment so soon in our relationship. I got a lot of those comments when I came out here, except from Avery of course. And my parents, but I don't want to bother them with this while they are traveling in Europe. It makes me more grateful for Lexy. I've been spending as much time as I can with her. She always answers when I call, and she's been the only one I'm comfortable confiding in about Mack being gone and how it makes me feel. She really talked me down last week.

"It's the way of life for musicians, Maci," she said. "You need to trust Mack and believe this is what's best for his career and for your future. You'll get used to it, and it'll get easier."

Do I want to get used to it? I knew dating a musician would be different. I mean, I watch movies. I guess I didn't fully comprehend the gravity of it. I've been distracting myself the best I can for now. I've read the entire stack of books that have been sitting on my nightstand since I pulled them out of my boxes on moving day. I came across Troy's letter again too. I don't know enough about him to judge whether my life could have been different in a good or a bad way, and I feel guilty thinking about it, but without Mack being here, it's easy to let my mind wander. I remind myself of Lexy's pep talk. This guy loves me so much, and I love him. He's sacrificing time with me to give us a life together in the future, in the best way he can right now. Moving here was such a big step for our future, but since that first week, we haven't really checked in or touched base on what's going on with our lives. We haven't had a lot of time to talk or do anything else. I seem to be able to keep it together during the day, but as soon as I lie down in a dark room, on a bed I should be sharing with someone else, I'm consumed by loneliness and my ability to talk myself down disappears. I've cried myself to sleep more often than I like to admit.

It's after one in the morning when he lies down next to me, the mattress dipping with the weight of his body.

I turn to face him. He studies my face, and even in the dim light, I'm sure he can tell I've been crying.

His gaze catches mine, and he brushes his thumb over my cheek. "What's wrong, baby?"

My voice cracks on the first word out of my mouth. "It's not what I thought it would be."

"What isn't?" Concern and confusion wash over his face.

I take a deep breath, knowing I need to be honest with him. "I'm happy for you, Mack, that you get to live out one of your dreams. I know it makes you happy even if you don't intend to do it forever. Maybe jealous isn't the right word, but you get to travel and do something you love every day. It's not how I thought it would be. I thought I'd move here and get to be part of that, part of your life. I thought I'd come here and everything would fall into place because we could physically be together, but I hardly see you more than I did before. I feel left out, like I'm living on the outside of your life. I love you so much, Mack, but I'm not happy."

I can practically see the wheels turning in his brain as he's processing everything I'm saying. I'm sure it felt a little out of the blue, but at the same time, how has he not felt it? Maybe since he's living the same life he was before with the added convenience of me already being here when he gets home, it's different. For me, nothing is the same anymore, and it's overwhelming.

"Mace, I'm sorry, I had no idea you felt that way. I love having you to come home to, and I miss you every second I'm away. What if you start coming with us? We have room on the bus. And we will be fine without the money you've been making at the café."

"That's not what this is about, Mack." I sigh.

When he stares at me, waiting for me to continue, I do. "It's not just about me not wanting to be a girl at home pining for her boyfriend. I can't be that girl who only lives her life around someone–for someone. I know it's partly on me that I need to figure out what I want to do, but I feel so lost. Avery, you, all my friends back home, you all have plans and goals and dreams. Then here I am, with no clue what I'm doing."

Even though it's dark in here, I can see his eyes well with tears, glistening in the street light glowing through the window. He didn't even get emotional the night everything happened with Avery. I know his feelings for me have only deepened in the last few months, like mine have for him. It's why it's been so hard to be away from him. I got a taste of what it's like to have him in my life, and it feels like it's being torn away. I'm not intentionally hurting him. I just can't continue living this way.

He looks like he's trying to collect his thoughts. "How can I help you, Mace? I have no idea how to make this better."

"I don't think you can. This isn't about you. I need to find my thing, my place in the world, not just in yours. I just–"

He cuts me off before I can get another word out, the rage in his voice shooting through the air around us. "This isn't about me?!" He sits on the bed, running his hands up his face, all the way through his hair and locking them behind his neck. "Maci, you're my girlfriend. We live together. You're the person I want to spend my life with." He takes a deep breath to try to calm himself, but the result is pain replacing the anger in his eyes. I've never seen him like this. "I know you moved here for me, but that doesn't mean I'm not in this relationship as much as you are. You can't act like I'm not a part of this." He tries to regulate his volume, but it still comes out like yelling. It's overwhelming. This is the first fight we've had, and I don't know how to handle it. My heart races, and I'm sitting now, trying to understand the scene in front of me. Before I can figure out what to say, he slides off the bed, his feet landing hard on the ground, and storms out of the room.

Mack came back to bed shortly after he stomped off. We both laid there in silence, closer to the edges of the bed rather than the middle, where we usually sleep wrapped up in each other. There was so much tension in the air I couldn't fall asleep until sometime after three.

When I wake, the other side of the bed is empty. I reach for my phone to check the time. 10. I have a gut feeling Mack isn't home, which is confirmed when I see a sticky note on my nightstand. *Going to the recording studio until our show tonight. Love you. -M*

I sink back onto the bed with my arms folded over my eyes. I just want clarity. I'm frustrated. I'm confused. Partially I'm irritated with how much Mack freaked out because he's usually good at communicating. He took it way too personally. This really isn't about him–at least I don't think it is. It felt like insecurity, but I'd never seen him like that.

CHAPTER FIFTY-TWO

Lexy: *I'm sooooo bored. The only people in this bar tonight are a bunch of college girls who are obsessed with your boyfriend's stupid band. Come keep me company.* I can hear her playful mocking tone in my head as I read.

I laugh before I sigh and close my book. Mack has only performed once since I've been here, and I had to work at the coffee shop that night. I don't feel like being around him until we can be alone and come up with a plan. But I haven't seen Lexy in a few days, and Mack will be on stage, so it's not like we will be hanging out anyway. He probably won't even notice I'm there.

I change into a pair of jean shorts and a tank top, not bothering to text Lexy back. The bar where Mack's band holds a residency is only a mile up the road–it's why he chose this apartment–and I'll be there before she has a chance to check her phone. I call an Uber because it's too dark and late to walk, and I run out to meet it in the two minutes it takes to arrive.

Spotting Lexy's bright blonde ponytail immediately, I head over to snag a seat at the bar. I find one on the corner by the ice well where I know Lexy will be the most, and hop up on the black leather stool. It also has a perfect view of the stage.

A group of girls celebrating a bachelorette party–the bride in a white sequin dress that looks more like lingerie and her friends dressed in equally scandalous hot pink dresses–squeal out orders to Lexy while I scan the room. She was not joking. This place is full of girls with glow in the dark penis necklaces, birthday and bride sashes, and groupie googly eyes. I guess I shouldn't be one to talk because surely someone else would classify my eyes as googly if they caught them the moment I spot Mack with his guitar in his hands. Damn, he's sexy up there. His deep brown hair has grown out–I don't think he's gotten it cut in the two months since I've been here. Sweat flings off the ends every time he shakes his head, and his image screams sex. *I can't remember the last time we had sex.* I forgot how much I love watching him play. Despite being focused on what he's playing, it's evident by the smile on his face how much he loves it, and I love that for him.

Finally, as the song ends, Lexy catches a break from the swarm of girls and hands me my go-to drink, which is whatever concoction she created for me on the day we met. I pop the cherry in my mouth then sarcastically ask her about all the fun she's having. The next song starts, and my eyes wander back to the man none of these other girls get to take home tonight. Sometimes I wonder how I lived so many years close to him, and never stumbled upon the connection we have now. There's no sense in wishing the past had been different though, there's nothing I can do about it. What I'm struggling with is not knowing how to alter the present, which is something I do have control over. I like California well enough, and I really love Mack, regardless of how frustrated I am right now. I just wish I was certain about more than that.

The band plays for another half an hour, and I help Lexy wipe the bar top while she loads her dishwasher. As soon as the crowd starts to dissipate, I look toward the stage. I stand and head in Mack's direction as he's gently placing his guitar in its case. I decided being here but not talking to him would be a little too petty. We aren't in college anymore. We are adults who live together, and I can't expect him to act like that if I don't.

The odor of sweat and spilled alcohol fills the air as I push through people heading in the opposite direction. Mack jumps off the side of the stage. I'm pretty sure he saw I was here during the last song and is coming to meet me in the middle.

My shoe sticks to something–God knows what–and I rub the soles against the cement flooring to get it off. When I look up, I freeze. I see Mack, but he's no longer coming toward me. Instead, there's a girl, who clearly was much quicker in getting to him than I was. She throws an arm around his neck and kisses him quickly and forcefully on the lips before pulling back.

Mack stands there, in a haze, which is the complete opposite of what I'm doing right now. I storm at him with enough intensity to definitely catch his attention this time. I stop right in front of them and shove her off Mack, harder than I intended, and she falls to the floor. I feel bad, but I don't have time to deal with her.

"WHAT THE FUCK, MACK... are you kidding me?!" My gaze shifts from the girl on the floor to him. Panic rushes through me, as I stare into his bloodshot eyes that are so dilated I can hardly see any of the green in them. "...WAIT. ARE YOU HIGH?!" He stares back at me like he's unsure what to say. I don't know how much time passes because it feels like it's only been seconds, but it also feels like we've been standing here forever. Either way, he doesn't make a move to say anything, so I turn on my heel and storm out the side door, letting it slam behind me. The cold night air stings my skin where the tears stream down my face. I pause for a second to take a deep breath and try to process what just happened.

Then I hear his voice behind me.

"Babe. Baabyyy," he whines, before a seriousness washes over his face, like he's sobered in an instant. "Mace." The deeper version of his voice pierces through me as I step backward. "I'm sorry, I messed up. I don't know what got into me. It won't happen again, I promise."

"No. This is a big deal. I TOLD YOU. You know this. This is the one thing, Mack. I'm supposed to be able to count on you." The bitterness in my words even rattles me.

"I know. I'm sorry. I fucked up." He steps toward me, but I back up. He stops in his tracks before he continues. "I was upset about not knowing how to help you, how to help us. I love you so much, Maci. Let's get out of here and go home and talk about this."

I fall to the ground, my knees propping up my arms as I scream into my hands. He bends down and touches my shoulder. My words come out muffled through my hands. "Talking about this should have been the solution before drugs." I connect my gaze with his. He's on his knees in front of me. "You're the one who told me I need to draw a line somewhere. I love you, Mack, but I can't do this. It doesn't matter why you did it." He tries to interject, but I cut him off. "I can't forgive you. Please go."

I redirect my stare to the roughness of the worn cement under me, unable to look at his high. By the time I glance up, Mack has been replaced by Lexy, who wraps her arms around me as I lean into her.

CHAPTER FIFTY-THREE

The coffee table in front of me comes into focus, and all of last night floods back. I sink into the couch, defeated. I'm upset and a little conflicted about my decision, but not enough to make me feel like I made the wrong one. Even if something is right, that doesn't mean it's easy, and even if my choice was made in a split second, it was the hardest decision I've had to make. Maybe part of me was looking for a reason to change our situation, but I didn't want this.

Making bad decisions is about more than just a choice of whether or not to do it, "getting caught up in the moment" or peer pressure. It's about making the first choice of putting yourself in certain situations where making the wrong choice is significantly more likely to happen. I think that's a lot of the reason people cheat, or in situations like mine, do drugs, and why some people never will. Of course I believe love can be strong enough to conquer everything, blah blah blah. But I also think just because it's capable, doesn't mean it always will, or should.

I know Mack loves me. I truly believe that. But love doesn't always win, and it sure as hell isn't always enough. It is absolutely his fault. I'm not saying the guy has to be perfect. I'm not even saying he couldn't question or wonder if one more night falling back into an old habit could provide him comfort and be worth the potential risks. He's human. I mean, it would be hypocritical for me to say he's not allowed to think about his options and how they could play out. I've had "what if" moments in the past wondering what it would have been like if I went to Costa Rica with Dean and while reading Troy's letter a few months back.

But it didn't mean anything because I didn't act on it. Mack did, knowing how strongly I feel about him doing drugs. If he was that upset from our conversation because he loves me that much, he should have come *to me* for comfort and to figure it out. Plus, *I* was having a crisis, and he proved I can't count on him to support me through it. We used to communicate so well, and he should know me enough by now to have faith we'd work through this. But as much as I love him and thought he was it for me, I don't know if I can forgive him for turning to the last thing he should have instead of the first thing, for crumbling what should be the foundation of our relationship–trust and respect.

I reach over and check my phone, the red bar on top letting me know the battery is almost dead. There are 4 missed calls and the same number of texts. I click on Mack's name to open our text thread.

Mack (11:47 p.m.): *Please pick up, Mace. I need to know you're okay. Please can we talk about this?*

Mack (11:52 p.m.): *I love you so much. That has to count for something.*

Mack (12:06 a.m.): *I know I fucked up. I'm so sorry. Please call me back, and tell me how I can fix this.*

Mack (12:59 a.m.): *Baby, I don't want to lose you. I can't lose you.*

I press play on the first voicemail, but as soon as I hear the break in Mack's voice, my phone falls from my hand, and my eyes fill with tears. Hearing his confidence slip is unlike him, and it almost breaks my heart the most.

I don't hear Lexy coming up behind me until she sits next to me. Wrapping her arm around my shoulder, she pulls me to her.

After a moment, she pulls back enough to look at me when she asks, "What happened, Maci? Is it about the girl who kissed him? I served her last night, but I'd never seen her there before. She's just some drunk, random girl."

"It's not that." I let out a small laugh flashing back to how crazy she seemed. "I saw the whole thing and could tell that girl was nuts. I don't think Mack would have had time to react to that. It was something else. I'm not ready to talk about it, but he broke my trust. How can I forgive him for purposely doing something he knew would hurt me?"

She doesn't push me on what happened. "Do you think he's really sorry?" she asks as she glances at the text thread I've opened again.

"I mean, yeah, but–"

She cuts me off. "Maci, Mack is a good guy. He helps me out at the end of the night, he's patient with any problems that arise at the club. Not to mention, you know how picky I am with who I let in, and *he* is my best friend, outside of you of course. The guy is obsessed with you. In the two years I've known him, he's never brought anyone else around. I've never seen him look at anyone else the way he looks at you. Hell, I rarely see anyone look at someone the way he looks at you. Is this truly something so bad he doesn't deserve a second chance?"

I contemplate her words. Am I being dramatic and overreacting? When she lays out the kind of guy Mack is, it feels like I am. But I recall the night Mack first said he loved me, and how he promised he wouldn't do something like this to jeopardize our relationship. Anger flows through my body as I recall the memory. I maybe could have let it slide if he was an ignorant guy or if I didn't know he used to have a problem with drugs in the past. But we had an actual conversation about how important this was to me. This is on top of him getting upset about my loneliness instead of comforting me. We are supposed to be in this together, and it doesn't feel like we are. I can't accept that.

"I think it is, Lex." I look at her, tears threatening to fall.

She sighs and pulls me into an actual hug, "I'm so sorry. You know you can stay here as long as you need."

When she stands to walk away, I look back at my phone and type my reply, having made my mind up about this. *I'm sorry, Mack, but there isn't anything that can fix this right now. You broke my trust, and I don't know what to do about that but take time to figure out what I want. I love you, but I don't think that's enough.*

CHAPTER FIFTY-FOUR

Mack lasts four days after our breakup before he texts me.

Mack (September 26th, 8:45 p.m.): *Hey... I know you want your space, but I just want you to know I'm thinking about you.*

Mack (September 28, 7:26 a.m.): *If there's anything I can do to help our relationship, let me know.*

Mack (September 29, 9:50 p.m.): *Sleep well. xo*

Mack (September 30, 3:15 p.m.): *Just letting you know we are filling in for someone at the bar tonight, in case you were planning on going to see Lexy. Didn't want you to be caught off guard.*

Mack (October 1, 11:37 a.m.): *Accidentally picked up my buddy's drink thinking it was my tea. Spit that coffee right out. Made me think of you :)*
Mack (7:13 p.m.): *I love you.*

Mack (October 3, 10:19 a.m.): *I came across some things you forgot. I'll bring them to Lexy's while you're at work.*

When I got home from the café, a pair of my leggings, my school hoodie and a few pairs of my underwear are folded neatly on one of the couch cushions. I go to move them into the closet but feel something hard between them. I pull out a CD. Wow, I haven't seen one of these in forever. Even though my car is old enough to have a CD player, Mack hooked up an auxiliary cord so I could just play Spotify. I wouldn't even know how to burn a mix anymore. I laugh, thinking about the time Avery and I genuinely thought we were going to get arrested when my dad caught us downloading music with LimeWire when we were 13. Mack is a professional musician though, so if anyone could still make one, it would be him.

I pull the silver disc out of its clear case. "Maybe Someday" is written in his handwriting in black sharpie across the top, a small heart next to the "y." Lexy is still at work, so I walk out the door, back to my car. Almost an hour later, I'm still outside, silent tears running down my face. I know every song on here was carefully chosen. There aren't any sad songs, rather only ones full of love and hope and about everything working out in the end. There's also a song the cover band was playing when we went to the Saturday Market together and a song from *Pitch Perfect*–the Anna Kendrick version of "Cups." It doesn't slip by me he put the live version of each song on the CD, knowing I prefer them. The very last song is his, the one he wrote for me. As far as I knew, it hadn't been recorded in the studio.

My heart is divided in two, half of it begging me to let it love Mack because he's still here trying, and the other half reminding me it's time to focus on loving myself. I leave the CD in my car's player and head back inside.

Mack (October 5, 8:06 a.m.): *I'm not giving up on us. I'm willing to do whatever it takes, Maci.*
Mack: *I can fix this.*

Mack (October 6, 3:47 a.m.): *Miss you more than you know.*
Mack: *Hope you have a great day.*

CHAPTER FIFTY-FIVE

It's been two weeks since I last saw Mack. The day after it all fell apart, Lexy drove with me while he was at the recording studio to pick up my things and bring them to her apartment. She doesn't have a second bedroom, but the hall closet fits most of my clothes, and her couch is comfortable. It works for now at least, and I'm thankful for her. Luckily, she only lives five minutes from Mack, so my drive to the café for work still isn't bad. I've been picking up as many shifts as possible while I figure out what my next step will be. I worry every day Mack will walk through the front door when I'm working since he was a regular here long before it became my place of employment. As far as I know, he hasn't been in once while I've been working. I'm not sure if it's out of respect for the space I asked for or if Lexy said something to him about staying away.

I haven't replied to any of his texts, mostly because I don't know what to say and partly because I don't trust myself enough to not just forgive him. Part of me desperately wants to forgive him, but the other part of me knows I need to take time for myself to figure out how to make things work, if that's what I want. I'm not ready to be in a relationship again because I can hardly stand to be trapped with my own thoughts. This isn't only about Mack's betrayal. That was just the catalyst that led me to look deeper into what I really want my life to look like.

I tie my apron around my waist and unlock the door before heading behind the counter. The bell above the door chimes, and I turn around to deliver the upbeat greeting I've been masking my sadness with. "Welcome to..."

He's already standing on the other side of the counter before I've finished turning around all the way. "Hey, Mace... Maci," He catches using my nickname and corrects himself, breaking his eye contact with me and looking down at his wallet in his hands. When his eyes meet mine again, they are glossed over. I wasn't exactly sure how it was going to feel when I saw him again, but I know at this moment it's not something I'm prepared to handle. He stands there frozen, gauging my reaction. I take in the man in front of me, and it takes everything I have not to leap over the counter into his arms. Outside of the look in his eyes, he's incredibly sexy. He's got on jeans with a gray and maroon baseball shirt and his black hat backward. It's a go-to look for him I've fallen in love with. My heart breaks all over again knowing this awkwardness between us might be his fault, but it's my choice.

I don't say anything in response and instead punch his order into the register. The air between us is thick, and I'm pretty sure feeling like I'm suffocating in it is the only thing that's keeping me from having a total meltdown right now. I try to keep it together as I reach for his card and swipe it through the machine. Handing it back to him, I focus on making sure our hands don't touch, but mine shakes too much. His thumb touching mine as he takes the card back from me is enough to break the fragile tape holding me together.

My resolve shatters. I turn and run toward the swinging doors that separate the front and back of the café, nearly crashing into Abby. She looks at me, then looks to where I'm assuming she sees Mack based on the realization washing over her face. I don't stop to say anything to her. I can't. I hardly make it through the doors before I fall against the wall, my back sliding down it as my face falls into my hands and tears flood from my eyes.

I try to steady my breathing, but I can't seem to get a grip. Looking at him overwhelms me. I feel out of control of my thoughts, my emotions and my life. *I miss him so much.*

After Abby gets Mack's food and helps a few more customers, she comes back to check on me and send me home. We both know I'm not capable of working anymore today, and luckily, she's understanding.

I'm digging through my purse for my keys as I walk outside, so I don't realize I'm going to crash until it's too late. He wasn't prepared for the weight of me falling into him. He stumbles back but doesn't let go, his hands holding me up at my shoulders.

"Are you okay?" Mack says softly, as if I'm going to break again at his words.

When I look up, I can see his eyes are red. I shake my head but don't look away. My tears are so quiet, I didn't realize they were back until I taste them on my lips.

"I didn't mean to upset you, Maci. I got my days confused. I didn't think you'd be here. I'm sorry." His words are genuine. *They always are.*

"It's not... You shouldn't have to... I'm sorry," I choke out as I fall into his chest, and he wraps his arms around me. I take a deep breath into his shirt, the cinnamon scent coming off him helping to soothe me. It's so good to be in his arms. Too good. I pull back when I've gathered my thoughts, and he reluctantly loosens his hold on me. "I'm sorry. I shouldn't be here with you like this."

"Hey, Maci, it's okay." He wipes the tears from my face, and I let him. "I'm always here for you."

I fall into his chest again. A few moments pass before I whisper, "I love my CD."

He pulls back to look at me, uncertainty all over his face. "Do you?"

I nod.

"Tell me what you're thinking, please," he begs.

"That this is hard. That I miss you. That I'm mad at myself for missing you. That I want to figure this out on my own. That I'm not sure if I can do this." I spit out all my thoughts so fast I have to stop to take a breath.

His hand slides to the side of my face, his fingers weaving into my hair. Pressing his forehead to mine and closing his eyes, he whispers, "I'm sorry. I want so badly to fix this, to take away your pain, and ease your fears, but I don't know what to do. I don't know how to prove how much you mean to me and for that to be enough. Do you think there's a chance for us?"

He pulls back enough to look at me, and I manage to respond without crying. "I promise this isn't just about you, Mack. As much as this sucks, I can't help but believe it happened for a reason. I do think there has to be more effort on your part. I know you made a mistake, and I trust you to always try your best, but I have to feel confident something like this won't happen again, and that you'll be in my corner when I'm struggling. I've also realized how much work I need to do on myself too. I don't think I'm ready to work on our relationship on top of that yet. But it's not fair of me to ask you to wait."

He grips either side of my face to hold my eyes on him. "Maci, I waited years for you the first time. You're worth the wait, however long it takes and whatever I have to do." He kisses my forehead before wrapping his arms around my neck and pulling me into him. Tightening my arms around his waist, I wonder if this will be the last time.

CHAPTER FIFTY-SIX

I sit on Lexy's bedroom floor, leaning against her bed, zoning out as my new best friend clips in her hair extensions. *The Bachelorette* plays in the background, but I can't seem to focus on any of it. I don't want to go out tonight, and for the first time, I'm glad it's taking her so long to get ready. Hesitantly, I pull my leggings off and jump into a pair of jeans because I know Lexy will roll her eyes and whine the entire way to the bar if I don't change.

"You need to get out of this funk," she says as she stares into the mirror and glues her false eyelash into place. "I have an idea," she declares, a wicked smile crossing her face.

Sighing, I roll my eyes, questioning if I look cute enough for whatever this plan of hers is or if I need to flip through her closet before we leave.

"You know that movie *Yes Man,* where Jim Carrey has to say "yes" to everything anyone asks him? Let's do that. For the whole weekend. You don't have work, and I'm not on the schedule until Saturday night. And you need some excitement in your life."

"Ugh, how about not? That sounds terrifying. Plus, I don't know... what if men are involved? I'm not ready for that."

"Maci, I love you, but I don't care. You are choosing to not be with Mack, and you still won't tell me why, which is fine, but I also refuse to encourage you to stay stuck because you aren't sure if he's going to be in your future. It's only one weekend, and what's the worst that can happen? We will set a few ground rules if it makes you feel better."

I already know better than to try and talk Lexy out of anything. Once she's made up her mind, there's no changing it. "Fine," I mumble, heading to her closet to pull out a flowy white tank top much cuter than the one I'm wearing. Before she turns off her curling iron, I twirl my hair a few times as she straps on her heels. She looks me up and down, seemingly mostly satisfied with my appearance, but tosses me mascara as we head out the door.

She climbs into the driver's seat of my dusty red Corolla, knowing I still hate driving in California. As soon as she puts the key in the ignition, The Used blares through every speaker. It's loud enough I know she wouldn't hear me if I started talking, but I know where we are going anyway. Even though the plan is to *potentially* get wild this weekend, we are creatures of habit, and it's rare we end up somewhere else, at least to start the night.

We pull into the parking lot of 3rd Base LA, and it's packed. It's busy for a Thursday, and it's only seven o'clock, but then I spot an all night Happy Hour sign posted in the entryway. The drinks are strong here, which is why it's usually our first stop, but there's no way we are getting a table anytime soon. We head toward the bar, where it's seat yourself, hoping there will be a couple of stools open while we wait. Of course there aren't any, so we stand next to a dirty high top table, in hopes we can snag it before someone else does. I scope out the scene, wondering if there's a plan I could come up with to get me out of saying yes to anything too wild. I realize my arm is resting on something sticky on the table just as I hear a voice from behind me.

"Do you need a table? I can clean this for you."

Weird, that voice sounds oddly familiar. I spin around on the heel of my boot Lexy made me wear. The moment I see the handsome man in front of me, I know if my arm still hadn't been leaning on the table, I would have fallen right over.

The server stands there, a row of dirty plates stacked on one arm and somehow balancing three beer glasses in his other hand. Sweat glistens around the edge of his blond hair. It's darker than I remember. I must be losing focus because even staring straight at him, I can't remember if his eyes are blue or gray. I can see the stunned look in them though–he's as caught off guard as I am.

Lexy looks at me, her brows furrowed, taking in the situation and trying to understand what's happening.

"Hey, I'm–"

"Troy," I whisper as he says his own name.

Lexy's eyes widen. "Troy... like Troy? Math class Troy? Troy who lives in Oregon, Troy?" She's not subtle at all.

Even though I've turned to face her, I can see a flicker of a smile cross his face, probably realizing I've mentioned him before. I'm surprised she remembers. I only mentioned him briefly when I came across his letter again recently.

"Mhmm," I mumble, my lips pressed together, eyes still wide.

"Yes, please," she tells him. Even though she's practically yelling at him because the TVs and people in the bar are so loud, it feels like she's talking from across the room because of the fog I'm trapped in.

Before I can register what just happened, Troy is gone.

He comes back with only a wet rag in his hand and doesn't say anything else as he clears and cleans our table.

I'm still standing here, frozen.

We sit, and I try to look over the menu but nothing my eyes scan over process in my brain. I haven't talked to Troy since before I found his letter. Well, since the party at Dean's house. It's been almost a year. He doesn't live in this state. How is he here? In California? In this restaurant?

I shake my head to clear my thoughts, looking up right as this memory comes walking back. He's wearing dark jeans and white Adidas, like the picture of him in my head. Besides that night, I never saw him in much other than a hoodie, so his black button-up shirt feels unfamiliar. It's also tight enough it stretches slightly over his body. He has a lot more muscle than I remember.

Lexy talks to him, being her outgoing and very nosy self. I sit there still stunned into silence staring at Troy standing in front of me. He tries to focus on whatever she's saying, but his eyes keep shifting over to me for split seconds at a time. All of a sudden, he cuts her off mid-sentence. "I'm driving out to Vegas this weekend with a friend. You two should meet us out there."

"I don't think that's a–"

"YES!" Lexy practically shouts as she kicks me under the table.

Shit. "Yes weekend." Of course this would happen.

Troy looks at me, his eyes questioning if I'm agreeing to this. I roll my eyes, leaning into my hands that are stacked above my elbows on the table. I'm probably coming off very dramatic, but seriously, how is this real? "Yes," I agree, and I make sure I'm loud and clear enough that I won't have to repeat myself.

Relief washes over his face, and I have a flashback to one of the last times I saw him, in the laundry room at the frat party. Lexy places an order for both of us, and Troy walks away, disappearing behind a door on the other side of the bar.

"Ummm, Maci," Lexy squeals. "Damn, he's cute."

I roll my eyes and sink my face into my hands. "I mean I know, but..."

"You need to have a 'yes weekend' attitude about this, girl! Come on, what if this is your second chance?"

I pull my head away from my hands to stare at her incredulously. "Coming from the girl who has been telling me to give Mack a second chance for the past month."

"You know I love Mack, and I support you making it work with him. But you're not having that, and I'm tired of watching you mope. Plus, this looks like a sign if I've ever seen one." At least she's honest.

"A sign of what?"

"Well, I don't know! But come on, what are the chances of something like this happening right after we declare 'yes weekend?'"

"Ugh, I know, it is a little crazy. I'm not ready for this. I don't even know what this is."

"It doesn't have to be anything you don't want it to be. Let's go have fun for the weekend and get your mind off everything you've been worried about lately," she says as she shakes my shoulders, as if it'll fling the negativity out of me.

"Okay, okay. He does look good, doesn't he?" My voice goes dreamy.

"He sure does. So weird, he looks nothing like Mack. I expected you to have a type." Halfway through her thought, Troy walks up behind us, and I can tell he heard what she was saying, despite it being so loud in here. I leave the question in his eyes unanswered as he sets our drinks in front of us.

Lexy and I spend most of the next hour researching things to do while we are in Vegas since neither of us have been before. Troy only stops over a few times to check on us. It's busy, and I'm okay with it. Seeing him is enough to process on its own without having to figure out what to talk about.

We cut ourselves off after our first drink–thank goodness no one asked us if we wanted another. I made sure Troy knew not to ask if he wanted us to make it to Vegas. The one time he did hang at our table for more than a moment, Lexy took the liberty of explaining our "yes weekend" rules to him–the only ones being nothing that hurts us or makes us broke. I'm already being way too good of a sport with this, so I made her promise we'd stop drinking so we could leave tonight and get the lay of the land on our own first. Plus, I want to have a good time before it's potentially ruined by whatever comes of this terrible idea. Thankfully, she agreed.

We are home now, quickly packing bags. It'll only take a few hours to get there, and since Vegas is basically open all night long, we will still have plenty of time to do something fun tonight. I fill my backpack with a few of my clothes, then head to Lexy's closet to pick out a few more. Let's face it, she has much better style than me, and it's only natural to want to look good in front of any person you've ever had feelings for.

We finally get on the road around nine thirty, blasting T Swift the entire way. As soon as we left, I found a cheap last minute hotel room at Planet Hollywood. I only booked one night, upon Lexy's insistence. As soon as we check in, we pick out the sexiest dresses we brought. I thought about saving mine for tomorrow night, but I deserve to dress up for myself as much as anyone else.

My dress is strapless, black, covered in sequins and so short that if I bend over, someone might see my underwear. Thank goodness it is crowded and dark in this city. Lexy's dress is silky and red and scoops low in the back. Knowing her and seeing the way her dress is smooth and flawless against her skin, I doubt she's wearing underwear. We stand in front of the mirror to fix our makeup before stepping back to assess ourselves. I do get jealous of how easy Lexy makes sexy and confident look, but right now, both of us look like total babes. I feel so incredible, I temporarily forget the reason we drove to Vegas. My stomach-churning experience from earlier is easier to ignore because we look so damn hot, and I'm excited to have a new experience for the first time since everything happened with Mack. Before we head out of the room, we each drink at least two shots straight from the bottle of tequila we brought to save money on what I'm guessing will be ridiculously overpriced drinks.

Neither of us have visited Vegas, or even been to a club since turning 21, so this is a new experience for us. We aren't quite sure where to go, but one of Lexy's coworkers told her the club at the Cosmopolitan was the best, so we should go there. Driving in, it took us a back way behind the hotel, so we haven't been on the Strip yet. Walking through the casino to check in and find our room was overwhelming with all the flashing lights and slot machines.

It was nothing compared to stepping outside onto the Strip.

This place is magical. The lights make everything sparkle–the hotels and restaurants and the dresses of every girl in our vicinity. As we cross the street, we watch the massive fountain at the Bellagio shooting off water higher than the building itself. Walking into the Cosmopolitan is another shock. The entire inside looks like a giant chandelier, strings of crystals forming beautiful designs from the floor to the ceiling four floors up, and there's a purple hue to all the lights giving the entire place an even sexier feel. We read the map and ride the escalator to the second floor, snapping a selfie on our way up.

After stepping off, we walk in circles until we see "Marquee." We head toward the entrance until we notice the line. Holy shit, it wraps all the way around the outside of the club. How are we going to get in tonight? We go to the end anyway and pass the time people watching everyone who goes by. So many drunk guys and bachelor parties whistle at us. Even a few girls stop to ask us where we got our dresses. Part of me is uncomfortable with the attention, but the other part soaks in the confidence spike I've been missing the past month. Avery is the type of friend who encourages me to work through my pity party and lets me know she's there for me. Lexy, on the other hand, is the type of friend who forces you out of your comfort zone. I try not to compare them because they are both different and important to me, but I'm thankful for Lexy's approach tonight.

Ten minutes into our wait, two very big guys in black suits approach us. "We'd like to bring you in through the VIP entrance," one of them says.

I stare at Lexy in shock and for what to do. She gives me a "you know what to say" look that makes me turn on my heel back to the security guards with a bold "Yes!"

We follow them past the entire line, and once we get to the entrance of the club and our IDs are checked, they lead us to a different entrance. Instead of going through the main part of the club, we walk down a hallway, popping out on the side of a bar. It's so dark and loud we can hardly see the guy we are supposed to be following. I can barely understand what he's saying when we reach the VIP table. All I know is we are being introduced to two guys sitting on the back of the curved leather booth seat. They both wear dress pants, and white button-up shirts that are hardly buttoned. Paired with smug looks on their faces and way too much gel in their hair, they look douchey.

On the small table in front of them is a giant crystal bucket with a bottle of Grey Goose, surrounded by tiny bottles of fancy water. On the tray in front are small glass pitchers of what I'm guessing are orange and cranberry juice. The guys in the booth direct us to sit with them as a very attractive blonde in a sparkly blue bra and black mini skirt appears in front of us. I can't help but look her up and down, snapping back to the moment when she asks us what we want to drink before proceeding to make them for us.

I feel very out of place and a little like a hooker, but I'm hoping nothing bad will happen with so much security around. Just in case though, I'm not willing to take a chance on alcohol that's been sitting out on a table, especially not after what happened with Avery. I never told Lexy. She could tell I didn't want to talk about it after Mack dropped me off at her apartment that night, and eventually too many days passed for either one of us to bring it up. I know she'd be more sensitive to it if I told her, but I don't like to think about it. That's why it doesn't bother me much when she sometimes jokes about me being overly cautious with my drinks. It's one of those things people typically don't realize is an issue or big deal unless they've experienced it themselves.

Before I pretend to take a sip of my drink, I lean into Lexy. "Lex, don't drink that, who the heck knows what's actually in these drinks. Better safe than sorry." She gives me a questioning glance, and I can't tell if she takes a real sip or not before turning to chat with the guys. I lean back and observe because I'm sitting on the other side of her, so it would be awkward to cut in on their conversation.

Shifting in my seat, I have this strange feeling of confidence for being escorted into the club while also feeling uncomfortable in my own skin, like I don't belong here. I end up taking a drink because I'm nervous and just hope for the best. A few minutes in, I'm still outside of the circle. Lexy tends to be the center of everyone's attention. I mean she's absolutely gorgeous, outgoing and confident all the time–not only on occasion like I am. I tug on the bottom of her dress, that's riding up a little too far. "Come to the bathroom with me? You have to say yes."

She laughs, grabbing her drink in one hand and my hand in her other, letting me lead her out of the booth. We get all the way into the privacy of the bathroom before we can hear each other. "This is wild!" I exclaim as we walk into the handicap stall together. Even if I'm only buzzed at this point, with how foreign this place feels, I'm much more comfortable with her than the alternative.

"So insane! I can't believe we just drove to Vegas on a whim! And got into the club because my best friend is a total bombshell." She waves her hand up and down pointing at my body before handing me her drink to hold while she pees. "Those guys are hot too, but please let's ditch them. They are so boring. I'd rather go dance."

Thank goodness.

We exit the stall to a bathroom much more crowded than when we entered. A pretty brunette in a blue and purple sparkly romper washing her hands at the sink looks over at us. "Are you two at a VIP table? I could kind of hear you talking."

"Yes," we say in unison and look at her while turning on the sinks in front of us.

"Just be careful. Those guys pay tens of thousands of dollars for security to bring them girls that match their "type." Their intention is for them to find someone to take home at the end of the night."

Damn. We are Vegas newbies over here, excited about a confidence boost that doesn't feel so great anymore. "We are definitely getting out of here," I say.

Maybe I'm less trusting because of everything that happened with Avery, but I think "yes weekend" rules can be bent for this.

Luckily, Lexy seems to agree, and we thank our new friend and make sure to sneak away in the opposite direction when we exit the bathroom. We don't want to leave because the vibe in here is exhilarating, despite the creepy situations going on at the VIP tables. As we walk down a ramp to get to the dance floor, the DJ starts remixing "I Gotta Feeling." Perfect. Nothing like a dance party with your best friend, lost in a crowd away from someone who wants us to practically be hookers to keep this night on the right track.

By the time we collapse onto our bed, our feet ache after walking around the Strip people watching and two hours of dancing in the club. We don't even have time to recap our night before we pass out on the huge white bed.

CHAPTER FIFTY-SEVEN

Sometimes when I drink a lot, I can't sleep more than a few hours, no matter how tired I am. That's what's happening now. It's only 9 a.m., and even though my body is exhausted from drinking and walking all night and getting back to our room around four in the morning, my mind is wide awake.

It could also have something to do with the fact Troy will be here later today. Last night before we left 3rd Base, Lexy made me write my number on our receipt. It hasn't changed in the past year, but she figured it was better safe than sorry. I deleted his number at some point, but when his text came through around midnight, I knew it was him. *"Hey, Maci from math class."* I nearly spit out my drink laughing, remembering that's how I entered my name into his phone last year.

I nudge Lexy, and she rolls over, trying to ignore me. "Lexyyy," I whisper. "I can't sleep! Let's get up!" When she stays silent, I add in an extra cheery voice, "You have to say yes you know!"

She turns over to face me and rolls her eyes, but it's followed by a laugh as she sits. "Okay, okay, let's see what we can get into today!"

I tie my hair into a low messy bun and check myself out in the mirror while I wait for Lexy. I'm slipping my sheer black coverup over my head when I hear my name. She's standing at the door holding two bottles of water that have been replaced with what I'm assuming is mimosa. I love Vegas. You can do whatever you want and be whoever you want when you're here.

When we swipe our room key and open a door that leads to the roof of the hotel, a rectangular pool surrounded by cabanas lies in front of us. The blue mattresses of the day beds are faded from the sun, with perfectly rolled white towels set on the edges. Off to one side of the pool is a stage where a DJ sets up his equipment. It's already 80° and perfect in the sunshine, and past the wall, we have a partial view of the Strip. It's like we are in a movie all over again.

We choose two sun chairs from the row behind the cabanas on the opposite side of the stage. I'm laying my towel on my chair when I look and see Lexy already laid back on hers, stripped down to her red bikini. She's wearing her matching red heart sunglasses over her eyes and scrolling on her phone. I'm not sure why it hits me all of a sudden–maybe it's the mimosa–but I'm overwhelmed with gratitude for Lexy. When Mack and I broke up, I was a little worried I would lose her too since she was Mack's friend first, but she's been here for me ever since I met her.

"Lex," I get her attention.

"What's up?" she replies in a distracted tone, not looking over from her phone.

I sit on the edge of my chair, the palms of my hands pressed into the plastic on either side of me. She puts her phone down when she feels me staring. "Everything okay?"

"Oh yeah, I just... I know mushy isn't your thing, but thank you. I seriously don't know what I would have done without you these past couple of months. You've been such a good friend to me since the day we met and an even better one since everything happened with Mack even though you didn't have to be."

"How could I not be your friend, Maci? Before you came along, I really only had Mack. As much as I consider him my best friend, he's still a guy, and it's not the same as having you around. I'm not sure what happened with his sister. I know you used to be close, and I'm not trying to take away from that. But you're my best friend, Maci, and I'm really glad that idiot dragged you here."

I laugh at how she twisted a joke into her words so she didn't have to get too serious. One of my favorite qualities of Lexy's is how she keeps the mood from getting too dark, and it keeps me going. She reminds me of Mack in that way. "I want to tell you what happened with Avery. At first it didn't feel like it was my place to say anything, or my story to tell, but you deserve to know, especially after being such a big help that night. If you want to know, I mean."

She sits up and faces me, really focused now. Even though Avery and I have gotten past everything that happened, we've drifted apart. It's not in a bad way. We both have a lot going on, and it's harder now that we don't share a lease, let alone live in the same state.

I'm not trying to replace her, but I trust Lexy. She is someone I can count on to be there for me no matter what and point me in the right direction when I have no idea what path to go down.

I spend the next few minutes filling her in on what happened both with Avery and then my breakup with Mack. The more I tell her, the more I see her piecing parts of stories together, understanding washing over her. I feel relief from sharing. I haven't talked about it with anyone other than Mack. It's like a weight has been lifted off my chest, like I've let go of both events a little more. Just in time to deal with something else from my past.

"Wow, Maci, I had no idea that's what was happening. Full disclosure, I knew about the drug problem, but I just assumed you did too. I'm so sorry. He wouldn't tell me what happened, or I would have said something. He said he wanted to leave it up to you to tell me when you were ready. Which was sweet, but also... Ugh, that makes me so mad at him. Especially since he relapsed. We worked so hard to get him clean." Frustration laces her voice, and her hand clenches around the edge of her sun chair.

"Please don't be mad at him. He's your best friend, and the last thing I want is to come between you two. There's no sense in ruining your friendship over it, and I'm sure he hasn't used since. It's just been hard for me to let it go. I wanted to work through our struggles before it got to that point."

"I get it. You know I love Mack, but that's seriously messed up, Maci. Ugh, maybe he was terrified of losing you and freaked out? Not that it justifies it at all, it just seems so out of character, at least for the Mack he's been the last year."

"Yeah, I know. I've been running it through my head on repeat ever since. But I keep thinking about how it feels out of character for the Mack we know, but he wasn't always this way, and I don't know how to trust the person he used to be won't come back."

She hesitates for a moment, like she's debating sharing a thought. "Do you still talk to Avery? Did she know about all this?"

"Yeah, we've been friends for way too long to let anything come between us. It's been a few weeks since I've checked in, though. I'm not sure she knows Mack and I broke up, and I doubt she knows about the drugs. She would have told me if she did. Either way, I don't want to bring her down with it when she just moved into a new house and is in such an exciting phase of her life."

"I'm sure she'll understand and want to be there for you. It sounds like she will. You know you're stuck with me now, regardless, but it still sucks. I'm sorry."

"It's okay. Time seems to be helping. None of it matters right now anyway. Can we talk about how wild last night was?"

"Can we talk about how wild tonight will be instead?" She wiggles her eyebrows, full of assumptions.

CHAPTER FIFTY-EIGHT

I wasn't able to convince Lexy to get our own hotel room for tonight. She's still sure Troy will show up with a smoking hot friend she'll want to hook up with, and we will either stay out all night, or the boys will let us share their room. Either way, she is set on the night going according to her plan. I rolled my eyes at her because as much fun as that could be, I haven't seen Troy in forever.

Even having insight into his head from his letter, I'm still very hesitant about the whole situation. I'm all for Lexy's positive thinking, but we don't know the friend Troy is bringing with him. What if he's intolerable? I doubt that's the case because Troy doesn't seem like someone who would hang out with people who aren't fun. But then again, what do I really know about the boy who sat beside me for two weeks in class? Not a whole lot. All of that on top of the fact I still think about Mack every day and wonder constantly if I made the right choice.

Still in our swimsuits and cover-ups, we head to the car, where we dropped off our things at checkout. We dig through our bags in the trunk for the dresses we have picked out for tonight. I choose a royal blue one I pulled from Lexy's closet. After growing up in LA, she has a lot more choices than I do. It cuts right above the knee with a slit that follows my thigh up a bit. The spaghetti straps lead into a much lower cut than I'd usually wear. Last night was more of a confidence boost than I expected, and I plan for tonight to be the same. So much has happened since I met Troy and he disappeared on me. I'm not interested in dating him, but I'm still human, and of course I want him to think I look amazing.

We walk back to the hotel and find the nearest bathroom. They are all so fancy here. There are couches in a sitting area when you walk in and TVs on the mirror in front of the sinks. I plug in the curling iron so it can heat while we do our makeup and slip into our dresses. Troy texted earlier to say they were getting in around 7 and to invite us to meet them at Ghost Donkey–a speakeasy inside the Cosmopolitan hotel. We finish getting ready at ten til, stopping back by the car, tossing everything we didn't need back in the trunk. We start walking away, but I swipe the keys back from Lexy and grab my toothbrush.

"Good thinking," she says with sex practically pouring out of her eyes. I certainly have no expectations for tonight. I don't know what I want to happen, if anything, but it is "yes weekend" and even if it wasn't, it's best to prepare for whatever Lexy has planned, just in case. We laugh when we get a few looks for spitting toothpaste out in the middle of the parking garage aisle. Ready as I'll ever be, we take off.

It takes us at least ten minutes to find the door. We ultimately had to look up hints because none of the employees we ran into would tell us if we were headed in the right direction. Finally, we find it–a huge dark teal door with a push bar on the front that makes it look like an emergency exit. There's a small pink and white donkey right above the bar indicating we are in the right place. Anxious to see who she's going to be spending the night with, Lexy pushes hard on the door, slipping through it quickly. I hardly have enough time to get through behind her as it starts to close.

The place is extremely small, so I spot them right away. Even if it wasn't, they would stand out because they are easily the most attractive men in here. Troy stands to greet us, dressed in his typical dark jeans and signature white Adidas, but he's got on a light blue button up shirt that matches his eyes and is tight in all the right places. His blond hair sticks up slightly and perfectly. He looks good–really good. I only catch a small glance of his friend before Lexy practically slams into him.

"Lexy," she says seductively and only inches from the man's face.

"Nolan." He laughs, his eyes grazing over her entire body appreciatively before he looks at me, reaching out his hand to shake mine.

Wow, he's attractive too, but his look is a little more preppy than Troy's, and for some reason he exudes a slight "I'm better than you" attitude. He apparently was in the same fraternity as Troy, but at a university in California. Honestly, I have no idea how all that works considering I went to one frat party in my life and probably didn't make the most of the college experience. They work together now.

"Maci," I respond as Troy's arms wrap around me for a hug. His cologne triggers my memory of the last time I had my arms around him on the back of his motorcycle a year ago. It's equal parts sweet and spicy, and being here is strange but warm and comforting at the same time. He sits down in the booth, sliding in so there's room for me on the end next to him. Lexy and Nolan are already curled in the corner talking about something. There's a deep red glow blanketing the entire room and twinkle lights fall from the ceiling every few feet. It's so dark I can hardly read the menu, and it all feels a tad too romantic for the situation.

"We already ordered Steak & Black Bean Nachos and the truffle ones too because apparently that's what they are known for, but I wasn't sure what you wanted to drink."

"Thanks." I look up from the menu, a sudden shyness coming over me. This is weird, like I'm living in an alternate reality where Troy didn't run off and we stayed friends–or became something more.

"So..." He looks at our friends. "Guess we don't have to worry about them getting along."

I haven't looked in their direction since I sat down, but now I see it's probably not going to be long before they are taking up one space on the bench instead of two. I love her, but it's so typical of Lexy. She might be right about at least part of the night. I'm never sure if situations magically play out how she predicted or if she just plays the role and makes it happen. Either way,

I'm glad things aren't awkward with Troy. I also hope I don't do something to change that, like getting drunk and bringing up his letter or something.

The nachos are amazing, and I ate way too many of them. I blame Lexy and Nolan because their ridiculous and unrealistic immediate infatuation with each other kept them from helping us. It is Vegas and "yes weekend," though, so who am I to judge? Troy leans back against the booth, pointing to the skillet, offering me the last chip. I take it and join him, sipping on my drink. This place is tequila and mezcal only, so that's what I'm sticking to tonight. It's not my favorite, but the last thing this night needs is a laundry room night repeat.

As I set my glass on the table, Lexy stands. "We are leaving," she says with a very telling smile on her face. "Don't wait up." She doesn't invite us to join them.

Nolan throws a couple twenties on the table and gives a small wave as he lets Lexy pull him toward the door.

"Well then." I laugh. It wasn't awkward before, but I worry it's about to be—even though it's not like the lust birds were participating in our small talk. He told me about his cousin who he moved in with when he got to California and how he met Nolan at a bar one night and found out they coincidentally are part of the same fraternity. I told him about meeting Lexy at the bar where she works and how we ended up moving in together. Luckily, he didn't ask how I ended up in

California in the first place or why I needed a new place to live. I do not want to get into anything regarding Mack. What a buzz kill that would be.

He looks at me, and his face goes serious. *Oh Lord.* I was worried about being too drunk, but maybe I'm not drunk enough for this.

"So... I have to ask. Did you ever read my letter?"

"I did... but not until a couple of months ago. How did you get it to me anyway?" I'm genuinely curious, it's been baffling me ever since I found it.

He shrugs. "Carley. I gave it to her one day before class. The week you showed up at my house and wouldn't talk to me." There's no hostility in his voice, just a reminder.

"You mean the class you never came back to?" I let out a nervous laugh.

"Yeaaah." He shifts in his seat, his eyes looking everywhere but mine. "They had an opening for the same class on opposite days that worked with my schedule, so I switched. I'm sorry about that." He looks at me genuinely when he says it.

"I get it." I do get it. Did it suck he left without saying anything? It did. Would dating Troy have prevented me from the heartbreak of Dean? Yes–though I don't regret my time with him. After that I found Mack, and it was like all of that was for a reason. Then he did the one thing he knew would upset me more than anything else and my heart broke again. I was lost after that. I'm still so lost, and everything is confusing. Maybe the situation with the girl who broke Troy's heart was similar to mine with Dean or Mack. If it was, I get it, or at least I can empathize. For a second, I consider telling him why I understand, but he cuts off my thought.

"You do? I'm guessing things didn't work out with Dean? At least I feel like that's a solid assumption based on the fact you're here."

He asked gently, but an old ache finds its way into my heart. I realize I haven't thought about Dean for a while, until this conversation. I don't want to start now. "A lot has happened in the past year," is all I decide to say.

Luckily, he can sense I don't want to talk about it and reverts back to a previous thought. "After I talked to Carley about asking you out, I changed my mind. I knew I wasn't ready to date again, and I didn't have the confidence you'd even say yes, despite Carley's insistence. But when you said yes to coffee and then our date, it kind of felt like it revived me from the pathetic state I was in. We had such a good time, but I didn't think it was fair for you to be a rebound. You deserve more than that. I wanted to reach out to you so many times, especially when you were at my house, but, well, you remember how that went... maybe." He laughs, surely recalling me being very drunk and kicking him out of his own laundry room.

I bring my hands up so my face can hide behind them, rolling my eyes at myself even though he can't see them. Pulling my hands away, I say, "Why on earth I thought it was a good idea to "catch up to the crowd" using a shot luge is still beyond me."

"On that note, want to take a shot?" He holds his hand up to get the waiter's attention. "Let's forget about whatever happened in the past and have fun tonight. We are in Vegas, and it's... what are you calling it? 'Yes weekend?' So, you have to say yes," he winks.

This time I let him see my eyes roll. Before my brain processes what happened, he leans in and kisses me softly on the lips, pulling away quickly and ordering a round of tequila shots for us.

CHAPTER FIFTY-NINE

"Ready?" Troy asks three shots later as he signs the receipt on the table.

"Do I have another choice?" I giggle, feeling like alcohol is literally flowing through my veins.

I stand dramatically and reach my hand for his, pulling him from his seat and tugging him toward the door. We are drunk now, but we find our way out of the speakeasy and back to the Strip much quicker than Lexy and I found our way in.

The second Troy pushes through the heavy metal door leading outside, the cold air hits me, instantly covering me in chills. As we wait at the crosswalk, Troy turns to me and rubs his hands up and down my arms, trying to warm them. When the light turns green he slides one hand down until it locks with mine, this time pulling me along behind him.

"Where are we going?" I question as we are halfway through what feels like the longest crosswalk. Seriously, is it safe for cars to drive on the Strip? It looks like there are a lot of idiots out here. How often does one of them run into the road? Wow, Maci, way to be morbid instead of focusing on having fun with this handsome man next to you.

"Not sure yet!" We make it to the other side of the street and start climbing the few steps to the walkway in front of Planet Hollywood. My feet are throbbing. I have no idea why I let Lexy talk me into heels, especially for a second night in a row, but it was one of the worst decisions I've made in a long time.

Moving to California has been a huge adjustment for me. It's not that I don't like it, it's just not really my style. I don't want the fancy clothes everyone wears and the fancy drinks I have to make at work every day. I like simple. Give me jean shorts and a hoodie, and I'm good to go. I cringe as I hit the top step and feel a blister already forming.

He looks at me, concerned. "Are you okay?"

"Oh yeah, you know. You can take a girl out of Oregon, but you can't take Oregon out of the girl. These heels are killing my feet. I'm fine, though. What do you want to do next?"

"Well, our room is right in here." He points at the hotel in front of us. *Convenient.* "We could drop your shoes off and get you something more comfortable. I think I saw a shoe vending machine in the casino. Who knew that was something that existed."

"YES!" I shout with a smirk. Partly because I have to and mostly because I want to get out of these shoes. I stand on my toes a little higher and kiss him on the cheek as we stand outside the hotel entrance, waiting for a couple to walk through before us.

The jolt of the elevator when it starts moving toward the 18th floor throws me a little off balance. I'm more intoxicated than I thought. Thank God we didn't get a drink to go because I'm at my limit. I'm past the point of feeling nervous, but not to the point of getting emotional, which happens sometimes. I truly believe everything with Troy is in the past and we are both in different places in our lives and tonight can just be fun. I'm not trying to take advantage or lead him on, but I doubt he thinks this is more than it is.

The elevator dings and opens to a long hallway. I'm not sure why every carpet that has an odd retro pattern reminds me of the Portland airport, but that's what crosses my mind. We walk down the hallway, my arm linked in Troy's. Without letting me go, he digs through his wallet to find his room key. Oh God, I hope Lexy and Nolan aren't in there. It didn't occur to me until this second. Only one way to find out. But also, Troy. He looks really good in that dress shirt. He also has the straps of my heels looped around his finger–he offered to carry them when I practically ripped them off in the elevator–and for some reason it's incredibly sexy. He unlinks his arm from mine as he turns to slide the key card into the door with his free hand.

Surprising myself, I pull on his wrist, twisting him to face me. In one smooth movement, I step forward, forcing him against the wall. I have the sudden urge to kiss him, so before I think twice, I do. The second our lips meet, my heels slip from his hand and hit the floor. One hand reaches up to cup my cheek and the one with the key card presses into my lower back, pulling me closer to him and deepening our kiss. He tastes like the lime and salt after our tequila shots, and I can't get enough.

A couple of minutes go by before he pulls back slightly, as if knowing I need to catch my breath. It feels like I'm dreaming; I don't open my eyes. I feel his breath against my ear. "I have wanted to do that for so long."

Simultaneously, our eyes open and connect, his look full of both lust and uncertainty. I feel like mine are full of confidence, and apparently, he sees exactly that because without breaking eye contact, he reaches toward the door with his key, pushing down on the handle when the lock beeps.

I bend down, grab my shoes and stumble into the room because he refuses to let go of me. I laugh, but as soon as I'm through the door and it starts to close, he pushes me against it, closing it all the way and silencing my laugh with his lips. My mouth opens enough for his tongue to slide in, tangling with mine. How on earth was I shivering five minutes ago? My skin radiates heat now.

His hands move from either side of my face, down my neck, then my arms. Linking his hands with mine, he starts walking backward, tugging me toward the bed. Sitting, he pulls me closer until I'm standing between his legs. His hands fall to my thighs, and he runs them up my legs, pushing my dress up until he reaches the lace that separates him from me. Without hesitation, I reach for the buttons on his shirt and start undoing them slowly. I briefly consider there's a chance Lexy and Nolan could walk in. Hopefully they don't come back anytime soon.

Troy grips me tighter, rubbing his thumbs along the sensitive skin at the apex of my thighs, and suddenly, I don't care about the risk. Our eyes lock. "What is happening right now?" he asks.

"We are having fun tonight. Like you said." I pause and drape my arms over his shoulders, my fingers playing with the short blond hair at his neck.

"Okay, but is this 'yes weekend' kind of fun, or you actually want this?" Being the spontaneous person he is, I'm surprised Troy stops to logic his way through this.

I'm not quite sure if by "this" he means whatever happens in the next hour or with "us," but I should be clear either way, especially after what he admitted earlier.

"I mean, I'm here in Vegas because it's 'yes weekend.' I was unsure about coming because I thought it might be weird. It's not at all. It feels like the past is the past, and I like you, Troy. But I also got out of a serious relationship recently and anything right now will be a rebound. It wouldn't feel right. You deserve more than that too. That being said," I drag out the last word with a smirk, "If you want to have fun tonight, there's no one else I'd rather have fun with right–"

He cuts me off by pulling on my hips so hard I fall back toward the bed and on top of him. I hide my smile in a few kisses on his neck before pressing myself up so I'm straddling him. He moves his hands to link them under his head and stares up at me–looking satisfied already–and I move to finish what I started with his shirt buttons.

It's weird being here in this moment because it's one I'd never thought I'd experience. I can't say it's something I haven't wondered about before, though. There are so many damn buttons on this shirt. Anticipation builds, more with each button I pop free. He must lose his patience because when I get down to the last two, he yanks on either side of his shirt, ripping it apart.

Moving onto his pants, my fingers follow the waist of his jeans, running along the edge until I reach the button, twisting it open before teasing his zipper down. I feel how hard he is underneath me as I glance back at him. My hands grip onto his hips, and I can see heat in his eyes. His hand reaches between his legs and mine, keeping eye contact. My dress is pushed far above my waist and the only thing between his hand and me is a thin layer of black lace. His finger hooks under it and tugs it to the side, the cold air touches me right before he does.

Between the alcohol and how clear my mind is from finally relaxing into a moment for the first time in weeks, I am more than turned on enough for his finger to slide in easily. He starts pulsing in and out, slowly at first. When he picks up speed, he uses his thumb to put pressure on my clit, and a tingling sensation shoots through my entire body. I fall forward with a moan, holding my body up on my forearms and just enough away from him that he can maintain access to me. My lips crash into his as a need for this moment overwhelms me. His finger twirls inside of me, matching the pace of his tongue in my mouth.

Unexpectedly, he pulls his finger out quickly, eliciting a gasp from me. I whine at the loss of contact, but before I can do anything else, he stands, wrapping his arms under my ass. My legs link behind him out of instinct. His mouth finds mine again as he adjusts his hold on me with one arm while he reaches around to his back pocket with the other. Still holding me tightly and with my help, he manages to kick out of his jeans.

Breaking our kiss, his teeth pinch the foil packet between his fingers and rip it open. He bounces me a little higher in his arm, as he pinches the condom out and slides it on. I hardly have time to be impressed with his skill before he's finished.

His blue eyes open enough to take in his surroundings, and as his other arm falls to my back again, he takes the few steps over to the full wall window that looks out to the Strip. He presses me into the glass, the coldness of it sending chills up my spine.

Pulling back slightly, he adjusts himself to align with me, pushing inside when he's ready. I suck in a breath as he fills me, and my eyes squeeze shut at the overload of sensation. He pulls back out slowly before thrusting in again, pressing me harder into the window, the frame creaking. His hips continue to pump into me, bracing me to the glass with one hand pressed into my hip. He laces the fingers of his other hand through my hair, tugging back enough to give him access to my neck. "Fuck," he mumbles against my collarbone, before kissing feverishly up my throat until he reaches my lips again. The instant our lips meld together, a heat wave shoots all the way to my toes. Pressure builds inside me as our kiss falls into sync.

Without enough warning, my orgasm rips through me, my breath catching and breaking our kiss. I can't tell if there are fireworks exploding in my brain or if the glow from the Vegas strip behind me is seeping through my eyelids. I tighten around him, and he pushes into me, harder and faster. My lips find his again, and I swallow his groan, trying to hold myself against the window as much as I can until he slows and stills against me. His forehead glistens with sweat as he presses it against mine before leaving a soft kiss on my lips. He pulls back from my face as he pulls out, all of my nerve endings firing off inside me as he does.

He sets me down and steps back slightly, only to lean forward on his hands which are now pressed against the glass on either side of my head. I adjust my feet under me in hopes they can hold me up. When our eyes meet, he smiles at me then links his hand with mine, pulling me back across the room, slowly.

"So much for dropping off your shoes and leaving. We got a little distracted," a smirk flashes my way. "Did you want to go back out?"

I shake my head slowly, as I take in the body in front of me. We never connected enough last year for me to see what was under his jeans and hoodie, but damn. I am glad I get this peek now, even if it's only a one time thing.

That last round of tequila shots hit me out of nowhere, and a burst of laughter shoots out of me, distracting me. Troy looks at me, questioningly.

"This is so random," I choke out between laughs. "Like, I don't see you for a year, after you bail on me, and I spent months wondering what the heck happened to you. Then we cross paths in a different state? What are the chances?"

His smile grows as he listens to my ramble. "Yeah, it's pretty wild. But, I'm kind of glad it worked out that way. Or that..." he waves his hand toward the window, "probably wouldn't have happened. And that would have been a shame."

"Definitely agree with that." My giggles transform into the most seductive look I can muster. "And if it's only tonight, we should make the most of it, don't you think?"

Instead of replying with words, he picks me up again, this time tossing me onto the bed.

CHAPTER SIXTY

Lexy gently shakes my shoulder, waking me. I groan as I squint one eye open to look at her, sunlight streaming through the window where the edge of the curtain leaves a gap. I turn to the clock on the nightstand. 10:07 glows in neon blue. I glance back at her, staring until my eyes adjust enough to take in the rest of my surroundings. The other bed isn't made anymore, and I'm assuming Nolan is the person rolled up in the sheets, sleeping. She smiles at me. "Hey, I was thinking we should head out since I have work tonight." I nod at her, gently moving Troy's arm that wraps around my stomach before sitting and rubbing my eyes.

I turn to look at Troy who is still asleep and rub my thumb along the side of his cheek until he hazily opens his eyes. "Hey, we're going to head out. We have to get home." He nods and without a word reaches up and locks his hand around my neck, pulling me into a soft kiss. His lips linger on mine for a moment and combined with the look in his eyes when he breaks our connection, I get the impression he's thinking it's a goodbye kiss too.

Taylor Swift's "The 1" comes through the car speakers as we pull out of the parking garage. It's a refreshing change of pace compared to the club music we've been surrounded by all weekend, but it's also fitting. We are both exhausted and sit in silence as we merge onto the freeway. The song fades, and Lexy glances my way. "So, do you think you'll see him again?"

I quickly replay last night in my head. Being with Troy was crazy. I mean, it was fun, and it felt good to escape this ache in my heart that has made itself right at home for the past month, but I'm still frustrated by myself. Regret is too strong a word; I don't feel that. I feel like this was a betrayal to Mack. I'm supposed to be figuring out my life so I can determine if there's a place for him in it. I'm not supposed to be sleeping with random guys. Troy isn't exactly random, but still. I choose to go with an answer my hangover can handle.

"It would have been fun if he was the one," I laugh at my own joke, "But, I don't think so."

"I think that's how it should be, but also the guy is cute as hell. Just saying."

"He's fun too. You two would probably have a great time together." I realize I'm both joking and completely serious. Lexy glances over at me, with an unreadable expression on her face, and doesn't add to the conversation.

I fidget in my seat, my mind wandering to Mack.

"What's up, Maci?" Her eyes shift from the road to me for a moment.

"I miss him." My voice cracks on the last word.

"You'll find your way back." She sounds sure of it.

I take a breath to rid my voice of its shake. "You know he wants to move back to Oregon someday? He wants to raise his family by Avery."

She nods, like he's told her his life plan too.

"I love that you two are close," I tell her genuinely. "But I also love that I got to share you in the divorce."

She laughs before growing serious. "Do you want that? A family with Mack?

I nod slowly but without hesitation. It surprises me.

"Then what's the problem?" Her eyes shoot me a questioning look.

"I think he's the right person, but it's just not the right time. Yet. I need to figure out a little more about what I need outside of him first. Does that make sense?"

She reaches over, shaking my knee gently with her hand. Somehow, I know she understands what I'm saying. "I think he's doing the same. He'd still take you back in a second, but he isn't just waiting around for you. He's working on himself too."

I turn toward her. "What do you mean?"

She hesitates, and I can tell she's warring with whether or not to tell me. "He didn't want me to tell you..."

I want to respect their friendship, but I also want to know. I remain quiet and let her decide.

"He's been going to therapy. For over a month now."

"What? He has?" I know he used to go when he first moved to California. He wanted to work past whatever relationship blocks he had in his head from his parents.

"Yeah. It's important to him that he doesn't end up like either of his parents. Which I understand. I know he failed at that for a moment, but he recognizes it. He's really trying. That alone makes him different from them."

"Wow. I'm proud of him for that. I mean, I've never thought he was anything like his parents, but still. Why hasn't he told me?"

"He's worried you'd think he was going so you'd take him back. He didn't want it to be the determining factor because he would have done it either way. Of course he wants to show you how serious he is about your relationship, but he's serious about who he wants to be too, regardless of what happens between you two."

I slide down into my seat, guilt overwhelming me. "He's been putting in effort this whole time, and I'm just over here sleeping with Troy. Ugh. I feel terrible."

"It's okay, Maci. You didn't know. It's not like you're trying to date Troy anyway. It was just sex." There's not even a hint of judgment in her voice. "But you know now. All you can do is decide if that information changes anything for you."

"Thank you for telling me. I know you're in a hard position."

She flashes me half a smile.

"So, tell me about your night with Nolan!"

CHAPTER SIXTY-ONE

It's been a week since Lexy and I went on our Vegas adventure. Troy ended up being the perfect escape. It was a little crazy we slept together–but it was nice temporarily ignoring reality. Now that I'm back, I'm also back to feeling lost and empty. I have to figure out what my next move is because I can't live on Lexy's couch forever, no matter how comfortable it is.

When my phone vibrates, Avery's name appears on the screen, along with an attachment. My lips stretch into a smile when I open a picture of our handwritten list we made in Florida last summer of places we want to travel. What I need to do at this moment is clear all of a sudden. Before I can work through my thoughts, my phone vibrates in my hand again.

Unknown number.

My gut tells me to answer it even though I normally wouldn't.

"Hello?"

"Hello, is this Maci Jackson?"

"Yes, it is. Who is this?"

"Hi, Maci, my name is Maria. I'm from the Human Trafficking Victim Rehabilitation Center in Costa Rica."

"Oh, hi!" I try to sound excited, but I'm racking my brain trying to remember why this lady could possibly be calling me.

"I wanted to reach out and see if you were available for an interview. One of our volunteers had to back out. I know it's short notice, but we are looking for someone who can fill the position immediately. Is there any chance you're interested?"

"Umm, yeah. Yes. I am. What would it entail?"

"We'd need you here by next week, if your background check clears of course. Our sanctuary is a place for women and children who have been rescued to have a safe place to work through their trauma and get caught up on education and life skills before they reintegrate back into society."

"Wow, this sounds like a dream. Wait, no, that came out wrong, I'm sorry. This is just something that has weighed heavy on my heart recently, and I would love the opportunity to make a difference with it. May I ask how you got my name?"

"A Mack Torres gave us a call a few weeks ago. He said you'd be perfect for a position."

A few weeks ago? We weren't together a few weeks ago. That was before I ran into him at the café. He's been trying all this time to get me to come back closer to him, and now he's helping me get this opportunity that's not in the same country? *God, I love him.* The thought crosses my mind without permission.

"Ms. Jackson?"

"Yes, I'm here! What do you need from me to get started?"

Fifteen minutes later I've squared away the details with Maria, and by the time I hang up, the divine timing isn't lost on me. Realization hit the second I saw Avery's picture. I need to get out of here. Like out out of here, somewhere new I can focus on figuring out what I want without any distractions of my past. I also knew it had to be a place we'd added to one of our many lists. I wish this plan could still include Avery, but I know it's not in the cards for us anymore. She and Miller moved into their house and have finally started wedding planning. A trip around the world without her fiancé doesn't sound likely. Getting this call just now, though, I feel like maybe everything is playing out how it's supposed to, like despite everything, this is fate.

I'm ready to lean into it.

CHAPTER SIXTY-TWO

This week was a whirlwind getting ready for my trip. I expedited my passport and called my parents. They are thrilled about this opportunity. I researched what I could possibly need in Costa Rica that would be hard for me to get there. I ate at all my favorite restaurants and spent as much time with Lexy as I could.

There was only one thing left I wanted to do.

Me: *I can't believe you did this for me, Mack.*

Mack: *I would do anything for you, Maci.*

Me: *I don't know how to thank you. This means a lot to me.*

Mack: *Let me drive you to the airport?*

Me: *Yes, please.*

Mack: *What time is your flight?*

Me: *Ummm, it's really early tomorrow... like 7 a.m. Is that okay?*

Mack: *Of course.*

Mack: *...do you want to stay at my place tonight? I'll sleep on the couch. Don't have to, just figured it'll be easier, and you won't wake Lexy in the morning.*

Me: *Umm, yeah I think that's easier.*

By the time I get my bag packed, it's been hours of contemplating how little I can get away with bringing for months in another country. I call an Uber because I'm leaving my car with Lexy. She hasn't had a car in a while–she doesn't really need one living a half mile from work–so I'm letting her use mine while I'm gone.

It's 9 p.m. by the time I get to Mack's. He answers almost as soon as I knock. Holding the door open for me, he doesn't say anything as I walk through. He's standing there in his plaid pajama bottoms and a T-shirt, which feels weird because I'm used to him shirtless. Uncertainty and nerves fill the air as I walk past him, dropping my bag in the entryway.

"Hey." My voice is barely above a whisper.

"Hey, Mace," he replies softly, closing the door behind me. "Umm, do you want something to eat? I'm sure you were busy today and forgot. I have leftover pizza if you want."

I can't stop the half-smile from how well he knows me. "Thanks, but I'm too nervous to eat."

"Are you excited though?" He leans his hand on the back of the couch, staying a few feet from me.

"Yeah, I am. This is exactly what I want, what I need right now. What I've been looking for is on the other side of tomorrow's flight." I'm confident in my answer because this feels right, like the next step for my life I've been searching for. But when my eyes meet his, I notice his hurt, as if me needing to go to Costa Rica means I don't need him. That's not what I mean, but part of me wishes I could backtrack anyway. "I was thinking maybe I'll just try to get some sleep. I have a feeling it'll be a long day tomorrow." I walk around the side of the couch where he's already laid out a sheet and a pillow.

"Please sleep in our bed."

I don't have the energy to argue with him, mainly because I'm nervous about my trip and not knowing what to expect, and partly because it's weird being at my apartment that isn't mine anymore. "Thanks," I whisper as my eyes lock with his. "I guess I'll see you in the morning?"

"Yeah."

I break our eye contact to walk to his room–what used to be our room. I head straight into the bathroom, brushing my teeth and washing my face. I wore my travel clothes here, leggings and a loose T-shirt. I planned to sleep in them so it's easy in the morning, and since sleeping with nothing on like I usually do wouldn't be appropriate. I opt to pull off my bra and leggings before I get into bed anyway and leave them on the bathroom counter before flicking off the light and making my way to bed.

As I fold back the blankets, I spot a picture frame on the nightstand. I run my fingers over the edge of it. I haven't seen it before. It's a simple black frame, but it has a picture of Mack and me from the hike we went on the day he played his song for me. As I crawl into bed, I unintentionally sigh so loudly I'm worried Mack might have heard and will come in here. Part of me wishes he was in his room. If I'm being honest, it's more than part of me. Despite the uncomfortableness currently between us, something about him still calms me when he's nearby.

"Mack?" I call out for him at a volume stuck between a whisper and loud enough for him to hear clearly, like it's as uncertain as I am about what to say when and if he responds.

The door cracks, barely enough for me to see him. His hand is on the doorknob, his head leans against the frame. I can see he doesn't have his shirt on anymore. "Everything okay?" His eyes find mine.

When I don't respond right away, he pushes the door open further, cautiously moving toward me until he reaches the edge of the bed. When I look at him, I'm not sure what he sees in my eyes because I'm not sure I can decipher my mix of emotions. Whatever it is, he kneels next to me, his eyes full of concern. "Are you okay?" he asks again.

"Yeah, umm, I wanted to say thanks again for doing this for me. I know things haven't been easy for us lately, and I know it won't get any easier by me going to another country. You didn't have to do this. I can't believe you even remembered me telling you about this dream."

"I remember all your dreams, Maci. How could I for-get?"

My heart beats faster with him so close. I'm torn. I leave tomorrow, and I'll be gone at least two months, probably longer because I know I want to travel more. After my contract ends at the sanctuary, I'll finally use my travel fund my parents set up for me. It's not fair for me to want him to kiss me, for us to try again, and I'm not sure I'm ready for that still.

He swipes his thumb across my cheek, before sliding the rest of his hand against my face. "I just want you to be happy, Maci. Get some sleep, okay?" He leans in to kiss me on the forehead.

As he goes to pull away, I reach up and grab his wrist, tilting my head back enough until our eyes lock again. At least in this moment, I know we want the same thing, but I'm not sure who will cave first. The way his eyes share a look of fear and desire, I know he's conflicted on what I want, and questioning if he should keep respecting the boundaries I've given him.

I lean into his palm that's caressing my face, closing my eyes and taking a breath. When I open them again, Mack is still there, frozen, studying my face. "I should go," he whispers, but his body language doesn't say the same.

"Wait."

The look in his eyes is a clash of hopefulness and caution. I'm nervous to tell him something he doesn't want to hear, but I'm confident I can ease his worries a little. A new sureness has washed over me since I walked into our apartment tonight. I know I never stopped loving him, and I also know I'm not upset with him anymore.

"Also... I want you to know I forgive you. I don't want to hold anything that's happened over you–or us–anymore."

If it was possible to see pieces of a broken heart fuse back together, I just witnessed it.

I don't know what will happen in the next two months–how that will change our relationship dynamic, or how it will change me–but right now I know I want to be with him. "Maybe you could stay with me?"

"For tonight? Or forever?" His question is laced with sadness.

Seeing my hesitation, and knowing forgiveness was a step in the right direction on its own, he adds, "It's okay, you don't have to answer that." Before I can say anything, his lips press into mine. I sigh into our kiss, and a wave of relief rushes through me. His hand slides back, weaving his fingers into my hair as he deepens our kiss. In one smooth movement, he's off his knees, pressing me back into the mattress and moving until he's hovering over me. His other hand runs up the side of my neck, as mine finds his hips. He kisses me as if intensity alone will be enough to make me choose forever.

My hands slide up his sides and down his back before pulling him closer. He relaxes into me with my gesture. Without breaking our kiss, he rolls on his side, turning me with him. His hand slides under my shirt, flat against my stomach, moving up until it's stopped by my breast. Realizing I'm not wearing a bra, he groans into my mouth. I can't help but smile into our kiss at how turned on he gets around me, more evident by the twitch I feel against my leg.

He slides his hand up further, catching on my shirt and pulling it over my head before returning his touch to me. His tongue tangles with mine as he closes the gap between us, his hand massaging my breast. The sensation from our skin touching like this and being closer to him than I have in months overwhelms me with desire. I'm already wet as I roll my hips into him. I hook my finger into both the edge of his pajamas and his briefs and tug down on them enough to free his erection. He helps me kick them off, still not breaking our kiss, as if he's afraid it'll snap me back to our reality if he does.

I somehow manage to get my underwear off despite his need to keep me close to him, but I only do it because I need to be closer. The moment the lace is around my ankle, Mack pushes me back onto the bed, hovering over me again. His eyes flash to mine, searching them for confirmation. As soon as my fingers thread through the back of his hair, pulling on his neck, trying to bring him closer, he grants my wish. He pushes into me, desperately, like someone gasping for air.

All of a sudden he nearly stills. His urgency from a moment ago slows, as he moves in and out of me at a torturous pace. Each time he pulls back, I crave the satisfaction that consumes me when he pushes back in and fills me. I want more while simultaneously feeling like it's enough. It's like he's savoring this, unsure if it'll be the last time, and I don't want to rush him because I'm not sure either.

He peppers kisses down my neck, and he continues to press into me, my hips rolling into his at the perfect time with each thrust. My orgasm builds, my stomach tightening as heat floods my body. The second it rips through me, Mack groans into my neck, and I know falling over my edge pushed him to his. He continues to pump into me, slightly faster than before as he rides us through our climax.

He stills on top of me, leaning into his arm, but doesn't pull back. Instead, his eyes lock onto mine and stay that way until our heart rate and breathing calm. Only then does he brush the sweat-soaked hair from my face, gives me half-smile and places one more soft kiss on my lips. "I'll be right back," he whispers then slips out of bed and comes back with a warm rag to clean me up. God, he's the best. Once he's done, he climbs under the covers, pulling me into his arms. "Are you okay?" His voice is nervous and quiet–missing the confidence he had before we broke up. I hate myself a little for that.

"Yeah... that was... it feels right when we are togeth-er," I say shyly, looking away from him like I'm embarrassed I've been trying to avoid it. Maybe I am. We are only partially on the same page.

"We are right together, Mace."

I know he wants us to be together. I know I need time for myself before that happens. The disconnect makes my chest tight. "It's not that I don't believe that... it's just... I don't think it's our time yet."

"When will it be 'our time?'" he asks with patience in his voice, although I can sense the invisible wall he's building back up around his heart.

"I'm not sure. Ugh. Maybe we shouldn't have done that." I sigh.

"Baby, please don't do that. I will never regret any time I get to spend with you." He rubs his thumb across my cheek. His ability to remain calm in this moment makes me certain his lapse of judgment with the drugs isn't a habit I should be worried about.

My voice comes out soft, my tears barely holding back. "I don't want to give you the wrong idea." Before he gets a completely wrong idea, I spit out the rest of my thoughts. "I love you, Mack. I do. I never stopped loving you. I want to be with you. But there are some things I need to figure out on my own first. I need my life to make a little more sense before I can give you and our relationship the attention it deserves."

"I want to help you with that," he pleads.

I scan his face. "I know, but this is something I need to do on my own. Please understand that."

"You know I will give you whatever you need, and I'll be here when you're ready."

I pause before I commit to the next words. "I'll be gone for months. I don't want you to stop living your life while I'm away. I want you to be happy."

It takes him a moment to register what I'm implying. Instead of responding, he just pulls me into him, his sweet cinnamon scent calming my nerves and lulling me into a few hours of sleep.

I stand on the curb in the departures drop-off area, teetering back and forth on my feet with my thumbs looped through my backpack straps as Mack shuts his passenger door behind me. When he turns to me, I try to reassure him the best I can, reiterating what I told him last night.

"Our time will come, Mack. I want it to. It just can't be right now. I need to get on this plane. And while I'm gone I have to be focused on me, on finding my purpose in life and making the difference that I want to. If we try this again right now, I won't be all in, and you deserve more than that. I know that's not fair to you to still not commit, but it's all I can offer right now."

He sighs like he understands what I'm saying but runs his fingers through his hair like it'll somehow dissolve the sadness he also feels. He pulls me into his chest before whispering into my ear. "I really hope you have the best time. I'm going to miss you so much."

"I already miss you," I admit.

"I'll be waiting when you get back." He pulls away just enough to kiss me.

"I'll see you then." I kiss him one more time before I watch him walk around his Jeep, climb in and drive away from me.

As soon as I get through the automatic glass doors, my phone vibrates in the pocket of my leggings. I open the text from Mack. It's a link to a Spotify version of the mixed CD he made for me. Another text comes through almost immediately.

Mack: *Just in case you wanted to take this with you.*

CHAPTER SIXTY-THREE

Me: *I cannot thank you enough for this experience, Mack. It was the most fulfilling two months of my life.*

Mack: *I'm glad, Mace. I was hoping it would be.*

I send him a picture of me with a couple of the women I worked with at the sanctuary.

Mack: *You're beautiful. And you seem really happy. I can't wait to hear all about it. When are you coming home? Any chance you'll be home for New Year's Eve tonight? I can pick you up.*

Me: *I didn't even realize it was New Year's already! Don't think this is because I don't want to see you. I do. But I'm going to stay a little longer. I spent so much time working, I didn't get to spend any time exploring or being by myself like I want. I'm on the bus now, headed to a small town Maria told me to check out.*

Mack: *Oh ok. Well, let me know when you make it there safely?*

Me: *I will. Thanks again, Mack. You're the best.*

I imagine getting off the plane when I get home and seeing him standing there waiting for me, like he was the first time I visited. My heart leaps at the thought, and I consider sending another text to tell him I love him, in case he doesn't know, but decide against it.

Holy sunrise, I'm not sure I've ever seen anything more beautiful in my entire life. The sanctuary was protected in the middle of the jungle, which was beautiful in its own way, but the sunrise I'm watching, over the crystal blue water and white sand, is like nothing I've ever seen before. This doesn't come close to anything in California. The orange and pink floods the sky, and even with the waves crashing into themselves, it's calm. The sand is untouched, as if the tide has just gone out, and I can't help but disturb its peace by leaving my footprints in it.

Maria insisted this beach was the perfect place to decompress for a few days and drove me to the bus stop this morning. Helping prepare women and children for the real world after being trapped in such a cruel one seemed impossible at first. I knew my work would be emotionally taxing, but I wasn't prepared for the magnitude of it. It turned out to be so fulfilling, though. My heart may not have been occupied by a boy for the first time in a while, but it has never been as full as it is after seeing how much of a difference I seemed to make.

I've walked a mile at least, but I haven't seen anyone. The waves have slowed, and the beach is so quiet I can practically hear my thoughts. I spot a wind-worn shack up ahead. Squinting doesn't bring it any more into view. Another hundred steps and I can tell it's a board shop. I'm too afraid to surf, but I think I could manage paddle boarding. Especially since the water is currently calm. Maybe they have someone who can teach me.

I glance into the shack but don't see anyone. Staring back into the ocean, I pep talk myself. When in Costa Rica, right? I'm a great swimmer, plus the waves have been calm for a while. If I rode on a motorcycle, surely I can do this too.

"Hey, do you have a boyfriend?" Chills race over every inch of my body as the voice hits my ears. I slowly spin my bare feet in the sand to face the shack again, and I lock onto brown eyes I knew I would recognize. My mouth drops open.

I melt at the smirk on his face from thinking the first words out of his mouth were clever. I take a step, my immediate instinct to leap into a hug, but I stop in my tracks.

No.

He hurt me. I don't miss him. How is he here? Where did he come from?

Suddenly, he's in front of me, his closed book in one hand. I vaguely hear the sound of my name as his other hand lands on my arm, and my stare transfers to where our skin touches. This was never supposed to happen again.

He drops his hand as he senses my apprehension.

Standing there in front of him, hardly a few inches from his face, I wonder if it's like this with everyone you've ever had chemistry with. Instant electricity buzzes inside me the moment my brown eyes meet his again, the feeling replacing some of the shock. I run my gaze over his body. The sun has stained his skin, and his hair is more golden than I remember. He's wearing the same stupid pants, except the bottoms have been zipped off. I love this moment more. Or maybe I hate it.

I realize only when he waves his hand in front of my face that I was gaping again. I have no idea if I'm more shocked he's standing in front of me or overwhelmed by how the morning sun hits his abs, which are more defined than they once were. Yup. Still the most gorgeous man I've ever seen.

"Oh, hi, sorry," I practically stutter. "I never thought I'd see you again." It comes out as more of a whisper than I intended. When my eyes meet his again, anxiety swarms in my stomach. Butterflies? The churning of jadedness? Who the hell knows. Either way, it's a feeling I intend to get rid of quickly.

It would be a lie to say running into Dean in Costa Rica hadn't crossed my mind. The thought flashed for a second when I was on the plane but faded away as I got more and more invested in the sanctuary. Plus, the likelihood of that happening was nothing, zero freaking percent.

It's been a year, almost to the day, since I last saw him. I wasn't sure if he was still here, let alone that our paths might cross. I was devastated for so long after he left and so torn up about the entire situation that made no sense to me at all. Mack helped me let go of everything and everyone from the past. He made me believe there was a reason for everything that happened with Dean, and I'm genuinely thankful for how it all happened. *Mack.* I forgot to text him and tell him I made it here.

"Maaaaciiiii," he says as if it's not the first time he's tried to get my attention.

"Yes, hi." Snap out of it, Maci, for goodness sake, get it together.

"What are you doing here?" The expression on his face is a mix of disbelief and excitement.

Oh, this I can answer. Get to rambling so you're distracted, Maci. "Umm, I've been working here, well not here, more in the jungle. Not really working, volunteering, for this place that helps rehabilitate women who have been kidnapped and trafficked." It's easier to relax thinking about my time here over the past eight weeks.

"Didn't you take a weekend class about that? That sounds perfect for you. Did you love it?" He seems truly interested, jumping into conversation like it hasn't been a year since we've spoken. Wait, he remembers that? I think I only said it in passing once. It might have even been a conversation I was having with Marcus.

"Yeah, I did," I say, a little stunned by everything. "How... are you? Do you like it here?"

"I mean, what's not to love? This view is incredible." He doesn't break his eye contact with me. "I traveled around at first, but I've been here for about six months. I work here in the mornings and surf in the afternoon. It's pretty great." He shrugs.

"Sounds perfect."

"Almost," he says wistfully, locking his eyes with mine but not elaborating.

The silence that felt perfect a few minutes ago now feels incredibly awkward. "Soooo, I was thinking about paddle boarding today. I only plan on being here for a few days until I head somewhere new but figured it was something I could try. Looks like you can help me?" I say while motioning to the hut behind us.

"Sure can. You don't want to surf? I can teach you."

"Yeah, I'm not that adventurous. Baby steps."

"That's not what I remember." He winks and the insinuation in his voice makes me blush.

For the love of me staying rational, please do not wink at me. It's like I'm back to square one, all the hard work I've done to be more in control of my life and emotions washes away with this golden boy's face existing in my presence. "Maybe tomorrow. One thing at a time. I just got here, and I haven't been in the ocean in months."

The smile he flashes my way freezes me in my place long after he's walked away to get me a board.

Am I in love? I'm positive. This is definitely my new favorite thing. I've been out here long enough that the skin on my nose is tight, and I know my sunscreen has worn off. I was worried I was going to fall, but my board hasn't so much as dipped its edge into the water. The only wet I got was from purposely splashing myself when my skin got too warm. I've stripped down to my jean shorts and black bikini top, and I'm sitting cross-legged, my paddle tucked under my foot. In front of me is like a National Geographic photograph–a soft, off-white beach, the palm tree branches swaying only slightly and the water is so clear I can see crabs scurrying around the ocean floor. I was comfortable within the first half hour and paddled a little ways from the shore, past where the waves would break, just in case.

My anxiety has faded, even as I stare toward the hut I know Dean sits inside, despite not being able to see him. As panicked as I was when I first saw him, it's become comforting. These past two months have been nothing short of magical. Maybe that's not quite the right word. It was eye opening learning how cruel the world can be, and to some extent it did take a toll on me. It's probably why seeing a familiar face feels so good. But I also got to experience the kind of forgiveness and love that is possible from people despite the darkness that exists. I know I was supposed to be the one changing the lives of the women I was helping, but my soul tells me they made a bigger impact on me. The way they were able to let go of the past because they realized it was truly the only way to move forward was beautiful. Being around them has freed me of a lot of the residual pain and guilt I've felt when it comes to Mack and everything else I've been holding on to.

I thought I had already let go of any leftover feelings when it came to Dean, but I was proven wrong as soon as his voice rang through my ears and our chemistry instantly resurfaced. Floating out here in the middle of the ocean, it feels like letting go of the past with him is the right thing to do, but once he's in front of me again, can I figure out how to let go of the pain I've harbored? What does it mean that I came here searching for myself and I found him too?

CHAPTER SIXTY-FOUR

The sun glows behind the trees by the time I spot Dean standing at the edge of the water waving me to the shore. I'm both reluctant and anxious to be back on land. When I get there, he takes my board from me. His shorts are hanging off his hips, and he smells like salt and sunshine. It's hard not to stare and want to follow him way too closely as he heads toward the hut.

"How much do I owe you?"

"Nah, nothing. It's the least I can do." He turns and lets his eyes connect with mine again, an unreadable expression in them.

"Okay, how about dinner?" I say somewhere between an unsure question and a statement.

A smile lights his face. "I know just the place."

Everywhere I go in this country should be in a movie, and this taco bar isn't an exception. There are little black wicker tables scattered over the sand, twinkle lights strung among surrounding palm trees. A guy in the corner plays a guitar, singing a song in Spanish I can't totally understand. Even after two months at the sanctuary, my Spanish isn't perfect, but the words flowing out of him sound romantic, and it's setting a mood. We wind through a few tables to the taco cart. "What do you want?" I ask, straining in the dark to read the menu written in black marker on a piece of cardboard.

"Surprise me. I'll get us a table." He points in the direction of the tables with a darkening view of the ocean, his hand grazing my still bare lower back before walking away. A burst of energy transfers between us where we make contact, leaving my skin tingling. Well, I guess some things don't change.

As I wait for our tacos, I scan in every direction except the way Dean left. When our food is ready, I loop the neck of two beer bottles between my fingers so I can carry all the paper trays in my hands. I ordered us two of each, knowing he's probably at least as hungry as I am.

"Mmm, thank you." He pulls the tacos out of my hands to set them on the table, reaching back up for one of the beers.

As he brings one of the tacos to his mouth, his gaze returns to where it was, on the waves you can barely make out crashing into the shore. His mood seems to have shifted. I wonder what happened and if I should say anything. Definitely trying to stay casual here since it's strange we're even in this situation–but nothing with him has ever felt casual.

His voice breaks through my thoughts. "I'm sorry about how I left."

More confusion washes over me until realization hits me. That was the last thing I ever expected to hear. "It's okay."

"I mean, not really. I had to do it, but I could have gone about it a little differently."

"You mean not after you sedated me with really great sex and before kicking me out of your truck." My laugh and eye roll happen simultaneously. I really do mean it as a joke. After connecting with Mack, the majority of my insecurities and frustrations around Dean dissipated. Of course I wondered what went through his head during all of that, but I had accepted I would never get the answers, like I'm assuming I still won't now.

He does his little laugh to himself thing that makes me feel more than I want. "Soooo, we had really good sex?"

Of course he focuses on that part. "Well, I thought we did."

His face gets serious. "We did." The corner of his mouth turns up in a slight smile, and his eyes wander as if stuck in a memory for a moment. "I like your sex, Maci. I like you."

I choose to temporarily ignore the fact he used the present tense. Not knowing what to say next, I shove the rest of my taco in my mouth.

"I want to be honest with you." I freeze mid-chew. Uhhh, more than he already has been? Is the person across from me the same Dean who left a year ago?

I finish chewing and swallow my bite. "You don't have to explain yourself. It's not like we were in a relationship or anything."

"I want to, though. There's a reason you showed up here, and maybe this is it. I've felt bad about it, even before I left."

I had started to raise my beer to my lips but set it down slowly, as if choosing not to multitask would help me hear him more clearly. I stare back, patiently waiting for him to continue.

"I made the official decision to come here last minute. It was right before that first party you came to at my house, remember? I wanted to see you so badly. But the second you got there, I panicked. I felt guilty we were hanging out so much, and I could tell–well, I had a feeling–you were starting to have feelings for me too even though I *tried* to keep it casual."

Of course I remember that party. It was the first time he told me he missed me and called me "babe." It was the first time I had real hope he might want to *really* be with me before I found out how misguided that was.

I can't help but look away, repositioning my gaze to my fingers fidgeting on top of the table. He reaches out, resting one hand on top of mine to still them, but I can't will myself to look at him when I speak. "I knew you didn't feel the same. It's okay, Dean. Sometimes it just works out that way–how it's meant to."

"Maci." He puts pressure on my hands until I stop talking. "You're misunderstanding me. I felt the same way. It wasn't that at all. I couldn't stay away from you. It's why I begged you to come back, but it scared me."

"Oh, I'm sorry?" I'm confused about what he's trying to tell me.

"No, that's not what I'm saying either," his brown eyes glisten from the twinkle lights above us as he laughs to himself. "That wasn't the reason I left. I left because I needed to do this for me." He pauses for a moment. "You know I graduated early, before you, before my friends. I felt like I should have more of an idea of what I wanted to do with my life, but nothing felt right. I had this feeling something was missing, and I needed to go find it. It had nothing to do with you. If anything, you were the only thing that made me want to stay."

Oh. This is the most upfront Dean has ever been, and I never expected to understand him or his choices after he left. I don't know what to say. Confusion over one thing was just replaced with another. Seriously, what am I supposed to do with this information? He picks up on my uneasiness.

"Wow, I do not know who possessed my body right now, you're probably wondering what the fuck just happened. I'm not sure I know," he chuckles while shifting in his seat. He seems embarrassed.

"Yeaaah, I might need time to process that." Honest words flow from me this time. I'm tempted to tell him how much his leaving impacted me, but it doesn't matter at this point. I'll be gone in a few days, and I'd rather leave that heartbreak in the past where it belongs.

He leans back in his seat, pulling his beer to his lips but not allowing his eyes to leave mine.

I jolt up in my seat, with a sudden realization. "Shit. I was going to find a hotel in town, but the day got away from me. I spaced." I pull out my phone to see if I have any service.

His hand reaches back out, this time covering my phone screen. "Chill, Maci, you can stay with me. My place is super small, but it's right over there." He points at the beach behind me. "We can walk to it."

"I've 'stayed' with you before, Dean," using air quotes for the full effect. "I'm not trying to make assumptions here, but I'm pretty sure it wouldn't be a great idea."

"Why do you think that?" He chews on his toothpick as he eyes me.

"Dean," I plead, hoping the tone in my voice is enough explanation. I'm not here for him. And eventually I'm going home to Mack.

"Okay, okay, I will sleep on the floor, PG sleepover, I promise." He winks.

Standing, he holds out his hand until I take it. He keeps them linked together, guiding me through the moonlit night as we walk across the wet sand to his place. When we get to his front door, he unlocks it, reaching only his hand inside to flip on the light. Before leading me in, he turns back. "For the record, I didn't mean for it to feel like I was kicking you out of my truck that day. I just didn't..." he pauses, his eyes begging me not to make him finish his thought. I nod and nudge him inside.

"Do you need anything?" He sets my backpack on the bed that's in the center of the back wall, held up by a wood frame. When he said small, he meant it. There's a little kitchenette and a two-person table off to the right and a door I'm assuming leads to the bathroom on the left, and that's about it. It's perfect.

"I'm good, I've been living out of this backpack for two months, so I don't need much these days. Thank you, though." Pulling my pajamas from my bag, I make a beeline for the bathroom, which is only four steps away. My shorts and bikini are folded in my hand when I walk out to Dean on his knees, laying a blanket on the floor.

"Dean." One hand flies to my hip as I stare at the back of his head until he turns around.

"Maci." He acts like he has no idea what I'm about to say.

"Don't be ridiculous, we can sleep together without sleeping together. We've done it before."

"Like one time." He smirks.

"Okay, well, if we did it once, we can do it again. We haven't seen each other in a year. There's no reason for you to be uncomfortable." Tossing my clothes on top of my bag, I grab his wrist with one hand and pull the blanket off the floor with the other. He gives me an uneasy smile and pulls his shirt over his head when I release him. Looking back as if he needs confirmation that was okay, I motion toward the bed. "Can you stop being weird? It's freaking me out."

Laughing as he flicks off the light, he mumbles something under his breath. When the mattress sinks under his weight, I turn to face him. "But thank you for the apology earlier." I'm trying to match the sincerity he's been showing me today, even if it all seems like an out-of-body experience.

"Can I tell you something else?" he whispers.

"Mhmmm." I'm tired from the day, but curiosity outweighs it.

"The only reason I didn't come into your apartment the first night I took you home, and why I resisted you at our sleepover... I didn't want to want you. I had a feeling it could potentially keep me from figuring out where I was going with my life."

"What made you cave?" I'm curious what the tipping point was.

"I know this makes me sound like a jealous asshole, but it was seeing you playing pool with another guy. Obviously I got that wrong, but I decided I had no choice but to give in if I didn't want to see you with someone else."

"But you left me anyway." It comes out as a fact, without judgment.

"I know."

I have no words in response to him continuing to validate everything I ever wondered. Again, I contemplate telling him how much his leaving shattered my heart but hold back. Instead, I close the distance between us, kissing his lips softly, noticing neither of us close our eyes. "Happy New Year, Dean."

His eyes fill with surprise, like he had no idea what today's date was. Maybe that's what pulled me to kiss him. He's been my only New Year's kiss, and it felt right, but now I have to ignore the chills that run straight to my spine and how badly the urge is to go back for another kiss. His vulnerability today is hitting me hard. As soon as I turn back over, Dean pulls me backward, into him.

CHAPTER SIXTY-FIVE

When I open my eyes, I'm disoriented, and my vision is blurred by the sleep stuck in the corner of my eyes. I rub them, the room coming into focus and my memory flooding back. Turning over, my hand flings out to search for Dean on the other side of the bed but falls straight to the mattress. Wait, did I dream all of this? Or did he disappear on me again? I'm in his room, so he can't do that. Can he? Sitting, I catch a glimpse of a crumpled receipt covered in writing on the nightstand.

Morning Gorgeous,

Had to leave for work. Come down for your surfing lesson when you're ready.

I smile and think back to last night. I can't believe Dean professed his feelings to me. After agonizing over all the possible scenarios of what he could have felt during the few months we were together, none of them were as hopeful as this reality. His disclosures seemed out of character for him, but maybe it's because I didn't really know him at all. I wonder how many people do? He's already let me in more than before. I wonder if it would be pushing my luck today to try and find out more. Do I want that? Am I setting myself up for something I can't handle or don't need right now? I'm leaving in a few days, and I have to keep going on this journey

I promised myself. And when I get home, Mack will be there, and we will give us another shot. Oh shit, Mack.

Reaching for my phone, I see there's already a text from him.

Mack: *Hey, Mace, just making sure you made it to your next place okay.*

Mack: *Just checking in again… a little worried I haven't heard from you.*

Whoops.

Me: *Hey, I'm so sorry, time got away from me yesterday. I made it here, and I'm safe!*

I change into my bikini as I wait for his reply.

Mack: *You scared me. I'm glad you're okay. How was your day?*

Me: *It was great. I learned how to paddleboard! And the craziest thing happened. I ran into Dean. What are the chances? So weird. I might try surfing today.*

He replies as quickly as I regret hitting send on the text. Panic rushes through me, knowing it wasn't the best idea to tell Mack that Dean is here. There's nothing to worry about, but I know he will anyway.

Mack: *Dean, your ex, Dean? That is crazy. Did you know he was there?*

Me: *No! I haven't talked to him in a year. Total coincidence.*

Seriously, I'm still in shock trying to wrap my head around the odds. The three dots indicating he's typing appear and disappear three times before his text comes through.

Mack: *I know I have no right to say anything, I heard you when you said you weren't ready for our relationship yet. But this is really throwing me, Mace. I don't feel good about it.*

Me: *Trust me, it threw me too. I never expected to ever see him again. But it's nice having a familiar face in an unfamiliar place. That's all.*
Mack: *Okay, you know how much I love you, right?*
Me: *I know. I love you too.*

Sure, I apparently still have chemistry with Dean. But that's all this is. I think. His admissions felt more like a clearing of conscience, and that's not enough to make me consider the possibility of it being more. Plus, I'm traveling. Then I'm going home where I'll try again with Mack because I do love him, and the future I want is with him. There's magic around traveling that distorts reality a bit. These new thoughts sneaking into my head are simply that.

Me: *I'm off to learn how to surf! Pray I don't get eaten by a shark! I'll talk to you later! Happy New Year!*
Mack: *Be careful, Maci.*

I'm not sure if he's talking about surfing or Dean, but I have a feeling he's less concerned about sharks.

I set my phone down, and my thumb runs over the note on the nightstand, covered in the most simple words from Dean. I wonder how much he's changed since I last saw him.

I shake away the stray thoughts this morning has brought into my head and lock the door behind me as I leave for the beach.

Yesterday felt like a walk through a haze with Dean–like when you wake from a dream that felt simultaneously vivid and clouded and for a moment you aren't sure if it happened in real life or only in your head. Unlike so many mornings during the months I pined for Dean and dreamed about him coming back, this time he actually appeared.

It's a strange and ever-changing feeling I haven't figured out how to navigate. Today already seems different, even though I haven't seen him. The shock and anxiety have been replaced with a sense of calm and comfort, as if this entire encounter isn't only a random coincidence. I'm more confident around him this time. I didn't even put on makeup when I left the house, not that I need it from this natural glow my skin has from being outside so much lately.

I slowly make my way down the beach, the nearly white sand cool under my bare feet. My hair has been lightened by the sun, and the salty air has created the perfect beach waves. Looking into the mirror this morning, a feeling washed over me that I belong here, even if I take Dean and Mack out of the equation completely. I'm not sure if it was a "here in Costa Rica" feeling, or in this place of not being tied down and having the freedom to do what I want and figure out who I want to be feeling.

I reach Dean just as a customer walks away from him. "You didn't leave me directions! What if I got lost trying to find this place again?"

"I wasn't worried about you finding your way back to me." He smiles as he looks at me. He starts walking my way, with sandy bare feet, blue and white striped board shorts soaked with salt water, like he's already been out in the ocean today. He's shirtless and... Okaay. Maybe I can't take men out of the equation. Especially because what was with that line he just gave me? How am I supposed to ignore statements like that?

This time yesterday, I was on a high from leaving the sanctuary, and I felt so much gratitude for Mack, thinking about the night we spent together before I left, and how I planned on going back to him. I swear. Even this morning talking to him, I felt confident in that belief. But now, it's like the shock wore off with the morning fog, and standing in front of Dean, I'm suddenly over-whelmed by how much he opened up to me. Then he makes a single comment laced with innuendo, and it cracked the wall I had built to keep all my feelings about him away.

Though, there still isn't a reason to assume. Just because he felt that way before, doesn't necessarily mean he does now. He could just be full of lines. Either way, the lines are feeling blurry, and I already feel myself naturally drifting over as if being pulled by an invisible connection.

Chill out, Maci, you're reading too much into all of this, and there's nothing to worry about right now. I'll focus on one thing at a time. I'm going to go with the flow like I did yesterday. If you take out the shock factor, it ended up being a great day. I'll ignore whatever the intention behind those words were and every other man-related thought. "So, I was thinking I could just paddle board again today."

"Nope, not happening. I'm playing hooky, and you're learning to surf. The waves are perfect, and the water is plenty warm enough."

"You really don't have to work?"

"Nah, this place is more of a locals' area. Not sure how you ended up on this part of the beach to be honest.

It's rare we get customers, and the boss doesn't care anyway."

I promised myself I would go with the flow today, and there would be no use in arguing with him. I've never been able to deny him. This hold he's always had on me whenever he's close is strange. Annoying. Frustrating. Magical. I don't know. What do I know right now? Dear God, Maci, we are living in the moment today. Snap out of it.

"Okay, let's do this."

Wrapping his arm around my shoulder, he pulls me toward the board rack.

CHAPTER SIXTY-SIX

Every muscle in my body is exhausted from trying again and again to stand on the board. At least another hour went by after I first successfully stood before I was able to catch more than one wave in a row. Dean has been so patient, and it was exciting when it paid off. He's got the biggest grin on his face as I paddle back to him after this last run. He looks proud of me, and the feeling is surreal. Am I trapped in a movie? Or an alternate reality? I'm pretty sure I am.

Pulling up next to him, I sit on my board, letting my feet dangle on either side in the warm, clear water.

"That was a good run!"

"Yeah, it felt great! Finally getting the hang of it, but also, you might have to carry me home because every part of me hurts." *Home.* The thought flashes across my mind that it was a weird choice of words, but it felt oddly right. I can't control the next words that pour out of me. "This is strange, right? It feels like a dream or something. What are the chances we found our way back to each other? I don't mean like that. That came out weird. I'm sorry. It's just, after you left, I hoped so many times you'd come back, but seeing you here now, I'm glad you didn't."

"Because you met someone else?" He doesn't appear jealous, rather genuinely curious. See, he doesn't have feelings for me anymore.

"No. I mean yes, I did. But that's not what I mean. You seem happy here, more at peace. And a lot less confusing than I remember." I laugh, reaching into the water to fling it at him.

"Hey now!" He leans back on his board, resting on his hands. "So, do I know this guy? It isn't Troy, is it?" This time his intention seems to cross over the line of simple curiosity.

"No." I chuckle. "I have no desire to date Troy. It was Avery's brother. I'm not sure if you remember her."

"Of course I do." He acts now as if everything we ever did together was important to him even though it contradicts the impression I got at the time. "Are you still seeing him?"

"Umm, it's complicated. That sounds cliché. We were together for a while. I moved to California to be with him, but we aren't together right now."

"Wow, that's pretty serious. Sounds like it could have been a dream come true, marrying your best friend's brother."

"Yeah, it was great." The entire situation was one I didn't know would bring me so much happiness until I was in it. It was easy to fall into our relationship when it already felt like family. Then sharing Lexy with Mack as our best friend created the perfect little circle.

"What about you though? You've been here a year. Have you met anyone?" I don't want to hear about his sexcapades, but a desperate urge to stay in Mack's lane without even considering crossing into Dean's washes over me.

"Sometimes I hang out with the tourists who come through town, and I've made friends with a few of the locals. But no one else has occupied my thoughts. It's not what I came here for, ya know?"

"Yeah, how is that going? Finding yourself?"

"It's going well, I think. I mean, I'm not sure what exactly I expected. I feel like I was overthinking my game plan for my life because I spent too much time comparing what I was doing or should be doing to what everyone else was doing. I have a clearer vision of what I want my life to look like now. I'm more connected to myself, like I can see my path as its own and believe what I'm doing in my life doesn't have to parallel anyone else's."

"What do you want that path to look like?"

"I definitely still want to travel. I've noticed being out of routine and away from home can be unsettling for a lot of people. It's not like that for me. Don't get me wrong, I love the routine I have here, but it's not like when I'm at home. I'm more in control of my ability to seek out freedom and spontaneity, if I want."

"I get that. Do you think you'll ever go back to Oregon?"

"I do. It feels right being here, especially lately. But Oregon will always be my home, and I do want to put down roots somewhere, so I have a place to return."

"I think I've learned more about you in the past 24 hours than in the entire rest of the time I knew you," I joke. I hope that statement doesn't make him uncomfortable or stop opening up because as different as it is, it's what I've always craved from him, and I'm not ready for it to end.

"This place kind of does that to you. Or maybe it's just you, Maci." Vulnerability fills his eyes as they lock onto mine with his statement.

"You could have told me this before, you know. I would have understood."

"Would you have?" He's not judging me, just asking. It's a fair question.

He doesn't push me to answer, nor does he change the subject as I sit there contemplating. Would I have understood? Suddenly, I've unlocked a new level of appreciation for Dean, but also for Mack. He let me go when I asked. Despite his feelings, he didn't try to hold me back from what I wanted to do. It wasn't because he didn't care enough to fight for me. It was because he loves me enough to prioritize what I needed over what he wanted. God, I love him. I also realize that as much as I loved Dean when he left me the way I left Mack, I was nowhere near as mature. If I had known the whole truth then, I would have felt just as hurt and wouldn't have been any more understanding than I was.

"I don't think I would have, at least not like I do now." His eyes stay with mine as an orange and pink glow of the sun invades my periphery. "I heard this quote once about having multiple soulmates. It was something like 'the one you end up with depends on the work you've done to evolve your own soul. Maybe there's a soulmate for every level of your journey.' Not that I believe in soulmates or anything." Maybe you should stop rambling, Maci. But he hasn't shied away from any conversation or confession since I've been here. At least not like he once did. "But in general, I think the concept could be applied to a lot. Like sometimes you can't possibly understand something until you're ready to hear it or until you've experienced something yourself that allows you to comprehend it in the way you should. Like maybe we can't be ready for some things until we are ready for it. I'm not sure if that makes sense."

"It makes a lot of sense, Maci." We stare at each other in silence for a moment before he asks, "You ready to head in before it gets dark out here?"

"YES! And I was hoping we could get more tacos, but I'm also exhausted. Any chance we could just eat at your place?" Thank goodness this conversation is over. The deeper we connect the more part of me leans into something I wanted for so long, and the louder a voice screams at me to knock it off before I never want to leave.

CHAPTER SIXTY-SEVEN

I make my way to the sink to wash the dishes, my stomach full of the most delicious steak I've ever eaten. Apparently in Costa Rica beef is one of the more affordable proteins, and I'm not complaining, especially since Dean knows how to cook them a perfect medium, smothered in garlic, onions and butter.

"What's your middle name?" I ask as if not knowing hasn't bothered me for a year.

Dean chuckles. "Lucas. Why?" He grabs a dish towel, taking a clean plate from me.

"Just wondering."

"Okay, Maci Rae."

I pause mid-scrub of the pan and turn to see his smirk. I had no idea he knew my middle name. I shake my head softly, turning back to the pan.

"So, how is Avery?" His amusement transforms into confusion as I freeze again, the sink water running over the suds-free pan and my energy instantly shifting. "Is everything okay?"

"Yeah, ummm..." I turn off the water and take a breath. For some reason, even though everything is fine between Avery and me now, I'm caught off guard. I feel the urge to tell him what happened, to fill him in on parts of my life he wasn't a part of. Being here with him now makes it feel strange he hasn't been around the entire time. I'm realizing how sad I am about how much of each other's life we missed. I don't know where to start or if he'd care to hear about my year without him.

"It's okay, you don't have to tell me. But you can if you want." He sets the now damp towel on the counter, picking up my hand in its place and leading me to the end of his bed where we sit, and he looks at me, waiting.

The sincerity in his eyes makes the decision for me. I start from the beginning, trying to leave Mack out of as much of the story as possible, but I can see a flicker of realization in his eyes when it slips.

"Wow, Maci, I don't know what to say. I'm sorry. That must be hard to navigate. I know she's your best friend, and you've always had a special bond. I could tell whenever you were together."

"Yeah, everything is okay now, though. She's always been my person, and nothing is going to change that."

I make a mental note to set aside time to call Avery and check in when I get to my next stop. I should really decide where that will be. And when–but later.

"Soooo..." I can tell he wants to change the subject, but his hesitancy makes me nervous. My gut tells me what's coming next. "Sounds like Avery's brother is a great guy." He doesn't ask a question, but his eyes are filled with them.

I come up with something to say quicker than I thought I'd be able. "Yeah, I'm thankful he was there to help with everything that happened."

"What did happen, though? With him. Are you tied to him the way you are to Avery? I mean, you've known him forever too, right?" His forwardness surprises me, although at this point, I'm not sure why.

I adjust how I'm sitting on the bed, pulling one leg under me. I'm uncomfortable but still pulled to be truthful with him. I've been grateful for the shift he's had around being open with me, and it would be hypocritical if I didn't match that. "We dated for a while. I moved to California, like I said before. He's super easy to be around, like it's always been with Avery. With added benefits, of course." I cringe. You're such an idiot, Maci. You can be honest without sharing every thought. I can feel Dean's eyes on me, and I'm too afraid to look up and read his face. My eyes stay on my hands fidgeting in my lap, and I try to recover by keeping it simple. "We had a good relationship."

"Why aren't you still with him then?"

"Initially it was because he broke my trust. I didn't handle it well. I panicked. I also realized I needed to take time to focus on myself before I could give our relationship the attention it deserved. Is that how you felt?" He starts to speak but I cut him off. "Wait, I'm not trying to say you felt that way about me. I know we weren't even in a relationship."

I try to keep rambling, but he gently holds up his hand to stop me. "Maci, I know I fought the title, but I considered us in a relationship. There was only you."

"Your communication said otherwise." The moment the words come out, my hands fly to my mouth as if I could shove them back in. "That was mean, I'm sorry."

"It's also true." He looks down at our hands where he's just interlocked our fingers. He doesn't seem to know what to add, so I choose to contribute more thoughts. I debated refraining the past two days, but I think he should know how much he hurt me because I'm getting the impression he has no idea.

"The night Mack and I broke up was the one time his communication failed. He was always good at it. One of the reasons I didn't let it slide is because I promised myself I deserved more." I pause. "Dean…"

His eyes hesitantly meet mine again, and his thumb rubbing over my hand freezes.

"You really hurt me."

He starts to apologize, but I cut him off.

"Please let me get this out." His lips pinch together, and he nods, letting me know I have his full attention. "I wasn't just hurt that you left without hardly any notice or explanation…" I take a breath to keep my tears in check.

He stays silent, watching me.

"I loved you. I was in love with you. I had never given anyone my heart that way. Maybe you didn't want it, but you broke it nonetheless. I was a wreck. For months, Dean."

He releases his hold on me so he can rub both hands up his face and into his hair. His fingers link behind his neck, his head tipped back slightly into them. He genuinely looks like he's in pain after listening to me. I didn't want to hurt him, but it was time for him to know. Regardless, I'm uncomfortable now.

"Sorry, that was a lot. I didn't intend to drop all this on you. I know it doesn't matter because we haven't seen each other in a year, but part of me felt like you should know. You don't have to say anything." I stand, getting ready to wash my face and wash away these resurfaced memories.

"Maci, sit down, please." He reaches out and runs his fingers down my forearm. I oblige him and sit cross legged on the edge of the bed, facing him.

"Do you remember when you came to see me on New Year's last year?"

I nod.

"Do you want to know what I said that night?"

"Ummm…" I search my memories, but I can't seem to remember anything but his thoughts being cut off by a customer.

"Not to you." He laughs to himself. "I was on the phone with my mom when you surprised me."

"You talked to your mom about me?" I know I heard the end of their conversation, but I'm still surprised.

"My mom, my dad, Marcus, Aden."

"I didn't know guys talk about girls like that." I crack a half-smile.

"We don't really." He shrugs. "At least I don't, but you're not just some girl. When I mentioned you for like the third day in a row, Marcus looked at me like I'd lost my damn mind. I told him I had."

I don't say anything while I try to process.

"Once I had officially decided to leave, he asked me every day if I had told you."

"I love Marcus. He's my favorite friend of yours."

He smiles like it means something to him. "My mom was the worst bugging me about it. She wanted to meet you."

"She did? I would have liked that."

"I know. That's why it never happened. It would have made things harder than I had already made them."

"So, what did you tell her?" I'm trying not to get my hopes up about what he's saying, but my heart flutters in anticipation.

He looks back down at our hands that are tightly intertwined again, like what he's about to say is embarrassing. "I asked her how you know you're falling in love with someone."

My mouth falls open involuntarily.

He looks at me, without saying anything else. We stay that way, with our eyes locked for what feels like forever.

"I'm sorry, Maci. I know that's not enough for the way I left you and everything else I should have done in our relationship but didn't. I'm sorry I made you doubt how I feel about you." It didn't escape me that he used the present tense again, and I wonder if it's intentional.

I take a breath and rub my thumb over his hand. "It's okay, Dean. I've forgiven you for that. It is what it is. We can't go back, and I don't want to."

"Can I ask you something?"

"Anything."

"Did you love him too?"

"Yes."

"Do you still?"

His questions should feel invasive, but for some reason I don't mind. I look up, searching his eyes for an answer I know can only come from me. "Do you really want to know?"

"Yes." The hesitancy in his voice contradicts the word.

"I do love Mack. He helped me recover from that heartbreak. He gave me what I wanted from you–security, love, real commitment–and I fell in love with him for that and so many other reasons." I take a breath to judge his reaction. He looks defeated, but I continue anyway because honesty is the only thing that's going to get me anywhere. "I forgot about you because I had to, because it was the only way to move on and give myself a chance to be happy."

"I hate that I wasn't there to fix what I broke."

"Like I said, I'm choosing not to hold it against you anymore. But..."

"But what?"

"I don't know..." I shift on the bed.

"We already started this, we might as well finish it. Tell me what you're thinking." He says it like he deserves the punishment of hearing about Mack. It breaks my heart all over again. Still, he squeezes my hand, urging me to continue.

"It's just... Mack is great. He's the one who helped me get this volunteer job. He sent me away from him so I could be happy. I mean, who does that? And when things are good between us, I am happy. I wasn't capable of handling the heartbreak when you left, I think because I was so mad at myself for being blindsided. Coming to terms with that was hard. Missing Mack is different... almost easier. He made one mistake, but he tries his best to not give me any reason to doubt our ability to make our relationship work. He knows we are worth fighting for and is willing to work through life with me. He deserves the second chance I promised him, one I want to give him when I go home."

"I see." He pulls his hand away from mine.

I reach back out for him, and he doesn't stop me. It's my turn to recall what else was said that night. "But that's not what I was getting at. Do you remember what I told you on New Year's last year?"

"That liking me makes you want to throw up?" He says it with a straight face, and it makes me laugh.

"Okay, well, yeah." I can't help my smile. "When I came to your work that night, I told you I had never felt about anyone before the way I feel around you. I meant it then... and I still mean it now. I'm not saying I'm still in love with you, to be clear. That would be crazy. I hardly know you anymore, or at least I'm still learning about this new you. But the way I feel when we are together, it's different from anything I've felt with anyone else. It's electric. I can't help but wonder how things could have been different between us. I'm also not sure you ever really stop loving someone."

I think I shocked him into speechlessness. He wasn't prepared for that flip in my admission. Or maybe he doesn't know what to say because he thinks I'm crazy. Maybe he had feelings for me a year ago, but it's been a year, and with everything he's confessed, none of his words have been directly admitting he's still interested in me.

"What are you saying, Maci?" He says it slowly.

"I'm saying... I'm confused and conflicted about a lot. I came here certain I'd go home to the only option I had in my head. I don't want this to be unclear: Mack is not my backup choice by any means. But I also never expected to see you again. I'm not confident about how you feel now compared to how you did before... but I need..."

When I don't finish my thought, he confirms what I had assumed based on him actively participating in this conversation. "My feelings haven't changed." He's confident. "What do you need?" he adds calmly.

"I don't want to make any promises or lead you on..."

Dean's fingers pull away from mine, and he threads them through my hair. "Maci, tell me what you need, please."

"If any part of you doesn't want our story to be over... I need you to kiss me right now."

The words have barely left my lips before he pulls my face toward his with his firm grip on the back of my neck. His mouth crashes into mine with an urgency that sends a shock through me, but as soon as my lips part for his, it turns tender, and we sync immediately as if it hasn't been a year.

A few minutes pass before he pulls back just enough to look at me. Then he kisses me softly once, as if he truly doesn't expect anything else. "Ready for bed? I just finished a book I think you'd like."

I nod and smile at him, then head to the bathroom to brush my teeth. Peeking back at him over my shoulder, I catch his thumb brushing over his bottom lip, the same way it did after he kissed me for the first time against his truck. The flutter in my stomach isn't so different from that night either.

CHAPTER SIXTY-EIGHT

I roll over, my eyes still closed. I feel around on the other side of the bed, much less surprised than yesterday that Dean is already gone. I rub the sleep from my eyes and sit. Once I can see clearly, I immediately spot today's note.

Hi Beautiful,

Your breakfast is on the stove. Tortillas are on the counter. Can't wait to see you.

I read his words twice more. They might not be a love letter but compared to Dean's level of vulnerability a year ago, it nearly feels like it. I walk over to the kitchen area of Dean's studio and smile at his second sweet gesture of the day. I slide the eggs onto a tortilla and roll them up. I'm not sure if that's how they eat it in Costa Rica, but it looks good to me.

I might have been able to ignore the chemistry I felt around Dean once he was out of the picture and I'd convinced myself there was more to a good relationship than electricity, but it's too hard to ignore it now, especially when he seems willing to give me the pieces that were missing before. I know I can't possibly be in love with Dean again yet–that is, if you ever stop loving someone you've loved in the first place. As much as he feels like all the good parts of Dean I remember, I also know he's grown, and I want to spend more time with that version of him, learning all the things I missed over the past year to know for sure.

Can you be in love with two people at once? I'm certain I love Mack, but I can see myself falling for Dean all over again, as quickly as I did the first time if I let myself.

It's hard to wrap my head around how I'm stuck in this dilemma in the first place. I truly never expected to ever see Dean again. Yet here I am, tying the straps of my bikini before I head down the beach in search of him, like we are on vacation together and never skipped a beat.

When I get to Dean's surf shack, he's speaking to a young local boy in Spanish. He catches sight of me, smiling in the middle of telling the boy to go wait by the water, I think. He must be giving him a lesson.

"Hi." He leans closer like he's considering kissing me but then pulls back.

"Thank you for breakfast."

"You're welcome. I also got your board ready for you, if you're comfortable being out there by yourself. I have a few lessons to teach today, but I'll be close by if you need me."

"Perfect. And then when you're done, we can get more tacos?"

He laughs. "Yes, we can always get tacos." Leaning in again, he kisses my forehead this time before taking off in a jog toward the water.

It's not as late as it was when we called it a day yester-day. Dean finished his last lesson about an hour ago and has been in the shop closing up for the day. By the time he signals me in, I've stopped trying to ride the waves in favor of letting them lap softly beneath my board as I lie with my face to the setting sun. The water is warm, and the vibrant sky makes it so peaceful.

When I make it to shore, Dean is there waiting. He takes my board from me, but instead of walking it to the shop, he lays it gently on the sand. I look from it, then back at him. He takes a step closer and drapes his arms over my shoulders. "Hi."

"Heeeey." I smile, my hands finding his waist as if this is a moment we share every day. He looks at me like he's debating if he should tell me what he's thinking or say nothing at all. "What?"

His fingers tug gently on my hair, already almost dry since the last time I was under the water. "Every day I've been here I've thought about what it would be like if you were with me. It's surreal to look out onto the water and actually see you. I can't believe you're here."

I smile and lean into his chest, not having the right words for a response. A few minutes pass. I could easily stay in this moment, standing here in front of a beau-tiful orange and pink sky, with the quiet lapping of the water on the shore. My stomach, however, isn't on the same page. I'm not surprised, considering I skipped lunch today. I pull back slightly. "Can we get tacos now?"

"As many as you want." He grins before bending down for my board, tucking it under one arm, looping the other back around my shoulder. When we get to the stand, he pulls away to hose off my board before setting it back on the rack. "Do you want to rinse off before we get food? There is a shower right behind us." He asks it as a question but starts walking off before I answer him.

Behind the hut is a shower surrounded by at least seven foot tall cement walls. It's almost entirely private with an open space to enter. Dean turns on the water, stepping back, reaching his hand in a few times to test its warmth. When it's hot enough, he motions for me to go first.

The water flows down my body, and I'm struck by the memory of the first time I was at his house. I was caught off guard when he got in the shower with me, but damn it was hot. Okay, Maci, stop. Get it together. If your mind goes there, there's no coming back. Would it really be that bad though? I'm planning on being here for only another day or two. I'm not in a relationship. I'm living in the moment. Yes, I'm living in this moment. Make a decision, and go with it. Before I can make a move, his voice penetrates my thoughts.

"What's going on in that head of yours?"

Decision made. "Ummm, I was thinking about the first time we showered together..."

He takes an assertive step toward me, backing me into the wall, the water hitting the ground behind both of us now. His hands move to the wall next to either side of my face, his forearms caging me in. "After the first time we had sex." His recall of the memory is evident on his face, heat apparent in his eyes.

I nod, not being able to focus on finding the right words. His face is so close, it's almost out of focus. If I barely moved, our lips would brush. My eyes search his, trying to determine if we've both made the same decision. One of his hands finds my hips at the tie of my bikini bottoms. He pauses, as if also judging whether or not we are on the same page. My teeth sink into my bottom lip as I wait for his move. Let's be real, as I hope for it.

His other hand moves to the side of my face, sliding into my hair that's half wavy and dried from being in the ocean earlier, and half wet from him pushing me through the shower spray. The moment he closes the gap between us, it's like electricity shoots through the water. The air around us feels super-charged. There's no turning back from this. I wouldn't be able to stop myself if I tried. My mouth parts for his on connection, and his tongue wastes no time melding with mine. I find the back of his neck, pulling him closer. An urgency flows through me, as if I've never experienced this before and need to as quickly as possible.

We aren't even under the stream of warm water, but my body is on fire. My hands fall to his waist, my thumbs gripping the V at the edge of his board shorts. Damn, how could I have forgotten how hot he is.

He pulls back and brushes a wet strand of hair away from my face. Leaning back in, he whispers into my ear, "Do you still want those tacos? We could go right now if you want." He's close enough to my face that I can feel his smile.

I shake my head. "Dean. Fuck the tacos."

"God, I was hoping you'd say that," he groans.

With his eyes on mine, his hands fall to each hip, simultaneously tugging a string on each side, allowing my bottoms to fall off. I kick them out of the way with one of my feet, my arms looping around his neck.

His forehead presses against mine. "Are you sure?"

"I'm sure." I keep my gaze locked into his so he knows I mean it. I don't think I've ever been more sure about anything. I don't care what happens tomorrow, or the day after, but I'm confident about what I want to happen next.

God, I'm so wet already, and he's barely touched me. I'm not sure I've ever been this turned on in my life. *I say that whenever I'm with him.* This guy rocks my world every damn time. His finger slips between my legs and slides in without any friction. My stomach contracts at the sudden contact, and my breath hitches. I almost fall backward but brace myself with my hand. A moan escapes me when his finger hits a sensitive part as he continues to slide in and out, at a much more sensual pace than he ever has. God, he feels good. It's never enough with him. I tighten around him as the pressure inside me builds. I'm so not ready for it to be over.

I pull my hips backward, and he tries to follow me, but I twist slightly to the side. He tenses, and confusion washes over his face. I tug on the strings of his shorts and he relaxes, pulling his hands off me to lean back and get a better view of the scene.

I take my time running my fingers across his abs, trailing down the V and catching on the edge of his suit. I tug off his shorts, lowering to my knees in the process and placing kisses down the edge of his stomach as his erection springs free and his shorts hit the floor. I wrap my hand around his length, feeling him grow as my tongue swirls around the tip.

Without warning, I take all of him in my mouth. I nearly choke at his size, but it's worth the hiss that escapes his lips. One hand gripping his hip, and the other softly pressed around his balls, I pull back slowly, running my tongue up the underside before sliding back down. His hands reach out to the wall on either side of him, and the groan coming from above me makes me envision his eyes rolling to the back of his head. No matter how confused he ever made me feel any day in the past, I never questioned whether or not he wanted me in the moment. Right now it feels like I'm all he needs, after all this time, and it's giving me a rush like I've never experienced.

His hand falls to my head, fingers running through my hair and tugging. I pull back worried I did something wrong. "Babe, I need to feel me inside of you. Like now."

He helps me up in one graceful pull, pushing me back into the cool cement wall. Our mouths press together and still, as he slowly pushes inside me. It feels like the last piece of a puzzle being pressed into place as tingles shoot through my entire body. His hands press into the wall on either side of my head, and his mouth falls to my neck, kissing gently along my collarbone as he thrusts into me.

His kisses make their way up my neck until he's close enough to whisper, "I thought I'd never feel you again. I missed you so much."

My skin heats from his confession. "So have I," the words tumble out of my mouth without thinking. I must mean them. I don't remember missing this lately, missing him, but being in this moment, how could I not? I must have suppressed it. His breath is warm and jagged against my ear and the moment his hand presses into my lower back, I can't hold off any longer. My orgasm explodes inside me, electrifying every cell. I tighten around him, causing his head to fall back a little, but he grips my waist, holding me close to him.

His eyes are full of so much heat, and the breeze hitting my wet skin isn't even enough to send chills through me. He keeps going, and I pray he doesn't stop. When I think my orgasm is fading, a second wave hits me, and I can hardly keep standing.

He pushes us through our joint wave of ecstasy but doesn't move away from me once it calms. Our lips lock again, and he deepens our kiss as if he didn't get enough of what he wanted. When he finally pulls back, he presses his forehead into mine. "God, I can't believe I was able to walk away from that, from you," he says barely above a whisper. I don't know how to reply, the feelings running through me make me wonder how I ever survived him leaving in the first place. "What else can I do to make you consider staying?" The connection I'm now certain he feels is evident in the way he admires me, hope sparking in his eyes like it's enough to keep me here.

"Can we just be here, right now, and not think about anything else?" As soon as the words leave my mouth, I regret how much they sound like I'm trying to brush off his plea. They don't convey how I feel about him, or this moment, so I quickly add, "I've thought about this moment so many times more than I want to admit, and I'm not ready to leave it."

The look on his face screams at me that the entire point of his words was to let me know we could replay this moment as many times as we want, but he doesn't say anything else. I choose to ignore it and lean into him. Wrapping his arms around me, we hold each other, until the sun sinks completely beneath the horizon and his voice breaks through the silence. "Ready for tacos now?"

We find the same table from the first night, and sit, freeing our hands of all the steak tacos we could possibly hold. I'm hardly sitting before I shove half of one into my mouth, so unladylike, but I don't care. I'm starving. We haven't eaten all day between being out on the water and our detour on the way here. I glance up. Dean leans back in his seat so far it teeters on the back two legs. A grin is plastered on his face as he stares at me with his arms folded across his chest.

"What?" I demand after I've swallowed enough of my taco.

"Nothing, you're cute. And I'm glad you're here."

How is it that the majority of the time he talked a year ago, I was flooded with confusion, but now, every single thing makes me want to melt wherever I am and stay there forever? I internally roll my eyes at myself. Get a grip, Maci. It's just really good sex. With the most gorgeous man you've ever seen. Who all of a sudden is willing to share every thought he has about you. The chemistry we share is unreal. That is something that has not changed at all.

Noticing I don't have a reply, he picks up a taco. I take it as an opportunity to share something else that's been on my mind. "I'm sorry I wouldn't have understood why you needed to leave. I wish you'd been comfortable talking with me about your need to come here."

He sets down the other half of his taco, giving me his full attention. "I'm sorry I didn't give you a chance to understand."

"Like I said before, I don't think I would have handled it well. I didn't handle you leaving well either way. It wouldn't have made sense to me the way it does now. I still would have been so angry with you. I would have thought it was about me, about not being enough for you. That *is* what I thought, and I'm not sure any explanation would have changed that."

"It doesn't mean you didn't deserve the truth."

"That we can agree on." I smile. "Can I ask you something?"

He nods.

"I was thinking this morning... the way you left Oregon and me, it's pretty similar to the way I left California." I pause before adding, "And Mack. I'm confident it was the right choice. Sometimes I feel guilty about it, like I'm being selfish and choosing what's best for me over someone I love. Did you feel like that? How did you deal with it?"

"Let me ask you something first. How much easier is it this time? Now that I don't have a lock on my communication skills?" He smirks.

I play along to see where he's going with this. "You don't make me want to throw up anymore."

He does his cute laugh to himself thing I missed so much. "Exactly. Part of me wanted to be all in with you, Maci. But my head was clouded with distractions. What I've realized is escaping here, figuring out my life, of course it was about me. But it *was* about you too. You might have wanted to be with me anyway, but you deserved to be with someone who could love you the right way. I couldn't give that to you at that point in my life." He pauses, adding the next words in a much softer voice. "If you truly love him, he deserves the best of you, and if that comes from this journey you're on, there's nothing selfish about that. He deserves more than the little energy that's left over after a long day of warring with your thoughts and fighting any unsettledness."

"Isn't working through challenges together the point of being in a relationship though?"

"At the end of the day, there is some work nobody else can do for you."

"Do you think you would have come back to me after you did the work you needed to?"

My question seems to surprise him, but he replies with certainty. "Yes. I didn't expect you to be waiting for me, especially after the way I left, but I was sure as hell going to try."

"I think sometimes things work out how they are supposed to, even if we don't understand it at the time."

"I agree." He chews on his toothpick and pauses for a second before he continues. "As hard as it was to leave you, and despite going about it the wrong way, I still believe I made the right choice–for both of us. Even if it means we don't end up together."

"What are you saying, Dean?" I lean forward, my elbows on the table.

He mimics me, leaning in close enough his breath hits my lips. "I'm saying I want to try again but be better this time. I want you to stay here, with me, at least for a few weeks." He reaches up and strokes my cheek with his thumb before dropping his hand to mine. My heart thumps in my chest as he adds, "To at least see if we deserve a second chance too."

I pause to consider his offer. "Okay."

CHAPTER SIXTY-NINE

It's Dean's day off, but he had to run to the shop to check on something. I reach into my backpack to pull out my phone, realizing I didn't touch it at all yesterday. I figure I should check in with Avery and Lexy since I've already been here longer than I expected. When I open my texts, there's one from Mack.

Mack: *Hey, just checking in.*

My stomach drops, feeling like anything but the direct truth is a lie. I'm not sure how to handle this since I agreed to give Dean a chance to see if we deserve another one. I get the urge to hear his voice, so I hit the call button instead of replying to his text.

Mack: Maci, hi. Is everything okay?

My heart flutters at the soft voice he saves for me.

Me: Yeah, I had a free minute, so I thought I'd call. I wanted to hear your voice.

Mack: You know you can call anytime. How are you?

Me: You're always checking in with me. Tell me about you, what's new?

Mack: There is actually something I've been wanting to tell you.

Me: Oh yeah?

Mack: I talked to the guys about quitting...

Me: Your band? What?! Already?

Mack: Yeah. It's been great adventuring to all these new places and having new experiences with my music, but I'm ready to settle down and figure out what I want to do with the rest of my life.

Me: Wow, that's a big deal, Mack. What did they say?

Mack: They weren't exactly happy, but they understand. They asked if we could finish the next set of shows before we talked about it again, but they know I'm done either way. Our last show will be at home. Oregon, I mean. Do you have any idea when you're going to be back? Did you decide where you're going next?

Me: Not yet. I'm going to stay in Costa Rica for a few more weeks before I go somewhere new.

There's a pause on the other end of the line.

Mack: Because of him?

My pause matches his while I think through what I want to say.

Me: I don't know. It's not *because* of Dean. When I said I wasn't ready to be in a relationship with you, I meant I wasn't ready for a relationship with anyone. It's this place. I feel... free. I don't know how else to describe it. The past two days I spent out on the ocean were beautiful and peaceful, and I had no worries. It's nice being somewhere new, with no real routine or responsibilities. It's not that I'm dreading coming home to real life, it's just nice to be away from it for a while if that makes sense.

He takes a deep breath on the other end of the line as if he's trying to give himself time to find the right words.

Mack: It does. That's how I felt when I was touring. It was exciting to be somewhere new, doing something I love. Yeah, it's my job too, but it felt way less part of the daily grind than anything else.

Me: Are you sure you aren't going to miss it too much?

Mack: I'm sure. Maci?

Me: Yeah?

Mack: I don't know how to fight for you when I'm not there and he is.

The vulnerability in his voice shoots straight to my gut, and I wish I could hug him.

Me: You know how I feel about you, Mack. I think I just need some time to have my own moments of freedom like you did, before I'm ready to settle down too. We're young.

Mack: I can understand that. Even if I was always going to end up back in Oregon, I had to go experience California for myself. I just miss you.

Me: I miss you too.

Mack: You know I was thinking, if I had a more regular job, we'd be able to set aside time to travel. We could go to a new country every year.

Me: I would love that.

I say it because it's true. It sounds like the perfect balance between the responsible routine of an adult and adventure with someone who would make both those things enjoyable.

Mack: I love you.

The front door swings open, Dean walking through.

I pull my attention back to my phone.

Me: You too. I'll talk to you later, okay?

I hang up and put my phone face down on the nightstand. I'm not trying to hide from Dean that I was talking to Mack. He knows the internal conflicts I have, but I do want to give him my full attention.

"Hiiii." I sit on the edge of the bed, and he walks toward me, settling between my legs and leaning down for a kiss.

"Hi."

My conversation with Mack is fresh in my mind, and I can't help but think about what happens with my life once I go home. "What do you think I'd be good at?"

"What do you mean? You're good at a lot of things." He winks.

I roll my eyes. "Nooooo. Like for work. I'm not sure what I want to do when I go home. What do you want to do? Have you thought about it?"

"I have been, more recently." As he's talking, I scoot back on the bed, lying on my side and reaching my hand out for him to join. He does, mirroring me. The sun comes through the front window and shines in a streak across his shoulder.

"I'm not sure if what I want to do is a job... but I had this crazy idea the other day."

"Oooh. Tell me." I bring my hands to my face and fold them under my head.

Dean reaches out. My eyes follow his fingers to where they run along my charm bracelet from Mack, resting on my wrist. He rubs a few of the charms between his fingers before pulling his hand away and connecting his gaze to mine again. "My degree is in sociology."

I nod. I knew that.

"I think it would be cool to go spend a few weeks in a new country, learn their history, their cultural norms and of course the best local food places. Then spend the next few weeks giving tours to Americans. Or at least helping current tour guides with translations. I don't know. It's cool learning about how different people are in other parts of the world. It's something people tend to take for granted when they travel just for famous landmarks."

"Wow, Dean. That's an amazing idea. If it's not a real job, you could make it one. I envy your ability to pick up languages. I heard you talking to the kids you were giving lessons to yesterday. I spent two months at the sanctuary and can only speak Spanish well enough to barely get by. But... didn't you say the other day you wanted to go back to Oregon at some point?"

"Yeah." His eyes roam over my face; I'm not sure why. "I would like to have a home base, and I wouldn't want to be gone the whole year. Being gone too long makes me dissociate from reality a bit, and I miss my parents. They are getting older, and I don't want to regret not spending more time with them. Sophie too."

My heart melts at his words. At least once a month for the past few years, I've had a mortality crisis imagining life without my parents, and realizing it's inevitable. "I love all of that," I whisper. *I still love you.* The thought floods my mind, taking me by surprise. I choose to ignore it for now.

He reaches over to tuck a loose strand of hair behind my ear and doesn't pull away after. "So, you don't have any ideas about what you'd like to do?" His tone isn't judgmental, just curious.

"Not really. Come up with something amazing for me, like you did for yourself." I laugh.

"You loved volunteering at the sanctuary. Are there paying jobs like that?"

"I haven't looked into it much since we didn't have internet there. But the woman in charge, Maria, was talking about how they are opening another location in Spain. And in that weekend class I took, the professor told us about a program they have in Oregon that helps victims of trafficking in Portland. Did you know how prevalent it is there? Most people don't, but it's unbelievable. Their building isn't too far from Eugene, maybe a half an hour."

"If you got to choose, which location would you?"

"Umm... I'm not sure. There are pros and cons for each. I wish there was a way to choose both, but if I had to pick, I'd say Oregon. I miss my parents and Avery, and if I moved home, I'd also be determined to convince Lexy to move."

"Tell me about her." His hand moves from my face to my waist and pulls me in close to him as he listens to me ramble about how great my best friend is.

CHAPTER SEVENTY

The routine we created came easily and naturally. Nearly every morning Dean heads to the beach to work. I wake to a sweet note with some variation of how he can't wait to see me and to come to the shop whenever I'm ready. Some days I bring a book from his stack on the floor by his bed. Some days I paddleboard while I wait for him to finish working. Every day we surf together for an hour or two before we head back to our place. I love the days as much as our nights together. The groundhog-ness of it hasn't felt boring at all even though it's as comfortable as if we'd been doing it for years. Nothing has felt too serious. He hasn't questioned when I'm leaving, or asked to define whatever this has become over the past three weeks. I'm glad because I don't want to think about it, though I know I'll have to eventually. I've been blissfully ignoring everything lately.

Dean sits at the small kitchen table reading, and it's rare we aren't attached at home, so I'm taking it as an opportunity to finally respond to Lexy's text from earlier.

Lexy: *Hellooo, Maci!! Are you alive!? I haven't heard from you in like three weeks!*

Me: *I'm sorry, things have been... crazy.*

Lexy: *Umm, yeah. Mack told me you ran into Dean?! He's kind of freaking out. What is going on over there?!*

Me: *I don't know... I've been living in this bubble, pretending the rest of the world doesn't exist. I don't know what I'm doing, but I feel freer than I ever have.*

Lexy: *And Dean is in this bubble with you? What's his deal anyway? Mack said something about him breaking your heart before you two got together?*

Me: *Yeah... It was a misunderstanding... Sort of.*

Lexy: *So, you just forgave Dean for hurting and abandoning you?*

Lexy: *I'm sorry, I know this might be coming out wrong through text. I'm not mad. I'm just trying to understand. It's hard since I didn't know you when everything happened with Dean. Plus, I've had Mack in my ear about it since he hasn't heard from you.*

Me: *You can't tell him any of this, Lex.*

Lexy: *Promise.*

Me: *I left for the sanctuary truly believing whenever I make my way back home, Mack and I would have a second chance. Or we'd at least try and see if it was right this time around. When I finished my volunteer work, I was even more certain that's what I wanted. But then I ran into Dean out of nowhere. Like, more of a freak occurrence than when we ran into Troy. I'm in another country for goodness sake. How can I ignore that kind of sign?*

Lexy: *The same way you kind of ignored Troy?*

Me: *This is different. I never dated Troy. I didn't have the chance to fall for him. But Dean... there was always something different about my connection with him. Mack feels like home, but when I'm near Dean, it feels like I can't live without him.*

Lexy: *Dean feels the same way about you?*

Me: *Yeah, I think he does. The first few days I was here he was super open about everything he left out before. The past few weeks, it's like I'm in the twilight zone. We just go about our days like it's normal to just surf, eat tacos and have sex... really great sex. Like... mind blowing, Lex.*

Lexy: *What you're saying is you've been holding out on me?!*

Me: *I didn't want you to feel like you were stuck between Mack and me.*

Lexy: *Soooo, the real question is... this mind blowing sex. It's better than with Mack?*

Me: *It's different. I try not to compare them. I always feel comfortable when I'm with Mack. Whatever moment we are in, he makes me feel like I belong there, with him. That's something I never really had before. But the chemistry I have with Dean... it's just. It's like the world stops and nothing else can matter until I'm touching him. Have you ever experienced that?*

Lexy: *Yeah... actually, there's something I wanted to talk to you about.*

Me: *Oh, hey, Dean is coming over here. Can it wait?*

Lexy: *Yeah, totally. I'll talk to you later.*

Me: *Soon. Love you!*

"Hey, babe, whatcha up to?" Dean falls onto the bed next to me.

"Talking to Lexy. I've been bad about checking in. Time has been weird lately. What are you up to?"

"Nothing, just wanted to be closer to you."

"You were five feet away at the table." I laugh and shove on his shoulder hard enough he rolls onto his back. With Lexy's conversation fresh in my mind, I decide to ask something I've been curious about for a while now. "Do you believe in chemistry? Like between two people?"

He lies there for a moment like he's contemplating his response. "I didn't." He's still talking to the ceiling as he continues. "But when you showed up here, I knew it was you before you turned around. It freaked me out, but after that I couldn't deny it anymore. Especially since that wasn't the first time I felt weird around you."

My first reaction is to be offended he thinks being around me is weird, but my mind flashes back to all the times I knew he was there before I saw him—at the pool table the night we had sex for the first time, when I was studying at school, the day he made me play hooky before he told me he was leaving. Each time it happened, I questioned how it was possible I just *knew*. It was exactly that—weird. I also thought I was the only one who felt it. "That wasn't the first time?"

"No. I've always felt this pull toward you. The first time I saw you and the night we actually met had me really tripped up."

As much as I want to revel in everything he's already said, my brain processes his out of place words. "Wait, what do you mean 'the night we actually met?'" My voice trails off before I add, "You're making it sound like you knew me before we met."

"Mmmm," he hums quietly under his breath like he's nervous to continue.

"It's okay, Dean. Tell me. I don't want secrets between us anymore." I say it gently, but my heart races as I wonder what has been left unsaid.

He turns to face me, his hand reaching up, fingers threading through my hair. His brown eyes search mine as if they are looking for confirmation he's safe to share. After a moment, he speaks. "You were wearing a strapless gold dress two Halloweens ago, right?"

I nod slowly, my brows pushing together in confusion. That was a week before my birthday, a week before I met Dean.

He continues. "Your hair was falling in your face, but I kept catching glimpses of your smile." He smiles briefly at the memory. "Unintentionally, I kept singling out your laugh from everyone in the bar, despite how loud it was in there. I was drawn to you. I kept seeing you visibly shiver from being cold, and all I wanted to do was warm you up, even though I was so fucking cold myself."

Recognition washes over me. I remember seeing him too. "George of the Jungle."

A smile lights his face, and any hesitation he had before about telling this story is gone. "Yeah, I lost a fucking bet." He rolls his eyes, but continues explaining the night as if he's an excited child at show-n-tell rambling about his favorite toy car. "Okay, so, I tried to fight my way through the crowd after you and your friends won the contest so I could introduce myself. I had been seeing Julia for like a week at that point, so it was probably a dick move, but I swear I couldn't *not*. That's when you all got on the bar. You looked so... happy to be with your friends, and I loved that for you even though I didn't even know your name. I was telling Marcus I'd be right back and looked away for only a few seconds. By the time I turned back, you were gone."

I interrupt his story to tell him how much I wanted donuts. "I wonder what would have happened if I didn't."

"I thought about it for a few days before shaking it off. I mean, our town isn't exactly small, and I had no way to find you. Then you showed up at my work and started talking to me... Right away I knew it was you. God, Maci, it was like the Universe was giving me a second chance.

It's why I wasn't completely honest when you asked me that night if I was seeing someone else. I didn't want to risk missing out again. I couldn't."

Every time he makes an admission that erases my thoughts about him never feeling the same way I did, my heart reaches for him a little more. "Why didn't you tell me you'd seen me before?"

"I almost mentioned it when I saw the picture of you and your friends in your apartment. I knew you were different than every girl I'd met, but I was still trying to convince myself you weren't."

I change the subject, feeling his guilt wash over him. I don't want him to feel that emotion anymore. "I'd never done anything like that before, just randomly talk to a guy, let alone ask him out," I admit.

"Why did you?"

"It was like I physically couldn't stop myself from get-ting closer to you. Every time I was around you after that, it was like... it wasn't enough. I don't know how to describe it. It happened when I wasn't around you too. I'd get a text from you, and I'd crave to be near you." The next part comes out as a shy whisper. "It scared me. Especially because that didn't seem to be how it was for you."

He laughs like I'm being ridiculous as he twirls a strand of my hair around his finger. "When I wasn't with you, it was easier to talk myself down. I fought it hard. You can ask Marcus. But being with you here, it's even more than it was before. I want you near me all the time. It takes a lot for me to not be touching you every second. There's something undeniable between us." He says it with no uncertainty.

"More than just sex?"

"More than just really great sex." He smiles again and pulls me to him.

CHAPTER SEVENTY-ONE

Dean is giving a surfing lesson to a group of tourists today, so I came back to our place to wait for him. When he walks through the door, a pang of emotion hits me like I've missed him more than I can bear even though we were only apart for a few hours.

"Hey, babe." He smiles as he wraps me in a hug. Even if he hasn't brought it up, I can tell he's been treating every moment like he's thankful for each one. The fact he doesn't take it for granted makes it easy to want to stay with him here forever. "I was thinking we could make a bonfire on the beach tonight?"

Once the fire is going, he tosses a few more pieces of wood on it before going back into the house to grab me a blanket. I never changed out of my jean shorts and black bikini. I've practically lived in them since I got here, and it would be hard to talk me into anything else. I sit in the sand, hands folded over my bent knees while I wait for him. It's beautiful here. Where we are staying there's hardly any other houses, and because it's more of a locals' spot, if anyone else is around, it's never too rowdy or loud.

We are in our own little world. The ocean in front of me is lit by the moon, and the waves crashing softly into the shore complete the perfect picture. How is it possible for a place like this to exist?

My thoughts are interrupted as Dean's shadow falls over the sand, and he lays a blanket across my shoulders. Sitting, he wraps his arm around me, pulling me into him and kissing the side of my hair. The fire flickers in front of us, and even though I also have a blanket, chills cover me. There's been a shift in the air around us. I noticed it the moment he sat down.

Silence stays between us for a few minutes before he speaks. "I could stay here forever if you were with me."

The confession hits me straight in the heart. I try to process the word "forever," and it nearly knocks the wind out of me. Since he started being upfront, I've noticed Dean doesn't speak without choosing his words carefully. Everything he says feels calculated and intentional. My brain tries to find an escape route. "But Oregon is your home. Aren't you going back eventually?" I haven't twisted my body to face him.

"This past year has been incredible. It was exactly what I needed. But it still always felt like it was missing something. I'm sorry I didn't realize you were the final piece before, but I know you are now."

I can't help looking at him, his golden blond hair tousled like he's been running his fingers through it and his brown eyes as dark as the shadows behind him. This is the first time I've noticed how much his tan has deepened in the past month since he's been spending even more time out on the water now that I'm here. He stares back at me like what he's about to say is obvious. "Kind of feels like wherever you are is home."

I pull my eyes away from his and lean back into his chest. I pause first until I'm certain about what I want to say. "I wish we could stay here forever too." My heart breaks as the words I mean more than anything I've ever said come out in a whisper. He stops breathing. I can feel the way he laid it out there, and in a second I stole his hope. I think I've known all along I couldn't stay here. If I get in any deeper than this, I know I'll stay, and I can't. I have to do this for me. I have to go off by myself and figure out who I want to be, discover who I am on my own, and not define my life by a relationship. Even if it's a man who makes me feel the way Dean does. There's so much I want to do and see alone, and more I need to learn before I can commit to someone, before it's fair to choose.

We stay on the beach by the fire until there's nothing left but embers–without saying another word. Silence fills his house from the time we rinse off in the shower until when we crawl into bed. We're facing each other now, close enough to feel his body heat. One of his arms is wraps around my waist, and the other is under his head like a pillow.

His shaky voice breaks through the silence, begging me. "Please, don't leave me."

"Dean, I have to. You know I do, just like you had to when you left me." I don't mean for it to sound spiteful because I'm not.

"It's not the same this time, and you know it." He comes off angrier and more frustrated than I think he intended, his eyebrows scrunching together.

"That's not fair." I sigh. "Please don't make this harder than it already is."

His features soften. "I know. I'm sorry." His thumb brushes across my cheek before finding its place on my hip again.

Even with the lights off, I can see his face from the glow of the moon through the window. I keep my eyes on him, without wavering until my heart starts to hurt too much to keep them open.

Just go to sleep, Maci. Tomorrow is a new day. Everything feels less dramatic when it's not the middle of the night. When daylight hits, he'll understand. He has to. He knows what this feels like… but that was before these past few weeks. Is what he feels now really too different from what I felt when he left me?

I lie there for what feels like forever, my thoughts turning around in my brain, fighting a battle with my heart. I thought he was selfish for leaving me because I didn't understand. Dean of all people should get why I need to do this, and it feels selfish he acts like he doesn't.

I wonder if he is still awake. How could he be sleeping? I refuse to open my eyes and check, but I wish we could talk this through, find some understanding, come up with a right plan I'm not sure exists. His hand leaves my hip and softly touches my face, tucking my hair behind my ear. He doesn't say anything, and I get the impression he thinks I'm asleep. His hand hasn't moved though. It just rests where it stopped, holding my head with his fingers threaded through my hair, like he's worried I'll float away.

With my eyes closed, I don't see it coming.

"God, I love you." It's soft, and it sounds more like a prayer to change everything, rather than a statement. My heart reaches for his, but I don't move, knowing he doesn't think I can hear him. But I did, and it takes all the willpower I have left to keep my heart from succeeding in its final attempt to change my mind. Despite my eyes being closed, a tear escapes, sliding down my cheek.

I love you too.

CHAPTER SEVENTY-TWO

The day after I made my decision, everything was more or less the same as it had been. We didn't talk about it; we didn't feel like we needed to, I guess. Maybe he realized he couldn't change my mind and there was an unspoken understanding between us. We made the most of it. He took the day off work, but we surfed for a few hours in the morning. We ate tacos, and we made love.

Love. Ever since he said those three little words, I've been running them through my head. Each time I ask myself if I feel the same again, my mind replies with a resounding "yes." Falling in love with Dean was inevitable from the moment I saw him on my 21st birthday. Something inside me knew it would happen. It's what pulled me back to a complete stranger. With him, it was out of my control, like I had no choice in the matter, like our souls are magnetized whenever they get close enough.

It feels different than it did with Mack. With Mack, it was a gradual thing, like our hearts slowly got closer and closer until I woke up one day realizing I loved him. It's as if I got to go through the experience of falling in love with Mack, while my heart already knew how to love Dean from the beginning. It's probably breaking some law of the Universe to love them both so much at the same time.

I haven't let go of Mack, despite him all but disappearing from my mind these past few weeks. Although less frequent, I still question whether leaving him the way I did was the right decision. I miss the comfort of him and the security of a future he was working to build for us. I miss all the little things he did because he knows me so well and feeling like being with him was *just right*. But then there's Dean, and falling into the uncertainty of the future has been calming and freeing in its own way. It's easy to love both of them. How do I choose?

I'm not sure. Maybe that's the real reason why I decided to just choose myself.

The sun rises over the ocean as Dean swings the strap of my backpack over his shoulder, ready to walk me to the bus stop–exactly four weeks since I arrived on New Year's Eve. We woke up tangled together but haven't spoken a word since. Reaching for my hand, he intertwines our fingers, pausing to look down at them before we go.

We arrive at the bus stop with a few minutes to spare. Taking off my backpack, he loops the straps over my arms until they settle on my shoulders. His hands slide to either side of my face, gripping the back of my neck and pulling me to him. The moment our lips touch, hot tears burn my eyes. I taste them as he deepens our kiss.

After a moment, he pulls back, wrapping his arms around my neck and squeezing me to him. My eyes are pinched tight in an effort to trap my tears, but they open at the rattle of the bus as it arrives, the wheels kicking up a small cloud of dust as it screeches to a halt. Tugging back from him is the only thing that makes him loosen his grip. Our eyes lock for a second before I walk away. He looks at me like he's trying to memorize my face, in case he never sees it again, and it makes every step heavier. When I reach the door, I don't look back the way I did when he pulled away from me a year ago. But this time it's because I worry he will still be standing there.

CHAPTER SEVENTY-THREE

I did the craziest thing I've ever done. Even though I told Dean I had a plan because I didn't want him to worry, I didn't. The day I decided I was leaving Costa Rica, I thought about where I wanted to go next. Avery and I had our list of places we dreamed about going, but nowhere in particular was pulling at my heart–maybe because it's currently torn and trapped between two men.

Hoping for direction, a memory resurfaced–the date I had with Troy at the beginning of senior year. When I asked him where he'd want to travel, he thought it would be cool to show up at the airport one day and take the next available flight.

That's exactly what I did.

When the bus dropped me off, I headed to the ticket counter and asked for the next flight I could catch.

On my walk through the terminal, I pass by an airport convenience store, a spinning metal rack filled with books stationed at the opening. *Eat, Pray, Love* sits at eye level, the colorful words drawing me in. How have I not read this book? Maybe because it was being saved for the right moment.

I pull my credit card from the inside pocket of my backpack. It's hooked on my charm bracelet, and I pull that out too. I took it off the night Dean was playing with it and haven't worn it since.

I clasp it around my wrist while the cashier swipes my card. As I reach to grab my receipt, I notice a charm I've never seen. I bring it closer to my face and run it through my fingers. It's a silver surfboard and would blend in perfectly with the others to someone who didn't have each one memorized.

Dean.

I snap back to reality when the cashier waves my card at me and take it before walking to my gate. I get there with ten minutes left until boarding begins, so I pull out my phone. I debate sending a text, but my curiosity gets the best of me.

Me: *Hi. Can I ask you something?*

He replies immediately.

Marcus: *What's up, Maci!*

Me: *It's about Dean.*

Marcus: *I expected it to be. How was Costa Rica?*

Me: *Sounds like you already know? Haha*

Marcus: *I'm not surprised.*

Me: *Do you think Dean would have come looking for me when he got back?*

Marcus: *Yes.*

Me: *You seem so sure.*

Marcus: *I am.*

Marcus: *Even if you hadn't run into him first, it would have been inevitable for you to find each other again.*

Me: *Marcus. Are you a secret romantic at heart? Haha*

Marcus: *Nah, just haven't seen two people click the way you do.*

Me: *Why didn't you say anything? Especially after you saw me with Mack.*

Marcus: *It didn't feel like my place to interfere. But like I said, I'm not surprised you two found each other again.*

Me: *It feels like you're implying we are soulmates or something.*

Marcus: *Aren't you? I've known Dean my entire life, and I've never seen him like this with anyone else. He wouldn't feel that way if you two weren't connected.*

I turn my phone off and zip it into my backpack as my boarding zone is called.

Finding my seat, I lean back into it, closing my eyes. What am I doing? Should I have stayed with Dean? If Maria had never suggested that beach, I wouldn't have run into him, and I'd probably be on a flight back to Mack right now. What does it mean that Mack is responsible for introducing me to Maria? It's strange to think about. I don't know, and every cell in my body is filled with agitation. I originally wanted to go on this trip to focus on myself and decide the direction for my life. It frustrates me that I can't seem to convince myself anything matters besides choosing between Dean and Mack.

I know it's too much to ask, but I wish the answer would just appear. In an attempt to distract myself, I open my book. As I'm reading myself to sleep, I start to believe I don't need to figure it out this second. I need to enjoy this trip. I need to take some "me time," and when my soul is rested, maybe I'll be ready for the answer. I keep reading until I drift off, dreaming only about the food in France, with neither Dean or Mack there eating it with me.

Half a day later, at 4 a.m. local time, I land in Paris, the city of love. I find it ironic this is where I ended up considering love is my main obstacle right now. I'm both excited and terrified to be here. I know I didn't really have a plan once I left the sanctuary, but at least I had gotten to the point where I felt comfortable in the country. I had a direction to head based on Maria's suggestions, and then I ran into Dean before I needed to formulate a longer plan. Now I'm in a new country where my ability to speak the language is even worse. The scariest part, though, is that I'm alone.

Despite having spent two months with women and children who have been trafficked, I'm not concerned about traveling by myself. Between everything that experience taught me and the class I took in college, I'm confident I know how to be as safe as possible. Not to mention, after everything happened with Avery, I've been hyper-aware of my surroundings.

What I worry about is being truly alone. It's not something I have ever done before. All through high school, I had Avery and then into college too. Even though she had Miller, she was always there for me, and either she or the girls were around if I needed company. Getting serious with Miller also aligned with me spending time with Dean and then Mack. Once I moved to California, I had Lexy when Mack wasn't around.

Now, it's just me. All alone. By myself. With nothing familiar except the thoughts in my head. Why did I feel called to do this? What am I hoping to get out of it? Is clarity too much to ask for? But what exactly do I want to clarify? I keep telling myself there will be a magical moment that tells me who I want to be and where my life should go from here.

When I get in my cab to head into the city, I send a quick text to my parents letting them know I made it. My phone rings immediately, surprising me. They are an hour ahead of me in Egypt, but it's still early. We chat for a few minutes as they get ready to head out for their daily adventure. I'm still driving by the time I hang up, so I check the time difference in California. 8 p.m. That's perfect timing before she heads into work.

Me: *Hey Lex, just checking in. I'm in Paris!*

Lexy: *What! That's cool! Alone? Send me pics!*

Me: *Yup, I left Dean yesterday... He said he loves me, and I freaked out and left.*

Lexy: *Oh wow. And he wanted you to stay?*

Me: *Yeah, he did.*

Lexy: *You walked away from him when nothing was really wrong. Do you think that means anything?*

Me: *I didn't think of it like that. I think I was having a little trouble telling if real love and real life were the same thing. Like, we can't stay on a beach in Costa Rica forever. So, what happens when we leave? I feel like the only way to know which life I want is to step back and think about it.*

Lexy: *Yeah, that makes sense. Have you talked to Mack at all?*

Me: *Not in a couple of weeks. How's he doing?*

Lexy: *Not great to be honest. He's been playing new songs every time he's at the bar. They aren't great, Maci. I mean, of course they are amazing, and the guy still has* *the voice of an angel. But they are sad as fuck. It breaks my heart a little.*

*   **Me:** Ugh, I don't want him to be sad. I never wanted this to hurt him.*

*   **Lexy:** He's miserable without you. The first show he played after you told him you ran into Dean, he was a mess. I don't think he's had anything to drink... or worse. But he let some girl kiss him after the show. I happened to look up right when he did. It wasn't more than a minute later he came and sat at the bar and basically collapsed in front of me. He said he thought it might help, but it made him miss you more.*

*   **Me:** I feel bad, like I haven't considered his feelings at all the past few weeks. I got so wrapped up in Dean. I couldn't think about anyone else when I was around him, not even Mack. And it's messed up that hearing he kissed someone else makes my stomach turn when I did way more than that.*

*   **Lexy:** I'm not trying to make you feel bad or pressure you into coming back just to be with him. I want whatever is best for both of you. He's just my best friend too, and it's hard to see him like this, ya know?*

*   **Me:** I know, I'm sorry. I'm thankful he has you.*

*   **Lexy:** I think when you left, he thought you'd come back to him.*

*   **Me:** That's what I thought too.*

*   **Lexy:** Well, you can't have both of them. What are you going to do?*

*   **Me:** Hope being in the city of love provides me with a magical answer? Haha*

*   **Lexy:** Haha yeah good luck with that. Let me know how it goes. Miss you!*

CHAPTER SEVENTY-FOUR

On my flight here, I paid for Wi-Fi so I could find a place to stay. I found a cute Airbnb in Place de l'Estrapade, which is apparently a quiet, perfect part of the city. It's within walking distance of everything I might need, a short cab ride to everything I want to experience while I'm here, and I got a discount for booking a month at a time. Hopefully I love it.

After checking in, I take a nap and plan my day. It's probably crazy to go all out right from the start, considering I have so much time here, but after 12 hours on an airplane trying to decipher my thoughts through *Eat, Pray, Love* insight, I need the distraction.

I step out of the cab after a 20-minute drive, and the Eiffel Tower stands in front of me. It's incredible. It's much bigger than I expected. I flash back to being in Vegas with Lexy and seeing the imitation one outside of the hotel named after this city. If I thought Vegas was sparkling, it's nothing compared to what lies in front of me now.

The spontaneity that landed me in France at the end of January doesn't pair well with the clothes I packed for Costa Rica. It's freezing outside. My body is covered with goosebumps under the only hoodie I brought, but the sun is shining, making it feel warmer than it is. I've walked past at least four different street musicians, all unique in their own way and all incredible. The chaos of the entire area is thrilling, full of artists who love what they do so much they are willing to compete for people's attention in the freezing cold.

After a few hours of wandering, I head back in the direction of my home for the next month. The entire cab ride I couldn't help but think about Avery, especially since she should be here with me. She's one of the best parts of my life. I appreciate her friendship and everything she's done to make my life better, more than she might know. I think about how important Dean's friendships are to him and how many times he insisted I get better about keeping in touch with Avery more. I love him for that.

I find a little French restaurant right around the corner from where I'm staying. While I wait for my food, it takes me far too long to figure out the time difference. Once I realize it's an appropriate time to text her, I search for a thread I haven't opened in a while.

Me: *Hi! I made it to Paris, and it's perfect. Well, almost. It would be even better if you were with me. This trip has been incredible already. Thank you for the part you played in sparking this decision. Well, you and Mack too. That sibling connection really worked out for me here. I've been trying to figure out what direction I want to go next in life. There's been so much confusion and so many questions I haven't found answers to yet. But the one thing that's never changed is I think about you every day. You're the best friend I've ever had, you're my family. I love you and miss you a ton. Here's the view from my adventure today! Wish you were here!*

Avery: *OMG, Maci, it looks incredible. I wish I was there! You must have best friend ESP because I was just about* *to text you. I know this might be a lot to ask, considering it would mean being around Mack for a few days, but I can't imagine my wedding without you standing next to me. Miller and I decided on a date yesterday. Since it's going to be small, and since we are paying for it ourselves, it's going to be in 3 months. When are you planning on coming home? Please tell me you'll be here. If not, I'll bribe Miller will a hundred games of pool to change the date.*

Me: *I wouldn't miss your wedding even if I had to find a way to walk across the ocean. Just tell me when and where.*

I wake the next morning, somehow managing the jet lag alright, and head out to explore my home for the next four weeks. I find a patisserie to get breakfast, people watch by a small fountain, and chat with a few of the locals.

I can already see why it's nicknamed the city of love. Love is everywhere in the air here and not just in the romantic way. Flowers line every balcony, most people only work 35 hours a week, there are boulangeries filled with fresh bread on every corner, and not a single person seems to be worried about indulging themselves in pastries each morning. Even their drinking fountains dispense sparkling water like hydrating yourself is something that deserves celebrating.

Before heading back to my flat, I wander into a small flower shop where I'm greeted by a cute, old French man.

"Bonjour," he exclaims! "I haven't seen you here before."

"Bonjour!" If I'm going to be staying in a locals' area I need to at least make an effort, but the word comes out sounding funny. I'm used to speaking broken Spanish. He chuckles but doesn't say anything else, letting me continue. "I'm Maci. I just got here. I'll be staying for a month, so I thought I'd make my place more homey." I walk the row of bouquets, finally landing on a bright bunch of yellow daffodils.

"That is a beautiful choice. I'm Theo. My wife and I have run this shop for almost 40 years now."

"Wow, that's amazing. You must really love it."

"I would love anything as long as she's with me." Endearment is clear in his eyes as he thinks of his wife.

I pick up the daffodils, sticking my face close enough to inhale their faint scent. "I wish I had that." I say it quietly, but he hears it anyway.

"Ahhh, trouble with love?"

"Something like that," I mumble. "Were you always certain your wife was the one and this was the way you wanted to spend your life?"

He laughs quietly, but it's enough to visibly vibrate his weathered body. "My wife will tell you she knew well before I did, back when I was young and free, that we would end up together. We met in the mountains one weekend while skiing. She was on holiday, but I worked at the resort. She was looking for someone to start a life with, and I wanted to live a new one every weekend. You can see who got their way, thank goodness."

"So, you're happy here even though it's nothing like what you imagined for yourself?"

"Turns out, it's better than anything I thought I wanted. But I never would have known that if I didn't trust my gut and try a different way."

"Yeah, well, my gut isn't being helpful." I laugh, trying to keep the mood light. "I keep telling myself I came on this trip to figure out what I want to do with my life. It seems silly I'm focused on which man I want to spend it with instead."

"Ahh, but don't you see, life is love. You learn to love yourself, and you find other things and people to love too. That is exactly what makes a good life." His thought echoes what Elizabeth Gilbert said about love being one of the only two things people care about when it comes down to it. I just struggle with the idea that I'm ready for it right now.

"How can I love someone else when I don't feel complete enough to be loved?"

"Just like any of these flowers, you can enjoy yourself, your life, other people, even before they are fully grown. The most beautiful thing will be when you learn how to love each other, use each other to help grow into someone you love, and create a life you love more. We wouldn't be surrounded by people if they weren't supposed to help us. Don't forget that. Don't let your fear hold you back from sharing your love with someone."

"What if I figure out who I love and there's not enough time to build that love and focus on all the other things I love too?"

"Toss aside your doubt, my dear. There is always time. It may have taken a while to figure out, but look at this city. We discovered what we value most: good people, good food, good energy. We work harder on shorter days to create the time to enjoy all of it. Once you figure out what's important to you, you'll find the time to love and grow together."

"I need to figure out what is most important to me."

"You will. You are in the city of love! It's bound to help you figure out the secrets to your heart."

CHAPTER SEVENTY-FIVE

The routine I've fallen into is lazy in a way that has given me a newfound energy. I wander the streets with my bakery treat of choice and stay out in the fresh air as long as possible. Some days I find a park where I sit in the sunshine and read, and other days I adventure out to see the sights. I've explored the Pantheon, been to the Louvre, seen the Notre Dame Cathedral, but mostly I search out the street performers. I love the simplicity and joy they seem to seek out for their lives.

After those first few days, I was able to keep my mind off both Mack and Dean for the most part. I spent most of my time helping Avery make last minute decisions for her wedding and enjoying the laid back energy of Paris. My intention while here has been to simply soak up the pleasure of traveling. I've decided to go to Thailand for a couple of months before I fly home for the wedding, and I've promised myself that by the time I leave Asia I'll determine a path for my life–in regards to work and love.

While neither man gave me an ultimatum, or are necessarily waiting for me, I know making a choice will ease everyone's mind, and it's only fair. I've also been coming to terms with the possibility I could go home and neither of them want to be with me anymore. If that's the consequence of my choices, it's something I will have to accept.

I learned a lot these past few weeks by immersing myself in the culture. Experiencing the way people live here–as if there's no rush, as if giving into love is all that matters–has helped me let go of my need to find a bigger purpose immediately. I have a better grip on reality and control over my perspective. The thought I keep coming back to is if focusing on what I currently love most is enough to guide my life.

I don't believe either man was a rebound, and I know I love them both differently. But even if I can choose which one I love the most and predict who will make me the happiest, how do I make sure I can be enough for them too?

Every few days, I've gone to Theo's shop to buy new flowers for my temporary home. We chat about life and love and of course flowers. Today I stop by for the last time to say goodbye before I leave.

"My Maci!" he exclaims as I walk through the propped open green front door.

"Theo! I need the best bunch you've got! It'll be my last one." My room reservation is almost up, and once I got to the point where I was comfortable and it was starting to feel like home, I knew it was time to leave.

"Ahhh, you've discovered the meaning of life and you're ready to head back to yours?" He smiles, having listened to me on more than one occasion over the past few weeks.

Searching through the bouquets lining the wall in front of me, I turn his way to respond. "I don't think I've figured it out as much as I've made peace with the fact there is no way around choosing."

"Ahhh, so you have chosen your path?"

"I've been avoiding the actual decision…" If you can be both calm and anxious at the same time, that's what I am. "Being here, and hearing it from you a dozen times, has made me realize love is the most important thing to follow in your life. I know I need to make a choice, but there's one thing that's holding me back now. What if the things I think are most important to me turn out to not be the right things in the end?"

"Sometimes what we love most changes, especially as you change. But if you worry about what you might love next, you'll never be able to fully enjoy what you love right now. You have come in here every time and picked out the same yellow daffodils because you love them the most. If you were concerned about a day you might not love them as much anymore, or a day I might not have them, you would miss out on all the days you could have enjoyed them. We never know how this moment will connect to the next million. All we can do is choose what we want in the present. It might not work out like we hope, but you might end up running a flower store with the love of your life surrounded by joy every day."

I run my fingers gently over the top of a bouquet before picking it up, paying, wishing him well, and leaving his shop for the last time.

CHAPTER SEVENTY-SIX

When the cab drops me off, I lower the magazine I took from the plane. It's flipped to a page of a street in downtown Phuket that was, well, picture perfect. I asked someone at the airport for directions, and after a short cab ride and 30 minutes of wandering, I found it.

I think.

The scene laid out in front of me is hardly recognizable compared to the picture. The magazine showed a row of pristine white and light pink buildings with intricate gold embellishments bordering every doorway and window. But when I study it next to the real thing, disappointment washes over me. The white is dirty, the pink is faded and dusty and instead of feeling peaceful, the street is chaotic and crowded.

Putting the magazine in my bag, I walk until I find the first coffee shop I come across. It's simple inside, with off-white walls and small two person café tables lining the side opposite the glass display case and counter. I order a tea and find a seat by the front window.

I laugh to myself when the barista drops off my drink. Every time I'm in a coffee shop it's not lost on me I never order coffee. I love that Mack hates it too. It was such a little joy in our relationship. A list of other things I loved about our relationship flood my mind. I soak in the memories before allowing myself to dig deeper.

My goal while I'm here is to make a decision, and that's not going to happen if I'm not honest with myself. By that, I mean asking my best friend for her opinion. I've successfully avoided a conversation with Avery about this for months now, but I'm ready to talk with her about it.

Me: *Can we talk about Mack?*

Avery: *Of course. I've been waiting for you to bring it up. I'm sure it's been hard since you know I'll struggle to be objective. But you're my best friend, Maci. Whatever direction this conversation goes, know I just want you to be happy in the end. That's all I want for both of you.*

Me: *What has he told you?*

Avery: *I feel like... everything. About the drugs–which I swear I never knew about. I would have made him tell you or told you myself if he hadn't. That he messed up, that he wasn't supporting your need to grow, and how much he regrets not trusting you to work things out together. I'm not trying to make excuses for him, and he's never used it as one, but working it out and sticking around was never something our parents modeled.*

Me: *It can't be a factor, though. I mean look at your relationship with Miller. It's great. I know it was a mistake. I've forgiven him for it. I really do love him, Avery.*

Avery: *Then what's the problem? What's holding you back? Dean?*

Me: *I'd be lying if I said he wasn't a factor. I love them both so much in their own way. I had this shift in Paris where I realized that love should be more about finding things and people who help make you better, rather than someone who "completes" you. I think that's an important factor in deciding who is right for me.*

Avery: *I've seen you around Dean in the past. I mean this in the nicest way, but you were unsure of yourself the entire first half of your relationship and for months after. That's kind of the opposite of better, Mace. Do you think it's still like that?*

Me: *I don't. Dean has shown me he's willing to grow and work on things. He already has. I also have more confidence in myself now. I'm not willing to settle for less than I know I deserve, and I wouldn't have stayed in Costa Rica with him if I wasn't sure.*

Avery: *I'm happy he's made changes. Do you feel like Mack has grown too?*

Me: *I'm starting to see he has. I noticed our fight and what followed was out of character for him. He also told me he is quitting his band to work toward new goals. I know that's a big deal for him.*

Avery: *Yeah, and moving home and getting that new job. It's perfect for him, I think.*

Me: *He's back in Oregon? What new job?*

Avery: *He didn't tell you?*

Me: *I didn't talk to either of them while I was in Paris.*

Avery: *Oh wow, okay. I feel like he should be the one to tell you this, but... yeah. He moved back a couple of weeks ago... He's living with us until he starts his new job in the fall. His middle school music teacher offered him a job teaching music at the after-school program. He thought it would be perfect for him to work with kids who could use a good role model and maybe don't have support at home. It's funny you both ended up falling into the same type of thing, helping kids who need it more than most.*

Me: *Wow, that's amazing. This seems like a direction that would really make him happy. I wish I was there to see it.*

Avery: *The question is if you want that enough. You could be the right person for both of them. I don't think Mack would have started making these changes if it wasn't for you. As his sister, I'm beyond grateful for that, but it also sounds like Dean is better off for knowing you as well. I guess the main factor then is which one is capable of making your life better in the way that would be most fulfilling to you?*

Me: *That's my dilemma. I truly believe both of them are good to me and could be great for me.*

Avery: *Let's try something. Tell me what you think your life could look like with both of them and what your favorite parts of it would be. Start with Mack.*

Me: *Okay. Hmm. I guess it changes things if he's already back in Oregon. I loved California because I got to be with him, but I'd rather call Oregon my home. He once told me he thought it would be fun to find a house in your neighborhood and start our families together. I think about that a lot, how great it would be to raise our kids and continue to help each other through life the way we always have. Mack would be such a good dad. I've noticed people tend to end up exactly like their parents, or completely opposite, based on their perspective of how they were raised. I know Mack would give our kids everything you two never had. Just thinking about that makes me want to be there and be a part of it.*

I send the text before continuing. While I'm typing, Avery sends back an entire page of crying emojis.

Me: *And imagine if I could convince Lexy to move to Oregon too. Sharing a best friend with Mack is fun, when we are together anyway. Almost all my favorite people would be in this perfect little circle. It almost seems too good to be true. I love the idea of his new job. You were right to say we both are drawn to helping people in the same way. I've* *been researching the nonprofit that helps rescue women who have been trafficked in Portland. I could easily work there and still live in Eugene. Thinking about the life I could have with him, with you, it overwhelms me in a good way. I can't imagine there not being anything I wouldn't love about it.*

Avery: *Mack said he invited Lexy to come visit for his final show. I can't wait to meet her! That entire vision sounds ideal, of course because it overlaps with a dream I would love to be reality. BUT as great as it sounds, it would mean nothing if you could be happier in a different life. Tell me about your future with Dean. What would that look like?*

Me: *Nearly the complete opposite.* I send the text, followed by another with just laughing emojis.

Avery: *How so?*

Me: *With Dean, Oregon would be a lot less of a home and a lot more of a home base. He came up with an amazing idea for a job he could work wherever we wanted to go. We talked about going to Spain because Maria is opening another sanctuary there where I could work as a paid volunteer. Once we were ready for another adventure, I think it would be easy to find remote work wherever we go. I'd miss everyone I love, like I do now, but I would convince you to come visit us wherever in the world we were. We'd also come back to see our families and friends on holidays or between adventures. As much as the consistency and comfort of what I imagine my life with Mack to be sounds amazing, I've also been enjoying the freedom and chaos during the past couple of months traveling. We are young and have plenty of time to settle down. It could be amazing to focus on making an impact on the world and spending time just on us first.*

Avery: *Can't say that doesn't sound like a good life too. As long as you ask me to come visit when you end up in Australia. Sounds like you've really thought out both of your options.*

Me: *You'd be invited to every place we go. You have to start crossing countries off our list for yourself! You know, Mack also said something about making travel a priority once a year, but that's more like vacationing.*

Avery: *He mentioned that to me too. Mace, I don't think there is a right choice or a wrong choice here. There's just a choice. Unfortunately, it's one only you can make, but know you will always be a huge part of my life no matter what. If you want to be with Mack, I'll love every second of and everything about that. If you want to be with Dean, I'll be supportive and happy for you, and I'll love Dean because I'll know he's what makes you happiest.*

Me: *I'm just nervous reality won't live up to whichever vision I choose, but there's no way to control 100% of the situation or know how else life could have been. I just have to think about all this and confidently decide by the time I come home. I can't wait to see you.*

Avery: *Exactly. And nothing is ever going to be perfect, but I know whichever route you take, it'll be the right one, and you'll make it work. But also, because I know you have this idea in your head, I'm reminding you that just because Miller and I found each other so young–your parents too–there isn't a deadline for starting the rest of your life. There's no rush. We just happened to stumble into our time. Maybe you figure it out before you come home, maybe you don't. Either way, it's all going to work out for you when it's your time too.*

Me: *You read my mind. Thanks for this, for being you. I'll talk to you soon. Text me after you sample cakes this weekend!*

I put my phone away and look outside to the street as one car cuts off another and loud honks blare from every direction. I wonder if it happens often, the picture we have in our head of how things are or were not aligning with reality. I expected to walk into the heart of this city and see the magazine picture come to life. When it wasn't that, it felt like such a letdown. I worry something similar would happen in my life. Both of the scenarios I came up with talking to Avery are lives I would happily live. They are also dreams over which I don't have complete control.

When I decided to give things with Mack a chance, I worked it up in my head to be this picture perfect opportunity for a relationship–girl falls in love with best friend's brother, and a happily ever after is inevitable. Did I put so much pressure on it being perfect that anything else didn't seem like enough? Subconsciously could that have been more of the reason I initially left than the night he made one mistake?

What about Costa Rica? I walked onto that beach, and it felt like a dream too. It looked like I was on a movie set. The way the waves crashed onto untouched morning sand, with the sunrise adding a pink hue over every-thing, it was the definition of no filter needed. Then Dean came into view, and it was like a scene straight out of a romance movie you joke about being unrealistic. Was it really that magical, or was it just a dream finally playing out, so I thought it was? I wonder if that's a thing too.

Is my memory of my time with Dean simply misplaced nostalgia? Like thinking back you remember things bet-ter than they actually were because that's how you wanted them to be; I hoped for it to work out between us for so long, did I make it up to be more than it was in my mind?

I need to figure out if it's possible for the vision I have for my life to align with what it can realistically look like and if the scenarios I played out with Avery are within reach.

By the time I leave the coffee shop, never ending circles of thoughts are running through my head about the possibility life could look like an edited picture depending on your perspective. Without being near either Mack or Dean, I thought maybe it would be easier to sort out my thoughts and make a decision. Apparently it won't be. I asked the barista for a suggestion for a safe place to stay and a good place to eat. After checking into a small hotel up the road, I head off to find food.

CHAPTER SEVENTY-SEVEN

I must be lost. The further I walk down this road, the sketchier it feels. Everything in me says to turn around, especially when the street becomes a cobblestone alley, and the sun starts to set behind the buildings. I keep walking anyway.

A neon "open" sign glows in the window ahead. Finally I'm in the right place. Upon opening the door, a little bell dings, and a beautiful blonde woman looks up from behind the cash register to greet me. This is not what I expected in the middle of Thailand, but here I am, and if I've realized one thing lately, it's that life is full of surprises.

The girl introduces herself as Brooke and sets a menu in front of me. Before she walks away, I tell her to bring me whatever she recommends; that I eat almost anything.

When she returns, I can't help speaking my thoughts. "You're not who I expected to be my waitress anywhere in Thailand."

She laughs. "I get that a lot. I came to visit a few years ago, right after I graduated college. I wanted to go on an adventure before I had to join the grind of American adulthood and do what was expected of me, but I loved it here so much, I never went back."

"You didn't even go home first?"

"Nope!" Her eyes drift to the corner of the room as if she's recalling a memory. "I sent my roommate back home another month of rent and told him to get rid of all my things. I haven't looked back since."

"Wow... that's..." I sit shock, my fork paused in midair on its way to take my first bite of the spicy pineapple curry she placed in front of me.

"Crazy?" She laughs.

"I was going to say amazing. I'm kind of doing the same thing. Not the staying here forever part–I don't want that–but the finding yourself part. Did it work for you?"

"It depends on who you ask." A sad expression washes over her face before she recovers. "What I can tell you is I don't regret it for a single second. You only get one life to live, so you have to live it the best you know how, ya know?"

"Yeah... but how do you know what that looks like? I used to think maybe it could be a gut feeling, but my gut doesn't seem to know a lot these days... except that this curry is the best thing I've ever tasted. Holy shit." I shove another bite into my mouth. This place is the definition of a hole in the wall, a hidden gem somewhere it shouldn't exist.

She laughs, pulling out the chair across from me to sit down. I'm the only customer in the dining room. "Start at the beginning, and let's see if we can figure it out." She leans forward, resting her chin on her fists, ready to listen.

Right then, a group of five gentlemen walk in wanting a table.

"Damn," Brooke says when she sees them and turns back to me. "Okay, I'm saying this because my gut tells me you won't think it's crazy. I live a few streets over from here. I work tomorrow during the day, but maybe after you can come over, and I can help you sort through this?"

"That sounds great." I'm excited to have a new friend here so soon after arriving.

She writes an address, her number and the name of something on a piece of receipt paper she pulled from her apron and slides it my way. "Tomorrow, go to the other place I also wrote down. You won't regret it."

"Thanks, Brooke. I'll see you soon."

She gets up to help her new customers while I finish my meal. When I'm finished, I leave double the cost of my meal in the baht I exchanged my colon for at the airport and walk back to my very small hotel room.

After taking a much-needed shower, I slip under the thin white comforter. I grab my phone off the night-stand, pulled to reach out to the other Torres sibling today too.

Me: *Hey*

Mack: *Hi. How are you?*

Me: *I made it to Thailand!*

Mack: *That's great, Maci. It's been on your list forever. How was Paris?*

Me: *It was amazing. I'll miss my daily morning trip to the boulangerie. The French really understand the value of bread. You know how much I love bread.*

Mack: *Maci, you love all food.*

Me: *I'm an equal opportunity foodie.*

Mack: *So, you're going to try deep fried crickets while you're there?*

Me: *Ummm... to be determined.*

Mack: *hahah keep me posted.*

Me: *I will. How are you?*

Mack: *The past few weeks have been really good.*

Me: *Why didn't you tell me about your new job and that you moved home?*

Mack: *I wanted to. I'd rather do these things with you. But I didn't want you to think I was doing all of this just to entice you to come back to me. I want to do what I can to be the person I believe could make you happy, but I also understand that right now you're already doing what you need to be happy. This trip you're on... despite me missing you and wishing you were here with me, I know it's more than just traveling for a few months. You're creating a part of your life that will help mold you into who you want to become. I want that for you.*

Me: *Thank you for saying that. I've been kind of feeling like you didn't understand.*

Mack: *That's my fault. It's easier for me to be vocal about how much I miss you because it's always on my mind, but I truly want you to get everything out of this journey you need, regardless of how long that takes.*

Me: *I hope you know it's not that I don't want you with me. I just feel like it's something I should do on my own.*

Mack: *I get it. Not that there's a timeline for anything, but I had to remind myself I've had more time than you to figure out what I wanted for my life. When I graduated, I picked up my entire life to move to California. Playing music and touring was my version of doing something I loved while also figuring out what is most important to me. You deserve to be able to do the same thing.*

Me: *But we weren't together then. You didn't have to worry about letting anyone else down. I don't want to let you down.*

Mack: *I love you, Maci. Every part of me wants us to end up together, but the only thing that would truly be a letdown is if you chose us when it's not the right choice or* *time for you. I've never stopped believing we could create a life we both loved together. I have faith this can work out for us, but whatever you decide, I won't regret all the time we've had together and every second I spend loving you.*

Me: *You always know what to say to remind me why I love you.*

Mack: *Just letting you know how I feel. I never want you to have any doubt about my feelings. Have fun in Thailand. Bring me home a cricket.*

CHAPTER SEVENTY-EIGHT

Based on Brooke's suggestion, I take a 30-minute car ride to Phang Nga Bay, which is a little northeast of the town where I'm staying. You can take canoeing tours into the sea caves, and I'm excited.

Where the car dropped me off, I can't see past the tropical trees. There's an overwhelming sound of birds. I don't see them, but there must be a lot because it's loud–and beautiful. It's also hard to breathe. The air is so palpable, it feels thick as I inhale.

I take a deep breath before pushing my way through the hidden path. I'm rewarded with a view unlike any-thing I've ever seen before. As much as I loved Costa Rica, its beauty is hardly comparable to what lies before me. The sand is whiter than any I've ever seen. The water is at least ten shades of teal and turquoise while also being crystal clear. It's odd it doesn't smell salty.

Massive boulders covered in foliage line the edge of the bay, looking as if they are floating slightly above the water. Out further, islands are sprinkled amongst the morning haze. I don't see the caves but head toward the canoe hut.

Once I get checked in, the guide, Nattan, helps me drag my boat to the edge of the water. As I climb in, a baby shark no bigger than my arm swims by my foot.

This is incredible. I'm thankful I took this leap. I'm still not sure what I expected to get from my journey, but this moment right here is worth all of it.

It's not until I start paddling out that I realize the caves are under the boulders. There's a hardly noticeable gap under them we must go through. Okay wait, maybe I take back how excited I am. That looks terrifying. Get it together, Maci. You're here, and you have to make the most of this experience or you'll regret not doing this.

Following the instruction of my guide, Nattan, I point my canoe in the direction of the cave and lie down with my back flat against it. As I float under the entrance, the rock is less than a foot from me. Condensation drips onto my face, claustrophobia threatening to send me into a panic, and it's even more difficult to breathe.

Using my hands, I gently push against the ceiling until I'm inside the cave. When it opens, Nattan turns his lantern on, and a rush of cool, damp air replaces the rock around me. I sit up to take in my surroundings. It's dark, but I can make out an entirely new world. Years of being worn by water has created hundreds of different designs in the rock, seemingly etched into the walls. Stalactites hang from the ceiling by the smallest connection, like icicles. Stalagmites rise from rock platforms that rest above the water level near the edges of the cave. Both have a slight sparkle, making them look as if they are intricate decorations. When Nattan holds the light higher, I scan the colony of bats, all sleeping and hardly disturbed by our presence.

Before we headed back to shore, we released a beautiful flower and leaf peace offering with candles. It's called a Krathong and designed to thank the Goddess of Water. It was the perfect ending to the experience, and I'm glad I pushed past my fear of going into that cave.

I'm gaining a new appreciation for difficult experiences that lead me to truly cherish the good in life.

CHAPTER SEVENTY-NINE

I take a hot shower and change before walking to Brooke's. Grabbing my phone off the charger to let her know I'm on my way, my heart skips at the name attached to my newest notification.

Dean: *Raul from our taco place asked about you today. He said he missed seeing you every night.*

Me: *We really ate there a lot, didn't we? I miss those tacos.*

Dean: *I miss you.*

Me: *I miss you too.*

Dean: *It's not like the first time. It sucked when I left you, but I pushed it out of my mind. I thought I could do that again this time. But how much I miss you now, I can't figure out how I did it before.*

Me: *Things were different this time. You were more open with me, I was more confident with you. We were in a beautiful place without any distractions of life. It's like when I got to Thailand yesterday, I discovered this hole in the wall that took me forever to find. The food was amazing, but I also wondered if it would have seemed as good if I didn't compare the magic of it to the hard journey it took to get there. I wanted things to work out with us for so long, part of me wonders if we just got swept up in the romance of* *that and of Costa Rica and if our relationship would be different if we were in the real world.*

Dean: *The REAL WORLD?! Seriously, Maci? What do you think that even means? Were you not there with me? YOU are real to me. And this thing between us feels pretty damn real too. How can you not see that?*

Me: *It's just different, Dean. I'd like to believe love could be the only driving force in life, but eventually I have to get a job and not live in a fairy tale.*

Dean: *The real world is whatever you make it. Me being here for the past year proves life can be what you want it to be. If ours looks like a fairy tale, then shouldn't we just appreciate that?*

Me: *Do you think we could keep up the way we were living?*

Dean: *I do. I've been looking for remote jobs that would be perfect for us. We could go wherever we wanted. I can't think of a better dream. Can you?*

Me: *So many people never get to live their big dreams. What makes us special? What makes us the exception?*

Dean: *We have each other. Anything is possible as long as that's true. I can feel in my bones the impact you're going to make on the world. I want to be there to see it, and I know I can help you make your dreams come true.*

Me: *I'm sorry, Dean. I promise I want to finish this conversation, but I have to go. My new friend is waiting for me. Text me later, okay?*

When I get to Brooke's cute one bedroom apartment, she wastes no time wanting to hear the details of my dilemma. I can't put a finger on why, but telling a total stranger all my personal thoughts sounds like a good idea. Maybe an outside perspective is exactly what I need.

I share with her the short version of the past year and a half, the visions I shared with Avery, along with my jumble of thoughts from the past week and my recent conversations with both Mack and Dean. She listens intently the entire time without saying anything, waiting until she's sure I'm finished.

"I wouldn't say I'm qualified to give advice by any means. I'm far from perfect and have made more than my fair share of mistakes." She doesn't elaborate. "But here's what I do know. When you choose the right path, it's kind of like my restaurant. It's a slice of heaven amongst the chaos. Right?" I nod. "Still doesn't mean there aren't people who focus on what's wrong with it. The location is terrible, a few dishes on the menu could be better, the chef is a little grumpy, and we are closed three days a week. But focusing on the negatives is a choice. Discounting the beauty in something because of details that throw you off is not a productive way to go through life. Nothing in the world is ever going to be perfect in every way. It's not possible. Whether you choose Dean or Mack, something will inevitably happen that's less than ideal. I think it's a matter of finding a balance between appreciating the magic in something you love, while tying yourself to the reality that you might not always see it, and that's okay."

"Wow, that makes a lot of sense. I think I've been expecting the answer to be so complicated that I'm overlooking how much of it is simply choosing a perspective."

"I vote you make a decision and then promise yourself you won't look back. Speaking from experience, it's hard–like really hard–to never wonder "what if." All you can do is know there's a reason you made the choice you did and accept it isn't fair to keep someone else from living their life because you aren't confident about how or if you fit into it. Your perspective is what makes your choice right."

"I think you're right." I'm determined to make a decision and lean all the way into it when I do.

"I can't say I wish I was in your shoes, that's for sure." She laughs. "But I believe in your ability to figure this out."

"Thanks. It helps just talking through it. Now, tell me all about you and how the hell you ended up here."

CHAPTER EIGHTY

Dean: *Good morning, Maci. I just wanted to check in with you because you seemed conflicted last night. I thought I'd share what I was thinking, so there isn't any added confusion coming from my end. The first time it was my choice to leave, and I know that's on me. I hate thinking about how things could have been different if I didn't make that decision. I didn't fight for you and give into how I felt then. If I haven't been clear enough, I'm doing that now. I'm sorry it took me so long to know I needed you in my life. I was scared before. I wasn't who I needed to be to commit to you. I knew the second you showed up on my beach I wasn't conflicted anymore. I know you're worried things might be different if we try a real relationship somewhere else, but there's a reason you found me thousands of miles away. There's no way we can chalk that up to coincidence. This past month and a half has been hard without you, and I don't want to live the rest of our lives this way. I want to make this work. What do you want?*

In all my back and forth between the two of them, there's one glaring difference I noted last night when Brooke was asking me questions about my story, something I didn't realize bothered me until then. It's a variable that matters when it comes to choosing my path.

Me: *I want to know you can keep showing me this side of you when we are outside of our own bubble. I want you to be able to tell me you love me when you know I'm awake.*

Dean: *Every side of me belongs to you, wherever we are. I'll show you I'm the right man for you and tell you how much I love you every damn day. Let me.*

CHAPTER EIGHTY-ONE

I spent five more weeks in Thailand before I left. After a few weeks on my own, I stayed with Brooke for a week, and then I met up with my parents in Chiang Mai for a couple of weeks. It was exciting to see them after so long, and I couldn't think of a better way to end my trip.

My phone vibrates with a text as the TSA agent scans my boarding pass. I assume it's Avery, but when I see the name, my chest constricts, tears instantly welling in my eyes.

Dean: *I just got back to Oregon. I need to see you. Please tell me I can see you when you get home–that we can talk?*

I stare at the words until the security agent yells for me to step up to the conveyor belt. I drop my backpack into a bin and quickly type out my reply.

Me: *Of course we can. I'm actually about to board my flight home for Avery's wedding.*

I toss my phone in the security bin, catching the glow of an incoming call as it disappears into the X-ray. Who is calling me? I wipe at my eyes as I walk toward the scanner. Once I get through, I notice the missed call and voicemail.

It's from Mack.

I press my phone to my ear as I walk to my gate. *Hey, Mace. I heard from Avery you'll be out here for the wedding.*

His voice makes my stomach flutter. I haven't heard it in so long. *Look, I don't know what or if you've decided anything. I've been trying to give you your space, but I know it's going to be hard when we are stuck in the same place. I thought I'd at least remind you where I stand so there aren't any surprises. Despite giving you space and focusing on my other dreams, I love you. I never stopped. I hate you're not here with me. I have been sober every day since you left, and I hope when you see me, you see how hard I've been trying for us, in case there is still a chance when you're ready. I know this weekend needs to be all about Avery and Miller, and I don't want to take away from that, so I wanted to get it out now. Avery said you land tomorrow before the rehearsal dinner, so I'll see you then. I love you.*

I play his message again just to hear those three words at the end one more time.

Making this one decision will completely alter what my life looks like and in turn impact who I become. I made a pro/con list of what makes me happy and what I love most about each of them. I forced Brooke to sit through hours of playing devil's advocate with me. She finally looked at me and said, "Maci, none of this matters. I've known you long enough now to know who you don't want to live the rest of your life without, but I'm not going to tell you because you know in your heart too. One of them will get hurt in this situation, but if you don't decide, everyone will."

She's right. I've reflected on everything I've learned on this journey, and I know who I'm choosing. I'm ready to be with him and start the rest of our lives. But I'm so close to being home, I'd rather talk to both of them when I'm not a world away.

After what feels like forever, I make it off the plane and head toward the exit. Pulling out my phone to request an Uber, I look up to see which direction I need to walk and freeze in place.

This can't be real. I squeeze my eyes shut before opening them again just in case I'm seeing a mirage.

I'm not.

My heart beats so loudly I can't hear any of the surrounding chaos. All the air around me disappears, and I can't breathe, but at the same time it's like I'm taking a real breath for the first time in months.

Him.

It's him. After all these months spent figuring out who compliments my life and this version of me best, my soulmate is standing in front of me. Before I ever decided, I think part of me always knew.

I go to move, planning my path to him. I take my first step, and that's when our eyes lock. Hope is etched on his face, but he doesn't make a move, waiting for me, for a sign he should be here.

My head shakes as something between a smile and a laugh comes over my face. I can't believe it. My teeth sink into my lip in anticipation, and then somehow he's already in front of me.

My backpack slides off my shoulder and hits the ground right before I fall into his arms, knowing more than ever, I am exactly where I belong.

ACKNOWLEDGMENTS

The basic storyline of *And Then There's You* has existed since the day I silently declared writing a book a dream, nearly a decade ago. For ten years, I never told anyone else about this goal, and when I wrote the first few chapters, I had convinced myself I'd go through the entire process alone–just in case I couldn't do it.

I've never been so thankful to myself for accepting I was wrong. There's no way I could have done this without the people who have been by my side during this journey–the blinking cursor has stared back at me so many times as I've tried to find the right words to say for those people. I'm not sure what I came up with is anywhere near good enough, but here it goes:

Brooke, thank you for getting to know my characters as deeply and intensely as I did, and for loving them despite any of their flaws. Thank you for loving me when I hated them and my story and questioned bringing them to life. Thank you for protecting my book and defending anything that exists in my world–sometimes even more passionately than I did. Thank you for riding this roller coaster for me. You stayed up late to work through scenes and bounce ideas around. You grew with me. You let me cry. You gave me pep talks. You read my mind more often than not. *You wrote me a freaking song.* You read my first shared sex scene aloud to our friends so I could get the feedback I was most nervous for. You're more proud of me than anyone else–it's not unnoticed. I don't remember how it happened, but somehow you became my assistant—the best damn assistant ever. I love you so damn much. Thank you for being my person. Oh, and thank you for my first book swag. As you know, all my other sweatshirts have now become obsolete.

Katherine, first and foremost, thank you for remaining my friend even after every time I fought you on an edit. One of the quotes that inspired the direction of this book is, "I think we have multiple soulmates and the one you end up with depends on the work you've done to evolve your own soul. I think there's a soulmate for every level of your journey." Somehow, because of a million little choices we each made, our paths crossed. The first part of our friendship was spent working together to improve our lives physically, mentally and financially–crossing off other goals. Then we joined forces for the biggest project we've ever undertaken. A million choices had to be made, countless paths had to be walked down for us to land in this place of life where we were both ready and capable of accomplishing our dreams of becoming a published author and editor. Thank you for being ready in alignment with me. Thank you for your ability to zoom in and out simultaneously—which made this book so much stronger than it started. Thank you for all the commas—I'm sorry if any part of this unedited acknowledgment section makes you cringe. I honestly, actually just could not have done this without you right now.

Alexa, thank you for helping turn my middle of the night meltdowns into giggle fits. For your help with writing exercises. For finding so many perfect songs to create the perfect playlists. For the brainstorming sessions. For reading my book all the way through so many times and never once complaining you were sick of it. My book crew wouldn't be complete without you.

Steph, thank you for your mental health check-ins. Thank you for becoming so invested in my characters, my story, and my journey. Thank you for every nice thing you made sure to tell me with every constructive criticism you shared. Thank you for my writing desk so I could stop making my body so angry. And thank you for coming around to Dean and giving him another chance after the shit show he initially was–he appreciates the change of heart.

In the words of Dean… "My parents are great and will support anything I want to do… even if it's crazy." Mom and Dad, you've been my biggest and best cheerleaders my entire life. Thank you for your pep talks, your love and support, and for not being embarrassed of your daughter publishing a book full of sex scenes. My own wanderlust, my ideas for this story, and my belief in myself to write it all wouldn't be part of me if it wasn't for you both.

To my husband, who may or may not ever read this. Thank you for loving me and supporting me through this journey–I know it hasn't been all Costa Rica sunshine. Thank you for sacrificing time together so I could chase this dream. Thank you for listening to every rant and ramble and idea I've needed to speak out loud. Thank you for sharing my book with every single person you talk to, believing in my writing even after you only read one scene. And obviously, thank you for all the research you helped me conduct. ;)

Amber, thank you for bringing my poorly pencil drawn vision for my cover to life. It's everything I envisioned and more–you created an image that captures the essence of my story before even reading it. It's beautiful and perfect. Thank you.

Thank you to my book club–you were truly the catalyst for starting this process. I hadn't read much since college, but in April 2021, I stumbled across the *After* series, deciding I wanted to get back into reading. On a whim, I posted about it, asking if anyone wanted to read it with me–that was the day our book club formed, and I found my love and excitement for reading again. You've all been my best cheerleaders and support whenever I've needed it. I know for certain, without this step in my journey, I would not have become an author. Special shoutout to Sarah, Danyelle and Kerry for reading early drafts and sharing all the feedback and emotions with me!

Caitlin, thank you for letting me share part of our personal story within this book, and thank you for letting me heal our friendship. I'll never be able to explain how much you mean to me. My life is the adventure it's turned out to be because we started going on so many together—thank you for sticking with me through all of the memorable ones.

Heather, my first author friend. Thank you for selflessly guiding and mentoring me on this crazy journey of self-publishing. Thank you for helping me finish this process strong and with so much confidence. Mostly thank you for answering my 87 million questions. I'm so excited to see where our author and personal friendship goes from here! Check out Heather Garvin's most recent releases *Make Your Move, Crossing the Line, Take What You Can*, and *Give Nothing Back*.

Thank you to my best friend, Heidi and to Carla @whereonplanetearth for helping me paint the perfect vision of Thailand. And Melissa for naming Mack's band–I'm obsessed with it.

Thank you to network marketing for existing–specifically Beachbody (BODi). Building my business for seven years created the time and financial flexibility that provided me the opportunity to pursue this dream of writing and publishing a book. Without this company, I also wouldn't have met my editor and the majority of the other friends who helped turn this book from an idea to a 405-page dream come true. I'll forever be indebted to the girl I was seven years ago who took a leap with Beachbody because she believed in herself and her ability to change her life–it's helped me accomplish that in more ways than I ever imagined.

Final thank you goes to every friend, every follower, every reader who has sent me kind words and/or hyped up this book. To everyone who answered a poll when I needed guidance on what's realistic. To everyone who opened up with me in private conversations about relationships. This book not only exists because of you but is even better too.

More by Tisa Matthews

If you loved this story, check out the **Finding Home** series on Kindle Unlimited.

And Then There's You is book one, following Maci's love triangle with Mack and Dean.

I Love You, So What? is book two, following Lexy and Troy's story.

Can We Just Be Happy Now? is book three, following the story of Dean's sister Sophie, and Troy's best friend Cooper.

Tied Up In Riches is book four, following the story of Brooke and Marcus.

While books three and four can be read as stand-alones, books one and two of the series should be read in order for the best experience.

Home is an extended epilogue featuring a POV chapter from each main character in the series! It's meant to be read after you've finished the series!

Unhitched is a standalone, modern-day romance jam packed with 2000s nostalgia and swirled around with the turning 30 identity crisis. It's written by a millennial for millennials.